ALSO BY ANDREA HAIRSTON

NOVELS

Will Do Magic for Small Change

Redwood and Wildfire

Mindscape

COLLECTIONS

Lonely Stardust

A Science Fiction & Fantasy Pick for *Kirkus Reviews'*
Best Books of 2020
An Amazon Best Book of the Month (September 2020)
in Science Fiction & Fantasy
Best of September 2020 in *io9*, *The Nerd Daily*,
Chicago Review of Books, and *Ms.*

"*Master of Poisons* is sheer, undiluted brilliance. Epic, courageous, unapologetically fierce. The world needed an epic fantasy from the unstoppably creative mind of Andrea Hairston, and it's right on time. This is a prayer hymn, a battle cry, a love song, a legendary call-and-response bonfire talisman tale. This is medicine for a broken world."　　　　　　　　　　　　—Daniel José Older

"*Master of Poisons* makes me laugh, gasp, and dream of the world we are so desperately holding on to and of a better world yet to come. . . . I am so grateful Andrea hasn't given up on us! May she keep gifting our world with her expansive imagination throughout the years!"　　　　　　　　　　—Sheree Renée Thomas

"Nobody does it better than Andrea Hairston, and if you doubt it, just open *Master of Poisons* and follow her into the light."
　　　　　　　　　　　　　　　　—Pearl Cleage

"You could practically smell the brine, hear the gulls by the sea, and taste the nut butter and sweet mango slices. . . . This is a vast world that you are dropped in."　　　　　　　—*WOC Read*

"Andrea Hairston's writing is not to be missed. Her fantasy is rich with evocative detail, stunning and original, and her characters are deeply humane and engaging. This is the kind of fantasy that expands your mind and warms your heart."　　　—Martha Wells

"Hairston weaves a rich tapestry of folklore and adventure, inviting readers into a well-developed, non-Western fantasy world, while navigating pressing issues of climate change and personal responsibility. This is an urgent, gorgeous work."

—*Publishers Weekly* (starred review)

"This book's lyrical language and unsparing vision make it a mind-expanding must-read."			—*Kirkus Reviews* (starred review)

"*Master of Poisons* is a lush, literary fantasy novel full of folklore and magic."					—*BuzzFeed*

"Hairston's prose is unique and poetic. . . . This is a challenging book: sometimes challenging to read, sometimes challenging to our complacency. It has atrocities in it, but also some moments of sublime beauty. And it's definitely not quite like anything else I've read."					—*Fantasy Literature*

MASTER OF POISONS

{ A Novel }

Andrea Hairston

TOR
DOT
COM

A Tom Doherty Associates Book
New York

MASTER OF POISONS

Copyright © 2020 by Andrea Hairston

Interview copyright © 2020 by Daniel José Older and Andrea Hairston. Used with permission.

Map by Pan Morigan

A Tordotcom Book
Published by Tom Doherty Associates
120 Broadway
New York, NY 10271

www.tor.com

Tor® is a registered trademark of Macmillan Publishing Group, LLC.

The Library of Congress Cataloging-in-Publication Data is available upon request.

ISBN 978-1-250-26056-7 (trade paperback)
ISBN 978-1-250-26055-0 (ebook)

Our books may be purchased in bulk for promotional, educational, or business use. Please contact your local bookseller or the Macmillan Corporate and Premium Sales Department at 1-800-221-7945, extension 5442, or by email at MacmillanSpecialMarkets@macmillan.com.

First Edition: September 2020
First Trade Paperback Edition: August 2021

Printed in the United States of America

0 9 8 7 6 5 4 3 2 1

Dedicated to Ama Patterson (1960–2017)
Friend, Poet, and Conjurer

DRAMATIS PERSONAE

The Arkhysian Empire
Djola, Master of Poisons, northlander
Nuar, northlander chief, Djola's brother
Samina, pirate, Djola's wife
Tessa, Djola's daughter
Bal, Djola's daughter
Quint, Djola's son
Rano, captain of Djola's guard

Azizi, Emperor
Master of Arms
Master of Books and Bones
Ernold, High Priest of Mount Eidhou
Master of Grain
Master of Money
Master of Water
Lilot, cook, companion to Queen Urzula
Kyrie, Iyalawo of Mount Eidhou, Samina's sister
Queen Urzula, pirate queen, Azizi's wife

The Green Elders
Awa, Garden Sprite
Bal, Garden Sprite

Yari, the griot of griots
Isra, shadow warrior scout
Neth, Garden Sprite
Jod, Garden Sprite
Cal, Garden Sprite

Holy City
Mother, Awa's parent, smoke-walker
Father, Awa's parent, builder
Kenu, Awa's brother
Hezram, High Priest of Ice Mountain
Tembe, Iyalawo of Ice Mountain, supporter of Hezram
Rokiat, Hezram's horse-keeper
Meera, empire citizen, Awa's friend

At Sea
Pezarrat, pirate captain
Healer, pirate
Orca, young man, captive
Vandana, woman from beyond the maps

Weeds and Wild Things
The Bees
Mango, an elephant
Soot, a wild dog
The Behemoths
The Goats
Fannie, a horse
The Crows
Amethyst, a river
The Trees

BOOK
I

1

Djola

We are more likely to deny truth than admit grave error and change our minds. Even in the face of overwhelming evidence or imminent destruction, we refuse to believe in any gods but our own. Who can bear for the ground to dissolve under their feet and the stars to fall from the sky? So we twist every story to preserve our faith.

Djola thought to steer the Arkhysian Empire away from this terrible yet mundane fate. He was forty-three, handsome, and fearless—arrogant, even—the Master of Poisons and in the Arkhysian Empire, second only to Emperor Azizi. When poison desert appeared in the barbarian south and the free northland, didn't he warn Azizi? For twenty years as it crept through river valleys and swallowed forests, Djola pleaded with Council and begged good Empire citizens to change their ways. As long as sweet water fell from the sky every afternoon and mist rolled in on a night wind, everybody promised to change—tomorrow or next week. Then crops failed and rivers turned to dust. Good citizens now feared change would make no difference or was in fact impossible. Who could fight the wind?

This morning, despite being fearless and arrogant, Djola retreated into a cave overlooking the Salty Sea as half-brother Nuar calmed his warhorse, a gift from Djola. Samina, Djola's pirate wife, had urged him to ride out with Chief Nuar and discuss his map for the future, since he'd refused to share secret plans with her. Sand swirled beyond the cliffs, a storm brewing, blunting the sunrise. Nuar wore pale cloud-silk robes over a lean muscled body, flimsy protection if the storm was fierce or poison, clothes for ceremony and celebration, not travel.

Mist got tangled in Nuar's crown of gray hair then drizzled down craggy cheeks. He gestured at the rising sun with an eagle claw, an official exchange, not a brotherly farewell. "Your map to tomorrow won't persuade Azizi's Council," Nuar shouted over the wind.

"You haven't even read it." Djola groaned. "You always imagine the worst."

"You should too."

"I do. My map is an escape route." Djola stepped deeper into the shelter of the cave. Bats clung to the ceiling, clicking and chirping like drummers calling protective spirits.

Nuar stroked his dappled horse, who shied away from a mound of bat dung. "Council is weak men who can't talk to rivers, read a poem in the dirt, or catch the rhythm of roots in their bones." Nuar had been singing the same song for days.

"Council has me for that." Djola forced a smile. "I seek ancient conjure that would guide us."

"You're a tame *savage* to them, an *Anawanama* who can't tell what storm is coming till it smacks your face. Council won't accept ancient conjure from you." Nuar mounted the horse and nodded at cathedral trees clutching the south edge of the cliffs.

"Ancestors still smile on you here." Frothy red crowns heralded new growth. Midnight berry bushes spilled purple blossoms over the edge. "Poison storms spare this cove and the canyons beyond."

Djola pointed at a sand squall skipping in from a new inland desert.

Nuar grunted. "A bit of bluster and not poison. It won't last." The horse glared at Djola and strained against the reins, eager to trot off.

"No one has tamed me," Djola declared.

"Azizi is a coward." Nuar never liked the emperor, never understood how Djola could be a friend to their old enemies. "To preserve the Empire, Azizi and Council will sacrifice *Anawanama*, *Zamanzi*, and all the other northern tribes. They'll sacrifice their own citizens, just like in Holy City."

Djola spat. "High priest Hezram bleeds children for gate-conjure in Holy City. Azizi does nothing like this."

"You're a fool to trust any of these men." The horse snorted agreement.

Djola stared at plump dark shadows swaying above them. He wanted to shout, but why disturb bats drumming themselves to sleep? "Of course I don't trust them."

"When we were young, you wanted to charm elephants and jackals, pull fire from the air, even ride behemoths and sink pirate ships." Nuar's voice cracked. "To protect our villages, like the heroes of old."

"No shame in that."

"Unless you're the buffoon who betrays his own people."

"A clown and a traitor? Is that how you think of me?" Djola hugged himself. Their mother had died when he was nine. He'd never met his father and grew up on the run, till half-brother Nuar found him. No People to hold him, just Nuar. "I chose a different path, brother, but am guided by the same spirit as you."

"Huh." Nuar scratched a scar on his chin from a blade meant for

Djola. An old wound, it shouldn't itch. He'd always defended his younger half-brother against other chiefs, even when Djola joined the Empire's warriors. "You're no traitor, but . . ." Nuar gazed out. "They call this Pirate's Cove now." Water sparkled. Red rock-roses drank the mist and enchanted hummingbirds. Green and purple wings blurred as the birds dipped beaks into eager blossoms. Nuar sighed. "*Anawanama* and *Zamanzi* roamed here once, free."

"A few rogues flaunt the law, but no one steals our children or locks us up with the emperor's blessing. Peace for twenty years." Djola had seen to that. "Your eyes are full of yesterdays. I look for our tomorrow. *Lahesh* conjure."

"*Lahesh?* Who can trust tricksters and dream tinkerers?" Nuar closed his eyes and laid the eagle claw against his cheek. "My Empire crops whither and blow your way. Azizi's promises are dust."

Djola wanted to press Nuar to his heart, taste the morning together, and remember their mother and wild adventures from their youth—not argue. "I don't need to trust them. I'll persuade them. My map has something for everyone."

Nuar's cloud-silk robes snapped in a gust of sand. He spread his arms wide. He raked the air with the eagle's claw. "I know the weather. Do you?"

"We are the weather. Your words, brother." Djola's voice reverberated in the cave. Startled bats chirped a warning he felt more than heard as they flew into darkness away from intruders. "We can't leave Azizi and Council to map tomorrow alone."

"No." Nuar shuddered.

Djola squeezed his hand. "What chance do we have if I don't risk everything?"

Nuar donned a turban, and draped fine mesh across his mouth. Storm protection for the bit of bluster? He made a crossroads sign with the claw over Djola's heart, a blessing, then trotted off. Djola watched until a sand demon obscured man and horse. The orange whirl was more debris than bluster. Djola felt achy and jangly, as if he should have taken better care with his words. The wind might turn fierce, snatch older brother from his horse, and smash him on the rocks.

"Fatazz!" Djola cursed an orange sky. He should head home, but he wasn't ready for another sandstorm—sweet or poison—or a fight with his pirate wife. He just wanted to kiss Samina's purple-tinted lips, hold the deep curve of her waist, and taste the raintree scent on her skin one last time before heading to Council. Samina could fortify him for the battles ahead, if she had a mind to. The sand settled and the storm sputtered out. Djola squinted at shadows. Nuar had already vanished into the trees.

A good storm-sense didn't mean older brother was right about everything.

2

Awa

When Awa was a twelve-year-old Garden Sprite, Green Elders declared Smokeland a true realm of vision and spirits. Awa and the other Sprites were not to fear or make fun of sacred space as most people did. Smokeland was a vast territory of possibilities and maybe-nots, but never very far from what was happening right now. Smoke-walkers were intrepid adventurers exploring the unknown, dream tinkerers who shifted the shape of the everyday.

Awa never told the Green Elders or anybody, but she'd become a Smokeland-believer at six. Whenever Mother's spirit faded away like smoke on the wind, Awa held tight to Mother's breath body, sometimes for hours. Awa sang, told herself stories, or talked to bees and wild dogs until Mother returned from Smokeland with herbs from nowhere in this world. Awa hugged cold from Mother's thoughts, shook dead weight from Mother's bones, and combed fearful snarls from her wiry hair. Watching over Mother's breath body was a lot to ask of a young daughter who had snarls and sorrows of her own.

Awa's older brothers would have felt duty-bound to report a smoke-walking witch woman to Father. Being a good Empire citizen, Father would have turned Mother in to the high priest in Holy City or killed her to avoid shame, so guarding her breath body during illicit adventures fell to Awa.

Mother and other smoke-walkers reported slogging through a border realm of enchanting freaks and monsters. Before entering Smokeland proper, they were harassed by lightning bolts and spears of fire. Jellyfish explosions and poison dust cyclones were also common. Worst was a cold, dark emptiness that seeped through skin, erasing thought, desire, and fear. To survive the border-void, smoke-walkers often drank a cathedral seed and cloud-silk potion to lift their minds above despair. This *Lahesh* potion *eased* the journey, but did not *cause* it. Even drugged, many people never made it through Smokeland's border realms. Their spirit bodies got lost in the emptiness or stolen by high priest Hezram for his conjure. Their breath bodies withered to bone and then dust. Awa thought of it as poison desert in the mind.

The first time she wandered to Smokeland was in the company of bees. It was the day before her twelfth birthday. She and oldest brother Kenu had opened an elephant corral left behind by thief-lord raiders and let the beasts run free. Angry villagers who wanted to sell the elephants chased after them, but the elephants escaped. Father was outraged. Awa ran away from him and Mother arguing over *true love* and *some other man's child*.

Awa followed friend honeybees as they flew sideways into the woods. Which woods, she could never say. The forest surrounding Father's lands was ancient cathedral trees whispering to one another up in the clouds. Bronze-colored bark was dappled with purple moss. Feathery needle-leaves started out red and turned green with age. Cathedral roots were as thick as Awa and oozed an oily scent that made her dizzy. In her childish memory, Smokeland-terrain got tangled with the everyday. This first time, Awa was disappointed not to find a border of fiends, exploding jellyfish, and void-smoke. She landed in a field of wildflowers by a cathedral tree grove. She moved at the speed of thought, spinning endlessly around a drop of water as it slid down a leaf. In a blink she raced from riverbank to valley to rocky peak.

A beehive the size of an elephant rested inside a tree trunk cavern. Swarms of workers buzzed about, stingers hot with venom. Dancing distress, they smelled like ripe bananas. Awa saw no reason for alarm. Trees and bushes were heavy with flowers. The ground was a mosaic of petals. Deep-throated blossoms bulged with fragrant nectar. Inside the hive, the queen pushed an egg from her abdomen into a cell every minute. Workers spit nectar into the queen's mouth. A thousand nurses buzzed over a developing brood. Drones were fat and frisky. Bee paradise.

Sentinel bees clustered around Awa's mouth. She was afraid they might sting her. Was she the danger? They spit honey and venom on her tongue, a bittersweet concoction. Night fell like a dark curtain. A cold scar moon hung overhead, a desperate lantern in deep dark. Sentinels wagged their butts and buzzed away from the giant hive. Awa flew among a thousand thousand bees toward Smokeland's border, where flowers dissolved and cathedral trees crumbled into poison sand.

The slash of moon dripped blood. Confused bees flew into the ground. They ate their own wings and stung rocks. Faceted eyes clouded over and sparking hearts burned out. A thousand thousand wings flew ahead of Awa and turned to smoke. She choked. Confronted with the famed horror of the border realm, Awa tried to slow down, tried to turn back for bee paradise, but she no longer had the speed of thought. Her mind was sluggish terror and then blank as void-smoke enveloped her. A taste of the sentinels lingered in her mouth. A stinger caught in a tooth pricked her tongue. Venom flowed to her heart and she swooned.

Father and other good Empire citizens claimed there was no

realm of imagination, no true land of visions and spirits. Smoke-land was sleepwalking sickness, drunken dreams, or Green El-der nonsense. That explained tattoos, burnt hair, and the treasures folks brought back from their adventures. Smoke-walkers know-ing what they shouldn't or couldn't was another matter. Father couldn't explain that away. He just insisted Mother's exotic herbs and concoctions were family secrets.

Southern thief-lords sold or burned any woman who knew too much. Northern savages sliced smoke-walkers from navel to chin to expel demons. Priests and witchdoctors poisoned their breath bodies and stole spirit-blood to power gate-spells or do other con-jure. This was a living death. Good Empire citizens locked up smoke-walkers to train for priesthood if they were men or drain as transgressors if they were women. And a *veson*—what *Anawanama* northlanders called someone who was neither man nor woman—had to declare for one or another horrible fate: living as a man or dying as a woman. So . . .

Awa returned from her first Smokeland trip to Mother's garden and let the Smokeland-knowledge taste sweet on her tongue then swallowed it quickly unspoken. That made her muscles lumpy and her joints wobbly. She snorted wisps of border-void and felt dizzy.

Father was still yelling at Mother about an unruly daughter who'd end up like witch-woman Kyrie: wandering a cold moun-tain, bloody and bitter, childless and without love. Mother dis-tracted him with a sack of jewels and coins while Awa struggled back to her everyday self.

The scar moon was low and the sun about to rise over Moth-er's garden. Silver-leafed herbs brooded around the well and spice-bushes scented the air. Awa focused on cinnamony aromas. The everyday was as compelling as Smokeland. Mother must have car-ried Awa's breath body back from the forest.

"Forget the elephants." Mother pleaded with Father. Her

willful hair was braided down in thick plaits. Her brown cheeks sagged. "This *unruly* child has brought in a treasure." Counting the money, Father didn't notice the wild pup licking Awa's face. Mother chased him off before Father put a bolt in his furry hide. Dogs harassed the goats who had no fat to worry away. "Selling Awa has saved your farm," Mother said.

Father looked up from his money bag at the tumble-down corn crumbling in the fields. Fruit trees were covered in a fuzzy scale. Goats bleated at kids sucking their dry teats. Father had stolen all the milk. "We'll see if the farm can be saved," he said. His eyes were flicks of flame, his trim beard patchy. "We'll see."

Awa's face was flame-hot, her hands cold. They were selling her on her birthday, like a savage girl nobody wanted to feed anymore.

3

Surprise

Djola climbed along the ragged cliffs, agile and practiced. He dangled a moment over a dark tidal pool, appreciating his strength, the salt air, and white-water birds diving for fish. He grabbed three shells, not yet sun-bleached, for the children, and a rare spiky urchin for Samina. He jumped over the pool and ran through a maze of caves and canyons toward their cozy cottage. He chuckled. Home looked like driftwood caught in a rockslide. Tree limbs obscured a broken chimney.

A secret hideaway meant dusty rides to the capital city, ten days on the Empire road or more, if he had to wait out storms. He hated leaving for Council before repairing the chimney or helping Samina fix the windcatcher. Rotating bundles of reeds cooled hot days and warmed chill nights, but were making such a racket, nobody could sleep at night or think during the day.

Samina stood on the roof by the windcatcher. A sweaty tunic hugged her muscled buttocks and thighs. Her face was the golden brown of nearby cliffs. Silver tattoos snaked under one blue-violet eye and over the other. Silver and blue lip-tint matched her eyes.

Strange to him once, beautiful now. Djola married Samina for peace and found love.

Mumbling about broken tools, Samina replaced a bent cross-beam. Reed-wheels rotated softly again, like wind whispering in the bushes.

"You've fixed the windcatcher despite broken tools," Djola called up to her, "and I must be going. I'm long overdue."

"Who travels far in storm season, even on a warhorse?" She leapt down in front of him. "Everyone will be late, even those who live close." She searched Djola's face. "You didn't show Nuar your map, did you?" Samina knew Djola better than anyone.

"We talked a little about it."

She balled her fists and pounded his chest. "You smell of bats and sea urchins."

He held up the spiky purple shell and grinned at the delight in her eyes. "Yours."

She cupped it gently. "How do you find these?" She pressed her body to his and kissed him, a slow dance of tongues and lips. "We should take a ride on the waves."

"On that flimsy raft? When I come back." He displayed three flat star discs. "For Tessa, Bal, and Quint."

"Not a crack or blemish, three perfect shells." Samina shook her head. "Master of Poisons? Why aren't you Master of Weeds and Wild Things?"

"Azizi invited me to the stone-wood table and named me Master of Poisons."

Samina set the shells in a window. "You can't name yourself? Use your true name?"

"Who masters the wild?"

"Exactly!" An old argument flared out of nowhere, like a poison storm bursting from static and shimmer. Why blame him for the weather? Why fight over the price of tree oil and mangos? Over too many fruit trees going to flower but not to fruit? Over the taste of sand on every breath? Djola agreed, something must be done, that's why he headed to Council.

"I don't want you to go," Samina declared. "We could take the children to Eidhou Mountain, visit my sister. She sent a bushel of mangos."

"Your sister will be at Council."

"Sister Kyrie can take care of herself."

"So can I."

"On Mount Eidhou, the air is sweet, the rain reasonable."

"For now. We'll go when I come back. You'll be fine here while I'm gone."

Samina poked him. "The gods of the crossroads are tricksters."

"Only Nuar and my guard know this place and the guards get lost. Inland villagers think we're pirates."

"I *am* a pirate. We used to raid this coast." Samina sucked back tears. "Twenty new funeral mounds in the village——a ghost village soon. Let us come with you."

"When Council sits, rebels rile the people up and priests snatch children to bleed for conjure spells. The capital is no place for you all."

She took a battle stance. "No one tells me my place."

Djola raised his hands high. "True. But we agreed to make this our home. You feared Kyrie would turn our children into rebels."

"I don't know anymore. Would that be so bad?"

"Rebels chase a hopeless cause. They're in disarray, a mob."

"You twist my words against me!" Samina paced around him, a captain on a floundering ship. "Just because you argue well doesn't mean you're right."

Djola retreated to the kitchen, to the smell of ripe mangos, cardamom, and kola nuts. He plucked a slice of warm nut bread from a basket. His Aido bag lay on the table stuffed with map scrolls, Kyrie's mangos, and Samina's pirate charms.

"Where is everybody? I must say good-bye." Djola climbed to the loft and poked blankets and pillows then glanced into the rafters. A fly twitched free of a half-formed spiderweb. Samina raced out the back door to an empty yard. Half the sky had turned orange again.

"Their cloaks are gone." Djola stepped beside her, touching his shoulder to hers.

"They snuck away. While your men readied the horses."

Djola headed to the corral hidden in the trees. "Most of the horses are gone."

"Quint saw something at the ruins by the village boneyard yesterday. Something for you. I heard him tell his sisters. That's where they went. Zst!" Samina cursed. She never let the children out when storms threatened, even if they wore cloaks *and* mesh veils. "They'll get lost. Or worse."

"Nuar says this is just a bit of bluster."

"Nobody doubts Chief Nuar's storm-sense, still . . ." Sand demons danced in from the table land and joined forces at the canyon walls.

Djola hugged her. "We'll find them."

Djola and Samina scrambled through a tunnel too dark and treacherous for horses. Samina led the way with a smoky torch. They'd reach the village boneyard in under an hour. Djola refused to imagine the worst, Samina's influence. Pirates saw opportunity in every direction. Horse tracks at the corral had been clear. Djola's guard, twelve seasoned warriors, rode with the children toward the canyon maze— Quint's idea. Their six-year-old son was always plotting mischief and keeping spirits high. The sky looked threatening, but sand demons collapsed in fickle winds. His guards were northlanders: *Ishba, Sorit, Kahoe*—tribes that aligned with *Anawanama* chiefs after the Empire invaded. They could handle storms or rogue pirates raiding for slaves.

Rano, the captain, was as fierce as a snow bear. He'd come through war and twenty years of peace with Djola. Rano doted on Tessa, Djola's eldest daughter. When she was born, Rano pledged to die for Djola and his family. Drunken bravado perhaps, but almost true. Tessa probably talked Rano into this adventure. She had a diplomat's tongue and a pirate woman's charm. Bal, the middle child, must be guiding the troops—she knew the maze better than anyone.

Djola touched Samina's back. "Don't be upset. They've planned a surprise."

"Why didn't anyone tell me?" Samina picked up the pace.

"Then it wouldn't be a surprise."

She turned to him with skeptical eyebrows and downturned lips. "You know I hate surprises and secrets."

He dodged her doubt. "This is your fault. Or your grandfather's." Pirates who tried raiding from the cove perished in the canyon maze, until her grandfather mapped a tunnel route, left over from when this was *Lahesh* land. Samina inherited Grandfather's maps and convinced Djola to build a hideaway near the entrance.

"No. Tessa, Bal, and Quint hope to delay you another day."

"We'll find them in less than an hour. I can leave after lunch. The light lasts long."

"Not as long as you think."

"Warhorses will make the Empire Road before dark."

The ancient boneyard was a gently sloping field covered by whistling acacia trees. Poison storms had taken their toll on nearby farms. Grain and fruit rotted; soil blew away; yet whistling acacias held their ground. Temple ruins to forgotten gods poked through prickly branches. Ancestor mounds, stone tombs, and funeral pyres were scattered among the trees. Everyone was buried here: citizens, northlanders, pirates, and people nobody remembered. When the wind blew, ancestors spoke through acacia gourds—fat bulbs along the branches that ended in knife-sharp thorns. The thorns discouraged hungry herds, and wildflowers growing in the thicket drew bees and hummingbirds. A perfect place to speak to the ancestors.

Djola and Samina smudged soil on their foreheads and whispered praises to sacred ground. Warhorses flicked tails at pesky flies. Djola's guardsmen shuffled their feet and offered sheepish grins as fifteen-year-old Tessa raced to her parents. "We'd have made it back in time, but Quint ran off with the old codex." She had Samina's watery eyes, sturdy physique, and flinty nature. "The words had faded. Why give that to you? So he's hiding."

Samina peered down the village road. "Hiding? Quint gets lost so easily."

"Don't worry." Bal jabbed at Djola with a fighting staff. "Captain Rano is on his trail." She had green-flecked dark eyes like Djola's. "Rano says he'll teach me to be the best tracker." Djola groaned when she got him between the ribs. "You say I have a fighting spirit, yet you ride into battle and leave me behind." Twelve-year-old Bal wanted to go to Council and protect him from scoundrels and haints.

Tessa sucked her teeth. "Quint's mad you're leaving, *before* taking us up the coast to hunt old conjure books."

"You won't find ancient *Anawanama* spells to save us." Samina shook her head. "That's all been lost, even old *Lahesh* wisdom."

"Not all of it," Djola insisted. Samina couldn't argue with that.

"Why go to Council if storms rage and masters ignore you?" Tessa stood in Djola's face, bold as a pirate captain, speaking for her brother, sister, and Samina. She threw her arms around Djola's neck. "Please stay. You can do more good here than in the capital."

Djola stroked his daughter's weave of braids. "I wish that were true." His resolve cracked. Was he a fool, banging his head on Azizi's table, betraying his own people?

Captain Rano stuck his face through a ruin wall. "Quint's in here. I just can't reach him."

A sand demon swirled down the village road, dust from the north, from Nuar's crops. Ancestors whistled a scratchy tirade as Djola and Samina struggled through thorny branches into the ruin. Trees had reclaimed most of the temple ground. Quint was tucked in a crossroads altar at the top of a tower, eyes filled with tears. He clutched a codex wrapped in metal-mesh. Rano stood under him.

Samina climbed stairs that ended in broken limbs. "How'd you get up there?"

Quint took a breath. The altar listed to one side, snapping a branch. He froze.

"He went up and down before, to get the codex," Bal said. "I was too heavy."

Samina shot Djola a desperate glance. He winced. Quint and his sisters had risked everything for an empty book. The altar-tower rattled as the sand demon closed in. "Jump!" Djola shouted.

Quint flew from the altar as the tower collapsed behind him. Samina bounced on a branch, sprang high, and snatched him out of the air. Cradling her son, she slammed butt-first into Rano's shoulder and chest. They fell against a grassy ancestor mound. Rano was knocked senseless. Samina and Quint rolled away unscathed.

Quint thought if they couldn't find him, Djola wouldn't be able to leave. Nobody scolded him. Rano praised Quint's courage, although the words came out garbled. Quint gaped at the addled captain then sank in a corner, pouting.

Bal poked him. "The gods of the crossroads smiled on us."

Tessa kissed the knot on Rano's head. She and Bal danced up and down the stairs and rolled across the ground until Quint was giggling and prancing around the cottage with them. Samina prepared a feast, for the guardsmen too. Djola let Quint sit in his lap when they sat down to eat: fish in a mango sauce, nut bread, plantains, and cardamom rice.

"This food tastes better than usual." Quint savored the last morsel and leaned back into Djola's full belly.

"You need a bath!" Samina wiped mango from Quint's cheek and brushed sand from his hair. He tugged her toward Djola and the three of them almost spilled onto the table. Djola's breath caught in his throat. Giving up the old ways, fighting for the Empire, he never expected to raise three children with his pirate love.

"No more climbing through ruins for old books!" Samina tried to scowl and failed, and so avoided Djola's eyes. Outside a distant wind wailed. She blamed him for sandstorms and high-spirited children. Unreasonable. She indulged the children as much as he did—so they could belong to themselves. Bal sang an ancient *Anawanama* song to the crossroads gods.

> *Crossroads tricksters crack you apart*
> *Truth upside down and inside out*
> *Right side wrong and backside front*

"You still remember that?" Djola had taught her when she was little. Quint clapped a rhythm and Tess added harmony. Djola glanced around the table, lifted his wineglass, and leaned into Samina. Silver tattoos around her eyes were snowflakes in a midnight sky. "You all are my heart beating."

Samina pulled away and started clearing up the last of the feast. "You're losing the light. If you're going, go now."

Djola packed Quint's blank codex with his travel cloak. Tessa gave him spells to avoid danger on the road. He clasped her neatly-written scroll to his chest. Bal offered her fighting staff. "No." He smiled. "You'll need it to keep everyone safe, while I'm gone."

Rano had recovered his wits and protested when Djola sent three guards to the cliffs and three to the village to watch over his family. Only six guards would leave Djola vulnerable at Council. "It's just for a short while." Djola hugged the children, then eyed his wife.

"Twenty years. Why does it still have to be you?" Samina slugged him and headed out the back door, fussing over crows in the berries, fussing at Djola really. No hug or good-bye kiss, no fortification for the battles ahead. Pirates made terrible wives.

He slammed out the front, rattling bamboo wind chimes. He cursed willful witch women as he mounted his horse. "Who else?" He shouted at Rano. "If not me, who?"

4

The Griot of Griots

Green Elders in cloud-silk travel robes stood around Father. They were smooth-cheeked, eyes outlined in black kohl, ropes of hair knotted with seeds. Green and red mica glittered on their palms. They gave Father another money bag and strode into Mother's Smokeland herb garden. Awa shook her head. They'd come from the sweet desert to take her away. Her chest tightened as they played drums, flutes, and hunter's harps. Were they all *vesons*, neither man nor woman, playing every instrument, eating little flesh?

Awa's three brothers gaped at strangers who jingle-jangled as they talked. Her brothers were headed off to apprentice in Holy City at the southernmost border of the Empire. They'd live and work a few weeks' ride from a thief-lord fortress. With such experience, they'd be important men someday, maybe advisors to the emperor. They looked foolish, smirking and grabbing their crotches. She caught oldest brother Kenu's eye. The smirk slid off his face.

"Don't play the fool." Kenu jabbed his brothers.

"Kenu could build a tower to the stars," Father shouted. "But you'd rather your sons be beggars or pirates."

"When have I said that?" Mother shouted too.

"I hear what you don't say, woman." Father quieted down.

"Do you?" Mother shook her head. Father only heard himself.

"When barren fields drink our sweat and a blight steals the harvest, I hear you."

"You sound like a high-nosed Elder." Mother flicked a finger under the tip of her nose. "All the time talking down to me."

He ground his teeth. "Awa will learn good conjure."

"Any conjure can be perverted. Even Green Elder spells." Mother sneered. "You know this better than I do." She didn't want Awa to go.

Father clutched the money bags and tramped away. He'd lived with the Elders, learned poetry, masonry, and metalwork, before inheriting his brother's farm and his brother's witch-wife, a woman too wild to love. Kenu said Father hated those years in the enclave—fasting or eating bugs, spouting jumba jabba all day long, and walking on hot coals. Father had ugly purple scars on the bottoms of his feet and a cache of secret scrolls and spells. City chiefs, thief-lords, and priests clamored for his building conjure. He'd even built a gate for Hezram, high priest of Holy City, and earned a sack of sky rocks. Still, Father regularly cursed the Elders for ruining his life. Awa hugged her knees, panicked. A lapsed Elder selling his daughter to an enclave didn't make sense.

"What's this face?" Mother pinched Awa's nose and tried to smile.

"I don't want to go," Awa said.

"Green Elders risked their lives to find you." Mother gathered Awa close. The lightning tang of Smokeland clung to them both. "Elders roam the forests, plains, and mountain cliffs, collecting stories and talking folks out of foolishness."

Awa scrunched up her face, unimpressed.

"They're free." Mother's usually bright eyes had gone misty.

"They have adventures across the Empire. They know a detour around the poison desert and wander to northern lands beyond Mount Eidhou." She tickled Awa's sides. "Elders sing songs and tell stories all day long. You'll love that."

Awa perked up. "Will I come back a griot storyteller to tell you tales?"

"Perhaps." Mother's lips trembled. "Yari, the griot of griots, has chosen you."

Awa glowered at the Green Elders. She spat out the bee stinger from Smokeland. It burnt her tongue. Yari was a legendary griot, a walking library who knew something about everything. Still, "I don't want to go."

"Would you rather be sold to a transgressor hut to get bled for high priest Hezram?"

"Why sell me at all?"

Mother bit her lip and traced the snake birthmark on Awa's scalp that wiggled to her eyebrow. She smoothed a snarl of hair and whispered, "I'll poison your father for stealing you from me. On your birthday." She clenched her jaw, serious. "His favorite bread."

"Oh." Awa felt uncertain about poison. Did Mother mean to kill Father?

Mother blinked away tears. "With the Elders, you'll map all of Smokeland. Think on that."

Awa loved to draw maps and plan visits to faraway places, but getting sold away from the family wasn't a story she'd told on herself. She clutched a honeycomb from Smokeland, her only possession, and stared at Kenu. The snake birthmark along his cheek quivered and his nose flared. He wanted to cry.

There'd be nobody who would do everything he dared. Not just freeing the elephants, Awa poured water in Father's wine so he wouldn't get so drunk. She stole forbidden scrolls from his bag for

Kenu to read in the night. Kenu whispered to Awa about the village girl whose eyes were so deep and dark, he got lost in her gaze.

Why didn't Kenu protest?

Elders were dragging Awa off to hot coals and worm meals. There'd be nobody for Kenu to share secrets with; nobody to make up funny stories to save him from Father. Two days ago, instead of getting drunk and beating Kenu, Father laughed over Awa's tale of dogfish men chasing mud maidens and washing away in the rain. Father even blamed the elephant escape on Awa, not Kenu. How could Kenu let Father sell her to his enemies?

Awa clung to Mother. "I'd rather stay with you and brother Kenu."

Mother's face ran with tears, but she said nothing.

"Bugs in your hair. You're a mess." Kenu tried to laugh. Her younger brothers had no problem chortling. Who would they laugh at tomorrow? Kenu chased them off.

"A bee." Awa pouted. "They don't make a mess."

"I know." Kenu touched the snake birthmark on his cheek. "Don't forget me."

"I won't." Awa wiggled the snake on her forehead. "What'll you do in Holy City without me? Don't make the high priest mad."

"I won't. I promise." Kenu held her so close, so tight she couldn't breathe.

The Green Elders were gentle yet firm as they pulled Awa away. The sun was a white disk in gray. Awa kept looking back until Mother and Kenu disappeared in the mist hugging the herb garden. Awa wanted to shriek. What good would that do? She forced herself to remember every Smokeland moment. Drawing a map in her mind was better than burning with rage.

5

Storm

The first week of Council was as unreasonable and frustrating as fighting with Nuar and Samina. In an afternoon break, Djola escaped to a south wall of the emperor's citadel—a maze of domes, columns, gates, and towers. He was a solitary figure in an *Anawanama* travel cloak and mesh veil. The third void-storm in a week roared through the capital.

This wasn't a regular wall of sand blowing in from distant dunes and blotting out the sky. Rogue twisters popped up here and there from nowhere, from static and shimmer. People barricading windows were too late. Whirligigs snaked through the streets, searing cheeks, burning lungs, and desiccating ancient cathedral trees. The library's onion domes were engulfed in sooty sparks. Stone turrets swayed in a shower of static. Wooden shops and hovels rattled. Thatched roofs lifted up and spun away.

Djola took perverse pleasure in this spectacle. The good citizens were primed for change. Tonight's Council session would be better: hope was on the other side of a lethal storm.

An elephant staggered down a riverstone alley toward the citadel's iron gates. Harassed by an angry mob, the elephant flapped her ears and trumpeted. A squall of soot and sparks chased her and had good citizens charging for cover. Djola chuckled at false bravado. The squall wound itself tight behind the elephant's tail, twisting and sparking with a fury and then disappeared. Nobody ventured forth to take up the chase. Who could say where else a poison whirlwind might dance? Twisters vanished and the air cleared. Blue-green water sparkled beyond the docks. Djola opened his cloak. Rogue elephants and demon storms fueled his resolve. A sea breeze would cool his temper.

The elephant stomped distress, calling to family, pleading for rescue—no elephant reply, just horses and men hollering in the distance. Maybe she was the last of her clan to survive. A massive beast roaming behind the emperor's citadel without a handler was strange. How had she gotten to the back alley? No guards raised an alarm. They were busy patrolling capital streets, quashing unrest. Djola was right to leave Samina and the children behind. Council always faced riots these days.

His heart warmed to see the wild elephant, a fellow northlander, a rebel defying the odds, making her own way. What would a simple bolt or spear do against an angry elephant or thousands of anxious citizens for that matter? The People needed vision, a map to tomorrow. Djola was the Empire's greatest mapmaker. He stroked the spell-scrolls in his bag, years of hard work. Samina's wisdom was there too. She would tell him to be careful, patient this evening at Council. He could do that. Soon was better than never.

The elephant shook off a cloud of dust and sparks. She wandered across the alley, her trunk writhing in front of her. The freak storms were like sandpaper. Blisters on her back glistened with blood. No longer dodging a mob or a whirlwind, she poked a jagged, broken tusk at an empty grain bin and stumbled through a dry water trough.

"Have you come to Council with a petition from the animal-people?" Djola sat down at the edge of the wrought-iron gates. "No? Well, I'll tell them for you: disaster is upon us."

His feet dangled between the bars. Mist condensed on coppery skin, and a sea breeze wafted through dense black hair. The weather shifted so quickly. As the sun disappeared into the Salty Sea, his eyes flickered in dwindling light. His moustache drooped and itched his lower lip. He was clean-shaven except for the mustache, a northern custom that made him look *savage*—or worse, like a Green Elder!—to folks in Arkhys City.

Samina urged him to grow a beard, do any masquerade that might gain access to people's right minds. Djola refused. An itchy beard would aggravate him and impress nobody. Samina had a head for gazing at stars, navigating the seas, or reading books, not face-to-face politicking. After hearing petitions, Council would curse and argue all night. In the morning, Emperor Azizi would do nothing, and more people, animals, and grasslands would die, unless Djola forced Council to admit truth: no hope without change, no change without sacrifice.

The elephant bellowed, tears darkening the wrinkled skin around her eyes.

"I know." He'd rather be home too, at the north edge of the Eidhou mountain range with Samina, waiting for the moon to rise over the Salty Sea, making love in the sand.

The elephant caught Djola's scent and halted below him. She lifted her trunk, exploring his secrets. He smelled of crossroads conjure and root work, of sweet water and mint tea, of ink and musty parchment. He put his hand through the bars. The elephant got a whiff of mango and cathedral nuts and moved in close. Djola emptied the food from his bag for her. Her thin ears radiated heat as she gobbled this scant food offering. Mangos in the mountain groves were still plentiful. After the last sweet morsel, she wrapped her trunk around his hand, marking him with her scent and gathering in his. The two finger bones at the end of her hairy nostrils tickled—a tale for Tessa and Bal. His daughters loved elephants.

"Whayoa!" Emperor guards not from his loyal escort appeared at Djola's shoulder, burly, hairy fellows with weapons ready. Southern barbarians?

"Hold." Djola gripped their spears before they did anything foolish. The elephant trumpeted. "Run." Djola spoke *Anawanama*, his mother's tongue. The guards wouldn't know a northern language, but the elephant might. "Leave this city while you have the chance." The elephant raised her trunk, beckoning him to join her. "No. I must stay."

A scrappy guard pulled his spear arm free and said, "Did a caravan lose this beast?" Djola blocked him. The elephant lumbered down a path to the foothills of Mount Eidhou. She must smell fruit trees and mountain springs. The passageway was wide enough for her, and Mountain Gates would open for an escape. Djola smiled at good decisions. The scrappy guard grimaced. "Someone has lost a fortune."

"That's a wild one," Djola said.

"There aren't any wild elephants left." He smirked at Djola.

"Poison desert is chasing the last few into the city," Djola declared. "A pity."

"Why waste pity on lumbering beasts?" Nobody wanted to hear about elephants and bees dying off. Samina and Nuar were right about this. "Our children starve."

"Zst!" The second guard hushed his comrade with a curse. A guard shouldn't argue with a master—even a clean-shaven northlander like Djola.

"I love my children too," Djola said, defensive. Everyone assumed northlanders sold or abandoned their daughters *and* sons without a thought.

The second guard managed a smile. "Petitioners are waiting."

"Yes." Djola watched the elephant disappear. "I make a map to tomorrow for all."

Forest-dwelling *Anawanama*, desert-rogue *Zamanzi,* and other so-called *savages* north of Arkhys City had grown restless under the Empire's fist. Djola couldn't say or think *savage* without wanting to argue with the word, take it back, turn it around. Why should proud people slave and starve to feed greedy Empire citizens? Southern thief-lords around the Golden Gulf also chafed against taxes, desert winds, and the rule of law. They preferred to let the best blades claim the most riches.

Samina once saw Djola as the architect of peace, a hero who turned northern tribes and southern thief-lords into loyal subjects of Emperor Azizi. She fell in love with a master of the impossible. Everybody was ready for peace back then. Twenty years gone by and Djola's peace had frayed with each dry riverbed and bleak harvest. Southern barbarians grew bolder, raiding Empire caravans and tree-oil strongholds. Northern tribes did the same. And now there was a plague of void-storms. Nothing to lose with death coming from every direction. Samina was right to worry.

Djola refused to scratch his hind parts, tug his mustache, and wait for someone else to act. "We save each other," he declared.

"Is that so?" The scrappy guard drew Djola into a dark archway and blindfolded him. "Jackals roam these corridors, and hyenas. They chew traitor hearts and suck spy bones."

"What a way to die," the other guard groaned. "We know the safe route."

"Safe?" Djola muttered.

They hurried through a maze of passageways back to the Council chamber, back to unsettling truth: they could all—master, thief-lord, guard, emperor, and elephant—lose everything.

6

A Mission

Awa was exhausted. Long-legged Green Elders had marched for a week, hardly resting or eating, rarely talking. They shared names only once. Awa remembered Yari, a *veson* with dancing braids and a singer's voice, and Isra, a spiky-haired barbarian with a throaty laugh. No one else—she'd been too sad or mad to pay attention.

Yari gave full purses to farmers who sold daughters and younger sons to stave off ruin. The farmers were desperate, like Father. But Yari never bargained, even when the girls were skinny and sickly and likely to slow them down. A few boys ran off, back to their farms perhaps. Isra railed against treachery and warned Yari to save some sky rocks so they wouldn't starve. Yari shrugged and kissed Isra's cheek.

Mother was wrong. A Green Elder journey through the wild country wasn't an adventure filled with song and wonder. Scrambling over roots and loose rocks took most of their focus. They traveled mountain tunnels or rugged goat paths, avoiding solid elephant roads. At night Yari whispered explanations to sullen faces while Isra and the other Elders kept watch. Most good citizens had forgotten that elephants first stomped wide thoroughfares from glacier-fed lakes to fruit forests. Awa knew this already. She and Kenu had read elephant escapades in Father's scrolls.

High priest Hezram collected tolls on the elephant roads, even far from Holy City. If travelers couldn't pay, they were sold to pay the debt or sent to transgressor huts to be bled. Hezram declared Elders enemies of the temple and banned them from elephant roads. He paid a generous reward for captured Elders. Mother spoke truth. Yari, Isra, and the others risked their lives to collect Sprites. Crafty farmers sold Yari their daughters then turned *vie** in for a reward. Mercenaries hunted them. No Elders sang for fear of ambush.

Goat paths challenged muscles and joints. Awa hurt all over. When Elders stopped for water and a few berries, they also rubbed achy ankles. She wished she could have gone with Kenu to apprentice in Holy City next year. Building a tower to the stars had to be better than running and hiding for your life. The other Sprites cut their eyes at her, suspicious. She had no one to trade stories with, even the bees in her hair were quiet. Did Kenu feel as lonely as she did?

Awa fell asleep in the middle of swallowing a mango slice and ended on someone's back, her head bouncing against spongy braids. Elders passed her from back to back until she woke from dreams of riding an elephant and slid down. Fear twisted the faces of the other Sprites. Awa counted sixteen. When she'd fallen asleep there were only eight, including her. Isra put a hand to her lips to stop her asking a question.

The six Elders were shadow warriors, fading in and out of view, as quiet as sweetgrass fluttering on a breeze. They spoke with their hands and mimicked jackals and crows to cover noisy steps. Awa

---

* *Anawanama* pronoun for *veson*

might have marveled at griot tales come true, but she was sweaty and hungry and wanted to sneak back home. A stupid idea. No girls ran off. Father would turn her away or sell her off to someone else. Mother would weep and brother Kenu would fuss, but they'd take Father's side. And then where would she be?

Isra marched the Sprites down a shallow creek and halted suddenly, still as stone. They were being tracked. Awa gulped breath. Her heart felt louder than the cricket serenade. Behind them, Yari drummed and sang. *Vie* pulled fire from the air, a bright blue column of flame that lit up the trees from root to crown. Another griot tale come true.

The trackers emerged from the trees. They stumbled over their own shadows, hissing and spitting, wobbly as drunks. Yellow cloaks snagged on branches. They were Hezram's warrior acolytes. Spears, swords, and bows slipped from their grasp. They collided with one another and collapsed in the mud. Yari's drumbeats made Awa woozy too. Isra tugged her and the other Sprites farther downstream. Awa's head cleared as the drumming got fainter.

Isra squeezed her hand. "Yari drums the warriors into a stupor and steals their weapons." Isra took great pleasure in this. "You could learn to be a shadow warrior too." Awa didn't want to be any kind of warrior. "Holy City swords and bows will fetch a good purse. That means a feast tomorrow and supplies for our long trip home."

"Where is home?" Awa thought Elders were always on the run with no real home.

"We usually make home, every day."

Awa didn't understand this answer. "Oh?"

"Nothing but danger to eat here. No time for home."

Before Awa formulated her next question, Yari and one of Hezram's acolytes trotted down the creek, chatting and smiling like two friends. They both carried a bundle of weapons.

"Only the youngest dropped all the way to sleep." Yari grinned. "I had to reason with the others." Awa wished she'd seen that.

Isra grumbled. "How much did reason cost?"

"A few bags of herbs."

The acolyte trailing Yari was bumps, bones, and unruly hair. He couldn't have been more than fourteen. He threw up in the fragrant tonic-bushes that grew along the creek. Awa and the other Sprites jerked away.

Yari held him up. "Hezram drugs his warrior acolytes."

Isra groaned. "We were lucky. This squad didn't know your tricks." Isra gripped the boy. "I presume Yari *persuaded* you to join us." The acolyte nodded. "Welcome, but you'll be the last to join."

They headed into hot, wet forests. *Anawanama* territory, where Hezram's acolytes wouldn't follow. Warm rain poured through the leaf canopy, drenching everybody. Slippery roots battered exhausted feet. Isra paused inside the fragrant trunk of a cathedral tree that rose above the clouds. A swarm of demon-flies lit up the dark with pale blue light. The Elders shouted and laughed with one another in savage tongues. Sprites huddled together and whispered. The former acolyte sat alone like Awa. He shook his head and coughed.

Awa rubbed sore toes and listened to the other Sprites complain. What good would that do? She drew a map in the dirt, noting the twists and turns they'd made on their march. There were gaps when she'd been asleep. She drew what she could imagine. Yari ambled close and offered her a gourd of fruity liquid. Awa gulped this down. Her mouth tingled and, after a few moments, everything looked clearer, brighter.

"What was that?" Awa stared into the gourd and clutched Yari's hand.

"Juice from midnight berries helps night vision."

"Does it hurt to pull fire?" She had a thousand thousand questions. Yari took the empty gourd and almost stepped on her map. "Watch out!" she yelled.

Balanced on one foot, Yari peered at her work. "*Anawanama* always know where they are. Blindfold them, spin them around in a maze, then bury them in a hole. They'll point and say that is west to the water and there is east to the mountains and sweet desert." Yari stuck corn stalks in Awa's dirt map. "There is your father's farm, right? Behind us is south to Holy City and the Golden Gulf." *Vie* drew the Salty Sea and *Mama Zamba* mountains. "March a little north along the sea and you reach Arkhys City. After that, free lands beyond the Empire's grip." *Vie* drew a clump of trees. "We head east through *Anawanama* territory."

Awa studied Yari's additions to her dirt drawing. "I've never been all the way to savage woods."

"Savage?" Yari frowned, then smiled. Demon-flies glowed behind swirls of *vie*'s hair. "The *Anawanama* remember your mother. Does she remember them?"

Awa shrugged. "*Anawanama* have map-sense and storm-sense too." She said what Kenu told her. "They read the wind, feel thunder in the dirt, but have no words for left and right."

"I can teach you *Anawanama*. They see more colors than *Lahesh* do."

Awa wondered: If a person learned *Anawanama* would she have a map of the world inside? Would she get a storm-sense and feel the wind and rain coming? "Can I learn both? And their stories?"

"Yes."

Awa forgot throbbing feet and hugged this prospect to her heart.

"This is my mission." Yari sat down next to her and drew a crossroads in the dirt. "To be a bridge, from the ancestors to tomorrow."

"Is that why you had to buy so many Sprites?"

Yari stiffened. Anger or terror flitted across *vie*'s face. Perhaps both. Awa wanted to take her stupid question back. Yari leaned close and spoke with a scratchy voice. "You all will conjure a new world." *Vie* patted her hand, as sad as Father staring at sick fruit trees and dead goat kids, as fierce as Mother planting Smokeland herbs that resisted poison sand. "Men like high priest Hezram want to steal the future. We can't have that now, can we?"

Awa puzzled *vie*'s words and shook her head. "I guess not." A Smokeland bee clung to a tight ringlet and buzzed.

"You're a bridge also." Yari sounded excited. "Perhaps you can teach me bee-talk."

Bees liked Awa and she liked them. How could she teach that?

7

The Emperor's Council

Djola pulled off the blindfold and shrugged free of the scrappy guard. The vast Council chamber with its high ceilings and sky windows was tucked in the middle of the citadel. Djola counted twenty doors, each wide enough for two elephants walking side by side, and leading to who knows where. Only Emperor Azizi, his guards, and Lilot, the chief cook, knew the safe ways in and out. Treachery here meant a difficult escape. Stone walls were thick to hold secrets and traitor screams. Enemy blood was easy to mop up—the floor was polished marble, quarried up the coast by northlanders, which people no one would say. *Lahesh* tinkerers? *Lahesh* animal masks hung on the walls: a menagerie of fire-breathers about to pounce. Djola chuckled.

The *Lahesh* say: *Steel is sharper than any claw and only people spit fire.* Nobody thought so-called savages had much to offer the Empire. But Djola knew better. If he mastered *Xhalan Xhala*, ancient *Lahesh* conjure, he'd wield the power of Smokeland in the everyday. He'd touch a withered tree and feel what caused void-winds to blow across the land. He'd clasp a man's hand, taste his breath, and know his dreams. Djola would be able to see what might be, even call it forth.

Dizzy at the thought of such power, Djola leaned into a *Lahesh* mask, a creature with metal-mesh hair, ruby eyes, and stone teeth in a maul the size of his head. The dusty fire-breather made him sneeze. *Xhalan Xhala* was a formidable challenge, a *Lahesh* spell of spells, a closely guarded treasure, conjure that might break a mind. Samina would not approve and Nuar never trusted wily shadow warriors who married their enemies, but—

"Ignorance won't save us," he whispered to the mask. Wielding *Xhalan Xhala* to halt the poison desert, Djola could show Council, his wife and brother, and everybody that he was indeed a master of the impossible.

Dinner candles dribbled away. A waste of beeswax, it was still light. The high priest of Arkhys City and Council masters sat in roomy chairs around the stone heart of a long dead cathedral tree. They held their heads and sulked in their beards. No one touched a feast of roasted goat, spicy tubers, seaweed, and nut butters except flies and a cheeky rat. Emperor Azizi had a strange fondness for rats.

Djola slid into his chair. *Anawanama* spells carved in the arms tickled. A *savage* chair for a *savage* master. This used to irritate him, but his chair sat next to Azizi's now. Djola tossed cheese at friend rat, a sable fellow who'd sat in his lap on occasion. Truth be told, Djola liked rats too. Masters groused, as if purple tides, crop failures, and thief-lord raids were the rat's fault.

"Don't indulge the nasty beasts." The Master of Grain stood barefoot on the warm hearth stones. A tent of wood piled shoulder high threw flames up into the chimney. Grain's blue eyes sparkled against black skin as he soaked in heat like a panther gathering energy for the hunt. He was young, shrewd, and on the rise. A beardless northlander who'd disavowed his tribe (no one knew which one) to join the Empire, Grain had good reason for hating rats. He reminded Djola of himself, twenty years ago.

"Another poison storm ripped through the capital. Two dead." Grain shuddered.

"So much unrest." High priest Ernold rubbed crimson tattoos on his brown bald head. Gravy stains on his priestly robe looked like blood. He strode among Azizi's helmet-mask collection: a hundred warriors with thick necks and bulging eyes, all stolen from vanquished northlanders, tribes whose names had been lost. "Hezram in Holy City offers Dream Gate conjure to Azizi. Blood sacrifice would stop poison sand and bring order. Security."

"Kurakao!" The Master of Water praised the gods. A handsome rascal, yet this evening his silver eyes were dull gray, his strong back and shoulders hunched, his smooth skin sallow. "We should accept Hezram's offer."

The Master of Money, Water's twin brother, also had a sickly pallor and a hoarse wheeze as he agreed. "The price will only go up." Hard to tell Money and Water apart. Both were Hezram's toadies on Council, Ernold too, though he'd deny it.

Djola smacked the table and rattled empty plates. "You'd suck blood from our people, our *children*, to make spells for order?"

"Transgressors who offend the gods aren't our children," high priest Ernold said.

"Hezram does blood conjure with children in Holy City?" The Master of Arms tugged a red beard frosted silver. An incurable idealist, he burped sour breath and patted a belly poking up from broad hips, a dumpling burial ground. "Shame."

"Yes, but . . ." The Master of Books and Bones worried crumbs on his plate. The knotty beard on his sagging jowls was egg white. His eyes were black beads. He hugged a coarse cotton robe. "Griot storytellers claim freak storms never touch Holy City. Inside Dream Gates, weapons or weapon-spells turn on the men wielding them."

Grain snorted. "Half the city lives in huts, bleeding for these impregnable gates."

"And the glory of god. Bleeding is an honor for the fallen," Ernold declared. Grain laughed outright at priestly nonsense. Arms scowled. The other masters squirmed.

"Mixing blood and tree oil to conjure Dream Gates is illusion solution. Outside Holy City, poison dust still blows, devastating the land." Djola was losing patience. "From the mines to the farms to the forests, we must work together to reclaim the land, change our ways."

Money shook a mane of black hair. "We can't afford change."

Djola rolled his eyes. "You're against change on principle."

"Hope enchants you." Water shook his own mane and guzzled wine. "You step in dung and see the next harvest, not shit on your boots. Transgressor blood is cheap."

Djola poured water in his cup. "Cheap like a poison oasis in the desert."

Water stiffened. He'd stab Djola in the back if he could. "Speak plainly."

"That wasn't plain enough for you?" Djola downed his cup in one gulp.

"How much spirit debt for a Dream Gate?" Books and Bones worried waist beads.

"Only the conjurer of the gates incurs a debt." High priest Ernold squirmed in his chair. "He'd be an honored hero-soldier sacrificed to win a war."

"You don't believe in spirit debt. You piss on the old religions." Grain poked the embers. "You burn sacred cloth, cut tongues out, yet people still believe."

"War is brutal and pointless." Arms picked goat from his teeth. "I hate war."

"Are you joking?" Money and Water hooted together.

"War is a joke, but peace is more entertaining." Arms leapt in the air, twisting his hefty torso, flapping his cape like wings—an agile dancer, a formidable warrior. He landed by the goat cheese, chased rats away, and stuffed a creamy ball in his mouth. Grain smiled at his antics. Arms punched Grain's shoulders. Flirting? They whispered to one another and laughed.

"We must be serious." Money shoved his picked-over feast away. Water mirrored his brother's disdain. They spoke together, an irritating habit. "War is coming."

"May catastrophe come when I'm dead," Books and Bones sighed. "Why struggle? What comes, comes." Djola had hoped for the old librarian's support, not philosophical farting and groaning. "We aren't gods. Tomorrow belongs to them."

"Gods don't care about time." Djola gripped the librarian's ink-stained hands. "Tomorrow never comes and today belongs to us."

"True." Books and Bones bit his chapped lip. "And the past hasn't gone anywhere. Still . . ." He'd rather be in the shelves with his books.

Djola had to keep an eye on his mood. "We count on your wisdom and insight."

The door beside the warrior masks creaked and swung open to the Council antechamber. Yesterday this door opened on to a dim tunnel. Azizi's guards claimed citadel rooms changed places and hallways shifted also. Djola laughed at himself for believing tall tales for a second. A simple trick to make identical rooms and fake hallways—Empire illusions.

In the antechamber, blindfolded petitioners waved scrolls and shoved each other. They were penned in by ropes and surrounded by guards. Djola gasped as half-brother Nuar barged to the front of the mob. Gray hair puffed around his blindfold. Anger was chiseled across his sharp chin and high cheekbones. Djola bristled. A home ambush had proved insufficient. Chief Nuar had come to argue with Djola in front of Azizi and Council.

The black and brown mudcloth cloak draped over Nuar's long

limbs matched stolen drapes hanging at antechamber windows. A provocation. Under the mudcloth, he wore a leather and copper-mesh tunic, outlawed *Anawanama* armor—another provocation. Nuar carried a sweetgrass basket with braids of green and brown bark undulating along the sides and across the top. The beautiful design irritated Djola.

"Collect petitions, then guide them out," Arms commanded. Petitioners threw scrolls in the air. Most clattered against the walls and landed in the antechamber.

"Wait." Djola turned to Nuar and spoke *Anawanama*, their mother's tongue. "What can you say that I don't know?" The crowd veered toward his voice, toward an echo of the ancestors. Djola flinched as they pleaded: *Bad things are coming. Save us. Save me.*

A few petitioners elbowed Nuar. He drove them back and boomed in Empire vernacular, "Master of Poisons, we intend to survive." Nuar scrunched his face under the blindfold as if at a bad odor. "You feel too good about yourself"—he leaned over the ropes—"standing in the path of a deadly storm like an idiot." Perhaps Nuar saw Djola on the annex wall watching the mob chase a wild elephant.

"I would learn the storm's secrets," Djola said. "Ignorance won't save us."

"You gave up the old ways hoping to be worthy, more than a *savage*." Nuar switched to *Anawanama*. "Where are the women? How do you decide the world without them?" He shook his head. "You call down ruin. I should sit at the stone-wood table. The Empire has made you an enemy to yourself." Older brother had found a good argument.

Djola sputtered, caught off guard. "Get to your petition, man."

Nuar lifted the basket high and spoke Empire vernacular again. "I don't bring words for Azizi and Council to dismiss. I bring the bones of my great, great, great grandchildren in a basket of the ancestors."

Petitioners shouted curses and threats. Arms signaled an end to the audience. Nuar tossed the basket. Bouncing off the closing doors, the basket landed at Djola's feet. Money toed a braid of green and brown bark. Djola snatched the basket up and hugged it.

Nuar was the first northern chief Djola talked to the peace fire. Nuar gave up ambushing Empire caravans for farming. Other chiefs followed his lead. Empire crops ruined the land in ten years. The soil was now unfit for basket trees. Only sweetgrass held on. If nothing was done, it would all be desert soon. Nuar came to Council to warn them, to speak for the ancestors and the unborn.

"We'd make a fortune selling sweetgrass baskets that hold ancestors and the future," Money said. "But savages won't sell sacred vessels."

"Anything might be in that basket," high priest Ernold said. "Nuar's an old scoundrel."

"He tells us to choose carefully or suffer high spirit debt," Grain said.

"Jumba jabba," Ernold muttered.

"You could sell other baskets," Djola said, "and avoid spirit debt."

Azizi was late. His esteemed masters argued over heroes and debts, over a glorious past and a ruined future, over untamed northlanders and rebels rioting outside the citadel. The Master of Water proposed conquering barbarians south of Holy City, but the war chests were empty. Arms wanted to collect back taxes, but who could or would pay up? Money and Water wanted to sack a floating city across the Salty Sea. They suggested masquerading as barbarians. Arms laughed. The Empire had no conjure against the superior defenses of the floating cities. The best Arms could do was send warriors to die in a futile siege.

Djola said little and listened for truth underneath their words.

Hope had become a bad habit. The alternative was despair, and Samina prevented Djola from indulging in that. She'd probably encouraged Nuar to come to Council.

"Xhalan Xhala!" Djola murmured. He would bring Smokeland to the everyday, conjure truth from illusions, from possibilities and maybe-nots.

What else could he do with the bones of the future?

8

Iyalawo

Y ou know every other spell." Emperor Azizi's voice echoed from a hallway. "You must know Dream Gate conjure."

Azizi stormed into Council followed by Kyrie, Iyalawo—wise woman—of Mount Eidhou and Samina's older sister. The masters jumped to their feet. Azizi barely acknowledged them. He focused on Kyrie.

"You're as bad as mobs rioting at our gates."

Lank gray hair fell over rheumy hazel eyes and made him look older than Djola, yet he was scant thirty-nine. War stole his youth, treacherous peace his middle age. His bones ached and his vision blurred. Azizi had become a bitter old man, seeing enemies and traitors even among his staunchest supporters.

"Why do you thwart me?"

"I am for you." Kyrie lowered her head.

She trailed Azizi as he limped to the stone-wood table. Short, round, and crisscrossed with silver tattoos, Kyrie was a fortress of knowledge and power. Jewels nested in a cloud of silver hair. Silk tunic and pants floated over an agile form. Her moon face was nothing like Samina's, yet her voice was almost identical to Djola's wife's.

"I've never conjured Dream Gates." Kyrie's musical accent made Djola ache for Samina like a youthful lover. She nodded at chief cook Lilot lurking in the shadows. Older brother was wrong—the women were here! Kyrie was Djola's staunchest ally. She'd support his map to tomorrow. "Hezram perverts *Lahesh* conjure."

Azizi turned and loomed over Kyrie. "Do what you can do."

"Arkhys City shelters too many citizens and foreign refugees." Kyrie used Samina's inflection for a fact not to be argued with. "We can't feed them all from Mount Eidhou."

Azizi hissed, a pot about to boil over. Masters shuffled their feet, tugged beards, and rubbed eyebrows. Azizi contemplated friend rat whose cheeks bulged with goat meat and seaweed. "Be reasonable." He feared Kyrie might let Arkhys City starve to save her mountain people and wild land. "Be generous." He dropped into a *Lahesh* waterwheel chair at the head of the table. "The fire's gone out. It's cold in here and dark."

"Iyalawo Kyrie, esteemed wise woman," Djola spoke over grumbling masters, "we ask for no more than your people, your land can spare."

"In *Anawanama* Eidhou means *all rivers flow from my heart.*" Kyrie scratched a fingernail across a rock wall and lit a candle with the sparks. "Plundering my mountain—"

"Eidhou is not your mountain, it's the emperor's," high priest Ernold said.

"Actually, nobody owns the mountains." Kyrie lit candles around the room. "I speak for Eidhou, as guardian and—"

"So do I." Ernold had been after Kyrie's mountain realm for years. If not for the conjure in her Mountain Gates, he'd have strip-cut sacred forests and declared Kyrie and her people transgressors who should bleed for the glory of the gods. "I know the mysteries and all that is sacred. Witches and witchdoctors make a carnival of faith."

Everyone went stone still, even the rat. Kyrie blew sparks from her fingertips into the fireplace and flames burst through a smoldering woodpile. "You've danced on the moon's cool white face and seen elephants fly." She called Ernold a liar to his beautiful face. "Yet I walk Eidhou's glaciers, taste the breath of cathedral trees, and cloak myself in wind and rain and snow. The mountain is my backbone. I—" She stumbled to a halt at Azizi's left side. Her stool was missing, her goblet face down, her plate empty.

"Kyrie always comes after supper," Djola said, swallowing panic. "Guards!"

"No sweets tonight." Water sneered as guards appeared from the shadows.

"In times of turmoil many believe that a woman at the stone-wood table is a sign of weakness," Ernold said, rubbing the crimson tattoos on his bald head. He'd persuaded Azizi to do this. "Even an Iyalawo of Kyrie's stature."

Grain frowned at Arms. "Besides Council, who knows she is here?"

Kyrie had conjured a wise-woman passageway through mountain forests to come and go from Arkhys City without notice. The best emperor-spies couldn't find her almost invisible path—a great escape route for an Iyalawo, elephant, or any *Wild Thing*.

"My men removed the beaded monkey stool last month, after Kyrie left the citadel," Arms muttered.

"Last month?" Grain glared at him, like a lover betrayed.

Arms turned to Djola. "I meant to tell you both."

"You didn't," Djola said.

Arms stiffened. He followed Azizi's orders even if they were stupid. Maybe he agreed with this one. Azizi waved the masters into their seats. Djola remained standing. Kyrie was essential. How could Azizi dismiss her without consulting him?

"Masters at your table spoil for war," Kyrie said. Her fingers sparked as if she'd scratched a rough surface. "They think I'm only good for carnival amusement." The air above the table burst into flames. Kyrie took each man's measure in the bright-as-day light while they gaped or fumed at her conjure. She was no better at politicking than Samina. Grain groaned and closed his eyes.

Azizi ground his teeth at her insolence. "So why do a carnival fire-show at Council?"

"Emperor Azizi," she glared at him, "do you no longer wish the Iyalawo of Mount Eidhou to sit at your table?"

The guards drew swords. Panic sweat made them reek. Kyrie would defend her mountain to the death. If even half the griot tales were true, Council was no match for her. She could burn them all right now and who would hear their screams?

"Zizi," Djola hissed a boyhood name in the emperor's ear. "I beg you, speak to her."

Kyrie bowed low, spreading her arms like wings. The flames overhead winked out.

"Give me a reason to bring your stool back." Azizi huffed and speared a hunk of goat. "I'd trust whatever gate conjure you'd offer."

"Every gate requires sacrifice. I conjure with the willing. No transgressor blood or stolen spirits like in Holy City." Kyrie spat at rogue sparks dancing on her fingertips. "The bushes, trees, rocks, and haints that power my gates do so willingly, for Mount Eidhou, for—"

"For love?" High priest Ernold interrupted her for the third time and sucked his teeth, disgusted.

"You prefer a spirit slave to a lover?" Kyrie glanced at scowling faces.

Azizi slammed his hand on the table. "Whatever it takes!"

"On this path, you'll destroy what you do love." She nodded at Djola and Grain, then bowed deeply to Azizi again. "I take my leave. I hope Council uses wisdom to guide you away from deadly illusion to a true solution."

Azizi trembled as he waved her away. Guards covered her eyes and led her out.

High priest Ernold grumbled. "We should lock her up."

"You fools would have done that long ago if you could," Grain shouted. "Have you looked outside? We need Kyrie's conjure book. Who else knows as much as she does?"

Yari, the famed griot of griots, knew more than Kyrie perhaps. But Yari avoided the stone-wood table. Djola bit his tongue before blurting this. Books and Bones grumbled about jumba jabba. The others joined in. Azizi whistled them silent. "Kyrie never stays away long."

Kyrie was bosom close to chief cook Lilot and to Urzula, Azizi's pirate queen wife. While the men dithered, Kyrie would lose her *escort* in the cook's maze. She'd find a way out, fade into the trees behind the citadel, and abandon Djola to the cowards and fools on Council.

9

Emperor Azizi

Djola, sit down with us." Azizi slapped his good friend's back. "Where did you get that basket—*Anawanama*, ancestor weave. It's beautiful."

"A warning from Chief Nuar." Djola set the basket in front of Azizi. "He thinks we've betrayed the living, the dead, and the unborn."

"That bad?" Azizi laughed.

Djola bristled. "Did you see the storm this afternoon, raising blisters on elephant skin and choking trees?"

"Chief Nuar's your half-brother, isn't he?" Azizi rattled the bones. "Nuar was always so colorful and exaggerated, like a carnival player." Azizi set the basket at Djola's plate. "Sit, please, and give calm council."

Djola dropped into his chair. Calm was difficult. Without Kyrie's mountain herbs, Azizi's health could fail. Without her groves and goats, Arkhys City might starve. Her missing stool meant Djola would have to get Books and Bones on his side or his map to tomorrow would go down from four to three. They needed everybody working together to turn back the poison desert. Did Kyrie think of that before mouthing off? Who listened to a shrill old woman? Djola glanced around the table. The moody librarian scowled at him. Arms had a stone face, still mad about following orders. Grain looked furtive, ready to bolt. Water and Money sniggered with identical contempt. Perhaps today wasn't Djola's day.

He considered gathering his family and following Kyrie and the elephant to the Mountain Gates. No master or witchdoctor in the Empire could breach Kyrie's conjure and enter the mountain realm without her permission. Nuar had stormed Djola's secret hideaway and urged him to take his family to Kyrie's compound. Samina repeated this grand idea, but why run from Council at the height of his power?

"You're worrying, Djola—I can feel it." Azizi nibbled a few berries. "What?" Two rats gobbled goat haunch, muttering rat pleasure. "They eat for their whole troupe. See the pouches in their jowls." Azizi pointed. "They risk angry cooks and wily jackals to carry a feast home to hungry mouths. Rat solidarity."

The rat nibbled Azizi's finger and he laughed. Then all the masters except Djola spoke at once. They lied, whined, and argued. They blamed fickle gods and anybody except themselves for poor tax revenue, thief-lord raids, and dwindling tree-oil harvests. They offered nothing new. Council was at the same standstill as last year, last week, ten minutes ago.

"Fatazz! We're lizards chasing our tails." Grain tapped a story on a two-headed talking drum with leather strands connecting the heads that he squeezed to change pitch. Ernold frowned at a *Kahoe* woman's instrument, but Grain was not afraid to play:

An *Anawanama*-hero of old was surrounded by the enemy. A *veson*, neither man nor woman, *vie* was the last soldier protecting the land. The enemy held the high ground. The hero refused defeat and rigged branches to beat fifty war drums as the wind blew.

Vie strung the shields of fallen comrades across a waterfall so that metal surfaces banged and clattered, then sang in many voices, high, low, and in-between. Echoes across the water sounded like a fearsome horde, an army risen from the dead. The enemy retreated in fear. The hero was the first shadow warrior. *Vie* turned death into victory.

Arms cheered. He appreciated a good warrior saga, Grain's sagas especially. Shadow warriors preferred cunning to spilling blood. Money squirmed at an *Anawanama* tale about a *veson*. Books and Bones blinked and yawned. He and high priest Ernold pretended to be bored. Water tinkered with a tiny wind-wheel contraption: a circle of reed paddles on a stick. Hot air from a candle made it spin.

"You're still worrying, Djola." Azizi rubbed his eyes. "Over Kyrie? You brought her back before, you'll do it again."

"Zst!" Djola cursed. "I only masquerade as a master of the impossible."

Azizi nodded. "Sometimes illusion is a good solution."

Sky windows above the Council chamber shifted to the blue-violet of Samina's eyes, the sun a threat of pink at the edges. The endless night had passed. The roast smelled rank. Rats shat in the gravy. Chief cook Lilot shooed the creatures away, laid out a fresh meal, and lingered in the shadows spying for Queen Urzula. She kept Azizi's wife well-informed. Bleary masters dropped their heads into honey cakes and cream. Not even Arms was hungry. Djola ate for the coming battle. Losing Kyrie need not mean defeat.

Azizi quashed a tremor in his hand. He chewed bark that dulled pain and held fever in check. He was the age his father had been when assassins struck. His father, mother, older brother, and sisters died sweating blood and spewing their guts right in front of him. Djola reached Azizi with an antidote just in time. Djola foiled countless assassination attempts before finally talking ruthless warriors to the peace fire. From a boy of sixteen, Azizi saw every shadow as danger, every kiss as poison. Yet he gathered the best masters from across the Empire and listened to Council before taking action. Azizi never desired power but was proclaimed supreme ruler of the Arkhysian Empire at nineteen.

For twenty years he worked to make one map of many people. He'd been cautious and neither cruel nor foolish. He outlawed slavery and transgressor huts in the capital. Southern barbarians, Green Elders, pirates from the floating cities, and even wild northern tribes were welcomed. Azizi opened the library to the poor, to women too, if they could read. He worked for order and peace, and took every raid, betrayal, and massacre to heart. Each new wasteland or dead water zone had him vomiting in the night. He loved the Empire, its people, fields, and creatures, its forests, rivers, and mountains too.

"Morning. Time is short." Azizi glared at them. "I need plans to stop poison desert. Why else call Council? I can agonize alone." He was ready to listen.

Djola scratched the whisper of beard on his cheeks. He shook his bones and stretched achy muscles. "A wild elephant was in the back court last night, at sunset," he said.

Azizi squinted at him. "I thought the wild ones were long dead."

"Not yet." Djola saw hope in an elephant's waddle into the trees.

"Hezram, Holy City's high priest, offers Dream Gate secrets to protect us from poison desert. I hear you're against his blood conjure." Azizi gripped Djola. "Bleeding the people, even transgressors, is a high price. . . . Yet you've offered nothing else, except elephant tales."

Djola grinned. "Fighting the enemy, you must avoid becoming one."

Azizi rubbed bleary eyes. "Give me an answer, not Green Elder jumba jabba."

"Not enough tree oil or blood for Dream Gate conjure, unless we sacrifice our forests, our people, and our children."

Azizi licked cracked lips. "You know this witchdoctor spell?"

"*Lahesh* conjure. I know enough to steer clear." Djola lied with half-truth.

"The *Lahesh,* a bold people . . . Everyone craves their wisdom . . ." Azizi stroked the arms of his *Lahesh* waterwheel chair then glanced at Kyrie's empty place. "Even the Iyalawo fears Dream Gate conjure." He sighed. "Foul winds blow through our streets. What else do we see?"

Good vision takes many eyes looking every direction. Green Elder words had been plaguing Djola all night, but he didn't let this slip. He unfurled his scroll of spells.

10

Wild Child

Isra led the Elders and Sprites deeper into the forests, deeper into *Anawanama* territory. Nobody tracked them, and Yari sang, eerie melodies in *Lahesh*. Awa stumbled along, edgy. Good Empire citizens told horror tales on thieving, murdering savages who sold their own children—or anybody's—to slavers. Mother had rolled her eyes and sucked her teeth at nonsense. Kenu said Mother's family was part *Anawanama*. In a good mood, Father teased Mother about being a wild woman; if he was mad, he cursed her savage heritage and Awa, her wild child. Kenu said farmers were suspicious of savages who roamed the forests and never settled down. "Rootless demons living at the edge." The edge of what? Kenu never said.

Elders ferried the Sprites across a swamp on a barge made from tupelo tree trunks. Hungry eyes looked up at Awa from water thick as mud. She jumped from the barge onto springy ground. A sour decay smell stung her nose as they hiked through cypress, tupelo, and other swamp trees. Yari sang to shy birds and bold bugs. Awa walked close to *vie* where the bugs were too enchanted to bite.

They came upon soot gray fields, farmland devastated by poison dust storms. Even wrapped in turbans and veils and wearing barbarian boots, the poison seeped in. Lungs burned and skin blistered. Isra cursed foolish farmers. Yari grew quiet and charged ahead, leading them up into a cloud forest. The misty air was a relief on scalded skin, but the climb was rough. Downhill in the gathering dark was worse.

Awa was ready to fall over and not get up when smoke from cook fires made her stomach howl. The smell of nut bread, yams, and fish brought water to her mouth. A clearing surrounded by houses on wooden platforms was a welcome sight. Palm-leaf roofs dripped water from a recent downpour. Brawny men in clown masks brandished rattles and spears. Warriors.

"Greetings!" Yari spoke—she recognized *vie*'s voice if not the shadow-warrior face. "*Anawanama* are never lost. They find each other in the dark, in a storm. They feel a heart beating in a prison cell and reach out with comfort. I need a story to guide me." Yari hugged the warrior-clowns.

"I was in Arkhys City yesterday. Council sits." One clown took off his mask, a gray-haired man with a blade chin and a deep voice like a djembe drum. He wore luxurious mudcloth robes, a chief perhaps. "A sad spectacle." He looked from Yari to Awa. "You bring new Sprites into an enclave. Djola wastes himself at Council, wrangling thugs and cowards, and every day more poison dust blows through our lands."

"We do what we can, Nuar," Yari countered.

"We must do more." A woman spoke. She wore mudcloth and a beaded headdress decked with feathers. "Azizi has no women at his stone-wood table. How can you chew your food with only one tooth? How can you speak truth with half a tongue?"

"No *vesons* since you walked away, Yari," Nuar added. "Azizi says you abandoned them."

"Azizi could follow me," Yari replied. "Why should I decorate his Empire table?"

"You could persuade Djola," Nuar insisted. "He'd listen to the griot of griots."

"Perhaps. But who would listen to him? Too much fear in the air."

Awa looked around, fascinated more than afraid. Village dwellings were tucked into a hillside. Naked children and old people came out with the stars. Women dropped from branches. Men stepped from under bulging tree roots. Brown people with sculpted features and black waterfalls of hair. They did Empire talk at first then switched to *Anawanama*. The Elders used savage talk too— words that never stopped rolling into one another.

Awa was dazzled by the musical language and carnival clothes, by parrot and orchid people and a moon girl with a star headdress. A boy in a hawk mask gave Awa mushrooms stuffed with something that tasted like fishy bird meat. Cooks must have roasted a big lizard from the swamps. Mother said swamps were disappearing and big lizards too, so northlanders starved. People in this village looked well-fed and they shared a feast with the Elders and new Sprites. Mother worried about everything before it happened.

Awa sat in a *house for wanderers*, a refuge on stilts for anybody on the way to somewhere. If you knew how to find this clearing, you were welcome. Dense palm-leaf roofs kept the downpour out. Awa ate until she couldn't swallow another bite. Young *Anawanama* sat around her giggling and teasing each other. They smelled funny— unfamiliar spices on their breath and strange oil in their hair. They looked at her sideways. She wrapped herself in their rippling words and a mudcloth blanket. The former acolyte sat behind her wrapped in a blanket too. They could have climbed down the stilts and run away. Shadow warriors might have been anywhere, yet Awa suspected, nobody would stop them.

Yari gave Father sacks of jewels, but Awa wasn't a prisoner or a slave.

Yari's voice rustled with the leaves. "These people will take you in if you don't want to travel on with us. They have a good life." In the stilt house next to hers, young women sang softly and twisted sweetgrass into ropes. Yari played a talking drum, squeezing the leather strands that connected the heads and tapping just so to mimic *Anawanama* words. "Whatever you want," Yari whispered.

"I don't know what I want, besides—" going home. Awa couldn't imagine staying with savages, even friendly, beautiful ones, her mother's tribe.

Were Green Elders any better than savages?

"Don't worry. When you know what you want, you'll do it."

"I draw a map every night in the dirt, to remind myself where I've come from."

"Good. You aren't lost."

Awa fell asleep to the talking drum and bees buzzing in her ear. In the morning she thanked the villagers, touching their hands to her forehead. They were puzzled by the gesture of respect a daughter made to relatives, but touched their cheeks to her palms. Yari and the other Elders slipped into a cave passage through the mountains without looking back. Awa followed, going the direction she wanted to go.

11
Djola's Map

The Master of Grain persuades northern tribes to share desert conjure: bunchgrass seeds that grow with little water; black aromatic rice and tough red beans that can survive a flood; midnight berry bushes that hold a hillside, bring light to the eyes, and turn sand back to soil.

Emperor Azizi closes mines that poison rivers. Tainted metals are illusion treasures. Azizi opens the dams and frees lakes and rivers. The Master of Water lifts the ban on mud and silt masquerade. He takes charge of waterwheels and oversees wind-and fire-works. He uses ancient Lahesh tinkering to reclaim deserts.

The Master of Arms makes sure no children go hungry. Food is rationed as during the last war—everybody lives on the same portions. Back taxes are forgiven. Arms runs the market. Who doubts his fair-mindedness? On market days, griots sing his praises and recall sacrifices of old.

High priest Ernold reminds people that tree oil is sacred and bans clear cutting for the glory of the forest and mountain gods. Kyrie and other mountain Iyalawos join Council and organize tree planting ceremonies under Ernold's guidance. Trees hold the mountains and the rivers. Tree song soothes us all.

The Master of Money works with weavers, planting basket trees and *fields of sweetgrass. Revenue from sweetgrass baskets, rugs, boats, and bridges will fill the Empire's war chests.*

Emperor Azizi asks every library from the Golden Gulf to the floating cities for wisdom. The Master of Books and Bones hosts griot gatherings on the steps of the Arkhys City library to recall old traditions and collect new ideas. Crossroads festivals are held during the scar moon. Griot storytellers and carnival players spread the word that change is coming and earn good fees. With fewer empty bellies, riots and rebel uprisings decline, and the People write their own spells for change.

12

Treason

A nd Djola, what will you do?" Azizi asked.

Djola had resolved to master *Xhalan Xhala* and find the cause and a cure for poison sandstorms. If Yari still refused to teach him the *Lahesh* spell of spells, there were other Elders. When Azizi's great grandfather conquered the northlands, he outlawed what he didn't understand, what he feared. Conjurers who defied his edict were put to death.

Green Elders wrote down the old ways before everyone forgot what they knew. Elders hid books in libraries across the world, where nobody would notice. Djola knew what to look for—*Lahesh* metal-mesh covers, impervious to most spells or poison. Yari had taught him that at least. While Council implemented his map to tomorrow, Djola would search for *Xhalan Xhala*. He'd told Azizi this, but only Azizi. The other masters would know soon enough.

"I'll help where I'm needed," Djola declared.

The Master of Arms leaned over the stone-wood table, breath caught in his throat. He ran a finger over Djola's calculations, delighted. Arms was easy to please. The burly idealist stuffed a honey cake in his mouth. He and Grain grinned at each other, while

Water and Money just looked uncertain. Djola's plan would make them richer men, but—

"Ten years living like . . ." Hope and fear warred on Azizi's face. "Which tribe does mud and silt masquerade? *Lahesh?*"

"Haven't the *Lahesh* died out?" Money slitted silver eyes.

"*Lahesh* live on among us," Djola said. "*Anawanama* do mud and silt masquerade."

"That's worse." Ernold rubbed his priestly skull. "Too much jumba jabba."

"Consult every library and all the storytellers." Azizi sighed. "Kyrie said as much."

Djola's words should weigh more than an old woman's. "All wisdom isn't written."

Azizi poked the scroll. "Is this a cure?"

"Precautions," Djola replied. "Until we understand what's happening to green lands." Money, Water, and Ernold smirked at *green lands.* Djola cursed softly.

Azizi groaned. "I'd hoped for—" He made a vague gesture.

"Miracles?" Djola said. "Miracles are hard work."

"Something faster"—Azizi had made speed a virtue in his Empire—"and not so complicated." He preferred elegant, simple solutions. "You'd have us live like Green Elders." Other masters grumbled agreement. "Who can trust bloodthirsty *Zamanzi* or corrupt barbarians to lay down weapons and share seeds and wisdom?"

Djola was ready for this argument. He circled the stone-wood table, shaking the sweetgrass basket of bones. "We give *Anawanama, Zamanzi,* and other tribes amnesty, a chance to catch their breath and raise their children, not bury them. You heard Chief Nuar. Void-winds blow over the northland. We offer them and southern barbarians a seat at Council, decent land to farm instead of storehouses to raid. No war on any border." He had them all nodding till high priest Ernold kissed his teeth, disgusted.

"More wise women on Council?" he said. "Kyrie isn't enough for you?"

"We aren't defeated," Water shouted. "Why surrender to women and savages?"

Books and Bones handed the scrolls to Djola. "Freak storms are on the rise. Dream Gate conjure could protect us tomorrow. High priest Hezram's offer is generous."

"Djola expects us to give away tomorrow without a fight." Ernold spat in the fireplace. "Hezram is Empire through and through."

"You'd trust a man who bleeds his own people?" Djola shouldn't have been shocked at their stupidity, but he was. "Hezram won't prevent freak storms and more ghost villages." He glanced up at the sky windows, the only windows in the Council chamber, dark eyes, blind eyes. No other master had gone out and experienced the poison storm. They felt safe behind citadel walls. "We must all dance to a new beat, dispel the void clinging to us."

"True." Azizi stuttered. "But the greatest empire—" As he got tangled in a coughing fit, Water chanted about the glorious Arkhysian Empire. Ernold and Money joined him. Books and Bones pounded rhythmic support. Arms pressed thin lips tight.

Water turned on Grain. "Where do you stand?"

"With the greatest empire," Grain replied. What else could a northlander say?

Grain stood up from the stone-wood table as sour faces turned murderous. Money, Water, and Ernold shouted lies about northlanders, transgressors, and *vesons*. They lambasted pirates, barbarians, and power-mad women then spooked themselves into turning down prosperity for Holy City illusions. When the sun finally made it over the foothills and shone through the sky windows, high priest Ernold accused Kyrie of being a traitor witch from the floating cities who wanted to destroy history's greatest empire. Kyrie, whose weapon-conjure turned back pirate ships and saved Azizi's fleet; Kyrie, who'd given her sister to Djola and arranged the imperial wedding with Pirate Queen Urzula.

"Kyrie forged peace on the Salty Sea," Djola shouted, his patience shot. "Her conjure book is the most coveted in the world." The end of days, and Ernold was making a grab for Kyrie's mountain temple.

Azizi dispatched guards to detain her. Too late, Kyrie was long gone.

Djola sneered at Ernold. "A wise man would have lured Kyrie in for one last Council, poisoned the wine, and betrayed her then." A wise man would have bitten his tongue. Too late now. "Kyrie will close the Mountain Gates and never leave her cliffs. Council gains nothing except an enemy at our back."

"And one at the table?" Water, Money, and Ernold ambushed Djola, talking faster than thought. They accused him of working with Azizi's enemies. Djola's scrolls for change and Nuar's basket of bones were proof that *savage* Djola was against the Empire's glorious way of life.

Djola faltered, weary from twenty years of pleading with men who poured libations to denial, weary of being the *savage* speaking jumba jabba nobody wanted to hear. His tongue tripped over words he'd said too many times. This was the opening they needed.

"Plotting with your wife's sister." Water shook his mane of black hair. "Those two witch women are as close as lovers."

Money stood over Djola, a hand at a hidden dagger. "Why do you betray us?"

"Answer them." Arms shook Djola.

Azizi's hands trembled. "You and Kyrie, traitors?"

"Kyrie and I can't betray what is already lost." Djola gestured around the table. "We've poisoned our days. We find a new way to live or perish." Hardly a rebuttal to treason, but he had nothing else to say.

Azizi turned to him, eyes pleading for a lie even. "What about that *Lahesh* conjure you've been chasing? *Xhalan Xhala*, the great spell of spells?" Desperate Azizi wasted Djola's *Lahesh* secrct on cowards and thugs.

"*Xhalan Xhala* is a tall tale." Ernold snorted.

"That's what you look for in the libraries"—Books and Bones worried his beard—"a conjure too dangerous even for Yari."

"Dream Gate conjure is harmless compared to *Xhalan Xhala*," Ernold yelled.

"Which is it, priest?" Grain scoffed. "Is *Xhalan Xhala* a tall tale or deadly conjure?"

"The griot of griots isn't afraid of *Xhalan Xhala*," Djola murmured. "Yari doesn't trust people to do right with sacred knowledge." Yari didn't trust Djola in particular.

"Can you stop poison desert with your plan?" Water shouted.

Djola shrugged. "I don't know."

Azizi clenched the table with trembling hands. He rattled goblets and dishes. "Neither you nor Kyrie know the cause of poison desert or an antidote."

"Your map to tomorrow is almost a cure." Grain gripped Djola's shoulder. "Isn't it?"

"Cure?" Djola should have lied to gain time, to regroup and fend off the other masters, but his arrogant tongue refused. What lie would last longer than a day, a month? "Kyrie and I don't know the cause or a cure."

"Honest to a fault." Azizi sighed. "Betrayal is shouting about poisons and offering crack-cruck measures before you know an antidote." His eyes were an angry blur. "You saved my life and helped me conquer all the green lands from the savage north to the barbarian south, from the west waters to the sweet desert in the east. But today you stab me in the heart with jumba jabba. I banish you for abandoning me during the Empire's greatest challenge. We must conquer the poison desert or die trying."

Djola gasped. Too shocked to beg for reason, too wise to plead for mercy, he attended to his breath.

Books and Bones looked stricken. Arms wanted to gut Money and Water and slit Ernold's throat. Grain slipped into the shadows by the *Lahesh* masks. Why go down for *Weeds and Wild Things*? Azizi avoided Djola's eyes. "Banished." Djola tossed his scrolls into the fire. Years of labor at the far edge of hope smoked and crumbled to ash. Too late, he spied daughter Tessa's scroll, his shield. It caught a spark and burned. Tessa would scold him for that.

"Defend yourself," Azizi commanded. "Change my mind."

Djola shrugged, nothing more to say. Denial was as inexplicable as poison sand blowing across fields and twisting down alleys. Death whooshed in Djola's ears and emptied his mind. His tongue went rogue, and he muttered, *"Basawili."*

"What does that mean?" Azizi asked. "More Green Elder jumba jabba?"

"A northern outlaw language," Books and Bones said. "Who knows savage talk?"

"Anawanama: not the end, more to come," Grain translated. "Roughly."

"Such a powerful conjurer makes a deadly enemy," Ernold said.

"We should execute Djola on this stone floor," Water said. "Savages have no honor."

The guards aimed spears at Djola. Arms and Grain bristled. Djola felt like someone had smashed his head.

"Execute?" Books and Bones blinked, as if waking from a trance. "I don't know."

Money, Water, and Ernold shouted at the librarian. Arms and Grain yelled at each other. Azizi pulled Djola close and whispered in *Lahesh,* "Fool, you should have lied. What can I do when Kyrie deserts me and the whole table is against you?"

"But banish me, Zizi?" Djola stared at him, blank.

Azizi squeezed his shoulders. "Go visit all the libraries in the world. Talk to wise men and long-winded griots. Find your *Xhalan Xhala* cure and be quick. You can do that, can't you?"

"I guess."

"Twenty years ago, you made peace from blood and bile and ash."

"Did I? That seems like a griot tale for children," Djola sputtered.

"You persuaded me to trust Kyrie and marry Urzula. You can find an antidote for anything. The Master of Poisons, yes?" Azizi gestured at the ashes of Djola's scrolls. "Take a few months. Bring us *Xhalan Xhala,* then we'll do the hard work for a good tomorrow." He actually believed Djola could do what he commanded. "Swear to me."

"I'd need a ship and—"

"I can arrange a pirate crew."

"Why pirates?"

Azizi smiled. "A rogue fleet will take you anywhere, and whatever you do, whatever desperate measures you need to take to find the cure, nobody will connect you to me. The People remain on my side."

Djola felt dizzy. "This was your plan all along."

"Not exactly . . . You insist we must always have many pots on the fire." Azizi whistled the masters silent and spoke Empire vernacular. "My decree is banishment. I'll hold each of you responsible if Djola dies before leaving Arkhys City."

Arms had a knife at Water's back and a sword to Money's

throat. They raised their hands high and backed away. "We are happy to let the Master of Poisons die at sea."

High priest Ernold stood in a splash of sunlight, teeth and bald head gleaming. Books and Bones had curled up under the table, like a scroll someone crumpled and threw away. Grain faded into the smoke by the fireplace. The guards who brought Djola to the table wrenched him from his seat and dragged him blindfolded through a maze of tunnels. Hyenas howled and laughed.

13

Pirate Queen

The cook's entrance to the emperor's citadel was close enough to Thunder River to feel the chill of Eidhou's glaciers in the water. Every breath carried the taste of spices, spirits, and bitter herbs. The scrappy guard yanked the cloth from Djola's eyes. Afternoon sun made him squint. He staggered, dizzy from wandering the maze, from losing his place at the stone-wood table. Disaster, happening too quickly to be believed.

Turning down the map to tomorrow, yes, but Azizi banishing his closest advisor, his most loyal friend? That was madness. Did every emperor eventually go mad?

"Basawili," Djola muttered as jolts of terror scrambled his thoughts.

"Why do you keep repeating that?" The scrappy guard shook Djola.

"He's lost his mind," the other guard said. "Wouldn't you?"

"He was always a bit off." The scrappy guard doused Djola's hot head with cold water from the river. "All the masters are." And the emperor too.

Death kept whooshing in Djola's ears. *Basawili* was his reply.

Not the end, more breath to come. An hour ago, he was one of the most powerful men in the Empire. Now he was a nobody who couldn't get a breath. Azizi was sending him on an impossible quest to find a quick cure. Djola clutched the sweetgrass basket. Nuar tried to warn him about Empire treachery. Samina too. He tripped and fell. Uneven stones in the courtyard scraped skin from his knees. The pain was slight, but cleared his vision.

No one from Council had been exiled in twenty years. Would he live to see his wife and children again? What happened to the family of a disgraced master? Did Azizi give a thought to that? Samina and the children would be safe at the hideaway. But they'd worry when he didn't return, when they got word of his exile. Djola's heart pounded.

The guards should just put a knife in his gut and get it over with.

"Do you understand what he's going on about?" the scrappy guard said.

Djola squirmed. "Where is Rano? He can get word to Samina, to my wife."

"He uses savage talk, reverting to old ways." The other guard patted his shoulder, not unkind. He raised his voice. "Courage, poison master. You can survive. Just do what the emperor asks."

"Fatazz!" The scrappy guard cursed as sparks flared from the cook's entrance. Pirate Queen Urzula emerged with a spark torch—lightning caught on a stick. The guards dropped to one knee, exclaiming at floating-city conjure. Wind nor rain nor sandstorm would douse Urzula's light.

"Have you lost your escort, my queen?" The scrappy guard kept his eyes lowered, but challenged Urzula for wandering about alone. "Emperor Azizi needs his wife to be safe."

"Who will attack me?" Urzula laughed. When a spark torch wasn't lighting up the dark, it could be deployed as a weapon, burning down buildings, boats, and men. "No worries." She extinguished her torch with gold dust. "I have many weapon-spells."

A witch woman from the floating cities, Urzula was wide and muscular, well-built for having babies and standing on the decks of pirate ships. Her skin was darker than Djola's, her hair cropped close, peach fuzz. Silvery white dots made half circles above her eyelids. A line of white crossed blue-tinted lips going from chin to nose—floating-city makeup. Like Samina, Urzula never adopted Empire style, even though good citizens thought she was a seductress.

She blew a dart and skewered a poison snake that dangled from the bushes above the guards' heads. "Are you men safe?" She chuckled.

An hour ago, Djola would have chuckled with her. There were too few pirates. That's why they didn't rule the world. That's why Urzula and Samina left the isolationist floating cities and married Azizi and Djola. *Lahesh* diplomacy: marry the enemy. Urzula could get word to Samina. They were friends.

"*Basawili*, Queen, I need your help." His tongue finally cooperated. He spoke Empire vernacular.

"*Basawili*," Urzula smiled sadly, undulating in schemes. The guards gaped at her sensual meditation, distracted. Urzula licked her lips. She understood politicking. "Djola would speak with me and I would speak with him."

The guards exchanged glances. "We must get to the docks." The scrappy one shifted from foot to foot. "We don't want to miss the tide."

"You won't. I know the sea better than you." Urzula waved them off.

The guards slumped against the railing on the bridge. Lilot, chief cook—and Urzula's true love according to whisper and gossip—strode out of the citadel maze. Outside Council's shadows Lilot was a bold presence, even wrapped in veils and robes for travel. Lilot's lips were tinged green, and she had red dots above her eyelids. They meant something Djola had forgotten. Lilot wasn't as sultry or compelling as Urzula, but she was just as formidable.

Urzula and Azizi's son and daughter accompanied her, children, ten and thirteen years old. They had their mother's fierce features, yet were lanky and lean like Azizi. They'd have been taller than Lilot, except for the cloth wrap that crowned the cook's head. The children also wore travel clothes. Urzula kissed each child. Then Lilot shooed them across the bridge with bird kites to fly.

"Lilot tells me your troubles." Urzula scrutinized Djola. Lilot heard everything that went on at Council and reported to her. "You've been wronged."

"Get word to Samina, through Rano. Tell him not to fight and her not to worry." Djola spoke slowly. "Tell her to take the family to Kyrie's realm."

Urzula nodded. "Lilot takes the children to my niece's ship. I miss them already."

Djola swallowed fear. "I miss Tessa, Bal, and Quint."

"Arkhys City is no place for our little ones," Lilot said. "The masters are rotten."

"Not all of them." Urzula gestured at the cook. "Lilot wants to poison half the stone-wood table, but I say that would mean war." She laughed. Lilot and the guards laughed with her. Urzula stepped close to Djola. "If there is war, nobody wins."

"Fool." Lilot snapped fingers in Djola's face. "Why not say what they want to hear?"

"Lies and illusions won't save us," Djola replied.

"Neither will spit on poison sand," Lilot muttered.

"Find an antidote for devastation." Urzula pointed to withered bushes and trees that had been savaged by yesterday's storm.

"Bring Kyrie back to the table." She touched Djola's cheek. Her hands were cool and rough. "My husband will welcome you both."

"Kyrie won't come back unless we change." Djola thrust the sweetgrass basket at her. "The bones of the future. Get this to Samina. Tell her I'm sorry for not following her advice. Tell her I love her."

"Of course you do." Urzula took the basket. "And you love the world."

"Sentimental slop." Lilot grunted. "Survive any way you can, poison master."

"Yes. We need you." Urzula gripped his shoulders. "Come back to Zizi with proof that what you told Council is true and find an antidote."

"Impossible." Djola groaned. "Zizi chose greedy masters over me."

"You asked proud masters to live like Green Elders and *Anawanama* savages for ten years. That's impossible. How could Azizi say yes and maintain power?" Urzula kissed Djola's dry lips and pulled him to her bosom. He felt less jumbled as she held his sorrow. "High priest Hezram angles for your chair but *Lahesh* tinkerers know something about everything. Go find a *Lahesh* spell nobody can deny, something better than Hezram's Dream Gates in Holy City and you'll sit beside the emperor again. Samina will forgive your foolish arrogance. She'll bring your children down from Kyrie's mountain to celebrate your return." She released him. "Come back to us all."

"A *Lahesh* antidote. Yes. I can do this." Djola repeated this as the guards marched him across the bridge and past Azizi's daughter and son. The children stared at him and let go of their strings. The bird kites flew up over the citadel turrets and vanished.

14

Elephant Memories

The Elephant stands at the foot of Mount Eidhou uncertain which direction to take. Her map for today and tomorrow is blank. As the sun hides behind steep cliffs, she remembers Djola, his scents, his laughter. Empire guards drag him down the alley behind the citadel, and she is sad. These are the same bad men who wanted to poke her with sharp blades last night. They scurry through sparse trees toward the Salty Sea. Djola stumbles along, his eyes glazed, his limbs rubbery. Will the guards eat him?

Once, long ago, when the Elephant was crossing a muddy river, her family lost to mist, her spirits low, Djola came riding by, smelling of fruit, ink, and good humor. He sat on a tall horse and watched the Elephant try to scramble up crumbling banks. The Elephant was young, her legs too short, and the mud sucked her strength. She was weak and hungry and expected any moment to be eaten. The wind roared in distant trees, carrying the scent of predators.

"How did you lose your family?" Djola called to her, using a friendly tone. "Run, little one, this way to me. I have a mango for you." He held up a piece of fruit and laughed. "A wild one, aren't you, and strong. You can do it."

The Elephant was exhausted and her legs gave out. She tumbled back into muck. The bank was too steep, too slippery. There was no way out.

"Want a bite?" Djola tossed the mango in the air. "Come get it." The Elephant loved mangos. She walked down the river toward him and tugged at a sapling on the bank with her trunk. "Good girl. Not so steep. Do you hear your mothers calling?"

The mud muffled sounds traveling through the ground. Only soggy jibber jabber reached the Elephant's feet. She tugged and tugged. From tough stem to sturdy roots, the sapling resisted her trunk. A young cathedral tree, it refused to join the Elephant in the river. She had to join the tree on land. Packed dirt was joy under her feet. The ground rumbled. Her family called, searching for her. The Elephant rumbled a message back to them. She promised to follow their sounds and find them, before anyone ate her. Djola held out hunks of mango. The Elephant grabbed them as she hurried by, scant nourishment for a long journey.

"You took the whole thing." Djola laughed again. The Elephant carried his sounds and smells with her as she hurried to her family.

Today, Djola does not laugh as Empire guards haul him toward the docks.

Other bad men on horses, hearts pumping, the smell of predators in their sweat, race after Djola and the guards. These men hunger for Djola's heart. The Elephant is close enough to see their eyes shine with fear as they draw their blades. The men do not see an elephant, only shadows. The horses catch elephant-scent and a glimpse of angry ears flared wide. She stands in an entrance to Kyrie's wise-woman corridor, hidden by rocks and laurel trees. The Elephant trumpets, flaps her ears, and throws up a cloud of dirt. The horses are spooked and dash back the way they came. The riders curse and spit. Some fall on the ground and are dragged in dirt. A few slam into cathedral tree trunks and shriek. The Empire guards shriek too. They drive Djola faster down the alley toward the docks. The Elephant steps out of the corridor to follow them.

"No, no! They'll kill us both." Djola waves at her to stay away. He stands near a gangway to a boat as the guards banter with a seaman. "Save yourself."

People gape at the Elephant, drop baskets and buckets, and holler. The guards talk faster to the seaman. Someone throws a knife toward her. It bounces off her shoulder. The Elephant flinches at the sharp pain. More blades appear, shovels and axes, and a fiery torch. But when family or friends (even people) are in danger, the Elephant can't abandon them. She takes another step.

"No. Go. At least one northerner should triumph today." Djola shouts and flails. The crowd is ready to pounce, but hesitates. "Run. For me," he pleads.

Reluctantly the Elephant backs into the wise-woman passageway. She fades from view to a chorus of gasps. The woman carrying fire takes a step closer to the entrance. "Kyrie's mountain shadows attacked me before, right here."

"Witch-woman shadows, yes, but no elephant," a man says. "The Master of Poisons must have conjured her."

Djola laughs, in a better mood. The Elephant is glad, but also sad as the guards throw Djola on a pirate ship bound for the floating cities. Other seamen shrink away from him, as if he were fire or a gang of sharp fangs. The Elephant hovers at the entrance of the corridor until the sails catch the wind and Djola is carried out to sea. When the ship is a pale memory on a deep blue horizon, she turns away from the water and back to decisions. This corridor led her to the sea, but a branch goes up the mountain. The Elephant has never climbed a mountain. No matter. There are too many hungry people by the sea guarding sweet water, grain, and fruit trees. The Elephant sends a message into the ground. If anyone is listening, if anyone is alive to hear her voice, they will know and understand the choices she makes, they will know the direction to take to find her. They will hear her and hope.

The Elephant doesn't forget this day. Hope is what she carries with her on the steep climb.

15

Filled with Now

Smokeland saved Awa. When she first joined the Green Elder enclave, she wanted Father, her two middle brothers, and even Kenu and Mother to die a thousand deaths. She also ached to hug them to her heart. This back-and-forth hate-love tormented her. She woke from dreams of her family with balled-up fists and an aching jaw.

Father had sneered at Awa's artistry, at her useless stories and dancing bees, but her sale had garnered enough jewel, cowry shells, and coin to send three sons from Holy City to the capital for grand opportunities—no matter how stupid or cowardly they were. Did Father wonder at her fate? Did Mother poison his bread? Would brother Kenu ever pour libations for her sacrifice or just laugh at a green-land freak?

Yari, the high Elder who brought Awa into the enclave, said, "Anything you believe could be wrong." Yari was a graying *veson*, the griot of griots, once advisor to Emperor Azizi. A trickster, *vie* had sparkling eyes and a lightning smile. Ropes of *vie*'s hair, adorned with seedpods, bells, and whistling reeds, danced even when Elders stood still for meditation.

Tapping and squeezing a double-headed talking drum, *vie* could seduce a snake or a crocodile. Yari's lovers—good citizens, barbarians, savages, witch women, Council masters, perhaps even Azizi—would fill a pirate ship. Who could resist Yari's charm or brilliance? Certainly not Awa.

"For wisdom you must intertwine passion, faith, and doubt," Yari said. "Like drumming four beats to seven or weaving Aido cloth, every color strong but a play of shadows for untrained eyes. A righteous person sings harmony with themselves. Holding contradictions and polyrhythms in your spirit, that's the basis of all conjure."

Other Garden Sprites did this easily. Bal, who joined the enclave a few months after Awa, could sound like a fleet of drums and a choir of voices her first week. Bal wove Aido cloth robes to disappear in and crafted flimsy sweetgrass into weapons, boats, and bridges. Awa was all thumbs. Her Aido cloth regularly unraveled. The best she ever managed was three beats to two on a drum and a single overtone when she sang. Drums, thread, and song were wasted on her. Indeed, Awa was so inept that—

"I worry Yari might sell me to thief-lords or abandon me to poison desert."

"Nonsense." Bal stood behind Awa on cliffs above the Salty Sea. They were becoming fast friends. Arkhys City's sandstone towers and domes shimmered far across the bay. "Why chant nonsense?" Bal's cheekbones were high and sharply etched; her limbs long, elegant, and muscled. Round Awa wanted to look like her. "Yari loves us all, but you the most."

"No." Awa raced along the cliff edge, doing a rock, water, and shell dance. Tons of black and white fish flesh jumped from the waves and trilled at her clumsy gyrations. When she flapped her arms, the behemoths mimicked her with stubby flukes. Bal applauded. "You're a shadow warrior, Bal. You carry shade with you.

You can hide anywhere and seem like a hundred warriors. What conjure can I do?"

"You call giants out of the sea and conjure moon-bridges to Smokeland. I can't do that." Bal pulled Awa back from the edge toward scraggly laurel trees. "We all love you. It doesn't matter what you do or don't do."

"People love you and sell you too." Awa hissed. Mother and Kenu had let Father sell her, so Kenu could build towers to the stars. "Love isn't enough."

Bal looked stricken. She hadn't told Awa who'd sold her to the enclave. Awa leaned close, hoping for this secret. Bal only said, "That's true, I guess."

"You must take better measure of yourselves." Yari, carrying lesson scrolls and nut bread, dropped down beside them from a jagged overhang. "You two know how to listen and, without losing yourselves, hold anyone or anything in your heart. This is grace." Yari wrapped long arms around Awa and Bal. Cloud-silk robes smelled of sugarbush and desert rose. "Grace is how you fashion something from nothing, Bal, and why you can traverse Smokeland's border-void, Awa."

"I thought it was spiders and bees, guiding us." Bal giggled.

"Laughter is good. So is sweat." Yari set down the nut bread and pulled out a double-headed drum decorated with Aido cloth and sweetgrass. Squeezing brown and gray leather cords that connected the black goatskin heads, *vie* modulated tones and made the drum talk. Ancestor words shook Awa's bones.

"Dance, read, and think on the measure of your spirit." Yari could drum a child into this world or reason out of a person's mind. "Move!"

Awa tripped over her feet trying to catch the beats. Even Bal groaned at tricky polyrhythms.

"Make your own music," Yari commanded. Bal sang several

harmonies with herself and worked her feet like a stampede. She pulled Awa into a furious dance. *"Fill yourself with now,"* Yari sang, *"tomorrow may not come."*

Awa kissed her teeth. "If the world ends, we won't be here to be sad."

"Are you sure? *Basawili*—not the end, more breath to come." Yari took off into the laurel trees. Songbirds flew from the berry bushes, grumbling. Yari was fast and relentless. Awa and Bal resigned themselves to being out of breath all day.

Good Empire citizens believed life in an enclave was dull and brutal: wandering, camping in drafty tents, eating grass and worms, chanting. People told many lies on the Elders. Where were the raggedy savages, liars, thieves, and perverts living like it was yesterday? Garden Sprites never had to walk on coals. Father had gotten those ugly purple scars on his feet somewhere else.

Father also claimed they bashed his head with jumba jabba. But Awa loved the discipline and adventure, the poetry and history, the animal lore and number play. Yari taught her ancestor tongues—*Zamanzi, Anawanama, Lahesh*—and signs and ciphers to map the everyday or hold tangled Smokeland memories. Awa practiced writing and drawing three times a day while Bal sang and sword danced.

Awa stood once in a herd of wild horses, memorizing hoofbeats before they vanished to who knows where. She drew a history of bees, tracked fish flight, and calculated the distance to the moon. Wherever the Elders made home, by the sea, in the desert, or on a mountaintop, Awa and Bal memorized the sky. Awa's torment over her family faded to an occasional ache, and Bal always hugged these sorrows away.

Best of all was Smokeland. Awa's trips beyond the border-void were long and luxurious. She mapped and catalogued many wonders. On one trip, Awa passed through a border realm of exploding jellyfish, lightning bolts, and deadening void-smoke. She barely held onto herself but came upon a village in the treetops: a weave of houses, balconies, bridges, and temples. Lovers with spiderweb hair and cloud-silk robes swayed in the branches. Their pleasure rippled through the leaves and through her body too. New aches surprised her.

In another region, Awa discovered underwater river forests undulating to the melodies of golden behemoths who sported white speckled fins. She swam beside creatures twice the size of elephants against the currents. She wove her song into be-hemoth sounds that she could feel but not hear as they swam among seaweed bushes and feathery trees. Iridescent eyes peered at her from murky caves, and tentacles reached out to greet or eat her.

The behemoths nudged the curious tentacles aside with a flap of tail flukes and a roar of bubbles. She laid her cheeks against cold skin, grateful for their caution. Exuberant behemoths flew with her out of the water and plunged deep again. In a third re-gion, a city of boats—floating towers with sails or spinning waterwheels—washed in on a blue-green tide and out again leav-ing iron horses and singing books on a rocky shore. Distant cook fires on the waves twinkled like stars. The metal beasts frolicked to the music the books made. Enchanted, Awa danced with them until they disappeared into caves.

Awa returned to the everyday exhausted and delighted after this long trip. While she'd been in Smokeland, weeks had passed and the Elders traveled beyond the maps to a wild side of the *Mama Zamba* mountains. They camped far from any barbarian or Empire city at a rocky oasis in the sweet desert. As long as the rains came and the desert bloomed, the enclave enjoyed peace and posted few guards. When the dry season unleashed deadly storms, foolish men became desperate. They'd attack anyone anywhere, even Green Elders who knew the most powerful weapon-spells in the Empire. Today was peace.

Yari cornered Awa and Bal at the cook fires. *Vie* smelled of cinnamon, jasmine, and sweetgrass. "Tell me, what do you say to people in Smokeland?"

"Nothing." Awa cringed, embarrassed. "My tongue knots up."

Yari feigned shock, rattling moth cocoon anklets. "Knotted tongue. You?"

"Yes. Me." Other smoke-walkers, their starlight hair glinting and volcano hearts pumping fiery blood, were too beautiful for words. "Nothing comes."

Yari turned serious as a knife thrust. "Avoid anyone whose heart is an ember."

Awa grumbled. "You told me before. A hundred hundred times."

"You might lose yourself in their eyes. Spirit slaves are Hezram's weapon."

"Not just Hezram," Bal interjected.

Yari bristled. Too angry to mask it. "Hezram is the worst."

"I've only seen a few," Awa said. "They were too sluggish to catch me."

"Don't count on the speed of thought." Yari danced around Awa, jabbing her with drumsticks. "Spirit slaves will suck your dreams and leave you hollow."

"I've never seen that happen." Awa dodged the sticks. "People make up terrifying lies about smoke-walking because they're afraid to venture beyond the everyday."

"True"—Yari halted—"but always play caution and risk together. Promise me."

Awa groaned. "Of course." She held up her charm bracelet. "I always carry bee stingers from a Smokeland hive."

"Good. Rehearse what to say to other smoke-walkers beforehand."

Awa had yet to meet Mother. Would she dare Smokeland journeys without Awa? Just in case, Awa decided to rehearse a speech for her. "I will."

Bal balanced on an arm, swirling her legs and a sword in figure eights, so elegant and deadly that Awa wanted to . . . what? "I'm tired of just guarding your breath body here and now," Bal declared. "Just waiting, waiting, waiting . . ."

"Practice patience," Yari said. "Shadow warriors can't let stillness be an enemy."

Bal rolled her eyes. "Who'd poison Awa's breath body in an Elder enclave and then live to steal her spirit body in Smokeland?"

"Don't underestimate our enemies." Yari's voice shook. "They may know as much as we do. Or more."

Did Hezram know more than Yari?

Bal jumped in front of Awa before she could ask. "Take me with you to Smokeland?" Bal knew what Awa wanted before Awa did.

"If I'm able, yes," Awa replied.

Yari hugged them to *vie*'s heart. "Of course you'll be able." Yari often acted like the sentimental Elders from carnival tales. Awa and Bal took secret pleasure in this. Every Sprite hoped griots would spin epics from their adventures, but Awa and Bal had an advantage. Yari was griot for all the Green Elder clans, the griot of griots, what Empire citizens called a walking library and *Lahesh* called a bridge, one foot in yesterday, the other in tomorrow.

Vie's tales were renowned in the floating cities, around the Golden Gulf, across the Arkhysian Empire and beyond where the maps ran out. Yari knew something about everything or at least more than most griots. *Vie* released Awa and Bal and smiled. "You'll travel together many times, to every region of your hearts."

"Really?" Bal asked. "You see this?"

"Yes." Yari's eyes filled with tears. "You shall make a new world."

Yari always said, *Each day, every one of us makes the world new.* *New* wasn't necessarily *good*, yet Awa felt certain that, despite experiencing many, many worlds, Yari looked forward to the one she and Bal would make.

16
Pirate Living

Djola's first weeks at sea were a blur. He was heart and stomach sick. Elephants trumpeted in his dreams, chastising him for poison sand blowing everywhere. He woke each morning not believing in the pirate ship that rocked under him or in the scoundrels who raided merchant ships and villages or in the story a griot might tell on the Master of Poison's defeat at Council.

He should have gone with Samina and the children to Kyrie's mountain. Bal loved waterfalls, Tessa the mango groves. Quint was happy anywhere they were all together. But the poison desert would chase them wherever they ran. To save them, he had to master *Xhalan Xhala* and conjure an antidote to poison sand.

Djola was an *honored* prisoner on the pirate flagship, a converted slaver with a large galley and several decks, ideal for Captain Pezarrat, his commanders, and their captives. Still, the food was disgusting—wormy meat, moldy bread, and sour brew. Djola threw up a lot and got into fights.

A northlander claimed giving up the old ways for a pirate life was better than being a corrupt master and chopping down the world to warm the emperor's ass. Djola broke his arm and ribs, and almost choked him to death. Luckily the northlander pleaded for his life in *Anawanama* before passing out. Djola pulled trembling hands from the fellow's neck. He put an ear to cracked lips and was relieved at the rasp of breath.

He shook the man and whispered, "The Master of Grain hid behind *Lahesh* masks and let guards drag me off. I persuaded Zizi to let *savage* Grain sit at the stone-wood table. I halted the Empire's assault on Grain's precious northland." Rage made him wheeze. "Zizi owes me his life, many times over. Exile? A pirate life?"

The barely conscious pirate moaned. He had dark skin and pale eyes like Grain. Djola dragged him to sick bay, set the arm, and wrapped the ribs. Nobody fought with Djola after that. He moved into sick bay, ate his meals there, and concocted *Lahesh* potions to calm his spirit. The old healer was grateful if Djola set a bone or shared a pain-killing brew. Wounded men wept in his arms, grateful too, for a cool rag at their necks or a hand to hold as they faced death.

At night, Djola burned tree-oil lamps and spent uninterrupted hours reading books and redrawing ancient maps. He charted routes along the inland waterway for Captain Pezarrat, always steering the fleet to places Green Elders might have hidden sacred books. He collected tales of void-storms devastating farms, villages, and forests. Searching for a pattern in a chaos of details was torture. Patience eluded him.

Four months gone since Djola sat at Council, almost five, and the sun was setting on a barbarian thief-lord village. The library at the beach was orange fire. Clouds of soot obscured other buildings. Djola had to persuade Pezarrat not to burn libraries or wise men. What could he learn from bone and ash?

The pirate fleet raced from the Golden Gulf to open sea. It listed so far starboard he feared it would capsize. The steer-man maneuvered into the wave just so, and the ship righted itself. The storm swell had seasoned pirates vomiting. Samina had hidden a sachet in his Aido bag: lavender, jasmine, and raintree blossoms from Smokeland. Inhaling her medicine steadied him.

Twenty raggedy vessels bobbed in unruly waves around the flagship. The hulls looked thrown together from shipwrecks and plundered docks. Patchwork sails were tucked away from the coming storm around driftwood masts. The rigging seemed frayed, chaotic. Too often foes thought one more storm would sink the pirate derelicts. Illusion. Pezarrat's fleet masqueraded as ramshackle yet Azizi had exiled Djola to the rogue with the sturdiest, fastest vessels. Merchant-patrols could never catch them.

A warship faster than storm clouds loomed on the port side. Djola made out the catapults and spark-torch weapons of the Empire Patrol, peacekeepers who'd condemn a pirate raid. Blades glinted in the last sunbeams. Archers crouched in the rigging. The Empire Patrol could ram through Pezarrat's rogue fleet, blasting boats with spark torches. Only Patrols had pirate speed and floating-city weapons. Queen Urzula saw to that.

The Patrol would attack the flagship first. Djola was unsure which side to fight on. As he pulled a knife from his boot, his hands shook. A warrior no more, he'd lost the taste, the will for killing. The Empire ship breezed by. Archers and spear-carriers waved as they pulled alongside the rig riding lowest in the sea. Someone played jaunty notes on a barbarian flute. Planks thunked the decks and joined the ships. A pirate crew lugged booty into the Patrol's hold. A bribe. Going in Azizi's coffers, no doubt.

Djola gagged. He'd come on deck to study the storm and clear his mind. That wasn't working. He hurried back to sick bay, a dark den, barely taller than he was. The old healer—whose name Djola kept forgetting—lit tree-oil lamps that hung from mismatched beams. Swinging lights made eerie shadows dance along the hull.

The old man was thin as a ghost, had three teeth, and five scraggly gray hairs. He looked ready to fade into the death lands, but was never seasick and never complained if Djola abandoned him to watch the sun set or a storm rise. Singing a barbarian ditty, the old healer trudged among bodies stuffed in bunks, slung in hammocks, and sliding on a lumpy wood floor. Djola had survived grisly battles, yet, to his surprise, these broken bodies made him as shaky as Azizi. He flexed twitching hands. Tremors persisted as he cleaned and dressed a knife wound.

"Pezarrat bribes Empire Patrol boats," Djola remarked. The old healer shrugged and attended to the loudest groan. Djola talked on as if to a friend. "He defies Urzula's peace and recruits men with few prospects: vanquished *Anawanama* and *Zamanzi,* orphans and the sons of outlaws, runaway slaves, and pirates who've lost everything to peace."

The Empire had drafted Djola when he was young, stupid, and lost too.

"Your hands shake." The old healer rubbed rheumy eyes. His jowls creased with pity. "Captain Pezarrat lives by ancient pirate ways. Don't let him see that."

Djola drank a cathedral seed and cloud-silk potion to quash the tremors. This bitter *Lahesh* blend blunted feelings without interfering with his mind, his work. Or that's what he told himself. A thrashing patient punched the old healer in the nose. Djola ran over and held the man till the fit subsided. Nothing more he could do except—

"I could conjure carnival illusions and frighten villages or merchant ships into quick surrender." He grinned. "Only a few casualties on either side. Books intact, no griots or libraries going up in smoke."

The old healer patted Djola's shoulder like he'd lost his wits. Djola shrugged off the hand. "This *is* possible." Hope was still a habit. "I'll persuade Pezarrat. He's greedy. I can use that."

The old man's bulbous nose dripped blood. He wiped it on a sleeve. "Captain likes to burn. Burning is easy."

Djola pulled an arm back in its socket. The wounded pirate howled. "My conjure will be easier. I'm the Master of Poisons."

"You were, yes."

Djola trudged to the next patient. He refused to believe that the ground had dissolved under his feet. Out the porthole, the stars sparkled in the sky. Djola would make an ally of the wind.

17

Out of Nowhere

It was five months and seven raids before Djola caught Captain Pezarrat alone on the upper deck, and then his mouth went rogue. No mention of conjure and carnival illusions for bloodless raids. Instead, he blurted, "Why head to Arkhys City?"

"Are you afraid to go home?" Pezarrat was as muscular and robust as Arms and always on the lookout for weakness. "Almost a year, maybe they've forgotten you."

"Why risk a run-in with an Empire Patrol you can't bribe?" Djola replied.

"I take my fleet where I want." Pezarrat poked the codex that Djola held. "And I let men read whatever nonsense we salvage from barbarians."

"*Lahesh* advice for lovemaking. A disappointing waste of parchment."

"Azizi loans me a mapmaker who guides us to where he wants to go." Pezarrat scratched beads of hair on his skull and peered at Djola. "For this, I pay one fifth from every raid."

"You pay so Empire Patrols don't sink your raggedy ships."

Azizi filled his coffers and blamed pirating on a banished master. "You hide half of what you steal."

"Patrols spare you, not me. Why?"

"Empire priests burned ancient codices. Barbarians collected them. We would know our enemies."

Pezarrat huffed. "Chief Nuar has a better storm-sense. Why not loan him to me?"

"Nuar would lead you into a trap." Djola tasted the air and nodded to the steer-man who turned the ship leeward. "I take you where pirates have never ventured."

"Pirates know the open sea, *Anawanama* savages the inland waterway." Pezarrat scowled. "And I trust no one."

A commander, whose sleek hair was twisted into a crown knot, approached the captain and held up a bark-paper scroll: *Anawanama* sacred paper made from mountain fig trees and outlawed in the Empire. Djola's name was written under a Vévé—the sun and moon circling a crossroads—a sign from the Master of Grain.

"This just . . . appeared." The commander spoke with a southern staccato accent. "Out of nowhere!" Kyrie must have folded time and space into a wise-woman corridor and sent a letter from Grain, maybe with word of Samina. "It won't open."

The commander jabbed a blade at the seal. The scroll spewed sparks. Silvery-blue flames devoured his pants and tunic. He shrieked and flailed. Pezarrat jumped away. Crewmen threw buckets of water at him. The fire blazed on. The commander tried to run.

Djola tripped him. "Kyrie's fire-spell protects the scroll. Use gold dust, not water. End his suffering quickly, before the flames spread."

Pezarrat hissed. "Do what he says."

Crewmen smothered the burning man in a fortune. Rivulets of gold seared the deck. Ashes drifted up into the sails. A horrible death. Djola shouted *Anawanama* nonsense, passed his hands through smoke, and pulled the unscathed scroll from the dead man's grip. A good jumba jabba show. He insisted they shove the corpse into the sea.

Pezarrat gestured agreement. "How does witch-woman Kyrie find us?"

"Bring me any letter that appears from nowhere," Djola said softly. News usually took months to travel across the Empire. Kyrie's conjure took no time. "Don't tamper with the Vévé seal or—"

Pezarrat gripped his throat. "Why not just toss the cursed thing in the sea?"

Djola pulled Pezarrat's hands from his windpipe. "Without my gold-spell to contain it, Kyrie's letter would keep coming back, trying to find me," he lied.

Pirates scowled and backed away. Pezarrat masqueraded cool. "What do I get?"

"I'll make you a weapon, acid-conjure to dissolve enemy resistance. Merchant ships and barbarians will surrender quickly. No pirate casualties."

Pezarrat slitted his eyes. "You really know how to do this?"

"I was a spy in a Green Elder enclave. I know many spells."

Pezarrat glanced at the commander's body. "I guess you do."

"I need supplies," Djola said. "The floating cities have cheaper prices than Arkhys City." And wise men, the world's best library, and even talking books. "A direct route across the sea, we're there in less than a month."

Pezarrat patted Djola. "My guard will get what you need for acid-conjure in Arkhys City. At the docks, we can even buy you a fighting woman from beyond the maps."

"Women from beyond the maps are dangerous."

"I like danger. You too, I think. We're alike." Pezarrat and his gang sauntered away.

Azizi thought finding *Xhalan Xhala* and an antidote would be quick. Madness. Djola dashed down to sick bay. His hands trembling, he unfurled Grain's letter.

Strength to you, Djola, in exile almost ten months
Nothing much has changed since my last letter
Azizi is as thin and brittle as dead leaves
Yari has disappeared—even I can't track vie
Northland chiefs chant war and call you and me traitors
Arms whines like a wounded dog
The other masters sit on their thumbs and blame you for speaking bad
    news aloud
Hezram presses for a chair at the stone-wood table—Azizi still puts
    him off
Queen Urzula hunts rogue pirates
She's torched fifty boats, after confiscating the cargo
No master crosses her
Kyrie cannot say if you receive my words
I know the rhythms of your heart and the inland waterway
I too would be an ally to the wind and stars and this connects us
Writing a fourth letter means I believe you receive these reports
I hope you find good conjure to conquer poison desert
Azizi expects a miracle
Something bold and bright to save the day, like from a griot's hero tale
We all need that
The crossroads gods are tricksters—power to your conjure hand

Nothing from Samina. Djola read the letter four times, as if words from Samina might appear or as if he'd missed news of her somehow and just had to read more carefully. How could Grain write such a letter? Who cared if Arms whined and Urzula chased rogues? Djola cursed Nuar and Yari, who must know Djola was in exile. Nuar should defend Djola against angry chiefs. Yari should persuade Azizi to do right instead of disappear.

At the fifth read, he decided Samina was wise to stay hidden, silent. His enemies hunted her and the children and would murder them. Three letters lost made his heart ache. What had he missed? Reading a sixth time, Djola could barely breathe. Grain should have written more—Djola was still in the dark. His mind was so jumbled, he couldn't think. He crumpled the letter and pressed it to his heart. Miracles were hard work. How would he do a miracle if he lost his wits?

18

Smokeland

A few months before Awa's fourteenth birthday, her hair turned thick as strangle vines. Her breasts were suddenly round and full, and muscles bulged. A strange woman with midnight eyes and sable skin burnished red looked back at her from lakes and streams. Bal declared her a great beauty who'd wreck someone's heart. Awa dismissed Bal's praise. She had no time for love. She mapped the clash of Smokeland territories—each region was many regions intertwined, a polyrhythm of possibilities. She crafted a calendar of Smokeland moods and drew the harmony of its seasons.

Once, covered in a swarm of bees, she skirted the borderland void and stumbled sideways into Smokeland. She hovered at a crossroads—a thousand thousand paths, bridges, and skyways intersecting. Dizzy with possibility, she stepped back to the everyday with the bees. Elders and Sprites marveled at static sizzling in her hair and crackling from elbows and knees. Bal claimed Awa had left no breath body behind on this trip.

"I've heard old *Lahesh* tales of full-body journeys, but only seen horses or wild dogs step sideways in and out of Smokeland." Yari rejoiced at Awa's prowess. "A smoke-walker like few others."

After practicing till her heart could beat in six regions at once, Awa dragged Bal's spirit body through the border-void and headed to favorite places. The treehouse village was deserted. Roofs had blown to the ground. Walls and floors had come apart and thumped in the wind. Shredded cloaks fluttered like ghosts in the shadows. Acid filled Awa's mouth. Her heart stuttered, off the beat. Calling on Sprite discipline, on hours of relentless meditation with Yari, she hauled Bal on to another region.

"We're leaving too soon," Bal said.

"That region was desolate, eerie. I can show you somewhere better." Perched on cliffs above the blue-green bay, Awa scanned the horizon for the boat people's sails or cook fires. On a clear day she could see a hundred hundred leagues. The boat people must have been very far out in the water.

"What do you look for?" Bal asked. She was a head taller than Awa now and two thirds as wide. Impatient, Bal rested her chin on Awa's spongy locks and muttered nonsense. Awa refused distraction and took her good time puzzling out an answer. Fog rolled in from the border-void. Dirty waves slammed refuse high onto the cliff walls, higher than the water had ever been before.

"Could sea level be rising?" Awa said. "From storms or . . ."

"You're truly baffled. Unusual."

"Not just that—" Awa felt abandoned by treehouse lovers and the boat people.

Bal jumped down to a ledge in front of two rusty iron horses with cloud-silk tails and feather manes. "You should have asked the boat people to explain their ways."

"I thought we could do that today."

"Ha! You thought I'd talk to them." Bal stroked a horse's tail and leaned her face into purple feathers. Both creatures came rattling to life, shaking seaweed and sand in her face. Bal squealed delight. The horses' hearts were golden wheels of light in iron-mesh cages. Red eyes blazed as they snorted hot steam. "Let's ride." Bal grinned. "Come on. You love horses." Bal sprang on a polished back and rode off.

The second metal beast climbed up a path to Awa and nudged her with a furry nose. Awa shrugged off anxiety and jumped on its cold back. Her horse followed Bal's to another ledge. The ride was herky-jerky, and the metal beasts made an awful clatter, as if each step ripped apart their innards. They meandered through rags and broken talking books. Fragments of ancestor story-songs filled the air.

Bal sang harmony, at home even in ancient music. Envy stole Awa's balance and she almost fell from the horse's back. She'd always been silent on Smokeland journeys, afraid of nothing in particular, just mindful of disturbing the mood. Singing joy with Bal was thrilling.

"If this is what boat people throw away, think what they must keep," Bal said.

The iron horses suddenly collapsed into shuddering heaps underneath them. Awa grabbed Bal and leapt clear. The beasts belched smoke, slid over a precipice, and smashed into the rocks below. A shower of wheels, mesh, and metal shards exploded up the cliffs. Bal reached her hand into destruction before it fell back into the sea.

"What are you doing?" Awa shouted.

"Thanks"—Bal hugged Awa to her volcano heart—"for saving me."

"Saving you?" Awa frowned at the sinking wreckage. Talking books gurgled and went silent. Dim red eyes faded to gray and sank. "Just now? That was nothing."

"Not just that." Bal shook her head. "Thanks for bringing me here, for—"

"Smokeland's no trash heap. Nobody throws things away.

Smoke-walkers take what they find back to the everyday and leave wonders for others to share." Rubble floated in the scummy bay. "Something happened to the boat people." Something bad.

"Ask them when you come back." Bal held up a gray marble eye and a slim golden wheel. Grinning, she put these treasures in a medicine bag made from Aido cloth that disappeared in the shadows. "I'm sure we could conjure iron horses in the everyday."

Awa marveled at the possibility. "Perhaps, but— Whayoa!"

A mob of empty-eyed spirit slaves tumbled out of a cave below them. They had translucent lungs and faint ember hearts. A rotten fruit smell gusted from cavernous mouths full of granite teeth. Seaweed decayed in their hair. Who had these smoke-walkers been before?

"Fatazz!" Bal drew her sword. "Yari said to avoid ember hearts." The spirit slaves jerked toward the sound of Bal's voice. She shook Awa. "Fly us away from here."

Awa gazed into empty eyes. Her mind was smoke, her feet heavy weights. Flight was impossible. She'd lost the speed of thought. The spirit slaves climbed up through brush, slow but steady.

"Let's go." Bal tugged Awa's arm.

"Maybe they are the missing boat people." Awa tumbled to her knees. Jagged shells pierced her skin and blood trickled into the sand.

The spirit slaves scrambled faster right toward them.

Using a chorus of voices, Bal sang harmony with herself. She tapped her feet and beat the hilt of her sword on volcanic rocks, creating dense polyrhythms that echoed around the bay. Thunderous reverberations assaulted the spirit slaves. Going every direction at once, they got tangled up in each other on a narrow ledge. Several fell down the cliffs into the bay.

Bal wrenched Awa back to standing and danced her away from the edge, a favorite routine from the everyday. Blocking Awa's field of vision, she hissed softly in her ears. "We must leave this region." Her breath was hot and her volcano heart pumped too fast. "You promised Yari. We must warn *vie*."

That jolted Awa's mind clear. "Spirit slaves are usually so much slower."

"They have a hungry look."

"Yes." Awa whisked Bal through the remaining regions of her heart, pausing only for brief glimpses. Swamps, grasslands, and deserts blurred together. They encountered few smoke-walkers and had to avoid spirit slaves in each region.

"Are there always so many with ember hearts?" Bal asked.

"Usually just one or two." They stood in Awa's home region under the giant beehive in the elder cathedral tree. Awa spied no spirit slaves nearby and sighed. Calm sentinel bees crawled across her shoulder. One got tangled in her hair and buzzed. "Never a spirit-slave horde before."

"You're brave to travel Smokeland alone." Bal used a solemn warrior voice. "We must tell Yari to weave a story of your courage." She pulled a tight curl-bundle of Awa's hair straight and released the sentinel.

"I'm never alone. I have the bees." Awa grinned. "I'm glad to have a shadow warrior along this time." She filled her lungs with the sweet expiration of the elder tree. "Take a deep breath. The hard part is leaving Smokeland."

Bal filled her lungs, and Awa flew them to the border-void. Bal ground her teeth as smoke invaded them. Awa felt as if she was home again, and Father, Mother, Kenu, and her younger brothers had just abandoned her in the desert to dry up and blow away while they enjoyed life in a lush oasis.

Bal whimpered. Caught in despair also, she was a heavy weight.

The border-void was endless, the smoke thick and sticky; escape seemed almost impossible. Sorrow began to fade along with the thrill of clutching Bal to her heart.

"We're too heavy and there's more void-smoke than usual. Sorry." Awa jabbed Bal's neck with a bee sting and then her own neck too. After sharp, burning pain, they swooned.

19

Vandana

Pezarrat dropped anchor at Arkhys City. No slaves allowed inside the capital, but trade at the docks was swift. Djola gave a supply list to Pezarrat's men. If Council spies saw him on deck, they'd send an arrow his way. Why give high priest Ernold or the Masters of Money and Water opportunity for murder? Djola paced the half-empty sick bay, muttering. He should get word to Rano for Samina or maybe word to Yari that he needed help. Yari was always ready to forgive. Samina too.

The old healer pointed at blood-soaked bandages on their patients. "They'll bleed out, unless we sew." Thread, sutures, and needles weren't on Djola's supply list. Nothing for sick bay was. "I'll get what we need." The old healer threw on a cloak.

"Can you deliver a message for me?" Djola stammered.

The healer scratched his few hairs. "I'll tell Pezarrat you do this."

Djola scribbled *Lahesh* to Yari and Samina. "To the *veson* who cleans the library. Bring me *vie*'s seal." The old healer took the tiny scroll and left him alone with wounded captives who groaned and whimpered. Djola downed half a bottle of seed and silk potion to lift his mood and dull his mind. He sank into a pleasant haze and watched the moon rise from inky water and climb high in the sky. Time dissolved.

The old healer returned carrying months of supplies and a scroll with a Vévé to the crossroads gods: the moon caught in a spiderweb. "Your friend had just finished scouring the windows."

"Friend?" Djola grunted. "No. Just someone I know."

"*Vie* promised to deliver your messages for no pay. A friend." The healer talked on. Djola heard little except, "Vandana is too old, too fierce for Pezarrat, but he bought her anyhow, for you." The healer offered Djola needle and thread.

"I don't sew flesh." Djola smacked his hand away. "I need conjure supplies."

A woman stepped in front of the old man and held up a *Lahesh* metal-mesh bag of poison sand. She was careful not to spill a grain. "I am Vandana." She dumped salts, lava stones, rare earth compounds, potash, dried bat dung, and crystals at Djola's feet. Dark as polished lava, she had big bones, big breasts, big hips, and four teeth filed dagger sharp.

Dagger teeth were supposedly common among warrior women on the far side of the *Mama Zamba* mountains, where the maps ran out. Vandana shook skinny gray braids at a captive whose wounds seeped blood. "Captain says you need help." She shifted to *Lahesh*—perhaps not her mother tongue, but well-spoken. "I told him, Vandana work medicine with you." She got in his face. "You agree?"

Pezarrat loomed in the doorway. "You pine after your wife." He'd bought Vandana to irritate Djola. "I hope your letter gets to her."

Djola forced a smile. "Vandana, you help the wounded. Can you sew? I'll do conjure for the captain."

Pezarrat disappeared up the ladder. Vandana shook her head

and lashed Djola's cheek with a whipcord braid, drawing a line of blood. "You make death for Captain."

"Acid-conjure means less death than fire raids."

"Maybe. Maybe just more raids."

"I'm trying to save us all."

"A man with a mission." She gripped him. "Captain says he dumps me in the sea, if you don't want me. I'd have to kill him."

Djola laughed the first time in who knows how long. "I want you."

"Good. Many need stitches. I teach you sewing tomorrow. No time now."

Vandana pulled a needle from a small bag at her waist and bent down to a captive. While Djola worked into the night making acid-conjure, she and the old man cleaned, sewed, and bandaged wounds. She babbled to her patients about flowers blooming in snow fields, eagles roosting by cliff cottages, and granddaughters clashing swords at dawn then sneaking off to lovers in the afternoon. "All done. They'll live," she declared.

"Thank you." Djola admired her bold spirit.

She snatched a lamp and tramped out of sick bay. Djola followed her to the hold, which was jammed with salt, northland seeds, baskets, and outlaw cloth. She slung a hammock over water barrels then pulled a knife from her small bag, a long knife that shouldn't have fit. She pressed the blade against his heart. "I sleep alone, knife ready, eye open."

Djola grinned. "You haven't come to kill me."

"You'd already be dead."

"But you could be a spy for . . . anybody."

"Pezarrat should send you a warm body."

"No." Djola held up the metal-mesh bag of poison sand. "I'm too busy."

"Studying void-storms?" She pushed him back toward sick bay. "Be careful there."

The next morning, Djola gave Pezarrat acid-conjure, and the captain raided a fleet of merchant ships. Djola refused to watch. He hid in his bunk and drank seed and silk potion. Victory was swift. Hulls turned to sludge and merchants surrendered. No casualties. "A man of your word." Pezarrat mocked him, but left him alone to work.

Djola spent the next days trying to neutralize poison sand. He lined a wooden bucket with *Lahesh* metal-mesh and wore a mesh veil to protect his face. He doused lethal grains with fire or water, then added concoctions of crystals, potash, bat dung, and lava stone.

The results were always the same: a spoonful of poison sand turned into a bucketful, which he tossed out a porthole. He should have worried about watery forests and behemoths, but despair and seed and silk blunted his concern. He needed to talk to wise men in the floating cities.

20

Orca

After a fifth acid-conjure raid, celebrations raged up on deck. Djola lay on his bunk in a silk-and-seed stupor, watching a spider weave a web—a crossroads-moon Vévé—in the open sick bay door. Pezarrat charged through the sticky strands. He clawed his face and spit spider-silk. "Vandana says you need a warm body."

Pirates dragged in Orca, a hefty boy with dimpled cheeks and a long, silky braid. Orca had been used so badly during the *celebration,* he could barely walk.

"No." Djola refused to invite a spy between his thighs. "No."

Pezarrat chortled. "Vandana fought off a gang of horny men. She insisted the fat one was perfect for you."

"If I don't want him, will you dump him in the sea?"

"Why keep spoiled meat?" Pezarrat and his men barged past Vandana.

Djola groaned at the blood on Orca's clothes and the suffering in his face.

"Give me a hand!" Vandana helped Orca to Djola's bunk.

Djola and Vandana tended Orca's wounds, gave him food

Vandana stole from Pezarrat's table and boiled wine made from Smokeland fruit. Djola held Orca's hand through the night while Vandana told tales of wild women from beyond the maps. Instead of dying out after plague and war decimated their people, the women crossed *Mama Zamba* and seduced thief-lords, good citizens, pirates, and slaves. Dazzled by free, wild-women ways and anxious for another life, a better story, their lovers went back over the mountains with the women and never returned to the Empire.

"Is this true?" Orca whispered.

"Yes." Djola squeezed the boy's hand, wanting to believe also. "True."

Orca's body healed quickly, but he was skittish, rarely spoke, and never left sick bay. He offered his body to Djola and looked terrified when Djola declined. Drunk pirates kept sniffing around him, so Djola told Pezarrat he wanted Orca exclusively. Pezarrat agreed. Acid-conjure let the captain triple his raids—as Vandana predicted. Sick bay was flooded with foolhardy pirates and wounded captives. Orca tended patients, doing what Djola hated. He had a gentle touch and a soothing manner.

"What else can I do for you?" Orca asked.

Djola let Orca massage tension away, but nothing more.

"You should learn what we know," Vandana declared. "You like doctoring."

Vandana taught Orca *and* Djola healing secrets from beyond the maps. Djola was excellent at concocting cures. Orca was better tending patients. Evenings, after brewing herb potions with Djola or patching up pirates with Vandana, Orca joined Djola climbing the mast. Birds hovered in warm updrafts, their delicate wing feathers gleaming. Djola liked dangling over the sea, feeling the swell in his stomach, letting the wind get lost in his hair. High waves broke across the bow and reminded him of Samina on a flimsy raft, cutting the water, naked under a sliver of moon.

Orca watched him sway over roiling water with terrified eyes. Vandana roamed the deck below, shouting at stars and gathering moonbeams for her small bag. Pirates who considered forcing her to their bunks feared how they might wake in the morning, or if they'd wake at all. She had an array of hidden weapons, yet was gentle, sentimental. She believed in dragging people back from death. Anybody was worth her efforts.

When the fleet reached the Golden Gulf, Pezarrat bombarded Sand Haven, a fortified barbarian city, with acid-conjure. Hundreds died. Vandana blamed Djola and stopped talking to him. This was an arrow in his gut. She still insisted Pezarrat bring Sand Haven books and live griots to Djola. The books were full of whimsy and fear. Griots spouted the same jumba jabba he'd already read about *Xhalan Xhala*: the power of Smokeland in the everyday; tomorrow from yesterday *right now*; sacred conjure too dangerous to be shared.

What did that mean? Djola was a terrible smoke-walker. He hated leaving his body to fly off to who knows where. He barely made it through the border-void his last trip with Samina. Wielding the power of Smokeland in the everyday was a daunting prospect. He'd rather concoct mixtures from stone powder, crystal dust, and potash. Babalawo wise men in the floating cities might know how to master the spell of spells. They might also help him neutralize poison sand.

After Sand Haven, Pezarrat hid the fleet in a cove to avoid paying Azizi his share. Orca climbed a mast without Djola. Vandana walked the deck and shouted to the stars. The old healer went off drinking with the steer-man. Djola sat alone in sick bay, puzzling poison sand, refusing to give up. *Every mystery could be solved.* Yari said this. Djola closed his eyes. He drifted close to sleep, calm, sober, his thoughts sharp. The puzzle yielded: void-storms appeared like Grain's letter, not from nowhere but perhaps from a wise-woman corridor or a bit of folded space.

Djola sipped a cup of soup. At the second mouthful, he spit it out. Too late. The bitter taste of lethal mushrooms hid behind garlic and honey. He carried antidotes for common toxins in his Aido bag, but these were potent, fast. One mouthful, and Vandana found him convulsing, an antidote clutched in a paralyzed hand. She helped him choke it down, babbling *Mama Zamba* sagas until his heart slowed, his breath was steady, and his strength returned. They took long breaths together.

"*Basawili.*" He thanked her and the crossroads gods.

Vandana hugged him. "I wish no death on you."

Djola drew knives from his sleeves and raced to the galley. Vandana followed, wielding long, diamond-tipped blades he'd never seen. They confronted the cook—a young idiot paid off by Council no doubt. Djola forced him to guzzle a bowl of his mushroom brew. In minutes, the cook foamed at the mouth, choked, and died. A kitchen boy cowered under a table. Vandana blocked Djola and let the boy run away.

"Little one not against us," she murmured in *Lahesh.*

Djola's hands trembled. "The cook killed himself."

"When do we go to home?" Vandana held his hands till rage subsided.

Djola couldn't go home without an answer to poison sand. He was certain it traveled through folded space, but why, how? "Soon I hope."

"Be quick, catch good weather. It's a long walk over ice walls, each one higher. Many steps to cross the backbone." *Lahesh* called the mountains that ran from Arkhys City to Holy City their mother's backbone, *Mama Zamba*. "Then is dry sand, stealing water from skin and eyes, no matter what you're drinking."

Beyond the mountains was the end of maps. Few travelers survived the sweet desert and glaciers to reach Arkhys City. Besides Yari, Vandana was the only one Djola knew. Warrior women with dagger teeth and diamond blades had been a tall tale he doubted until he met her.

"I must understand something first," Djola said.

"I know. I am patience. I have good to do in the meanwhile. That is living."

21

A Broken Tusk

Pezarrat marched into the galley with a phalanx of guards trailing behind him.

"Empire spy"—Vandana pointed at the cook—"dead from his own soup."

Pezarrat thrust a bark-paper scroll at Djola. "A letter appeared."

Djola snatched it. Leaving Vandana to clean up the galley mess, he dashed to sick bay. Orca, smelling of moon mist, hovered close as Djola neutralized Kyrie's conjure with gold dust, broke the seal, and read Grain's flowing script.

What you predicted comes true. Strength to you, Djola, in exile
No rainbow fish run the rivers—revelers at the Water Festival
  go hungry
Kyrie sends honey, mangos, and goats for Arms to distribute in
  the Arkhys market
Empire coffers are full, though few can afford taxes
Azizi hoards money for the coming wars over water, grain, and
  tree oil
I persuaded Council to build storm shelters throughout the capital

Shelters are Zamanzi *conjure against void-storms, and nobody*
    sneers
I waited, hoping we'd catch a culprit but after months of investi-
    gation Arms still cannot say who murdered your men
Only six were found—I saw the bodies—they put up a good fight
The other six are still missing
I suspect they protect Samina and your children, wherever they
    hide
Kyrie sends hope and power to your conjure hand

Djola let the scroll fall to the deck. His heart hammered at his veins.

Orca dug at tension in his back as Djola whispered, "They saved my life many times."

After he and Arms liberated Holy City, thief-lords surrendered and swore an oath to peace. Celebrating, Djola and everyone got drunk on tainted wine. Just a few warriors stood watch. Rogue barbarians mounted a cowardly ambush, no hope of victory, just terror. Sober Rano sounded the alarm and took a barbarian arrow in the shoulder pulling an unconscious Djola from a burning tent.

"My best friend, murdered, because of me." Djola gripped Orca's shoulders. "Tortured for my family, my secrets." Honorable to the end, Rano had died without revealing where Samina and the children were. He doted on Bal, Quint, and Tessa most of all—the children he never got to have. "Rano was a true friend."

Orca pulled Djola close, kissed his cheeks, told him to breathe.

"Has Kyrie gone mad?" Djola trembled against Orca. "No more hope for rainbow fish or Rano." His family must still be at the hideaway or on Mount Eidhou with Kyrie, who told nobody, not even Grain. "*Basawili,* Rano."

Vandana appeared. As Orca told her the news, Djola choked on sorrow. He was the fool Rano and his guard died for. Vandana grimaced. "Pezarrat says we'll be in the floating cities in a few weeks."

"He lies." Djola collapsed into Orca.

"We'll get there, eventually," Vandana insisted.

"Too long," said Djola, mumbling. He fell asleep in Orca's arms, grateful for the boy's warm body.

The elephant with a broken tusk trumpeted, flapped enormous ears, and spewed poison sand in his dreams. Djola shielded his face and called to her, bitter. "Did you hear? Rano and my men were murdered, but we'll reach the floating cities." Eventually.

22

Out of the Void

A wa's stomach gurgled at the smell of nut bread. Her head ached, burned, as if her hair was on fire. Bal caressed her cheeks and sang an ancestor song from the Smokeland talking books. Awa opened her eyes. They'd come through the border-void back to the everyday outside Yari and Isra's goat-hair tent. Isra was a warrior-scout from the south, an Aido cloth weaver, the love Yari always returned to. Some Sprites claimed Isra was a reluctant Green Elder, yet *vie* was the anchor to Yari's wandering spirit, to all their wandering spirits.

Awa shook off void-smoke clinging to her hair and smiled. Swampy wetlands turned silver in the twilight. Twisted tupelo roots clutched the banks of a gurgling stream. Demon-flies flashed green and blue butts, making love, eating foolish enemies. The enclave had marched from the northern desert to old *Anawanama* territory.

Yari and Isra carried their breath bodies around for weeks and set them on mats in this grassy knoll. A few moments in Smokeland could be days in the everyday. Moans and grunts poured from the tent. Bal pointed at a tangle of shadows. She and Awa giggled. Yari and Isra were noisy lovers. Both used many voices.

"Yari would kill me if *I* left your breath body unprotected and went off for a roll in the sand with a lover," Bal said.

Awa poked Bal's bony chest. "You don't have a lover."

"But if I did . . ."

"You don't!" Awa was jealous of Bal's shadow lover. "How long were we gone?"

"I don't know."

A wild dog shoved a cold nose in Awa's face and licked her hot forehead. They wrestled in the grass. The dog pinned her down and nipped her nose. She rolled him over and tickled his mottled tummy. Her headache faded and jealousy burned off.

Bal laughed. "Stray dogs always smell Smokeland on you."

"He trailed us from the border." The dog sprawled by Awa's side. She scratched his big smoke-gray head. "What did you see in the void?"

Bal broke off laughing, her breath suddenly short.

"Never mind," Awa said. "Shall I tell you how I was sold to the Elders?"

"You'd tell me that?" Garden Sprites were usually too ashamed to tell who sold them or why. Poison desert turned good citizens into slavers who stole children, who sold their own daughters or even sons to buy food or passage on a pirate ship to the floating cities. Sprites imagined horror scenarios for each other. "Are you sure?"

Awa shrugged. "It's what I saw at first in the void."

"Why risk the ire of—"

"It's not bad luck for Sprites to trade stories. Cowards made up that tale. Crossroads gods are tricksters, but they don't care what we say to each other."

Bal looked unconvinced. "I guess . . ."

"I want you to know me." Before she lost heart, Awa blurted her saga in coarse detail, no music or dance embellishments, no poetic flourishes. Even such an awkward telling made her feel better. Sold to save a farm and send her brothers to study in Holy City wasn't the worst Sprite saga. "Mother was right about Yari and Smokeland—traveling through the regions, understanding the rhythms, a treasure. But—"

"What?" Bal hugged away Awa's sadness. *"What?"*

Awa savored Bal's sweetgrass and iron scent before answering. "My family is a wound, but you're a balm." She stroked her friend's bold cheeks. "Now you tell."

"I can't," Bal stammered.

"Why not?" Awa trembled. The wild dog whined and licked them both. "Don't you trust me?" She loved no one more than Bal, except maybe Yari. "I told you everything. Even older brother Kenu's cowardice."

"I can't tell you, because—"

"Were your parents desperate savages selling daughters?"

Bal snorted at her. "Savages don't sell their daughters."

"Everybody sells their children. To slavers or brothels or enclaves."

"Empire citizens tell this lie when they steal *Zamanzi* or *Anawanama* daughters."

Awa didn't believe this, but decided not to argue. "Were you stolen?"

Bal shuddered. "My mind was blank in the void." She looked away, embarrassed. "I have no memories of before joining this enclave."

"Oh." Awa took a breath and scratched the dog. "What's that like?"

"Like carrying a bit of void inside you all the time."

"Zst!" Awa rarely cursed. Bad memories were probably better than none. "No memories at all?"

"Conjurers took my memories. It's supposedly easy when you're young. Somebody gave me to Yari. I wasn't sold. Perhaps Yari knows who I am, where I'm from, who my people are, yet even when I beg, *vie* won't tell me."

Awa almost said, *that's awful,* but kissed Bal's cheek instead. "Green Elders are your family and mine too. You can invent a past for yourself if you wish."

Bal took a breath. "A bold idea."

"Memory is a story written on your body, who you mean to be, now."

"What about truth?"

"Truth is what you do with the story." Awa jumped up and danced around the tupelo trees. Blue berries and purple leaves littered the ground.

"Yari says one of your gifts is weaving strong story cloth from a few threads." Bal hunched her shoulders. "Griots conjure the unknown from the known. Not me. I'm lost in the void, without a map."

"I love making maps," Awa declared. "I could help you craft one."

Bal jumped up beside her, smiling shyly, an unusual face for a fierce warrior. The wild dog wagged his hind parts, smacking them with a bushy tail. "Go ahead."

Awa observed Bal, as if she'd have to write her down in signs and ciphers, as if she'd have to mold her from cloud-silk and drum beats. "The green in your eyes is from far away, northland mountains or the floating cities. Long limbs belong to cloud forest folk. You sweat little, always cool, a child of the desert too. So, one parent from high, one from low, and whether *Zamanzi, Anawanama,* or barbarian, they risked all to shield you from pirate assassins or Empire thugs. Your parents sacrificed your memories of them to save you. Kurakao! They are to be praised, for if their daughter knew her true identity, conjurers would find her in dreams and betray her spirit to enemies.

"Powerful people feared you might grow into yourself, into your power, and come for them. Your parents wanted you to have your own life, your own story, not perish in theirs. Assassins hunted you and would have killed you when you were a child. It's too late now. You're a shadow warrior, well protected, even in dreams. Your parents gave you to Yari. Their wise plan triumphed. They loved you, saved you, and even if they've gone on to the death lands, their wisdom watches over you still."

Bal's eyes shone with moonlight. "You really believe that might be true?"

Awa nodded. "Why not?"

"Kurakao!" Too heavy to stand, Bal dropped to the mats, dragging Awa with her. Bal cried fat tears. After a moment Awa cried too and they leaned together. Their hearts beat slowly and breath was minimal. The moon vanished from the sky, and stars emerged, challenging the dark. Dew prickled skin, ants nibbled at knees, and the dog fell asleep, head and paws in their laps. When birds hopped close and sang morning rites, Bal stood up carefully. After such a long meditation, muscles might forget themselves. She pulled Awa up. The dog had disappeared.

"A past to guide my future," Bal declared. "I shall live in this story."

"Good." Awa liked Bal's story better than her own. "We shall live in it together."

So many spirit slaves wandering Smokeland was a bad sign—high priests perverting *Lahesh* conjure—but Yari was thrilled that Bal and Awa had returned to the everyday with ancestor songs, a new rock dance, and plans for the future. They never mentioned the golden wheel and marble eye from the iron horse, or the past Awa conjured for Bal. These secrets were theirs alone.

Yari rejoiced to see them so changed. *Vie* gave them each a *Lahesh* timepiece. Awa's was a waterwheel sculpture, Bal's a candle contrivance. They were thrilled to have such rare treasures. Yari was *Lahesh*, a tinkerer, fashioning whatever wim-wom came to mind. In days gone by, thief-lords and warriors had raided *Lahesh* markets stealing everything, even snatching people from themselves. Few *Lahesh* spoke their ancestor tongue anymore, but *Lahesh* tinkering, craftwork, and wisdom were coveted. Awa and Bal felt lucky to have Yari—the crocodile lover, the dream tinkerer, the trickster shadow Elder—bring them into the enclave.

"You won't be Sprites forever," Yari said, sucking down sadness. "You should think on who you want to be: Green Elder, Iyalawo, good Empire citizen, griot storyteller, shadow warrior, or something of your own invention."

Father had claimed story weavers were useless, lying windbags. She had proved him wrong. Griots made the world.

"At the crossroads, why choose only one role?" Bal said. "Why not be everything we want to be?"

Awa nodded, excited. "Like Aido cloth, every color strong."

Yari grinned. "The ancient languages have a word for sacred shapeshifters. I shall find this for you in time for your crossover ceremony. I promise."

Out of the void and into tomorrow. Of course, the void could follow you to tomorrow, but Awa and Bal danced for their good fortune.

BOOK
II

1

Visions of Fire

Djola guzzled a flask of cathedral seed and cloud-silk potion, a perversion of *Lahesh* conjure, but time was a demon tormenting him. Days on the flagship rushed by, like white water over a cliff, or dragged on and on, endless torture: ships, villages, and cities plundered, the taste of acid-conjure lingering in dead air as the pirate fleet chased a good wind. Almost three years lost to the sea.

Djola scratched a patchy beard. Shaving was too hard. No longer the clean-shaven northlander, he looked like a rogue pirate, scruffy and merciless. He stared from a cracked mirror to the book-booty scattered on the floor. Probably nothing he hadn't read. No word of his family, no word from Yari. Perhaps Yari was against him. Djola burped sour bile. A double dose of seed and silk was merciful, but hard on an empty stomach. His mind was as ratchety as a broken windcatcher. Vision blurred; sounds were muffled. He closed his eyes and let the pirate world fade.

Mangos on Mount Eidhou would be ripe this time of year, a second crop turning the air sweet. Samina and the children would help sister Kyrie with the harvest. All the refugees and renegades helped. Quint must be nine, Bal a fierce fifteen, and Tessa a grown woman of eighteen, ready for husband and babies of her own. Djola was missing their lives. Samina would have to be mother and father. Kyrie's towers were hot and dank, but Samina would fashion windcatchers and *Lahesh* wim-wom. She'd play talking books and her twenty-one-stringed kora harp till she melted stone mountain hearts.

Howling winds interrupted Djola's drugged reverie. He focused again on the porthole. Kaharta, the southern harbor city the pirates had just raided, smoldered on the horizon: red, orange, and purple, like a setting sun. Pezarrat still torched the bigger cities. Seed and silk blunted Djola's emotions, yet allowed him to focus on details at a distance—a good warrior drug. He peered out a porthole. A child on a shaky dock hugged a sooty goat and wailed. "Hush," someone yelled, "nothing to be done." Pezarrat raided Kaharta for Djola. "The best library outside the floating cities." It was Djola yelling. He kicked useless books. Three years and he'd learned almost nothing.

"I'm scared," someone blubbered at Djola. The wounded had arrived. Djola gathered a bloody pirate in his arms as the fellow gasped his last breaths: "My spirit debt, too high." A boy of fifteen, nobody should blame him for his life so far. "Will I suffer in the death lands?"

"No." Djola lifted his head so he wouldn't drown in his own blood. "People say, 'Living is free. No debts to pay at the end, just a legacy to leave behind.'" Djola repeated *Zamanzi* lies, excuses warriors invented for bad behavior. He wasn't a proper healer like Vandana. She knew stories to ease a body into the death lands.

The boy shivered. "Who could believe such a thing?"

"*Zamanzi*—"

"Savages believe anything." The boy came from a city like the one that burned, that had killed him. Kaharta was in a necklace of rich barbarian market centers around the Golden Gulf. A confederation of proud thief-lords, they'd seen better days.

The boy tugged Djola's sleeve. "Do *you* believe we carry no debts at the end? You're a Council master, a wise man—"

"Just a pirate like you and a *savage* even."

"No." The boy convulsed. "A wise man."

Djola flinched and surveyed the wounded. This lot had been burned or hacked so badly, they were only ten breaths from—

"Death costs everything you've got," the boy mumbled. "Nothing left to pay a spirit debt." He expired. Djola might have saved him if he'd gotten to him sooner.

"We lose everybody. Zst!" Vandana cursed at familiar faces who yesterday danced on the deck to djembe drums and calabash harps, who bragged about their exploits on land and sea, who drank wine from Djola's cup to prove they didn't fear assassins or anything.

Djola had wanted to poison these fools himself or rescue them: too late to do anything. Vandana closed her eyes on tears. Why mourn pirate rogues? They should mourn Kaharta's dead. Yet, Kaharta and the barbarian confederation looted villages on the Empire's southern border. Thief-lords fished out the Golden Gulf and filled it with toxic spew. Why pity anybody? Djola let the boy's body down gently. In exile, a man might lose his wits and nobody would notice. Sanity was an elusive shapeshifter.

"Too many," the old healer said. "What can we do?"

"Search for an antidote," Djola mumbled to the dead boy. "That's what I do." He yelled to the crew. "Don't bring in corpses, throw them overboard." In the swell of a storm wave, the dead boy slid against the bulkhead, eyes fixed on Djola. "You don't add to my debt." Djola stumbled over to books taken from Kaharta's library and jammed them in a barrel.

"We're lucky." Vandana glowered at Djola. "Plunder from best library on the Gulf offers ballast. Kaharta was unlucky."

He replied in *Anawanama*. "All Kaharta had was last year's smoked fish and wormy grain stolen from somebody. Gold nobody can eat."

Vandana smacked him with a book wrapped in *Lahesh* metal-mesh. "So many dead. For secrets we should leave hidden, forgotten."

In metal-mesh, this codex could have survived poison sand. Why protect what should be forgotten? Djola drew a bark-paper conjure book from the mesh and whispered its title. "Amplify Now. *Xhalan Xhala*. *Lahesh* Reckoning Fire." Words leapt at him: *no progress without sacrifice*. His heart jolted.

"A good one?" Orca stroked Djola's hand and passed fresh bandages to Vandana.

"Yes. The gods of the crossroads are tricksters." Djola read on, eager.

Lahesh jumba jabba was easier to understand than he'd expected.

2

Lovegrass

In the middle of a chilly night, camped north of Kaharta near the Bog River Gorge, Awa and Bal donned Aido cloth robes for camouflage and drank a midnight berry potion—fruit and herb conjure to see clearly in the dark. They warmed naked toes at the cooking coals and giggled. They were barely fifteen, untested, yet going out with scouts to defend the enclave—after the Elders got done squabbling.

Plump Isra, spiky white hair exploding from *vie*'s scalp, pinned lanky Yari down on bed cushions in their goat-hair tent. Yari always returned to Isra, the lover never too dazzled by Yari's charm to argue. Isra had will and vision to match Yari's and insisted Awa, Bal, and other Sprites were ready to join seasoned shadow warriors on a scouting venture.

Yari had doubts, but finally agreed on one condition: *vie* would lead the expedition instead of Isra, the enclave's best scout. To sweeten the deal, Yari promised Isra a new song.

Isra scowled. "An exiled master roams the Gulf hunting you on a pirate ship."

"Your spies are well-informed." Yari kissed Isra.

"He sends missives in *Lahesh* that you don't share." Isra tried to be angry. "Did he steal your heart and stomp it? Like the high priest of Holy City?"

"He's not like Hezram. More like the Sprites we have now. I worry about him."

"Were you lovers?"

Yari smiled. "He thinks I waste my time teaching Sprites."

"You seek news of pirates and old lovers from Kahartan warriors. Rascal—"

Yari drowned out Isra's protests, singing a favorite:

Stolen love tears you apart, but—
We can give love away
Make a bridge of the heart

Isra laughed as Yari promised a new verse on return. Thrilled, Bal gathered bow, arrows, sword, spear, drum, and calabash rattles. Awa had no instruments or weapons to take along and felt useless. She helped Isra and Yari load grain stores onto hardy goats, then packed up bedding, tent, Isra's loom, and the few books they carried with them.

Who needed to lug heavy tomes and delicate scrolls when Yari knew more stories than *vie* had time to tell? Before the enclave crossed the Bog River Gorge, Awa had hoped to visit the Kahartan library with Yari, the greatest library outside the floating cities, but Isra's spies said library and librarians were soot. Pirates had raided and stolen the best books. Awa sighed and pulled on climbing boots. Why bring a smoke-walker on a dangerous expedition when what you needed were warriors?

Isra and the enclave disappeared into the gorge, silent and slippery as fog. No barbarians would be able to track them as they scattered into the hills. Yari and the big-headed wild dog led the scouts and five pack goats the opposite direction through loose gravel and scrub brush. Keeping up with Yari's jaunty pace left Awa breathless.

The dog stalked a foolish party of Kahartans who, given poison weapons and midnight stealth, intended to ambush the Green Elders. Uneven terrain around the gorge was treacherous. Flash floods carved new canyons every afternoon. The barbarians slowed to a crawl. Yari sang, in many voices, a local song that laid out the best routes along solid rock ledges and sounded like birds, bugs, and wind in the bushes. Awa sang along, guiding the Sprites creeping behind her.

"I'm a map," she whispered in Bal's ear. "I know all the songs from around here." Kahartan thief-lords regularly plundered villages near their city, but had never learned the People's songs. "I've drawn this entire region many times."

Yari shushed her using the hand-talk of *Ishba* people. They perched above the enemy, invisible, though a keen-eared barbarian might catch whispered words under Yari's song-cloak. Shadow warriors nocked arrows, aimed spears, and drew their swords.

Bal, Awa, and the other Sprites hid in fragrant laurel bushes. Awa calmed her mind to map every detail of this encounter and tell a full story. At least she could do a griot's task.

Quiet voices argued in the staccato merchant tongue. Awa made out thirty Kahartans: burly, honey-colored men, with clipped beards and ropes of brown hair pulled tight in crown knots. Exhausted and dispirited, they shivered and cursed the sliver of moon that offered meagre light. They'd left horses behind somewhere with fallen comrades.

Defying the tales of Green Elder defenses, the troop had started as fifty warriors, surely enough to subdue griots, clowns, and *vesons*. They intended to steal grain, goats, and tree oil. Rock fields and steep climbs had broken Kahartan legs and too many necks. The captain called a halt in a dry streambed until sunrise. Dawn was less than an hour away.

By morning Isra and the enclave would be camped throughout the wooded hills on the other side of the gorge, a difficult site to ambush heading east from the Golden Gulf. A few archers in the trees could pick off anybody trying to scale the gorge. The Kahartans were already defeated. Awa rejoiced.

An owl screeched a love call and shadow warriors hooted in response. Jed or Jod—a scruffy, snub-nosed Sprite Awa barely knew—laughed at barbarians who didn't realize they were about to die. The berry potion made Jod's hazel eyes shine in the dark like a lion's.

"Our victory is almost too easy," he mumbled under Yari's owl masquerade. Awa and Bal smirked with him. How such stupid people had gained control of the Golden Gulf and all the land south and west of Holy City was a mystery.

Yari gripped Awa and shook the smirk from her face. Bal stopped grinning also. Even Jod pulled a mask over disdain.

Yari spoke with *vie*'s hands. Long fingers danced in Awa's face. "If I cannot talk sense the Kahartans will hear, you must guide our scouts back through the gorge to Isra. Nobody else knows the song-maps."

"Oh." Awa was Yari's backup. She wanted to ask why talk sense to stupid barbarians who chopped down forests, dug up mountains, and fished rivers till they were dead waters, but she just nodded.

"We're not better than anyone." Yari read her sullen silence. *Vie* gestured to all the Sprites. "We fall like leaves and fail like crops. Our blood dries up and our shadows scatter. We eat lies and think them sweet." *Vie* must fear death could be near and took care with last words. "Don't lose yourselves in petty pride. I almost died doing that."

"Don't die tonight." Awa gestured and hugged Yari, relishing the scent of desert roses. "Not losing myself in others' thoughts is one of my strengths."

"Is it?" Yari pulled away. "You shall find out."

Vie shook bristling braids loose, played calm-heart rhythms on the talking drum, and sauntered into the enemy's camp as bold as a sunrise. "I am Yari, the griot of griots. You've been chasing me and my people, so I thought I'd let you catch someone."

The Kahartans looked as stunned as Awa. They exchanged glances, drew weapons, but hesitated. "The griot of griots," the captain yelled, "is only a legend."

Whirling in Aido cloth, Yari disappeared and reappeared several times, singing harmony with *vie*self: *Warrior, warrior sweet enemy mine, will this be our last time?* A blotchy-skinned barbarian lunged and sliced shadows. He kicked dirt up in his oiled beard. Braids came loose from his topknot and blood dribbled from cuts and gouges.

The captain blocked a second lunge. "Save your strength."

"Yes. Why waste ourselves in battle?" Yari said. The wild dog chased the goats to the captain. "I bring you bunchgrass from the north that survives drought and sprouts after deluge. This we Green Elders can spare. But raiding us, you will die."

The captain sucked deep breaths. One hand hovered by his sword, the other over a pounding heart. The dog growled and Yari sang in many voices. The rhythm of the drum, the jingle-jangle of seedpods, and *vie's* hair dancing in the wind was hypnotic. Shadow warriors clanged swords and spears, and sent fire arrows over the Kahartans' heads.

Bolts landed in a circle, illuminating gray hairs, young boys, and battle-weary regulars who should have stayed home. Shadow warriors brandished blades in crevices and bushes, reflecting the firelight and creating a fearsome display from mist and shade. Even Awa thought there could be several hundred scouts.

The barbarians backed away. The blotchy one almost slid over a ledge. Yari gripped his cloak. Looking into his fearful, despairing eyes, Awa let go of the contempt in her heart.

"You have great numbers in your walled cities," Yari said. "But in the mountains, deserts, and swamps, you cannot defeat us. Take this offering, go home, live well."

The Kahartans shifted and wheezed, not the battle they'd expected. Who ever knew what Yari might do? *Vie* leapt in the captain's face, talk-singing, "You think: *Our homes are rubble. Fields are sludge. Babies eat soot or go hungry. Tomorrow the sun won't rise.*" Yari saluted the purple sky. "Yet the light comes."

The captain sputtered like a lover right before release. Yari motioned at Bal to play drum and rattles. *Vie* gripped several fire arrows and juggled, a trick learned from Kyrie, the witch woman of Mount Eidhou. Yari threw fire arrows at the feet of warriors who looked ready to crack. They blubbered tales of pirates and acid bombs laying waste to their city. Each warrior added a new horror, a secret defeat. An exiled master used his conjure to make Pezarrat unstoppable. Yari listened, hungry for details. The pirates stole books and holy relics. Only half of Kaharta survived and none of the grain stores. What the pirates didn't take, they burned.

"Rebuild what was lost. Give your children no reason to cry over your bodies. Make a new home around the gorge away from pirates. With a watch in the canyons, raiding parties are easily defeated. Try trade instead of plunder, a new life."

"Change is hard." The captain drew his sword, gripped Yari's arm, and pulled *vie* close enough to taste breath. "Why should I trust you?"

"I leave you your lives," Yari said, tender almost. *Vie* brushed dust from the man's beard. "I begin with trust."

"You're a crazy fool, but"—the captain raised his sword high—"I salute you. To life."

After a moment, the barbarians cheered with him.

"You're brave men. I'll tell your stories." Yari leaned into the captain. "Perhaps we'll meet again." *Vie* disappeared into shade and mist, a voice on the wind. "Be good to the goats and they'll honor you."

The fire arrows made a circle of soot in the dry streambed. The sun lit up the sky. The captain bent down to the bags of bunchgrass seeds on the goats. His troupe gathered around him. A few men glared up at the ledges. "Desperation forced us out on a clown's crusade." The captain held up a fist of grain. "Northlanders make a nut loaf and sour bread with this. They call it lovegrass."

3

A Different Story

The shadow warriors disappeared in the bright sunlight. Awa was glad to be hiding in dense laurel bushes. "Yari's charm worked." She gestured to Bal and released clenched muscles.

"Barbarians aren't stupid. They fear our blades, our numbers," Jod said, loud and bold. "I would too." He looked disappointed as the Kahartans withdrew in high spirits. "They deserve the death they offered others, not clown songs and gifts of grain."

"Do they?" Bal climbed down to a ledge, fading in and out of view.

"Showing off shadow warrior skill doesn't impress me." Jod sounded impressed.

Awa was thrilled to see what Yari's diplomat craft could accomplish. Griots were often peacemakers. She would need to learn this. "If we killed the barbarians, who would we be?"

"Alive, who will they be?" Bal always asked good questions, but why take Jod's side? "Barbarians will think the gorge is theirs to plunder, pollute, and kill."

"You talk as if the gorge is alive." Jod sneered.

"Why not?" Bal snapped at him. "When the world is dead, so are we."

Jod choked off laughter. "You actually believe Elder jumba jabba?"

"Some of it." Bal and Jod faced off as if to fight.

Awa stood between them. "You can't believe everything Elders say, but—"

"Grow up!" Jod shoved Bal to the edge of a ravine. "Barbarians would kill us without thinking."

"Maybe." Bal blocked Jod's second attack and put a knife to his neck. "Maybe not."

Jod grimaced at her skill. "Why are we on the run if they've been defeated?"

"No one has won." Yari stepped from the shadows and separated them. "Tell a different story."

"You know every story," Jod shouted. "Why know so much and live worse than savages?"

"That's your question, not mine," Yari replied. Awa wanted Yari to argue with Jod. Instead, *vie* led scouts the tricky way around the gorge to throw off trackers.

Awa argued with Jod in her head. *Anawanama* and *Zamanzi* lived better than poor Empire citizens, even as renegades on the run. They ate well and lived free. Father's farm had been headed for ruin. He had to sell Awa, so his sons could have prospects. Green Elders lived simply, not poorly. What good was a dank stone house, slaves who hated you, and dumb animals who couldn't take care of themselves?

As if to prove Awa true, Yari took them by abandoned farms and villages where groundnuts rotted, wells ran dry, and grain stalks crumbled. Poison dust raised stinging welts on exposed skin. They paused in a barn to get out of a foul wind. Two balls of rags trembled by a dead farmer in an empty corral: young boys too weak to moan or stand.

"They probably sold their girls," Yari muttered.

Scouts drizzled water on parched lips, and, when the wind died, threw the boys on their backs and trotted on, singing comfort.

Six days the scouts wandered, gathering survivors and refugees. A silent trek. Exhausted and numb, they finally reunited with the enclave in a green-land valley. The leaves on a hundred hundred trees whispered welcome. A stream rushing over rocks gurgled joy. Standing in a waterfall, Awa and the others washed the poison dust away and smeared on Smokeland honey to ease the sting. The story Awa told at the feast fires was of shadow-warrior bravery, Yari's wisdom, and barbarian resilience.

"Well done." Isra had slicked spiky white hair down with red clay for celebration. "What of the fields and forests?" *Vie* wasn't fooled by Awa's omissions.

"The land near Kaharta is dead," Bal said, "and poison desert spreads."

"We shall see if we're better at surviving than Kahartans are." Isra gripped Yari's waist. "You should be glad I didn't go and sent Garden Sprites with you instead."

"Why?" Yari drank a long draught of honey wine.

"I would have stopped you giving away our goats." Isra took the wine and drank a swallow. "I'd have let shadow warriors shoot our enemies and not waste fire arrows on air. I wouldn't have risked our children for news of an old lover."

Awa would soon be fifteen, a child no more. None of the Sprites were.

"It was your idea to take them with the scouts," Yari countered.

"Today the crossroads gods smile on you." Isra emptied the wine jug. "But I know these people. I'm one of them." Isra grew up around the Golden Gulf and raided villages and enclaves until Yari persuaded *vie* to run away to the Elders. "Change is unlikely."

"You changed." Yari grinned. "Or are you still a tight-hearted demon?"

"You can't charm everyone."

"I don't need to. I have you to protect me." Yari squeezed plump Isra and sang an untranslatable *Lahesh* love song.

Isra groaned. "When I'm not there and you dance into danger and charm fails?"

"Do you plan to leave me?"

"The gods of the crossroads laugh at our plans."

"We can laugh too!"

Isra drew Yari into their tent to finish arguing on the bed.

Everyone retired except Awa and Bal, who sat watching the sliver of moon rise. It had grown a little fatter. The wild dog rested his big gray head in Awa's lap, chewing the last of the feast scraps. Bal balanced on one arm, legs swaying. Awa knocked her over. They wrestled with the dog, then settled into a furry heap, toes in the warm ashes.

"What would you have done?" Bal asked. "Killed our enemies or not?"

"I don't know," Awa said. "I'm not brave like Yari, to risk dancing for the enemy . . ."

Bal stroked a tight curl at Awa's neck. "You'd have come up with a good story, I'm sure."

"You always say that."

"Well"—Bal touched the snake mark on Awa's forehead, eyes full of sloppy sentiment—"we *always* need a good map for our days."

Awa took secret pleasure in Bal's faith.

4

A Snake in the House

Amplify now
Every yesterday lives in today
We have many futures and each changes the past
Many possibilities get lost to the void
Imagine freedom and it is yours

F atazz!" Chanting verses from *Amplify Now* wasn't mastering *Xhalan Xhala*. Djola sipped a potent cathedral seed and cloud-silk potion. Tremors coursed through his body. "*Xhalan Xhala* changes all *that might be* into a single *what is*. Other possibilities turn into void-smoke."

He spoke *Anawanama* to the boy who offered him water, a mute child of nine or ten. Quint's age. "You must feed the void-smoke to the crossroads gods, or else it slips through a wise-woman corridor and storms the everyday. Feeding crossroads gods is tricky. The spell is almost impossible." The boy shrugged and thrust a cup at him. Djola pushed it away. "I need fire, not water. Calling fire is the pivotal spell. *Xhalan Xhala* is a spell of spells."

The boy stomped off, pouting like Bal. With Djola an *honored guest* on a pirate ship, Nuar would try to turn Quint into an *Anawanama* chief. Yari would be a better teacher. Sweet Yari, bold Yari went off to train Sprites, to *teach the future.* They had no future unless—"I was meant to find *Amplify Now!*" He shouted as if Yari stood near. *Vie* wouldn't teach him *Xhalan Xhala,* proclaiming, *Better for ancient wisdom to be lost than perverted.*

Why write down conjure unless you wanted somebody to learn it? Once he mastered *Xhalan Xhala,* he'd sweep away corruption and bring fools back to the peace fire. Yari and Kyrie would return to the stone-wood table. Djola would offer his family and everyone a good life.

"What words are you chewing?" a pinched voice demanded in Empire vernacular.

Djola almost threw a knife in Captain Pezarrat's placid brown eye. The rascal appeared in the sick bay door without a sound. *Lahesh* flame-cloth pants were cinched at his ankles and glowed in the dark. "Why are you here?" Djola also spoke Empire vernacular and slid the blade back up his sleeve. "I thought you—"

"You don't know me." Pezarrat's pockmarked face revealed little. He scratched tight beads of hair on a sun-bronzed scalp and watched Vandana and the old healer stumble around swaying bodies. "My ship, belowdecks or above."

Djola nodded. "It's your fleet, Captain."

Pezarrat held out a bark-paper scroll. A resin seal smelled of cathedral forests. "It appeared on my bunk. How does Kyrie do it? I don't even know where we'll go." Djola tucked the scroll in his Aido bag. "Why don't letters appear on your bunk? Is Kyrie trying to scare us?" Pezarrat eyed the barrel of books. "You tell that old mountain bitch how good we treat you. Books, meat, tree oil, a boy or girl or *veson* if you want."

Djola grunted at pirate largesse. Pezarrat got quieter. "You feed the whores your meat rations. Don't you worry they'll die a poison death meant for you?"

Djola fed them antidotes too. "Why waste worry? They're your spies."

"I have to pay Vandana and Orca two shares each."

"A share and a half," Djola muttered.

"Who wants to sleep near a man who conjures ghosts and bad weather?"

"Haints come of their own accord, and *we are the weather*."

Pezarrat chortled. He enjoyed their sparring. "You should join us." Half the pirate crew began as captives. "You've already paid a tenth of what you owe me."

"Surely I've reached a third by now."

"During every raid, you hide in your bunk, talking jibber jabber. Afterward you disappear in a scroll or codex." He looked down. *"Amplify Now."* He puzzled over the first image: a conjurer with one eye closed leapt in the air and touched a wheel that exploded into flames. "What does this jumba jabba mean?"

Djola chose his words carefully. *"Amplify Now* is a poor translation for the *Lahesh: Xhalan Xhala."* It felt strange speaking the name of the spell of spells out loud. Vandana took a sharp breath and dropped a needle in the middle of stitching a wound. Djola stared. Nothing had rattled her like that in a year of plunder and mayhem.

"You know dead languages? Speak, woman," Pezarrat commanded.

Vandana shrugged. She never looked in Djola's books. Orca couldn't read. Poor spies.

"Xhalan Xhala is conjure to call tomorrow from what we do yesterday and today," Djola said.

"No man makes time." Pezarrat frowned at another symbol.

"Flames from a crossroads heart. I've seen this squiggly Vévé before."

"Reckoning fire." Djola leaned close to Pezarrat. "Calling reckoning fire, a man risks burning up too."

"I don't believe in spirit debt." Pezarrat slammed the book shut. "You claim reckoning fire for yourself?"

"It's just a carnival dance." Djola forced a smile. "A trick on the eye."

"Azizi and Council welcome tricks. A book of *Lahesh* wim-wom might cut our tax."

Djola snorted. "Untested, *savage* conjure is worthless. Just tall tales."

"So you always say, yet you collect so much." Pezarrat and Vandana glared at scrolls and codices.

"Azizi would know how his enemies think," Djola said. "Tall tales reveal a lot."

"So this jumba jabba is a cheap thing, but not worthless." Pezarrat tapped *Amplify Now* against Djola's chest. "Tell Azizi, all men are the same. Don't waste himself looking for savage secrets, just grab their randy balls and squeeze."

"What about the women, the Iyalawos who rule the mountains?"

"Squeeze them too." Pezarrat sniggered as if they shared memories of violating women. "I don't fear Iyalawo Kyrie or any of them." He tossed the book out a porthole into the placid sea.

Djola flinched and bent down to a spy who'd gone to Bog City to poison wells and spread lies. A broken bone poked from a sleeve.

"This one also builds ships." Pezarrat stood over them. "He needs both arms."

Vandana gripped his torso and sat on his legs as Djola tugged clenched muscles to make room for the bone. He snapped the broken pieces together and held tight while Vandana wrapped the arm to a splint. The fellow passed out. Djola headed for a captive bleeding from her side.

Pezarrat blocked him. "Sometimes I think you should be a librarian or a priest and sometimes I think you have an assassin's cold heart." He wasn't stupid, just greedy and heartless. "I think you'll try to skewer me when you find whatever you seek."

Djola spoke *Anawanama*. "I'm worth more to you alive than dead. When a change comes, it'll be too late for you."

"I have no use for savage poetry." Pezarrat feigned understanding. "I intend to get rich, kill you before you kill me, and retire from the sea to the floating cities."

"*Why keep a snake in the house if she wants to eat you?*" Djola translated a line from *The Songs for Living and Dying*.

"All men are snakes."

5

Mortal Danger

No matter that Pezarrat tossed the book.

Djola had spent sleepless nights memorizing every word, every image. *What you know is always yours. Lahesh* conjurers could call fire yet stay cold. They felt the motion in stillness, sensed the truth in a lie, and changed the unknown into the known. They brought the power of Smokeland to the everyday. If Djola could touch a thing, feel its fate, imagine flowing in its time, he could pull reckoning fire and bring tomorrow to today.

"We've run out of splints and bandages," Djola cursed.

"I sent Orca to fetch the healing silk I stashed in my hammock." Vandana was sewing up pirates and captives in flickering lamplight.

"Thank you." Djola hated sewing flesh.

"How bad?" A delirious captive clutched Vandana. "Will Pezarrat take me?"

"Maybe." Djola drizzled a honey-venom potion into his and everyone's mouth, for strength and sleep. Tomorrow, captives had to be well enough to replace dead pirates or be sold to a farm, brothel, mine, or army. Weak ones would be tossed overboard along with pirates too broken to fight again. Captives were eager to join Pezarrat. They imagined a few years of easy raids and then retiring to a rich life in the floating cities. "Better to get off these ships as soon as you can." Djola wanted to turn his patients into rebels. No potion for that.

"I'm patience." Vandana finished sewing and touched Djola's arm. "Like you."

Djola snorted.

"I will take everything to home." Vandana held up a small bag. "A library from the floating cities."

"*Lahesh* conjure? Is that how you hide your long blades?"

Vandana smiled, dagger teeth glinting. "Old warrior women trek across *Mama Zamba* to Arkhys City. We can be spared and know how to come back to home."

When nobody else could be snatched from death, Djola shooed Vandana and the old healer away. He scrubbed the bloody floor with sand and salt water. He stripped naked and tossed his clothes out a porthole. Orca appeared toting hot water and a clean apron, shirt, and pants. He scrubbed Djola's skin, ate his smoked fish, and drank his wine, then feigned desire, a lusty display. He was relieved that Djola declined as usual. Orca put out every lamp except one so Djola might read.

"Do you still tell the captain you're pleased with me?" Orca's cheeks dimpled.

Djola smiled. "Yes. I want only you." This might mean danger for Orca.

"He thinks you'll tell me secrets, eventually." Orca curled up close, a hot ember.

"I serve the Empire and I miss my wife, our three children. No secrets," Djola said.

Orca kissed him. "Don't leave me when you escape. I know I could please you."

"You please me already." Djola took comfort in a warm body against his chest, but arousal was impossible. No failing on Orca's part. The boy sang soft nonsense and fell asleep. He could sleep through rats fighting over maggoty food, pirates screeching, and lightning storms breaking the night. Lulled by his breathing, Djola pulled out the letter. He almost forgot to neutralize Kyrie's conjure. "Patience." He sprinkled gold dust and broke open the resin seal.

I say again, I regret hiding among the masks when masters ambushed
    you at Council
Saving my own head

"What can I do with your regret?" Djola muttered. It helped to talk back.

Shadow warriors carry shade with them and hide in the bright glare of
    truth
What you predicted comes true—strength to you, Djola, in exile
Blossoms burnt by desert wind bear no fruits, no seeds
Clear-cut mountain slopes crumble away in torrential rains
Rotten groundnuts and berries mean songbirds starve
Fields overrun with beetles and mold produce little grain

Djola's hands shook. He'd witnessed this from Holy City south to the Golden Gulf.

Council condemns thief-lords, Zamanzi raiders, and city chiefs who steal
    children

Mobs slice up vesons, *blaming them for poor harvests, storms,*
    stillbirths, anything
Yari and other griots avoid the capital and hide out near
    Mama Zamba

"Fools! And is the harvest better?" No way for Djola to get a letter to the mountain backbone for Yari. "Zst!" If he could just talk
to Yari. They could do *Xhalan Xhala* together and make a stronger
spell.

Rebels masquerade as good citizens and nobody knows their plans

Djola scoffed. "They have no plans. A mob, nothing more."

Arkhys City wise men want a week each month in the library to them-
    selves
Azizi refuses to ban women even for a day, a wedding present to Queen
    Urzula
Tree oil from Holy City is abundant and nobody freezes on cold nights
The Master of Arms has a fresh supply of warhorses and more recruits
    every day
Empire coffers are full and warrior morale is high
Azizi won't give Hezram your chair

"He's unworthy to crawl on the floor of Council."

Money, Water, and high priest Ernold scheme for Hezram in secret
Trapped in Arkhys City, your half-brother, wife, and children are in
    mortal danger

Djola read these last lines a hundred hundred times. His heart
thundered; his breath was shallow. Orca woke with a start. He

stared at the scroll in Djola's trembling hands. "Poison?" His heart pounded too.

"Yes. In the letter."

Orca scooted away from the bark-paper. "Do you know an antidote?"

"No."

6

Living

Orca lit another lamp and dashed off.

Djola talked on to the walls, in *Anawanama*. "Grain is a coward who hangs in shadows waiting to see where the winds blow. Kyrie is holed up in her precious mountain. She won't leave her glaciers to help just a few people. My people." His chest tightened. Each breath was a stab. "Her own sister!" Djola pounded the deck. "Why write *mortal danger* to me when I can do nothing but go mad?"

Perhaps Grain hoped to shield himself from Djola's wrath, in which case Grain was a fool *and* a coward.

Vandana appeared with Orca in a *Lahesh* flame-cloth tunic that glowed in the dark. Djola barely noticed. "Assassins have failed the masters at Azizi's table, so this letter is the knife in my heart."

The last line read: *I didn't find out until too late. Kyrie sends hope.*

"How long has Grain kept this from me?" Djola shouted.

"Who knows?" Vandana knocked the knife that Djola dug into his chest from his hand. It clattered to the floor, loud enough to wake the dead, or maybe that was Djola howling. He shoved past Vandana and stepped on a woman too wounded to roll out of his way.

He cursed Kyrie, Grain, and pirates, priests, thief-lords, farmers, and good citizens then banged into a post and fell. Orca sat on his belly. Vandana cradled his head while he cried.

Djola woke the next morning shivering, yet his insides burned. His head was in Vandana's lap. She stroked his cheek. Orca curled against his back, snoring. Djola lurched to standing.

"You all right?" Vandana's stupid question and teary look sent him racing out of sick bay. Up on deck, a freak snowstorm slapped him in the face. He paced along the railing, snarling at a white sky falling into a gray sea.

"Nobody in the Gulf has seen storms like this in a hundred years." Pezarrat stepped from a snow squall wrapped in a white bear. The head had fangs. "Wild weather every week. Fools read ominous messages from the gods in any ill wind. I see opportunity." Djola wanted to murder Pezarrat then join his family in the death lands. Luckily for the captain, Orca had confiscated the blades hidden in Djola's sleeves, belt, and boots.

Pezarrat dodged balls of sleet. "I tell everyone ice storms are Djola's fault. Outlaw conjure. They feel better to hear that. Well, not better about you, but jumba jabba is better than crossroads gods laughing at you."

Djola backed away from Pezarrat and returned to sick bay. He downed a seed and silk potion. The day passed in a haze. Orca and Vandana were busy sewing wounds that had reopened. Vandana did Djola's work and hers. Orca brought him roasted bird stew. Somebody ate it, not Djola.

"Don't lose hope." Vandana sat down next to Djola. "Your family could still live."

"Hope might keep me alive," he replied. "It will also be torture."

"No. Despair is torture. Do something good. That is living."

"Everyone asks too much of me."

"Do they?" She patted him and went back to sewing folks she insisted were well enough to fetch a good price.

He swung from hope to despair twenty times a day. He almost killed Pezarrat a dozen times and also thought to poison himself.

Orca watched him closely. "In suicide, no honor for your family. Suicide serves your enemies. Vandana is right. What if your family lives? What if you're like the ancient heroes who faced down demons and saved their beloveds and everybody else too?"

Djola sneered at Orca but practiced pulling fire for *Xhalan Xhala*. He'd mastered many tricky spells: talking to rivers and trees, feeling the rhythms of dirt and water, reading the stars. Pulling fire required different talents: a storm of stillness in his mind, a sense of the heat animating everything. Many a conjurer had burned up trying to pull fire with a false gesture, an off rhythm, the wrong breath. For Djola the hardest part was the chill on his hand and at his heart.

Freak storms chased the fleet out of the Gulf. Pezarrat sold off contraband and headed to the floating cities sooner than planned. Djola rejoiced. Spies said Urzula might visit the floating cities. An audience with the queen meant word of Samina and the children. Hope was still a habit.

7

Love

Awa slipped Bal the smoked fish and crumble bread she'd stolen from the feast basket. They were both starving, sleepy, and Awa wanted to curse. The enclave had marched day and night, in and out of *Mama Zamba* caves and ravines, with only brief pauses for water and nuts. Now they paddled in several barges across a cold underground lake. Under what ground and toward which stars Awa couldn't say. She was a mapmaker and hated feeling lost.

Awa was sixteen, a grown woman, and Isra still kept her in the dark. They headed to a secret crossroads, a ceremonial ground where Sprites might become Elders, if they couldn't wait until the next big gathering of the clans. Jod and two other Sprites had decided to be shadow warriors. Waiting two years for the sweet desert gathering would be punishment, so Yari and Isra agreed to let them cross over early. However, Jod and his comrades, Cal and Neth, had to prove themselves exceptional. Yari dug up shadow warrior scrolls and prepared tricky questions. Isra dragged the enclave to a little-known region to test their scouting skills. If Jod, Cal, and Neth failed to stay hidden for a day, they would have to wait for the clan gathering to become Elders.

The underground lake was blue-green, liquid turquoise. Probably beautiful if your belly was full and your feet weren't throbbing. The air was thick and warm—the breath of an exhausted beast. Sunlight streamed from tree-lined holes in the ledges above them, illuminating gray, bronze, and red walls. The cave's wrinkled surface called to mind elephants wallowing in mud and spraying each other with clay.

A dream image—Awa was paddling in her sleep. Jerking awake, she ducked before hitting vines and strings of rock hanging over the lake. More wasted beauty. Why come this way? The barges passed into deep darkness, and Awa shivered. Isra had to know a better route. For some reason, *vie* wanted everyone to feel lost. Elders kept so many secrets and hidden scrolls. Awa was too tired to be annoyed. She'd be mad later when she had more energy.

This dark passage was the longest so far with no one lighting a torch. Something red smoldered up ahead—a bed of coals? Would Awa have to walk barefoot over fiery rocks to get out of the cave? Father's thoughts, not hers, still plaguing her. Awa gripped Bal, who was calm, in shadow-warrior form, singing a rhythm for the paddlers. Awa leaned into that. Even so, when the barge bumped solid ground, she shrieked.

Yari lit a torch and cursed. A path led up a steep incline. The red that Awa had spied was a flame bush glowing in a sunlit opening. Isra waved everyone off their barge. Bal leapt ashore and helped unload supplies. Two other barges bumped land and more torches were lit. Light didn't help Awa figure out where they were. Cold, hungry people tromped on elephant-skin stone and grumbled. Awa gathered Yari's books and stumbled off the barge. They had more books than usual, brought from a secret cache for the ceremony.

"Quit pouting," Isra whispered to Yari. "Sprites have gone out scouting since the gorge—why not let a few cross over early?"

"You insisted they were ready to scout, not me," Yari replied.

"But you led them into danger," Isra said. "You risked their lives."

"You brought Jod into the enclave and he has your heart." Yari frowned. "Jod draws spirit from elsewhere. He could end up a lapsed Elder."

Like Father? Jod was a pain, but not—"Someone who knows us and hates us and works against who we are?" Awa blurted this.

Isra put a hand to *vie*'s lips, crossing fingers then flicking them in the air to say, "Just between us." Clumsy hand-talk. *Vie* gestured at Yari, "Better to find out Jod's true spirit before he sits in a circle of Elders."

Awa headed back for a second load of books. She would never tell Jod that Yari had doubts. In fact, she never spoke to Jod. He brushed her off like dust from his boot on the way to fussing with Bal. Jod and Bal fought over anything. Jod was bigger and stronger than Bal, and thought he was smarter than everybody, but Bal was more skilled. She used his strength and arrogance against him.

Jod's Aido cloth always unraveled—he was a worse weaver than Awa and never carried shade with him. Bal could disappear in bright sun, like Isra, Yari, and the best Elder shadow warriors. Jod called Bal's skill cheating. Isra broke up fights between them before Jod suffered inglorious defeat or called in Cal and Neth for an ambush. Jod claimed ambush by his friends wasn't cheating.

Yari thought most fights were a waste of spirit. *Vie* scolded Bal for letting Jod bait her and Jod for letting Bal make him itch and steam and lash out. Bal never picked a fight with Jod. She just never backed down when he picked one with her. Bal being Bal made Jod want to fight. Why was Bal to blame?

Awa rehearsed a speech to argue with Yari: *We have to stand up for who we are.* She was always arguing in her mind with Yari, never face-to-face like Isra. She caught her foot on a root and tripped, Yari's books slipping from her arms.

"Let me help you," Jod said, rushing toward her.

"I can manage." Awa scowled at him, suspicious.

"I'll carry the big ones." Jod picked up heavy tomes and smiled at Awa blankly, as if they'd never met before. Hazel eyes looked right through her to Bal who tugged baby goats onto solid ground. "No problem." Jod toted the heaviest books in one arm. He was dressed as an Elder in a blue cloud-silk robe. A new bow was slung across his back; a diamond-tipped blade hung from his belt.

Jod ran past Bal and headed to the surface. He was good with a knife and better than anyone at giving Isra the answers *vie* wanted to hear. Isra praised Jod even when he was mediocre, and Jod would be an Elder before Bal, who was excellent at everything!

Bal had chosen to wait and gain more skill before crossing over. *Never let the enemy know your heart.* Bal hid jealousy and anger well, but Awa caught flaring nostrils and measured breath in Jod's wake. Jod being Jod and everyone thinking him handsome and brave made Bal want to fight. Was that wrong?

The enclave set up camp on a grassy saddle between mountain peaks. Tents were pitched, goats corralled, and water hauled in. A few weavers set up looms. Awa stared at unfamiliar cliffs. She had no idea where they were. If she chose griot for crossover, she'd have to do better at finding her way. Maps were tricky stories. Tell the wrong tale and you were lost. Tonight she'd read the stars and orient herself better.

"I wish it wasn't so steep," Isra said. "Up is great, but down. Zst!"

"Your knees are fine," Yari said. "This is the safest place for the crossover ceremony, since we're in such a hurry. Your idea."

"No, their idea." Isra pointed at Jod and crew. "Let's hope they don't fail."

Yari sighed. "This test is good for everyone."

Awa expected Jod to fail. Bal was fast and quiet and could track anyone, even Isra. After sunset when festival tables had been set up, Awa saw Jod steal an Aido cloth cape and sneak off. Stealth wasn't his downbeat. Awa lay on a table, staring at an inky sky, waiting for stars to rise. She always kept track of the nights. Bal appeared over her. Green-flecked eyes flashed light from the cook fires. Her chin was sharp, her grin crooked. A vision.

"Jod says I love him and he loves me, and that's why we fight," Bal said.

Awa lost a few breaths. She was jealous at the thought. "Do you?"

"Love him? No." Bal snorted. "Yari's right. Jod's cocky behavior is no reason to lose myself."

"Everyone makes excuses for Jod." Awa balled her fists. "Nothing is ever his fault."

"That's true too." Bal poked Awa's tight curls. A sluggish bee burrowed deeper into her hair. Everyone worried the bees might sting her, but they never did.

"Jod calls tormenting you love," Awa said.

"Don't be jealous." Bal leaned in so close, her features blurred. Awa closed her eyes and savored Bal's sweetgrass and iron scent. Bal pressed her lips against Awa's cheeks, eyes, and lips. "Jod doesn't know what love is." Bal's tongue tickled Awa's nose.

Awa giggled. She didn't know what love was either. If someone asked, she'd have no way to explain it. A griot should have a story for anything. Yari believed loving even an enemy could change them, but Awa knew that love didn't always work. She opened her eyes at a cool breeze across her body. Bal had vanished, leaving tingles and aches behind. The moon was a slash of light on the horizon. The stars twinkled overhead, laughing at her. Why would Bal love someone like Awa?

8

Lapsed Elders

Sometime during the night, without anyone noticing, Bal and a few other Sprites slipped with Elder scouts into the woods to track Jod, Cal, and Neth. In the morning, Awa helped cooks prepare a celebrate-new-life feast. When Elder eyes were elsewhere, she stole mango slices, goat cheese, and honey cakes smeared with nut butter. Why should everyone fast? Practicing hunger discipline never made sense to Awa.

Jod and his allies were resourceful. Nobody had found them by midday. Isra was relieved that they might prove worthy. Yari was suspicious and *vie* usually believed the best of anyone. As the afternoon wore on, Yari climbed the highest mountain and put a tube of wood and glass to one eye to see far. Panting and sweating, Awa and Isra joined *vie* at the peak.

"What do you see?" Awa asked.

"Lion and elephant war masks." Yari sighed. "*Zamanzi* fighting and dying over dust."

"The peace is broken." Isra rubbed swollen knees. "And the exiled peace-master searches for you."

"On a *pirate* ship." Yari clenched *vie*'s jaw. "He wants something. Some secret."

"He begs you to relent," Isra said. "I read his last letter."

Yari jabbed Isra. "You spoke against him before."

"I was wrong." Isra winked. "I thought you loved him once." Yari looked unsure of love. Awa had never seen this face. Isra gripped Yari's arm. "He's not Hezram. And Hezram's not your fault." Awa was baffled. How could Hezram be Yari's fault? Isra murmured in Yari's ear. "If the peace-master and Azizi met Awa, Bal, Jod, or any of them, *Xhalan Xhala*—they'd see tomorrow and resist men like Hezram."

"Perhaps." Yari put the tube to the other eye. "We should take care. The victors of this battle will steal whatever they can."

Awa frowned. "What do we have that *Zamanzi* want?"

Yari snorted. "They'll come for us no matter how little we have. So Isra tells us."

"You think so too." Isra took the tube and observed the *Zamanzi* battle then turned to the mountain opposite them. "I see veins in the leaves and the sleepy eyes of cats."

"I like watching birds," Yari said. "The colorful wing feathers."

"What a marvelous bit of *Lahesh* wim-wom you've made." Isra scanned to the foot of the mountain. Blood drained from *vie*'s face. Yari grabbed the tube. Isra sounded an alarm on a seashell and ran down the slope without a word, knee pain forgotten.

"What?" Awa tried not to panic.

"Keep watch." Yari thrust the wim-wom tube at her and ran off too.

Awa's skin prickled and her breath was short. This was a griot's task. Calling on Sprite discipline, she looked through the tube.

Bal cradled one of Jod's friends, Neth. Blood soaked his tunic. Neth pulled Bal's ear to his lips and spoke. Bal nodded, her face calm except for nostrils flaring once. Awa wished the tube brought sound as close as sight. Neth's hand fell away, his head lolled. Bal closed his eyes and indulged a silent scream before rushing into the trees. *Never let the enemy know your heart.*

A crow flew to Neth's body, quick to smell death. As it pecked, Awa looked to the arid plain on the west side of the mountain. *Zamanzi* warriors clashed, elephants against lions. In the east, three riders left the trees and headed along the Empire Road toward Holy City. Awa stuffed the tube in her pocket and hurried to camp in gathering twilight. Every story she made for what she'd seen was terrible. She wished they'd never come to Isra's secret place.

It was a moonless night, too many stars to count. The enclave came together around feast fires. Tents rippled in a chill wind. Fresh bread and stewed fruits steamed on the tables, food for a celebration, not a funeral. Griots set aside masks, seedpods, and bells. Deep djembe drums filled the mountain caves with somber rhythms. People huddled together and singers wailed. Jod and Cal never returned. They rode barbarian horses to Holy City with a stranger. Scouts carried Neth in and laid him in a rocky streambed grave.

"We are tested," Isra said. "Let's remember who Neth was and who we are."

Nobody had much to say about Neth. Jod and Cal were his best friends, his only friends. Neth was the Holy City acolyte who Yari talked into joining the enclave, the same time Awa joined. She remembered stealing food with Neth when they were younger. Why mention that or Neth ambushing Bal for Jod? Awa made up a story about collecting mushrooms and finding the best ones that was almost true—Neth loved mushrooms. People nodded as if they remembered her lie and covered Neth with rocks. Bal held the final rock. She told what Neth said with his last breaths:

A woman came to rescue the three of them, someone who knew Yari, Isra, and this secret place—an Iyalawo or lapsed

Elder who brought horses and flung curses at depraved Elders. One horse was lame, so only two Sprites could escape. She demanded a fight to see who was strong enough to go with her and who would die here. Jod stabbed Neth when he protested. Jod and Cal rode off with the lapsed Elder, leaving Neth to bleed out.

Bal ran out of words and dropped the last rock.

"Jod and Cal stole maps, conjure herbs, and Aido cloth to pay their way," Yari said.

"And books." Awa felt terrible for giving Jod special ones. Jod stuck a knife in a friend's chest, for a horse and a chance to ride off with a scoundrel. "I don't understand. We're not prisoners. They could have left any time."

"No family, no prospects, how to live?" Bal asked good questions. "Jod thinks he knows too much to live worse than savages. Neth told him tales of Holy City."

"I brought Jod to the enclave." Isra stomped around Neth's grave—a display of anger more than grief. *Vie* spoke the staccato barbarian tongue. "Be warned. Good citizens say that Sprites get perverted by Green Elders. Many of us live as neither man nor woman. What could be worse?" Isra paused. "Well, lapsed Elders are worse. They're traitors, perverts, and murderers."

The enclave hooted disdain. Awa flinched, thinking of Father. Was he really as bad as Jod? The enclave howled.

Yari hushed them and tapped the talking drum. "Perhaps Neth tried to stab Jod, and Jod killed him in self-defense." *Vie* turned to Bal. "You arrived just as horses were charging away, right?"

"Yes." Bal blinked, confused. "That's possible. I didn't see the fight."

Awa jumped up. "You and Isra saw the fight through the tube. Tell us what actually happened."

"Whoever knows that?" Yari shook ropes of hair. This mystery was a shadow warrior test. The entire trip was a test for all the Sprites.

"People who speak against Green Elders could be right." Isra kissed Yari's palm. "Everything we believe could be false. I know from my own life. Jod wore a mask, stole our secrets, our hearts."

Awa wanted to scream. "So how can we trust anybody or anything?" Other Sprites grumbled with her. "Is there a verse in *The Green Elder Songs for Living and Dying* to help us pierce illusions?"

"Look around. Anyone could betray us." Yari gave her an indulgent smile. Awa bristled. Yari drummed and danced from Neth's grave to the other griots. They donned bird masks, picked up drums, and followed *vie*. "Every day I think of leaving."

Younger Sprites and even Elders gasped.

Yari danced around them. "Every day you prove I'm wrong to doubt. Neth doesn't breathe anymore, but your breath makes my heart beat." Awa, Bal, and a few older Sprites rolled their eyes. Yari laughed in their sullen faces. "Every day we test our truth and if we discover a better truth, we change. Trust that." Elders snapped their fingers, agreeing. Bal joined them, but Awa resisted.

"Jod and Cal have decided who they mean to be and crossed over." Isra poured a cup of honey wine, spilled a few drops on the grass, then downed the rest. "Let's eat. The bread is warm." *Vie* sat at a feast table. "We celebrate new life."

Yari played infectious upbeats, lifting spirits. Stomachs growled and mouths watered. The fast had turned everyday food into a special delight. Awa wasn't hungry. Her stomach was sour, her mouth full of unspoken words. She and Bal sat close, rubbing shoulders and thighs. Bal tickled her clenched muscles and kissed her flaring nose. The griots blasted fire from their mouths and burned off the last of the foul mood.

Being rid of Jod and his friends was a good thing. Awa and Bal could celebrate that.

9

Everywhere Except Sick Bay

The sun was a white disk behind mist. Djola stood on deck by the steer-man. He practiced pulling fire, the key to *Xhalan Xhala*. His skin crawled and his mouth was ash. He couldn't call a flicker or spark, too jittery inside. No letter from Grain in a while. Maybe Pezarrat's course was too erratic to track, so Kyrie sent letters through a wise-woman corridor to empty sea.

The pirate fleet had almost gone to the floating cities several times, but Pezarrat always changed his mind. Steering clear of Urzula's patrol, the fleet dawdled in a northland cove—near what was left of *Anawanama* and *Zamanzi* territory. Spies alerted Pezarrat when *Zamanzi* warriors left their camps to attack caravans, and he sent in raiders. Pirates suffered few casualties and took whomever they wanted. *Zamanzi* often surrendered without a fight. The fleet was waiting for raiding-parties to return with captives.

On a ledge above the water, rogue twisters appeared from nowhere, from static and shimmer, and pulverized bushes and trees. In a blink, the storms vanished. A wise-woman corridor was more stable than that. These bits of folded space collapsed quickly. Leafless bushes flailed in the wind. Listless waves lapped against the flagship hull. Silvery haints hissed in the sails, sounding like Tessa, Bal, and Quint. A rope smacked Djola's back and dispelled visions. His family hadn't walked from the death lands to haunt him. They were prisoners, under house arrest or in a cell in Arkhys City. Azizi would never let harm come to them. Djola had to believe this.

"They'll come soon." Pezarrat stood at the prow haggling with good Empire citizens over the price of captives and a surcharge to ferry them to Thunder River, the Empire's northern border.

"Costly," a reddish brown citizen declared, a rich man who drank tree oil and transgressor blood for long life. This brew gave even the blackest skin a reddish glow. Djola was disgusted. He was on deck to vouch for the captives' health and guarantee a high price. Azizi and Urzula outlawed raiding for captives, so Pezarrat claimed desperate northlanders sold their daughters and even sons. Pezarrat's price was reasonable and his lie easy to swallow, even easier to repeat. Good citizens traveled to the cove to buy cheap labor for farms, mines, brothels, or who knows what. Djola was a part of this filthy exchange.

"Demon fog is slowing my people down," Pezarrat said. He and Empire men laughed at northlanders who thought fog was demon's breath.

Another minute without murder seemed impossible.

Djola tried to pull fire again. Kyrie made it look simple—a flick of a finger and she had a spark. Heat was everywhere. He needed to entice enough of it to—"Fatazz!" A ball of sparks burnt his hand. He threw the heat into the waves. Painful sparks dribbled from his fingers. He had yet to master chill hands or chill heart. Good citizens stepped away from his antics, alarmed.

Pezarrat smirked at their fear. "Conjurers get restless in fog."

Djola played the clown, splashing in a water barrel, muttering *Anawanama*. Kyrie knew how to call sparks and stay cool. She knew how to sit on her cold mountain and let his family burn in Arkhys City. He should make his mind a fortress and lock up his heart. Kyrie did that years ago when assassins poisoned the man she loved.

Lahesh conjurers spent a lifetime mastering *Xhalan Xhala*. Djola didn't have a lifetime. A mind-heart fortress might be the trick he needed for chill hands and heart, for feeling the motion in stillness, sensing truth in a lie, and changing the unknown into the known. Steam poured from the barrel and he groaned. Fingers were still on fire. Flesh didn't burn away, yet that's how it felt.

The good citizens ignored Djola. Pirates led a chain of *Zamanzi* onto the boat: girls who had yet to bleed and boys with high voices and smooth faces. Wounds festered around their chains. Mucous dribbled from noses. Djola avoided bloodshot eyes. As the flagship headed out, the children spewed on one another. If sold to the water, they'd have to get over that or puke themselves to death. Djola's *Anawanama* mother had slaved in a mine. She escaped to Arkhys City slums and died coughing up mine dust. What would she think of her son now?

"They're fine," Djola declared. "The waves make them spew." He tumbled down the ladder to sick bay, pushed past Orca, and downed a seed and silk potion. He stared out the porthole at the fog, waiting for the bad mood to blur. He sank into an almost pleasant haze till pirates dragged captives down the ladder and barged in the door.

"Stop." Djola used a command voice and stumbled to the door. "Turn around."

Pirates exchanged desperate glances. The old healer hid among empty barrels.

"Pezarrat's orders," the lead pirate said, a furry man with a muffled voice. "We got so many. Need to put them somewhere."

Djola took a wide stance, blocking the entrance. "Not in here. Somewhere else." Orca pushed past him and up the ladder.

Behind Djola, Vandana offered a dagger smile and a stronger accent than usual. "Every day, Djola is calling ornery wind and wailing haints to sails. He throws fire and freak ice storms at enemies. He loves the world, but he say, turn around, go back up."

A woman pirate, scarred and missing a few teeth, stepped up. "I know you, poison master." Djola didn't know her. He tried not to know Pezarrat's pirates. "Griots sing of your mother, a captive— yet one son a chief, the other a master. You've risen; so can they." Djola spat on tales Azizi paid griots to spread. "We've both risen," the pirate woman insisted. "Pezarrat stole me from Kaharta."

"In the mines and brothels, they work you to death and pay nothing," Djola replied. The captives were crying. A few slid to the ground. "Take them back up on deck."

Orca came down the ladder with Pezarrat.

"I said everywhere *except* sick bay." The captain waved the pirates away. "Get out of here before he turns you into weasels or slugs." The pirates herded the captives to the ladder. "You arrogant rascal." Pezarrat poked Djola's chest. "I should sell you."

"Who can afford your price?" Djola scowled. "Not even masters at Azizi's table."

"Those stingy cowards think I'd kill you for a few coins." Pezarrat chuckled, then whispered in Djola's ear. "In honor of your mother, I don't capture *Anawanama*."

Djola had *Zamanzi* blood too. That was a story he refused to share. He pointed at the children struggling up the ladder. "They'll spread disease. We'll all get sick, and there's nothing I can do. I needed supplies *before* the last big raid." He whispered, "You're captain, but I wouldn't take on more captives. Too dangerous."

"You wouldn't sell captives at all." Pezarrat gripped Djola's shoulders. "What's in the floating cities that won't wait till I make a little coin first?"

Djola was desperate to talk to Babalawo wise men who might understand the shimmer storms that appeared out of nowhere and left poison desert behind. Librarians could help him pull fire and do *Xhalan Xhala*. Urzula could offer more news of his family than Grain's letters. "I need supplies." Djola lied with truth. "For healing, for repairs, and acid-conjure too. We couldn't sink a bucket with what I have left."

"You exaggerate." Pezarrat studied Djola. "Azizi spares my ships not just for the bribes I pay, but for you. After all this time. Why?" He searched Djola's eyes. "You're a snake, aren't you?" He marched off.

The woman pirate and furry man fell ill that night. Vandana saved the man, but the woman died a week later. Vandana muttered we-warned-you curses. Unnerved, Pezarrat unloaded the captives before Thunder River and decided against more northland raids. The fleet struck out for the floating cities in bad weather. Relief, hope, and fear wrung Djola out. He hung from the mast and wept into the wind.

For two weeks, Djola paced the upper deck, trying to pull fire and cursing high waves. He never managed cold around his heart. Sometimes he sat and stared at mist, muttering in *Anawanama*, trying to talk to the ancestors. Pirates avoided him. Orca and Vandana made him eat and drink and poured potions in him for sleep. This evening, cold rain pounded Djola's head. Soft-spoken Orca shook him and mumbled.

"Speak up," Djola growled. "I can't hear you."

Orca shouted, "Vandana says we should make you gloves to hold fire without burning your hands." Djola squinted at flame-red palms and sparks flitting across the waves. Had he just called fire?

Orca pulled him toward sick bay. "Vandana says you know a good mesh-spell."

"I'm the Master of Poisons. I know an antidote for everything except poison sand."

"I don't want you to get sick or catch fire." Orca was as sentimental as Vandana. Or maybe Pezarrat paid him an extra share to be kind. Orca hauled Djola to their bunk. "You're shivering and too hot at the same time."

"What do you want?" Djola surprised them both with this question.

Orca rubbed Djola dry and stuffed him in a warm cloak. "What can I want?"

"I want to hold my wife, smell her skin, hear her scold me and the children. I want to see her ride the waves, half naked on a flimsy board. I'd love her wise counsel."

"Spies told Vandana, Queen Urzula travels to the floating cities to see her children."

Djola tensed. "Urzula knows everything that happens in Arkhys City. I'll beg her for news of my family. Tell Pezarrat this secret so he can stop threatening you." Djola sighed. "You must want something."

"I'll think about that and then tell you." Orca put salve on Djola's angry palms. "Urzula is wise. She'll help you, but—"

"What? Tell me," Djola commanded.

Orca's dimpled cheeks flushed. "You drink too much seed and silk. The last trip to the floating cities your mind was mush."

"Which trip? When?" Djola wanted to deny a trip to the floating cities, but he vaguely remembered a nightmare where he sputtered jibber jabber at Babalawos, who sneered at him. Had this happened? "No, I—"

Orca hugged Djola. "This time you must be clear."

In exile a true friend was a treasure, even if he was a spy.

10

Goat Treats

Two Goats bound from a crumbling ledge to the boulder wedged between a stone-wood tree and a piece of sky that fell long ago. The Goats love this climb. They lick salty minerals on the ancient tree then trot along a narrow ridge into the wind. Few creatures can reach them on the knife edge. The air is thin and cold; every step is slippery. They jump over a gap. Behind them the wild dog growls at someone. Big cats don't roam this high, only the foolish dog.

The Goats and dog have been friends since they were kids. The dog barks and lunges at a flurry of feathers. A golden eagle takes to the air, chirping and circling the peak. The Goats consider the bird, unafraid. Eagles only attack kids or a distracted goat, hoping to knock one down the mountain and feast. Not today. The dog keeps the eagles in the air. Yari, Awa, and Bal tramp up behind the dog, panting and chattering. They scramble and sweat.

"This is my favorite peak," Yari says.

"Worth falling for?" Awa asks.

"You climb like a goat," Bal replies. "Don't complain."

"Food is better at the top." Yari talk-sings. "Berries taste like sunshine. Cloud mist is the best wine."

Awa and Bal snort and blow their lips like horses. "Goat treats."

The Goats jump to the peak and scurry down the other side. Dewclaws are sharp and prevent slipping. They reach a rocky terrace, bathed in sun. Scruffy shrubs hold down soil. The Goats eat leaves, twigs, berries, and crunchy lichen. The dog wiggles through a rock tunnel to the terrace, avoiding the knife edge and peak, treacherous for his soft paws. He licks the Goats' faces, finds a warm rock, and drops down, panting. The Goats eat quickly, before Yari, Awa, and Bal arrive. They'll eat too and then want to turn back. Beyond the terrace, this sunny side of the mountain is sheer rock, nothing for even Goats to hold onto. Golden eagles fly about, diving down to catch something for the bleating mouths in their nests.

Bal and Awa come through the tunnel before Yari, who gets stuck. They each take an arm and pull. Yari tumbles out, laughing and jingle-jangling. The dog licks their faces and wags a bushy tail. The Goats jump over them, and they all chase each other around the terrace like kids. One Goat butts Awa into Bal. They stumble to the edge. Yari grips them and they sit with legs dangling over the mist. Everyone is laughing. The Goats put their heads on Yari's shoulder. *Vie* scratches a neck and around the eyes. Yari gives everyone food from a bag. The dog gobbles his smelly treat quickly, some greasy, dead thing. The Goats get sweetgrass and herbs treats. Awa, Bal, and Yari eat orange fruit and berries. Red fire streaks across pale blue sky over distant mountains. Yari points, delighted. They sit quietly as bits of sky fall and land in *Mama Zamba*'s bosom.

"Do you think falling stars could land near us?" Bal says.

"They have already, don't you think?" Awa looks around.

Yari nods. "The stars are our ancestors."

Awa and Bal groan and giggle. "And there's a bit of sky in everything."

"Even in you two." Yari plays a drum.

Awa shakes her head. "You say mountains, river, even dirt are ancestors."

"Don't you feel that on the mountaintop?" Bal stuffs a berry in Awa's mouth.

"Always take a moment to feel who you are: star, river, dirt," Yari says. Drumbeats match the words. Awa and Bal titter a second then close their eyes. Even the Goats and wild dog get caught in *vie*'s beats. When the song ends, Yari slings the drum over a shoulder and, full of sky and dirt, stands tall.

The sun sinks and eagles vanish to their nests. The Goats are full, but not enough time to chew cud. Cold seeps from the mountain and the Goats are glad for wooly coats. Awa and Bal shiver and bleat. The wind blows mist over their flimsy hides. Yari scratches everybody one last time. *Vie* slithers through the tunnel, singing. The dog nips at Awa and Bal, chasing them into the passageway. The mountain is full of music.

The Goats jump back over the peak and scurry along the knife edge. Still enough sun to see the way, but Yari lights a spark torch. Lightning on a stick. The Goats are used to this. Other creatures who prowl at dusk will avoid them. Awa and Bal cling to each other, sharing warmth. Their eyes glow in the dark. Yari's glow too, like big-cat eyes. The Goats skip down the cliffs, singing to friends below. Bellies full, spirits high, their troupe prances into the enclave.

11

The Floating Cities

The sea was rough all the way to the floating cities. At first, drinking less seed and silk, Djola's mind got *more* muddled. He lost days, weeks to shakes and delirium. One morning, clouds dissolved to clear blue sky, clear blue sea. Orca and Vandana joined him in the rigging. He'd spent the night, staring at black sky, black water, slowing his heart when it raced. He let it pound now.

A mountain range broke the seam between sea and sky, like the ridged back of a half-submerged beast. The floating cities were strewn around this island-beast in concentric circles. A beautiful sight. Coral reefs provided protection from storms, high waves, and enemy vessels. Pezarrat's ships crawled in shallow waters. The floating-city peace patrol—fast, well-armed boats—escorted them to harbor, setting an excruciating pace. Cottony clouds fluttered around library towers at the mountain's peak. Djola's heart fluttered as he took a deep breath. If Samina and the children were dead, high priest Ernold, Money, and Water would have made a spectacle of their bodies. Djola broke into a smile and climbed down the ropes.

Orca and Vandana followed. "What? What?"

"My family still lives!" He waved at stern faces on the peace patrol, thrilled.

"Another letter came?" Orca took Djola's arm.

"No," Djola said. "But no terror-tales means they're alive." He would have realized this sooner if he hadn't been addled.

This morning, no drug stupor, no useless regret or rage. His family was under house arrest. Soon, he'd free them. Floating-city wise men would help solve the void-storm and poison desert mystery. Last time, he'd been addled, unprepared. Today he had detailed reports and maps. Librarians would know what book or griot to consult for *Xhalan Xhala* and they'd arrange an audience with Urzula.

Azizi's pirate queen was more powerful than anybody at the stone-wood table. She'd help rescue Samina and the children from *mortal danger.* "The last months were difficult. Today the weather changes." He hugged Vandana and Orca and kissed their cheeks. Orca took out a blade and shaved Djola's scruffy beard. He rubbed the stubble with pumice stones and massaged perfumed oil into smooth skin.

"*Lahesh* call this mountain *Yidohwedo*"—Vandana pointed at the peak—"after the rainbow serpent who made the world from dung and water and taught the *Lahesh* to weave light and fold space."

"I see the rainbow." Orca clutched Djola. "Two rainbows."

Docking twenty-one boats took forever. Orca danced around the deck in fancy pants and tunic made from *Lahesh* flame cloth, a gift from Vandana. His mouth hung open as they approached a bamboo walkway circling the cities. Triangular towers anchored the walkway and marked the hours on sundials inlaid with crystals.

"Rainbow gods in the crystals are tricksters," Orca said. "We should step lightly." Sweetgrass bridges connected inner and outer walkways and swayed in the wind. "I've never seen anything like this."

"What about the last time we came?" Djola asked.

"I was too ill. I've only heard stories." Orca looked ashamed. Djola didn't press him.

"I first came here years ago with Yari. I was a spy pretending to be a Sprite." Djola repeated what Yari told him then: The floating cities were once four coastal capitals in the northlands surrounded by mountains of ice. An Iyalawo warned of hot winds melting the ice and deluges claiming green lands. City chiefs hired *Lahesh* tinkerers to rebuild fortresses, grain stores, mills, and libraries on barges near a cluster of islands—a volcano with peaks above sea level.

When Djola first saw metal-mesh domes, reed windcatchers, and giant sundials he thought he was smoke-walking. Yari said *Lahesh* tinkerers used Smokeland inspiration to design the cities. They mounted sturdy structures on even sturdier barges and anchored the new cities to *Yidohwedo*'s ridges in the shallow sea. They crafted bridges and underwater tunnels to connect the four capitals—east, west, north, and south. Pirates plagued early residents but eventually the floating wonders became the pirates' safe haven. *Lahesh* diplomacy—marry the enemy.

"What are the cities called?" Orca asked.

"Speaking city names out loud is bad luck," Vandana said. "Names were written somewhere and forgotten. Conjurers take care reading unknown spells out loud."

Orca pulled his hair back and wove a single braid. "Why not just *Yidohwedo*?"

"Then, serpent's name is bad luck too. Who wants that?" Vandana was staying on the ship. The bridges, domes, and waterworks reminded her of someone, some place that made her sad.

Orca stumbled behind Djola along the bamboo walkway, gawking at *Lahesh* wim-wom. He bumped into a fierce man with a parrot on his shoulder who chuckled at a wide-eyed pilgrim. Floating-city folks were short, stocky, and dark-eyed. Hair was dusted bronze, gold, or silver and cropped—tight beads like Pezarrat or peach fuzz like Urzula. Women had dots painted or tattooed around their eyes and reminded Djola of Samina.

His wife's hair was a silver bush with mischievous streaks of red. Her tattoos were intricate, silver snowflakes that caught the light, and she was tall, of mixed heritage, like the woman approaching them. Blue-violet eyes disarmed Djola, daring him to be a better man. Dazed, he clutched a stranger and panted in her face. The silver-haired pirate woman broke free and frowned brown eyes at him. Djola mumbled apologies and the woman walked on.

"So many languages I've never heard. Wind-wheels and waterworks," Orca exclaimed at a windcatcher pumping water. "Who builds such things?"

Djola leaned against a metal-mesh building that looked like an overturned basket—a merchant dome. "*Lahesh* tinkerers still make sure the cities don't fall apart or get swallowed by the sea. My wife has *Lahesh* blood and wisdom. She kept our reeds singing." A blast of white light blotted out Orca's face. Djola shut his eyes. Heat burned inside his chest. He wanted to call fire and incinerate the island paradise. What had they done against void-storms to help his family and all the families on the mainland? Who in the floating cities spent a breath on Samina, one of their own daughters, who gave her body to him so that pirates might live in peace?

"Are you all right?" Orca held him up.

"Yes," Djola lied. "Let's buy conjure supplies first."

The merchants stocked everything: *Anawanama* herbs and dyes, cathedral seeds and pulverized cloud-silk for *Lahesh* potions, barbarian dried mushrooms and holy water, *Lahesh* metal-working tools, Smokeland honey, wax, and herbs, rare earth compounds for acid-conjure, cloud-silk bandages, shadow-warrior spider cloth, even fermented midnight berries that cured night-blindness. Prices were fair, low even. Djola wasted no time haggling. He hired ferryboats to transport purchases to Pezarrat's ship.

Business complete, Djola led Orca across a sweetgrass bridge to a garden barge where Babalawos—the twelve wisest men in the world—and two Iyalawos gathered among voluptuous flowers to talk, argue, or let their minds wander. They wore violet robes and a weave of tight braids on their scalps. They sat on stools with Smokeland scenes carved on the sides and brandished iron staffs to evoke mountain and water deities. Speaking *Lahesh,* they welcomed Djola and Orca with fruit, nut-cakes, and honey wine.

The two oldest Babalawos remembered Yari's and Djola's visits many years ago. Djola let them think he'd become a Green Elder and Orca was a Garden Sprite. The old men were eager to hear his reports of the world—the women too. A drummer thanked the crossroads gods and called for silence. Djola told stories of void-storms popping up from nowhere, from static and shimmer, to devastate the land. He noted range, frequency, and severity then offered his folded-space theory. They snapped fingers, approving of his insight.

As he tallied animal and crop loss from poison desert, Orca held up scrolls of storms devastating green lands, painted in a vivid *Anawanama* style. Silver static and black ash made everyone itch.

"How do you know all of this?" asked a Babalawo who was Djola's age.

"I've seen it," Djola replied. "Kyrie gets reports to me."

Muttering, the Babalawos set down their cakes and honey wine. Djola cursed under his breath for letting her name slip. The drummer drowned out the grumbling. The eldest declared that idiots were ruining the mainland. Everyone agreed. They sang laments for *Weeds and Wild Things* on distant soil, but felt safe enough on their remote island paradise to joke: wild women and foolish men caused void-storms, and what cure for stupid people except to wipe them out? A catastrophe to cancel out disaster. Orca laughed at lewd gestures— people humping rocks.

The middle-aged Babalawo pounced on Djola. "Kyrie set a barbarian on fire with sparks from her fingers, then like a *Zamanzi* warrior ate his heart while he watched."

"Nonsense, Haji." An Iyalawo spoke for the first time. "Burning alive, the man's not watching anything."

"Perhaps Kyrie's folded space corridors are spreading void-storms," Haji shouted.

"You're jealous." The Iyalawo shouted over him. "You can't make a corridor."

"Women's conjure wreaks havoc with the everyday!"

"And men don't add to the void?" The Iyalawo rolled her eyes. "You lot tried to assassinate Kyrie behind Urzula's back. You're mad at Kyrie for surviving."

Haji poked Djola. "Follow your own theory to the source. I'll wager it's Kyrie."

Djola attended to his breath, willing himself to be patient. "What other ideas to stop void-storms and poison desert?"

"The mainland has doomed itself," the oldest Babalawo said. "You seek the impossible." Everyone nodded, poured more wine, and chewed at dried figs.

"You feel safe with your pirate ships and *Lahesh* conjure!" Djola closed his eyes on an image of the wise men and women going up in flames. Luckily he couldn't pull enough fire, or he would have blasted them. "We're wasting our time." He grabbed Orca.

"What language were you speaking?" Orca asked as they stormed off the garden barge.

"*Lahesh.*"

"The trickster's language." Orca smiled. "That's why the wise men laugh at us."

12

Libraries

It was a day's walk over many bridges to reach the biggest island *Yidohwedo* made as it reached to the stars. Djola's last shreds of hope were dissolving into panic, so they hired a canoe to travel the waterways to the peak-island in an afternoon. Colorful fish darted in and out of undulating seaweed and coral reefs. Curious sea turtles nudged their boat, and Orca and Djola took care with their paddles. The docks were jammed. Farmers came to tend vegetable and grain fields. Pilgrims in feathered hats headed for the observatory at the mountaintop: a stone fortress with windows to catch stars at dawn, twilight, and during the night.

Climbing the steps to the summit, Orca was breathless, yet he squealed at golden domes and sun-and-moon dials. "The griot of griots claims there are more than a thousand windows filled with *Lahesh* wim-wom: celestial wheels, tubes with eyepieces, star-catchers. Under the windows are scrolls and paints to create a record or render a vision."

"A thousand?" Djola darted by sweaty farmers. "Yari may have exaggerated."

"I hope it's true what *vie* said about sky windows." Orca

grinned. "Pezarrat didn't want you coming alone. He said you could escape through a window to another world." Orca was a terrible spy. "If you don't return . . . He says he'll kill Vandana."

"A lie. He'd sell her. What does Yari say about the observatory?"

"Special windows open to the heart of sparkling demons. At night, when darkness invites demons to hold still a moment in the sky, you might step through the window and greet them without fear of being eaten. No escape though. If you don't step back, you'd be lost in the dark between stars."

Lahesh whimsy cheered Djola. "When I visit Urzula go look through the windows."

Orca agreed, even though Pezarrat wanted him to tail Djola everywhere.

The library was the dim heart of the observatory. The whoosh of reed-wheels made Djola's skin tingle. *Lahesh* wim-wom kept the sea's dampness out. Adjusting to near darkness and cool, dry air took a moment. Shelves cut into *Yidohwedo*'s walls were augmented by wooden scroll-cases from the old cities. Books filled the mountain. On trips with Yari, Djola had roamed the library for days. He'd learned antidotes for everything and the language of dirt, water, and wind. Afterward they made love under the stars, whispering about wonders they might discover the next day.

"Who has time to read everything?" Orca peered into a cave of bark-paper codices.

Librarians wrapped in coarse cotton had black eyes and knotty egg-white beards like Azizi's Master of Books and Bones. Everyone reminded Djola of his other life. The librarians were cordial and sent word to Urzula—her residence was nearby—that Djola wished an audience.

Like the Babalawos, they lamented a ruined mainland and then drifted back into the shadowy aisles of books. The head librarian blamed greedy citizens and barbarians for void-winds and poison desert. "Only a fool brings a whole forest to its knees or plants corn without beans and gourds. Who shaves sweetgrass to a nub or gouges *Mama Zamba*'s bosom for poison metals to make baubles?"

Nobody listened when Djola talked like that. "Something clouds our minds and kills our spirits." Djola tapped his chest. "Poison desert inside too."

The head librarian pounded his desk. "Know yourself. Know the world."

"Yes." Djola was relieved to find someone who understood. "I've been practicing a fire-spell. I need your help, your wisdom, to hold chill in my heart and hands."

The librarian chuckled. "Don't believe the griot tales. Fire-spells are dangerous, but novices never burn to death. They can't pull enough fire."

"I need to pull a lot of fire."

The head librarian leaned close and grinned. "I have only modest skill, but I'll share a secret. Kyrie was my student. Of course, I can't take credit for her ferocity."

Djola smiled. "No, of course not."

"Clumsy at first but so much power, Kyrie was someone who might have burnt herself up. But I knew just what to say." He savored some insight he'd doled out. "What are you trying to do?"

Djola licked dry lips. He hadn't told anyone his plan. "If I dance *Xhalan Xhala* at the border between green lands and poison desert, reckoning fire might show what led to poison sandstorms. Then I could find an antidote."

"No," the librarian roared, "too dangerous." He switched to Empire vernacular and waved a spark torch, warding off evil. "Only a madman—"

"*Xhalan Xhala* is a prophet's tool." Djola effected a calm manner. "I could look at now and see the future and call it forth."

"You'd conjure one future. There are so many. You'd add to the void."

"No, a meal for the crossroads gods."

The librarian sneered. "Who can count on those tricksters?"

"I found a book in Kaharta," Djola said, *"Amplify Now—"*

"Amplify Now—in Kaharta?"

"Kaharta had the best library on the mainland," Orca blurted.

The librarian aimed the torch at Djola. "Rogue pirates burned Kaharta, looted the library."

Orca pushed the torch aside. "Pezarrat dumped the book out a porthole."

"Good. *Amplify Now* is a few notes written by desperate Elders." The librarian came to the front of his desk. He was taller than Djola. "What are you, *Sorit* and *Zamanzi*?"

"Anawanama and *Zamanzi*." Djola corrected him. "My brother is a chief—"

"You should know better." The librarian narrowed his eyes. "You can't rip up the fabric of ancient wisdom for a few convenient threads."

"I seek the whole cloth." Djola clenched a fist behind his back.

The librarian sighed. *"Xhalan Xhala* is sacred ritual, a lifetime practice. Who learns that from a book?"

"That's why I've come to you." Djola tugged the frothy cloth at the librarian's neck, cutting off his air. "We're running out of time. We have to do something. Soon."

"Stop." Orca pulled Djola's hands away and stood between them. "Forgive us. Too many months at sea. Loved ones lost. Djola would learn anything to master the spell."

The librarian rubbed his throat. "Nobody masters *Xhalan Xhala*—you surrender to it."

"I would surrender," Djola declared. "I would do anything."

"I'll bet you would." The librarian almost snarled, "I can't teach what is impossible."

"You mean you *won't* try." Djola's chest was fire again. "Ignorance can't save us."

The librarian pounded the torch on the rock floor. "You need a *Lahesh* conjurer, like Yari, the griot of griots and master of nothing. Who ever knows all the stories?"

Djola grabbed the librarian's rough cotton sleeve. "Yari hides from the world."

"Empire citizens call *vesons* abominations and string them up. Can you blame Yari?"

"Yes." Instead of pummeling the librarian, Djola raced down the corridor and out into the sunset. Great gulps of salt air quenched the fire in his chest and belly.

Orca scurried behind him. "We should come back tomorrow and reason with—"

"Librarians and Babalawos won't help. They think ignorant, foolish people have called disaster upon themselves—a cure for that is impossible."

Orca clutched Djola's shoulders, his face open, his smile deep. "You're a master. You can learn anything, even the impossible, without anybody's help."

Djola shrugged Orca off. "I'm not who you think I am."

"Of course you are."

Instead of arguing, Djola sent Orca to the sky windows and tromped across the ridge to meet Queen Urzula.

13

Fortress

Yidohwedo's head was the pirate queen's fortress, a serpent's face with fire eyes overlooking the sea. The queen's mountain chambers never went dark. Spark torches lit the night without burning tree oil and lasted who knows how long. This *Lahesh* wim-wom was one of the floating cities' most closely guarded secrets. Impossible conjure until *Lahesh* tinkerers mastered it. The floating cities could have shared their fire-spell with the world and saved a hundred hundred cathedral trees or more, but they were greedy, stingy pirates. Djola squashed a gout of anger.

Urzula sat alone in a courtyard on a stone bench, watching the sunset. A mosaic of crystals at her feet soaked up the last rays of light. "Too beautiful a night to waste in a cave." She smiled. If she had bad news, she wouldn't flash her teeth at Djola. Silvery white stars made half circles above her dark eyes. A white line crossed her purple-tinted lips going from chin to nose. She wore a tight tunic and loose-fitting pants gathered at the ankle—pirate gear. On *Yidohwedo* Urzula was almost unremarkable. "Why have you come to see me?"

Djola would not start with family. "The wisest conjurers in the world, Babalawos, Iyalawos, and librarians, offered nothing new to solve the poison dust mystery."

Urzula flicked her fingers. "Of course you know more than librarians and Iyalawos sitting in the middle of the Salty Sea."

"If they applied their wisdom to the problem," he retorted, "we could solve this."

She kissed her teeth. "You think you're the only one who looks for a solution?"

"They were patronizing, indifferent. They've already given up."

"Why should anyone trust a savage rascal?" Urzula glowered at him.

"We northlanders have much to offer the world."

"Do you?"

"I didn't come to burden you about void-storms. What news of my family?"

Urzula looked away from him to the water. "I hear of your adventures at sea."

"I hear Ernold and Money plotted against Nuar, Samina, and my children."

"Lilot says Council talk is of pirate raids—barbarian cities burn in acid-conjure and scoundrels steal *Zamanzi* children for brothels, mines, and warships." She blamed Djola for Pezarrat's breaches.

"*Zamanzi* villagers are easy prey with their warriors out raiding Empire caravans."

Urzula gritted her teeth. "So much unrest since you left my husband's side."

Djola stepped between her and the sea. "He banished me."

"The masters wanted to kill you. Should Zizi have let them?"

"You're my wife's friend. Have you seen her?"

"I travel the coast from the Golden Gulf to the *Zamanzi* north, trying to hold the peace against renegades." She lit a spark torch. "Lilot, my cook, watches over Azizi while I'm gone. Rebels run riot and Council plays into their hands." Lilot was a more powerful witch than Urzula. Griots claimed they were lovers, and Lilot was willing to do anything for her queen. "I'm here visiting my children. They study at the library."

"Did you see my children before you left?" Djola lay on the ground at her feet, his face in gravel. "Please. Tell me."

"They came to Arkhys City a while ago. Why do such a thing?" Urzula sighed. "I hear rumors of a trial. They live still."

"Alive, but in the hands of my enemies." He struggled up.

"Azizi's masters say you're a rogue pirate who deserves worse than death."

"My family suffers"—his voice cracked—"in my place."

"Azizi and the Master of Arms won't let anyone hurt your family."

"This is my hope." He leaned close. "Perhaps you could—"

"Samina waits for you"—Urzula's jaw was set, her dark eyes slits—"to finish your mission and rescue her and your children." She took his hand. "What will you do?"

Djola snatched his hand away. "I'll make my mind a fortress."

"Iyalawo crossroads conjure. You could lose yourself." Urzula sighed. "Do what you must do, but hurry."

Djola raced off, arguing with Samina all the way down the mountain. Why take the children to their enemies, even searching for him? Nothing reasonable occurred to him. Spark torches glittered on the walkways—weapons and nightlights. He wanted to steal one, storm Council, and blast his enemies like a fire-breathing beast of legend. But men had burnt themselves up trying to wield stolen torches. "Zst!" Djola longed for a flask of seed and silk.

On a barge to the flagship, Orca chattered about stepping through a sky window, being touched by a demon, and seeing wonders no one had painted before: a bridge of stars and a great blue eye watching over the light. "In sky windows, you see what you imagine."

Pezarrat ignored jumba jabba and agreed with Djola that lingering in the floating cities and paying docking fees was pointless. As the fleet headed out, Djola chased the old healer from sick bay and sat on a prayer rug with Vandana and Orca.

"I've lost too much time"—his voice cracked—"distracted or blank or addled from seed and silk." He held up a hand as they protested. "Don't argue. To master new conjure, I'll make my mind a fortress and seal my heart. Otherwise I'll go mad."

Vandana pursed her lips. "You'll be patient. You won't believe lies or crave seed and silk, but it'll be hard to feel anybody else's pain, joy, or fear." She stroked his face. "Take care to banish despair. Locked inside, despair will fester and ruin you."

"Samina and the children wait for me to rescue them," Djola sputtered. "I'll hold fast to memories of them." He thought of Quint's musical laugh as he soared through the air; Bal's pout when she couldn't ride to Council and protect him from fools and haints; Tessa's grin as she offered a scroll-spell for avoiding danger. Instead of a good-bye embrace, Samina balled her fists and pounded his chest. "My wife's hands always smelled of almonds and raintree blossoms. Conjuring these memories will clear despair."

Vandana grunted, unconvinced, but she sharpened the chisel and every needle. She mixed blue-green *Anawanama* dyes and silvery dust from *Lahesh* gate-mesh. Orca shaved Djola's head and chest. Peering into the cracked mirror, Djola drew Vévés on his skull and over his heart: a lattice of interlocking roads and spirals, shooting stars and spiderwebs that invoked crossroads deities.

"I'll also hold fast to my mission." His voice ached. "I don't know if what I seek is possible, if what I do matters . . ."

"Everything matters," Orca said. "That's what you say to me."

"I can't recall why my wife and I fought that last time." Djola poured a libation to the crossroads gods. "With this conjure and everything I do from now on, I ask for her forgiveness."

Vandana cut the Vévés into his flesh and filled the wounds with the fortress-spell.

14

Surviving at the Crossroads

When the stars aligned, Green Elder clans from across the Empire and beyond the maps gathered at a secret oasis in the sweet desert for a crossover festival. They honored the dead, welcomed the future, and celebrated freedom. Feast tables were laid out around a gurgling spring in a windswept canyon. Honey wine cooled in cisterns belowground. Potions were brewed, and Elders crafted masks, instruments, and dances. They found lost words and invented new ones.

Intoxicating aromas wafted from a dozen cook tents nestled in scraggly midnight-fruit trees whose roots dipped in the spring below. Berries had fermented in the rocky soil. Drunk crows hopped underfoot, screeching and teasing everyone as if they were honored guests. Wine from fermented midnight berries was a festival treat and made everyone's eyes glow in the dark.

Awa and Bal had turned seventeen and decided to cross over. Bal was as tall as Yari and as ferocious as Isra. She crafted powerful bows and sleek arrows that flew true. She forged *Lahesh* blades to cut through stone and metal. Everyone loved to watch her dance along tightropes and ridges, balancing anger and love. A true shadow warrior, Bal preferred cunning to spilling blood.

Awa drew sky maps, silver stars on dark brown cloth, for all the seasons. She wrote stories in *Anawanama, Lahesh, Zamanzi,* and barbarian tongues, for every region west of *Mama Zamba.* She knew a few dirt poems and the language of bees and trees. A true griot, she could puzzle her way through any knot, squabble, or mystery and then offer a good story. All of Yari's and Isra's Sprites did amazing conjure, and the Elders boasted about a bold new world coming.

The night before the crossover ceremony, Isra made a new loom and Yari crafted a double-headed talking drum. *Vie* decorated it with Aido cloth, cathedral seeds, and glass beads. Gifts for Bal— Awa was pleased and jealous. Isra and Yari wouldn't let Awa open a bag of story-spells and *Lahesh* wim-wom. Awa hoped this was her gift. As everyone gathered for the Sprites' last story celebration, Yari slipped with Isra behind a midnight tree and used hand-talk from the *Ishba* people. Awa picked berries across from them unnoticed, not spying, just overhearing.

"We haven't seen these people for years." Yari pointed at a man and woman, Elders Awa had never met, *Zamanzi* perhaps, with spiral scars on brown cheeks and thick locks arranged in a crown. "Anyone could betray us." *Vie* pointed at Bal talking with shadow warriors. "Our own Sprites."

"Not Bal. Stop worrying." Isra pulled Yari to the enclave fire. Awa joined them. Yari kissed the top of her head. Isra stroked her cheeks and whispered in Yari's ear, "Take better measure of yourself."

Griots told a story on the sentimental griot of griots and the fearsome scout *vie* loved:

Once, a great brood of Sprites crossed over, as many as would become Elders or who knows what tomorrow. After the ceremony Yari wan-

dered off to Smokeland, weeping and howling, "What world will these
Sprites conjure?" Isra feared doubt would rip Yari apart.

Despite great scouting skill in the everyday, Isra was a terrible smoke-
walker. Luckily a wild dog had Yari's scent and led Isra to Smokeland.
Yari was slumped against black lava rocks, tongue drying up, heart a
faint ember. The dog vanished, stranding Isra with Yari who was too
feeble to smoke-walk them back to the everyday.

Isra scolded Yari, "You rescued me, but the good or evil I do is not yours,
you arrogant wolf! Sprites belong to themselves. Let them fly!"

Yari's heart burned bright again and vie *brought them back to the ev-*
eryday. Yari grinned at Isra and said, "Never let the enemy know your
heart—until you marry them."

This could have been a tall tale but Awa felt the truth of it as
Yari hugged each Sprite. Isra touched a forehead to their open
palms then jumped on a boulder and shouted, "Yari won't mope
with me after you all cross over. *Vie* goes off to find an exiled master, an old lover." Isra sounded jealous and excited.

Yari jumped on the boulder too. "You said he's lost his way; go
find him."

Isra poked Yari. "Come back to me."

"Always." Yari kissed Isra. "You are my rhythm, my reason."

Sprites cheered the romantic scene, then Isra gave Bal the loom.

"I'll tell stories tomorrow," Yari shouted. "On all of you."

"My story too?" Bal asked.

"No secrets too dangerous to play on this drum—yours tomorrow." Yari handed Awa the bag of scrolls and wim-wom. "I give
you my yesterdays." Awa thought she might burst. Yari hugged her
and Bal until Isra pulled them all into a barbarian jig.

* * *

Awa passed her last night as a Sprite wandering vivid vision-scapes. Smokeland got tangled in the everyday. Iron horses with red eyes trotted across Father's fields to nibble Mother's berries. Kenu built a tower to the scar moon and smiled as she and Bal rode wild horses through waterfalls and across black lava sand. Behemoths danced in waves and doused Awa with warm, salty water. She woke, drenched and laughing.

In the dark before dawn, Awa and Bal outlined their eyes in black kohl, twisted seeds in unruly hair, and rubbed their skin with green and red mica. Over green shifts, they donned cloud-silk robes, light as air and warm as fire. Dressed as Elders, they poured a libation to the ancestors and gave thanks to the bees, cathedral trees, and spiders, to the seas, green lands, *Mama Zamba*, and the sweet desert. Who would anybody be without rock, rain, and sand? Filled with anticipation, Awa and Bal joined other Sprites singing and dancing on a carpet of purple sand-bells to the enclave circle.

Everything you believe could be wrong.

Patience, forgiveness, that is our song.

Elder musicians lost the beat and melody. Dizzy, they dropped kora harps and drums. The Sprites stumbled to a halt. Warriors in lion masks raced down *Mama Zamba*'s stone hills and burst through sand drifts carrying axes and swords: *Zamanzi*, ambushing them.

Nobody brought weapons to a crossover ceremony. Shadow warriors wore cloud-silk robes, not Aido spider-weave, and couldn't disappear.

Yari brushed unruly braids from a sweaty face. *Vie* clutched a heaving chest. "Something in the wine."

They were all drug-addled except the two Elders with spiral scars.

Awa gasped. "Anyone could betray us."

Zamanzi warriors surrounded them. Nobody put up a fight. Yari dumped salt into a gourd of water then guzzled it. Shock gripped Awa. She clutched Bal's hand. A *Zamanzi* war chief shouted commands and warnings in Empire vernacular. "Decide to live right or face the ax!" They'd come to *liberate* Sprites and *vesons* who agreed to be griots, wives, or soldiers.

Blood splattered across feast tables. Several Elders and Sprites refused to choose quickly and lost their heads. Bal lunged at a warrior twice her size. Awa held her back. He laughed. Three *Zamanzi* men doused a white-haired *veson* with tree oil and set *vie* on fire. The burning Elder raced across the enclave circle. Yari vomited on the purple sand-bells and howled.

The one who burned was Isra, Yari's partner of twenty-five years, the love Yari always returned to, the weaver who taught Bal to fashion spiderwebs into dreams and shadows into Aido cloth, the friend to horses and wild dogs, the scout who never let anybody get lost. Yari and Isra had rescued Awa before Father sold her to a mine, brothel, or Hezram's huts.

Isra died rolling in a sand dune. *Vie* suffocated the fire before it could spread to anyone else. Tears blinded Awa. Her breath was a wheeze. Her heart cracked and muscles gave out. She and Bal collapsed. The burly axman headed for them. Yari blocked him, sober and ferocious, hair a bristling storm cloud. The axman hesitated.

"*Basawili*, Isra." Yari spoke the *Anawanama* prayer for the dead, then helped Awa and Bal up. They almost fell again. "Not the end, more breath to come." *Vie* shook them. "Survive. Find each other." Turning to the axman, Yari shouted, "I choose griot."

"Prove yourself." Spiral scars decorated the axman's naked cheeks, just like the traitor-Elders. Thin braids with bones on their tips fell to his shoulders. He raised his blade.

"I know secrets about everyone and everything." Yari swaggered in full griot trance. "I've traveled farther than any griot and listened to many hearts. I hold all the people. I've persuaded emperors to peace. *Xhalan Xhala.* I carry the past to the future. Take heart in the story I tell." Looking at Awa and Bal, Yari chanted an epic in the language of *Zamanzi* ancestors:

When the Arkhysian Empire invaded the northlands, a petulant scoundrel, Mmendi, refused to surrender his horses, his women, or give up his fine tent to work an Empire farm and war against barbarian thief-lords in the Golden Gulf. Empire soldiers locked the rascal in a cage and took what they wanted. They paraded Mmendi's horses, children, and women, chained and branded, in front of him. The pampered chief went mad with grief, tearing out his beard, talking only to haints. The beard never grew back.

Seeing Mmendi raving, his people were subdued, beaten. One afternoon the captain of his Empire guard, Thalit, a strong woman with northern roots, recognized his true spirit. Thalit seduced Mmendi or he her—who can say? They ran away together, hiding and eating roots and rats at first, with no thought of much but survival and pleasure.

One night, Mmendi and Thalit raided Empire caravans for mangos, goats, and nut bread. Mmendi's people delighted in this defiance and deserted the Empire in droves. All the men shaved their beards; the women cut their hair short as a fighting woman's. They joined the rascal and his warrior wife and harried Empire caravans, outposts, and patrols. Mmendi and his people claimed the shadows, the caves, the night. They forced the Empire to withdraw from this desert.

Mmendi and Thalit's spirits guide the People still.

Awa looked from Isra's body to Bal, who trembled with rage. Yari's story craft and man-masquerade drew cheers and whistles from the savages. Yari hated that word, but they'd burned Isra alive—what else to call them?

"Only *Zamanzi* know the whole tale." The axman squinted at Yari. "How did you learn this? Unless—the walking library!" He lowered his ax. "You are Yari, the *Lahesh* griot who seduces husbands, wives, emperors, and snakes, who drums up the past and the future." He pounded the ground in front of the traitor-Elders. "I won't cut Yari's neck and risk *Xhalan Xhala*. Only a fool courts *Lahesh* reckoning fire."

Yari's name moved through the crowd like a sandstorm. Three chiefs clashed blades to possess the griot who knew something about everything. Bal snatched a sword from a careless guard and challenged the chiefs. Archers aimed bolts at her, but the war chief stayed their hands and let Bal fight. "For the show if nothing else," he growled.

The cocky chiefs underestimated Bal. They lunged at her half-heartedly, winking at women who huddled with horses and goats at the edge of feast tables. Bal slashed tendons and foreheads and danced away from disabled foes. Limping around with blood dripping in their eyes, the cocky chiefs skewered each other. A shadow warrior defeated enemies without killing. The war chief claimed Bal as soldier and Yari as his griot praise-singer.

"Join me," Bal shouted to Awa. "Wife is too perilous."

"Yes, choose," the axman said, "or die."

Awa's tongue knotted as the axman lifted his bloody blade again. *Zamanzi* considered women too weak-minded to be griots. Awa was no shadow warrior like Bal and desired no husband. What choice was this? As a warrior, she'd die quickly. "I choose . . ." She ached to pour a libation to the crossroads gods. No time. "Chief's wife."

"No," Bal cried, and Awa's heart wrenched. "Too dangerous." Bal dumped sword and spear at Awa's feet. "Don't leave me." She pressed her Aido cloth bag at Awa's chest. The axman did not notice. Aido cloth was every color strong but a play of shadows for untrained eyes.

While *Zamanzi* warriors laughed at Green Elder sentiment, Yari snuck a catalpa anklet in Awa's hand and whispered in *Lahesh*, "Survive. We will find each other."

"How?" Awa whispered *Lahesh* too.

"You're the mapmaker, the storyteller. You'll make a way."

The axman snatched a weeping, thrashing Awa away from Bal and Yari. He forced a bitter, intoxicating potion down her throat, locked her in a cage, and dumped her in a wagon with two other caged Sprites. Awa banged against the bars as the wagon lurched off. Bal and Yari faded in the mist. Two families lost.

Sprite discipline deserted Awa. Her spirit was too scrambled to make any sort of map for tomorrow. *Zamanzi* held her in a cage for ritual cleansing—drug potions, cold water baths, hot stones on her belly. The drugs made it hard to think right or feel herself. She was haunted by Yari's hard eyes as Isra burned alive and Bal's tearstained cheeks when she chose chief's wife.

Awa might have done mortal damage to herself, but Yari said, *Survive.* The moon turned to a pale scar leaking silver light, and her blood came with cramps and heartache for two families lost. Old men leered through the bars, happy she could produce *Zamanzi* sons and daughters. One must have been her husband to be. *Survive.* Awa blotted out mottled faces and recited from *The Green Elder Songs for Living and Dying.*

"Hush that noise," the axman declared one night. "Tomorrow, twenty-first wife."

Awa whispered every song, losing herself in the words,

rhythms, and rhymes. Better that than go mad. *What you know is
always yours.*

On Awa's wedding day, the southern barbarians raided during
the final cleansing mutilation. *Zamanzi* women were fracturing
her leg—to ensure she couldn't run away from a chief five times her
age—when thief-lords tromped in on elephants. They pierced her
husband-to-be with fire arrows. The ancient chief lurched into
her, trying to escape.

Awa caught fire too. The barbarians laughed as she rolled in
the dirt like Isra and smothered the fire. They let the old chief
burn alive, then wrapped Awa's burnt arm and set her broken leg.
Thanks to *Zamanzi* potions, pain was a distant throb. *Survive. We
will find each other.*

A thief-lord transported her to Holy City as a blood offering
to the gods of Ice Mountain. High priest Hezram paid well for
Sprites—good blood, no family, and not yet dangerous.

Awa's first transgression was singing tree song under the scar
moon, *actual* sacred cathedral tree melodies that only high priests
should know. She'd learned tree song in Smokeland. Her second
transgression was talking to the Amethyst River. The river was
sick. Anyone could hear that. A person didn't need medicine-
woman skill or priestly dispensation.

The barbarians didn't know that Awa was a smoke-walker.
Women supposedly polluted Smokeland. One transgression
meant exile, slave labor on an Empire caravan or merchant ship.
Two meant a slow death, toiling and bleeding for the glory of the
supreme god. For three transgressions, the punishment was spirit
torture too terrible to speak of.

Awa wanted to curse the crossroads gods, but she refrained.
Cursing the gods wouldn't help her survive.

15

The Future from the Past

Many conjurers collected fire-spells. They showed off at carnivals, throwing sparks, exploding leaves, even eating flames. Only the *Lahesh* burned through this moment to ones that were coming: reckoning fire. Everyone said *Xhalan Xhala* was impossible conjure, but Djola had yet to admit defeat. Samina would never forgive that. Impossible was what lazy, ignorant fools said when they reached their limits. Djola had to push beyond himself. Hadn't he always done that? He was the first northlander at the stone-wood table, and for twenty years, second only to Azizi! After mastering *Xhalan Xhala*, he'd sit at the emperor's table again.

Pezarrat and his pirates were well-fed and spirited. They cheered a clutch of merchant vessels sailing in on a good wind. Hefty boats with bright sails rode low in the water. Pezarrat hurled Djola's acid-conjure at one ship. When the hull dissolved into sludge and sizzling vapor, the other ships blew horns signaling surrender. Pirates looted the ships without suffering many casualties, although a few merchants lost their heads protecting trinkets. Grateful for an empty sick bay, Vandana and Orca joined the victory celebration.

They gobbled shrimp, drank too much wine, and slept like the dead on plush pillows and blankets—merchant booty.

Up on the deserted deck, Djola swept feathers, medicine bags, and discarded trinkets into the sea. A scar moon sank into rippling water. Samina's moon. He was clean-shaven and clear, his fortressed heart a faint smolder, closer to the chill he needed to pull fire. He found a merchant blade and stowed it in an empty sleeve. Dead merchants floated by, and he wondered if they'd been slavers. A few unlucky pirate lads floated with them. Djola turned away, unmoved thanks to his heart fortress. Orca and Vandana had helped him fashion silver-mesh gloves, cold conjure impervious to hot spells. Singing, he put on one glove and left one hand bare.

Two knobby-headed behemoths, their tail flukes almost the size of a ship, floated in a placid sea and observed him with unblinking eyes. A thrill shivered past his defenses. He'd only come face-to-face with water giants in Smokeland, never in the everyday. They wailed high-pitched long notes—a greeting? warning? question?

Djola displayed the silver-mesh glove and explained. "I'm practicing *Xhalan Xhala.*"

The behemoths sang again, rumbles and warbles that soothed his itchy skin. They ended with throaty chirps and a geyser of seawater. He offered one of Yari's melodies to them. The behemoths swam closer. Shell-encrusted skin and tongues the size of elephants dazzled him. Their eyes were spots of light as they warbled and chirped.

He climbed out on the bowsprit, dangled over them, and sang. *"You are the ocean and I am the air. The clouds are our children."* He mimicked their sounds as he ran out of words. One jumped close enough for him to touch cold skin. He filled himself with their oily chill. Shivering, he swung his legs up and climbed back to the deck. "Holding yesterday and today, I call tomorrow's fire."

Djola squinted his right eye at the catapult bowl used to hurl acid-conjure at merchant ships just hours ago. Caressing its waxed surface with the bare fingers of his left hand, he recalled the attack in vivid detail. Ships dissolved in his mind. Pain sliced him and stole balance. The bowl burst into flames. He wore a silver-mesh glove on his right hand and clutched the flaming bowl without burning flesh. The bowl turned to a puff of void-smoke. Dizzy and nauseous, Djola almost blacked out, dropping like a felled tree toward the deck.

A net broke his fall. Tangled in stiff threads was a letter with a resin seal. A sharp cathedral tree scent jolted him back to his senses. He patted his skull, surprised he hadn't cracked himself open. He gripped the railing and vomited. The behemoths stood on their tails, flapping long pectoral fins. Cavernous mouths dripped foam and seaweed strings. Djola sputtered at this wonder. The behemoths dove back into black water and disappeared. A flick of their tails rocked the ship.

Singing the sea giant's song, Djola grabbed the letter as it bounced free of the net. He hugged the scroll to his chest. It was damp and thick, a long tally of bad news. Why open that? He shoved it in his shirt.

16

River Children

Behemoths swim down the coastal waterway from one river delta to the next, escaping lightning storms and foul waters. Leagues and leagues they swim to reach cold waters to feed. More storms than ever churn up sour waves and tainted food. Many Behemoths have been hungry and sick. This water tastes good. Bubble nets are full, a good catch.

The pod is stuffed with krill, herring, and squid. Perhaps they won't starve. They must eat enough to swim back to warm waters where, far from sharp-toothed killers, babies are born and grow fat on mother's milk. If the pod keeps filling their nets like tonight, next year the river deltas will greet many young ones.

Djola's song is intriguing. The pod approaches the boat, cautious but curious. They sound out an image of land creatures, tall tree trunks, and cloth waves rippling in the wind. Djola's song is a short burst. The Behemoths try to make sense of his strong voice mimicking their songs. He adds new rhythms and melodies—a delight, a mystery. Two Behemoths circle under his boat and leap into the air, waving pectoral fins. Djola waves too, singing till he lays down on the deck.

A boat with singers is a good prospect. Some boat creatures are monsters, ramming hulls together and burning each other. They ambush sleeping Behemoths or those nursing young ones. Yet, these boats swim together, friends. Such a fleet might scare off the black-and-white killers who hunt weak or half-grown Behemoths. Surfing in the wake of a music boat is always fun. Singers twist the air with strings, blow hard shells, and beat dry, dead skin; they fling themselves around the decks.

The Behemoths hope to hear more music or play with the boat creature if he dives in the water. When the boats drop anchor, the Behemoths might even risk closing an eye to sleep. A grand day.

17
Calling Fire

Behemoths finished their song. Orca and Vandana took a woozy Djola down to his bunk, which was covered in drawings for *Xhalan Xhala*: a thousand thousand roads intersecting—the maybes and maybe nots of Smokeland. After pulling fire, he had to smoke-walk to the crossroads of crossroads, get there and back at the speed of thought—a mapmaker's spell. He knocked the scrolls away.

Difficult to map what he could barely imagine, even with *Anawanama* craft. Orca and Vandana hovered. Wine and garlic on their breath made him gag. His right eye burned, his left hand ached, from botching *Xhalan Xhala*. Djola curled against the bulkhead. He wanted to be shadows and ash and feel nothing.

Vandana poked him. "You practice *Xhalan Xhala* where I won't see. Foolish."

"Better to rehearse in the night," Djola explained. "No distractions."

Vandana lit lanterns. "Ignorant man huddles alone in dark. Brilliant man reflects light from his friends."

"I don't need more wise words." Djola smacked a barrel of books. He wanted to toss them into the sea.

"Every dawn, something is smoke." Orca fingered a singed stronghold-map. "He turned a barrel of pitch to ash."

"*Xhalan Xhala* should go beyond flames and soot to . . ." Djola sputtered.

"To what?" Orca whispered and massaged Djola's cramped shoulder muscles.

"You rehearse a dangerous spell you don't understand?" Vandana scowled.

"Understanding comes from doing," Djola shouted.

"Not always," Orca said. "I've seen you—"

"Do you report me to Pezarrat?" Djola pulled away from Orca's strong hands. "Is that why you smile in my face and dig at my secrets?"

"Of course he reports." Vandana sucked her teeth. "He wishes to breathe another day. I also tell Captain what you do. What does Pezarrat understand?"

Djola flailed. "Never underestimate an enemy."

Vandana slapped whipcord braids in his face. "If it's so bad, you need gods or heroes to save your world—"

"You're already lost," Djola muttered.

"No. It's time to pull together."

"All people are the same." Orca quoted Pezarrat. "We live in a pirate world. Everyone is thief, liar, and cheat."

"You don't believe that." Djola sighed. He'd sealed Vandana and Orca in his heart with Samina and the children.

Vandana poked his heart Vévés. "When you run to home, will you look to see if we follow?"

Djola gripped her hand. "I have no home to run to. They stole everything from me."

"You aren't the only one who suffers." Vandana spoke *Lahesh*.

Orca gaped at northlander talk. "*Xhalan Xhala* is warning. A rehearsal of spirit, not carnival show or vengeance."

Djola spoke *Lahesh* also. "Anything can be turned into a weapon."

Vandana licked dagger teeth. "Will you be weapon or something else?"

Djola circled her. "Griots say *Lahesh* have a stronghold across *Mama Zamba*."

Vandana laughed. "Griots also say *Lahesh* live a full-bodied life in Smokeland and walked an ice bridge to beyond where the sky falls into the sea. Tall tales."

"*Lahesh* walk among us, *changing us from the inside*." Djola spoke Yari's words.

"Truth, yes." Vandana held up her small bag, a *Lahesh* wonder of folded space. "*Lahesh* have not vanished. They live in everything we do."

"Will you teach me this talk?" Orca spoke Empire vernacular.

"So you can be a better spy?" Djola arched an eyebrow. "Or a master of stories?"

The sick bay door burst open. An arrow whistled past Vandana and nicked Djola's ear. Orca shoved Djola to the ground as a second bolt headed for his heart and landed in the old healer's eye. He'd been spying behind a barrel. He screeched and fell over dead.

Before the assassin let loose a third arrow, Vandana knocked the bow from his hand and ripped his throat with dagger teeth. The assassin crumpled, clutching a bloody neck. Shock and disbelief would be his death mask. Behind him, an old woman in a greasy apron carried pots of glowing coals. Jibber jabber drooled from her lips.

"Another assassin cook." Vandana wiped blood from her chin and pulled diamond-tipped blades from her small bag. "Bowman was telling you to burn our bodies and speak lies to Captain: *Djola misplaced wits. Almost set fire to ship,* yes?" She waved blades at the guilty look on the cook's face. "Alive, we don't go following bowman's plan."

"What you say against what I say," the cook declared.

Djola scrambled up. "Who paid you?"

"Halt." The cook held up the pots. "Or you'll burn with your savage books."

"I don't fear your scullery fire," Djola shouted, but Orca held him back.

Vandana crept toward the cook. "What if you die and can't say anything?"

Eyeing Vandana's blades, the cook edged toward the ladder to the deck. She missed Orca throwing a bola. The iron balls tangled her legs in tough leather strands and smashed a knee. She stumbled and fell back against the ladder.

Djola snatched the fire pots and smothered the coals with mesh-covered hands. The cook bashed her head against several rungs as she slid to the floor. Her breath rattled to a halt. Orca looked horrified as he untangled his bolo from her legs. He was inured to death, not killing.

"I've saved that bowman's life twice. The cook too." Djola set the hot pots in his sandbox. "How much money did Council pay them?"

Orca pulled purses from their bodies. "Gold, more than a triple share."

"The Master of Money is generous," Djola said. "Keep it. Buy your freedom."

Orca covered his face in kisses.

"Three dead." Vandana's swords had disappeared into her bag.

Djola shrugged. "The old healer was Pezarrat's spy."

"Still a waste of spirit." She raced up the ladder and retched over the railing.

"Ripping throats out doesn't agree with her," Orca said without irony.

"I think she'd rather use a blade than her teeth," Djola replied. "Who knows? She's from beyond the maps." He and Orca hauled the bodies to the upper deck and heaved them overboard. Pirates up early to clean and sharpen blades stopped work to stare. One clutched his neck and swallowed a curse.

"Assassins," Vandana explained and vomited again. Orca stroked her back. She sloshed wine in her mouth and spat. "Who but tigers likes the taste of dead men?"

Two behemoths burst into the air, barnacled mouths agape. They sprayed Djola with foul-smelling water. They plunged under the ship's belly and lifted it on their backs. Pirates tumbled to the deck and screeched—farm boys and blacksmiths, new to the sea.

The behemoths cheered Orca up. Even Vandana managed a sigh. The behemoths carried the ship several minutes, spiraling and zigzagging, making a crossroads Vévé in the waves. Djola was full of wonder. *Weeds and Wild Things* were sealed in his heart with Orca, Vandana, and his family. Djola sang to the behemoths. They set the ship back in the water, sang a long high note, and swam away.

"Friends of yours?" An ashen pirate gaped at Djola. He and the others backed away.

"I fill the sea with poison, how am I a friend?" Djola replied. Grain's letter burned against his chest. He dashed back to sick bay and sank down on his bunk. After a few calming breaths, he neutralized Kyrie's conjure. Silver-mesh gloves made it hard to break the seal and unfurl stiff bark-paper. He almost ripped it.

Grain dispensed with salutations:

Five years and the griot of griots has not come to Council
We could use Yari's wisdom
Ernold, Water, and Money poisoned Nuar
Your half-brother died a traitor's death on cold stone at Council
This morning, I carried Nuar's body to the foothills of Mount
  Eidhou
I led a mourning parade to Kyrie's gates for an Anawanama
  ancestor ceremony
Money and Water protested an honorable, if savage, *burial for*
  a traitor
Azizi refused to interfere with northland rituals
Arms and his warriors accompanied me to Kyrie's gates to guard
  the ceremony
Rebels, Green Elders, Anawanama, *elephants, and other wild*
  things were in attendance

Nuar dead. Djola's fortress heart raced. His hands shook. Half-brother Nuar and Djola had often clashed, yet they loved each other. *"Basawili."* Djola spoke the *Anawanama* prayer for the dead. "Not the end. I will live in your spirit." Nuar was the first northland chief Djola talked to the peace fire. With Djola in exile and Nuar cut down, many northern tribes would walk away from the Empire. An honorable funeral would forestall desertion only a short while. "Reckoning fire is how I'll mourn you, brother." Ernold, Money, and Water were dead men.

While Urzula, Arms, and I were gone, Ernold condemned Samina
  to a transgressor hut
Money and Water marooned your children in the desert
Ernold proclaims that Samina and the children have perished
I have searched everywhere
Nobody has seen the bodies

Money and Water blame Zamanzi *warriors or* veson-*rebels*
Arms insists the masters lie
Azizi doesn't know who to believe or what to do
The Empire could come apart
Kyrie communes with her mountain and sends hope

The letter burst into flames. Djola had called fire without meaning to.

18

Snatched from Herself

The temple at Holy City was an extension of Ice Mountain, built from stone and wood around ledges and caves. Inside high walls, a hundred cathedral trees strained toward the light. Gray leaves hung from flaccid branches. Rope and wood balconies connected the sparse crowns to Ice Mountain's cliffs. Hardly anybody worshipped in the temple. Most people climbed stone stairs and talked to the gods at the icy peak, as the ancestors did.

Awa trudged up temple steps with transgressors about to be bled. She never believed in angry mountain gods. Entering the temple, she chanted Yari's words: *You're the mapmaker, the storyteller. You'll make a way.*

Dream Gates glowered in the dark behind the temple trees. The gates' silver-mesh intrigued Awa: interlocking roads and spirals, shooting stars and spiderwebs—Vévés to call down crossroads deities, a dangerous lot on nobody's side. A continuous circle of gates enclosed the entire citadel in Dream Gate conjure. Beyond the gates in the mountain proper, cauldrons of blood and oil bubbled in caves with holes in the ceiling to carry away smoke. Awa spat out the foul taste.

Griots claimed life in Holy City transgressor huts was worse than death. Awa tried to tell her own story. She let her mind go blank rather than take in horror. *Survive.* One day had blurred into another for several months, and she'd managed to forget blood and stench and pain. But she was also forgetting the touch of grace in Isra's loom and the call to truth in Yari's talking drum. She even found herself doubting Bal's tricky harmonies. Could anybody have that many voices in them? Griot tales for children.

Awa did remember Mother promising to poison Father—yet for a moment, she thought she saw him, squatting in the temple, then her vision clouded. Acolytes sliced Awa on the stone floor. The pain was sharp at the slice but faded to a dull ache as blood oozed from her good arm into a metal bowl. Acolytes rarely cut her burnt arm for fear of tainted blood. Crows flew in the high windows.

"Probably hoping for dead meat." An acolyte chortled.

Awa knew these crows. She fed them berries to spite priests whose flimsy bows and bad aims were no match for crafty birds. "No berries here," she said.

"She's delirious." The acolytes laughed.

An inept or cruel acolyte jabbed Awa's leg. Blood spurted on his stub nose. She fought to stay conscious. Father's voice jolted her mind clear. Droopy-eyed, sallow, and paunchy, he haggled with Hezram, high priest of Ice Mountain and witchdoctor of dreams. It *was* Father. Here. Real. Awa swallowed an urge to yell, *Save me, take me home.*

A conjure woman had gotten her lover out of a transgressor hut. She taught Hezram a gate-spell, and he released the lover, a *veson.* Father hated Green Elders, but their spells were his treasure. He'd never part with a spell to rescue Awa. She closed her eyes on his haggard face. Fury would take too much energy. Calm helped her survive.

The acolytes dumped icy temple water on her head. "No sleeping."

Transgressors had to know their pain to earn redemption. Awa's thin shift clung to damp skin. She pressed ice on her burbling leg wound. The acolytes smacked her nipples and poked fingers in her navel. She let the ice drop. Bleeding out in the temple would be easy. "Death is a doorway," she muttered in *Lahesh*.

"Jumba jabba." The acolytes chortled at Green Elder nonsense.

"Nobody cheats me," Father roared and startled Awa and her tormenters. "Not even you. I'm a good Empire citizen."

"I know what you are." Hezram shook his silky brown beard and mane of hair. He was muscular and handsome, in his prime. Awa wanted to curse him to a slow death.

"You stingy barbarian, I deserve more than a few sky rocks." Father shook a bag of turquoise. "To build gates around the capital city will take more than a year. You must pay three times this much."

Father built stone bridges and cathedral-tree towers for priests and barbarian thief-lords. He hewed transgressor huts from mountain rock. He'd learned in an enclave to build anything with stone, metal, or wood. Perhaps he'd made the hovel Awa lived in. She wanted to curse him along with Hezram. Resisting the urge made her flame hot. The acolytes let her go and shook burning hands.

Father thrust the bag in Hezram's face, distracting the acolytes again. "You need me." He was foolhardy to challenge Hezram, who cheated everybody and locked up or tortured those who protested. Maybe Father had lost his wits. Mother could be using a slow poison, a few mushrooms in the bread each day.

"If you didn't need me, I'd already be dead." His eyes were bleary, his words slurred, maybe he was drunk. "I knew you when you were a common witchdoctor peddling tricks at carnivals."

The acolytes smirked and jabbed each other, hoping for torture.

They dragged Awa to the caldrons. They meant to take her in a cave on the other side of the Gates while Hezram dispensed with Father. Tembe, Iyalawo of Ice Mountain, found a mutilated dead girl yesterday in the temple—she was stripped naked with a head wrap stuffed in her mouth.

Priests claimed transgressors had done this. Awa knew better. Acolytes liked to cut souvenirs, brag about their exploits, and leave transgressors to bleed out. Awa wasn't dying like that. She cackled alarm at crows roosting in the crisscross of high beams. They cackled back. Swooping low, several shat on bald acolyte heads.

Awa observed the scrambling and shrieking placidly until she recognized snub-nosed Jod, grown muscular and bearded. Jod's lion eyes glowed in the dark as he punched the shock on her face—yet he didn't remember her from Sprite days. Awa wasn't Bal.

"Enough." Hezram hauled her away from them. "Tembe says you lot go too far. In the temple!"

"Just a bit of fun," Jod said.

"No more fun like that," Hezram replied.

Jod stood eye to eye with him. "You have Tembe to cushion your bed."

"Iyalawos marry their mountains." Hezram circled him.

"A stout-hearted woman could love a mountain *and* a man, if . . ." Jod took a breath. The other acolytes cringed. "If the man is worth the risk."

Hezram smiled. "Do you think you're worthy of mountain love?" Jod shrugged. Hezram sniggered. "I like your grit, but you've got blood and bird shit on your robe. Clean yourselves. Leave her be."

Awa clicked thanks at the crows. The young men grumbled and filled basins with water then removed outer robes. Hezram dumped Awa near the cauldrons. Pots bubbled day and night, filling the temple and Rainbow Square with a nauseating smell.

Spirit slaves had to be fed constantly to maintain Hezram's Dream Gates, Nightmare Gates, really.

"No one will do what I do," Father said. Hezram held up another bag. Father snatched it. Sky rocks spilled out. Whatever he did was worth a fortune. "Why the same dance every time?"

Collecting turquoise nuggets from the ground, Father caught sight of Awa. Blood drained from his face; his lower lip trembled. Did he recognize her? Awa wasn't a plump child anymore. Still, the snake birthmark was hard to miss. Brother Kenu had one on his cheek. Where was Kenu now? Perhaps he also built transgressor huts and Nightmare Gates.

Rage ambushed Awa and she spit anger at Father. Sentinel bees from the temple hive swarmed him. He took off with his bag of sky rocks, barging through half-naked acolytes. Awa crawled in a recess behind a blood cauldron and hugged her knees. She tried to calm herself and friend bees. Nobody should lose a stinger over Father. He and the acolytes scrambled outside trailing a trickle of angry sentinels.

Hezram dropped down beside Awa. Shrieks faded. Hezram peeked around the cauldrons, chuckling. Bees returned to their hive in a cathedral trunk tower. Hezram stood up and mixed tree oil with Awa's blood before pouring it in a cauldron. "Why are you still sitting there?" Hezram looked ready to drag her into shadows.

Awa coughed and cackled distress. A crow with a few white feathers in its blue-black wings flew in his face, scratching and pecking. "Zst!" He cursed and flailed. "I'm not dead meat yet." The piebald crow flew to the window that looked out on a glacier. The cold gray eye of god glared down on priest, citizen, and transgressor alike. Hezram sighed. "The gods must love crows."

Awa bit her tongue. Ice Mountain gods loved only themselves.

"They're a plague." Blood from a claw- or beak-wound trickled into Hezram's eyes. "Afraid of a few bees and crows?"

"I fear bees more than crows." Awa spoke truth. The banana smell of bee alarm, a buzz of wings by her ears, or a drop of honey on her tongue might land her on the other side of smoke for hours, for days, for who knows how long. Hezram and his witchdoctors hunted smoke-walkers and turned them into empty-eyed spirit slaves. That would be worse than the transgressor huts.

"Crows are welcome to my dead flesh." She clutched the throbbing leg wound.

"A crow with white feathers." He pointed at the bird watching from an altar. "Everything is wrong today, upside down and inside out. Even the bees." He scanned the rafters and grabbed a hot poker. "I hate omens."

"Stung to death might be better than a slow bleed." Awa bit her tongue too late.

"Your blood is precious. A shame to waste it." Hezram pressed hot metal against her leg wound. She lost sense for a moment. He threw cold rags in her face. "If you must take your leave"—he pointed to a belt of snakeheads hidden in his robes—"venom is faster."

"Poison snakes are rare in Holy City." A viper's head with full poison sacs hung from a slim cord inside Awa's shift and bumped her ribs as she bound the leg wound. "Dying slowly for god is redemption. Kurakao! I lose faith, sometimes."

"You hang on," Hezram said. "This is grace."

"Yes." Awa scrambled up. "Grace."

"You think I'm cruel, evil?" Hezram pulled Awa close. His breath was honey sweet, his sweat oily and red. "I won't be a drum that someone else beats, a road they walk to riches and fame. I won't be bled and boiled." He grinned at her, eyes wide, fervent. "The world is evil. A wise man does what he has to. I'm strong enough to prevail."

"Yes, but—" Awa ground her teeth. The cauldron chambers

were on the other side of the Nightmare Gates, so priests and acolytes could do what they wanted. And so could transgressors. Stabbing Hezram with the viper's fangs would be easy. Afterward, she
could follow the Dream Gates to the outside. Who would know
she'd killed him? Not Jod, he never noticed her. Awa groaned. She
wasn't a killer. Imagining murder was easier than actually doing it.

"What?" Hezram demanded.

"Everything we believe could be false."

Hezram laughed. "One thing is sure. The gods are indifferent
to our suffering."

"Perhaps we must be better than the gods."

"Perhaps you're a coward afraid to give up ghosts and face
death."

Awa met his gaze unafraid. "I seek redemption however it
comes."

His expression hardened. "Then you shall find it. Get out of
here."

19

Basawili

More breath to come. Not for Djola's family. They were all dead. Or just Nuar? *Nobody has seen the bodies.* Not knowing was torture. They'd died a thousand thousand times in his mind, because of him. Djola had mourned them over and over. He was finished with torture, with hope and struggle.

An icy wind grabbed his arm. Frigid air made him cough. The fleet must have hit an ice storm. Djola was too thin. He wasn't eating enough. The cold got to him under anybody's thick, hairy hide, and wrecked even drugged sleep. Actually, he'd taken enough *medicine* to stop his heart. Had the cold followed him to the death lands? He opened crusty eyes. White light blinded him. He blinked and squinted. The scent of almonds and raintree blossoms pierced woozy visions, organizing the view a little.

"Come with me." The scar moon spoke, a red slash on a gray horizon above hills and valleys of water, not land. He was still at sea. "Come to Smokeland. We have so little time."

Not the moon talking, but Samina—her words tugged him away from the everyday. He was thrilled and frightened. "No worry. Vandana and Orca stand guard." How could Samina know their names? "Hurry!" She used the voice not to be argued with, so Djola left his breath body on Pezarrat's ship and flew over a sea of behemoth eyes. Their icy geysers lifted him high.

"This way," Samina shouted.

Djola groped the cold, trying to touch her, pull her close. In one achy heartbeat, he passed through the border-void to Smokeland, going too fast for despair.

"I would spend these last moments with you," she said.

His last moments or hers? She drew him along a bridge of blurry starlight past icy comets to a winter region. "My realm now."

A stream, frozen midair as it rushed over a precipice, shimmered. Light from a hundred hundred surfaces bounced everywhere. The shadows of snow-dusted trees danced against the side of a white mountain. One hazy form blended into another. Leaves rustled and tinkled, and Samina whispered and whistled. Djola wished he hadn't swallowed a bottle of seed and silk potion. Suicide suddenly seemed foolhardy, cowardly.

"Where are you?" he whispered.

"Walking beside you." Her face was a snow squall, her heart lightning bolts. "And also in a transgressor hut, where my breath body burns."

He tasted ashes, but was calm. Knowing her fate would be relief. "Are you dead?"

"I'm not sister Kyrie. Still, I cheat death." She whirled about him. "I set fire to the transgressor hut before drinking a lethal potion and traveling to Smokeland. I smell that *Lahesh* potion on your breath and see the haze in your eyes." Her voice was gentle, sweet. "What are you doing, my love?"

He choked. "Kyrie sent me letters, but only from Grain, not from you."

"I wrote you many angry words, and love too, but I burned the scrolls. I'm not Kyrie. She found you with Grain's map-sense."

"You find me now."

"We find each other. Smoke-walking."

"Grain said you were in mortal danger—" Djola slipped on ice. "I've mourned you."

"What good was that?" Her voice echoed around the mountain. Snow rumbled in reply. Avalanches awaited her command. "I won't be sacrifice, spirit slave, or victim. I'm a guardian."

"You've found your way," Djola whimpered. "I'm lost."

"End torture in the huts, on the sea, in the woods and fields." Her icy words tickled his ears. "Do this to honor me. You're the Master of *Weeds and Wild Things*."

He almost sneered. "No one masters *Weeds and Wild Things*."

She sighed a gust of wind that blasted him over a cliff. He tumbled through snow and ice then gripped a branch and dangled over a ledge. "At first, failure is the map." She used his words to their children. "Come visit me here, where the dead linger and watch over the living."

He dropped to snow-packed ground. "What happened to Tessa, Bal, and Quint?"

"You abandoned us, that's what happened."

"Quint would be so grown up. Are they dead?"

"I burn to ash in a hut. Why ask me?"

"A mother's duty—"

"What of a father's duty?"

"Council stole my future and yours. I mourned the children too."

"What if our children live and you waste heart spirit?"

Djola didn't want to fight with her or hope she was right. "Still . . ."

"Enough mourning. Promise me." Icicle spears crashed around

her. "I won't speak of the children or revenge. Kill nobody in my name, not even yourself. Live, for love of me and the children." Dying in a hut and she was asking him to be reasonable. "Use the heartbeats you have left to do what you set out to do. *Basawili.*"

"How? Poison sandstorms travel faster than thought, like a void-wind from Smokeland devastating green lands in the every-day."

"You know more than you think."

"Stopping the void is impossible." Djola shook his head. "It travels through wise-woman corridors."

She drew him close. Cold lips brushed his forehead. "I should have taken the children to Mount Eidhou, but like a fool, I went to Arkhys City to find you."

"Not your fault," he whispered. His fault.

"Will you swear an oath on my last breath, to work for change, not revenge?"

Who refused a dying wish? "I will live for change not revenge." Djola wanted to hold her, comfort her. He reached out and hugged a frosty wind. "I've been practicing *Lahesh* conjure. *Xhalan Xhala* will be the proof I offer Azizi. For you, for the children."

"Good. Survive! Visit me whenever you can." Samina stabbed his back with a hot barb, and, in a blink, he was back in the every-day, sprawled under a porthole in sick bay, soaking wet and shiver-ing. Wounded men groaned around him.

"You were sleepwalking again." Orca wiped his face. "Too much medicine. Fever."

"We found you on the upper deck, behemoths singing, waves splashing you." Vandana gave Djola a hot brew.

Djola gulped it down. "How long was I *sleepwalking*?"

"Days. I worried you might never return from the border-void," Vandana whispered.

Orca rubbed Djola dry and held him till he was warm. He

asked a hundred questions about frost in Djola's mustache, the wound in his back, and the raintree aroma on his hands.

"Samina is the chill at my neck, the cold in my bones," Djola said.

Vandana nodded. Orca blinked, confused. "From now on I live for change," Djola declared and with the last of the brew poured a libation to the crossroads gods.

BOOK
III

1
If the Way Is Open

Amplify now
Every yesterday lives in today
We have many futures and each changes the past
Don't lose possibilities in the void
Imagine freedom and it is yours

Djola was patient, methodical, relentless. He let Samina's chill sink into him, and every day he pulled more fire without burning himself. Calling on Elder discipline, he glimpsed the crossroads of crossroads, a haven of possibilities. In sick bay, he brought more rogues back from death than ever before. Only a scar moon put him in a foul temper. Otherwise he was calm, a landscape smothered in snow.

The plunder pirates acquired using his conjure lulled Pezarrat. The captain praised ingenious weapons that took out defenses, killed nobody, and left survivors who urged quick surrender. Djola joined victory celebrations. He ate fire, called behemoths to sing, and disappeared in bright light. Everyone enjoyed the carnival display and the tonics he brewed from fermented herbs and roots. They marveled at his transformation.

Pezarrat hounded Orca for secrets, threatened to find a prettier boy to replace him, but other whore-spies were afraid of Djola's bed. "What if you turn them into rats, or worse make them wind in the sails?" Vandana chuckled. "At least a rat still lives. Who knows about the wind?"

Djola taught Orca shadow-warrior tricks and told him to sneak off in the night to a real lover. "I lust for no one," Orca said. "I want to study at night with you."

After every village or city raid, Djola spoke humbly with local conjurers and toured libraries that he'd saved from a pirate torch. He deciphered stone tablets until fingers blistered and bled. He read music cloth and memorized singing books until he was hoarse and wheezing.

Vandana filled her small bag with books, maps, and clown acts for *when I finally go to home.* She wrote scrolls that she never showed Djola. She was on a secret mission too, another snake in Pezarrat's house. Djola could hold her danger. She could hold his. Orca was a diligent student since being touched by a star-demon in a sky window. He catalogued everything in Vandana's small bag. He invented a spell that let her find any scroll, seed, book, or weed root. He even sorted her weapons.

"We almost have a good life," Orca said, yet—

More freak storms harassed the fleet, coming too fast and often sinking boats. Djola danced in snow and lightning, trying to make sense. He swam naked in cold seas whenever behemoths swam near. Stuck in a cove waiting out gale winds, he made *Anawanama* outlaw armor, impervious to wild winds and most weapons. Few conjurers still knew this ancestor craft.

Djola fashioned deep-throated djembe drums and a kora—a calabash harp with twenty-one strings like Samina's. His music kept spirits high. Pirates thought his trance dances were harmless carnival acts or Green Elder jumba jabba. Orca knew better. He pestered Djola and Vandana to teach him *Lahesh.* "You asked what I wanted? A trickster's tongue." Djola warned that every language changed the mind. Orca shrugged. "You say ignorance won't save us."

"Since when do you want to save the world?" Djola asked.

"Aren't I part of the world?" Orca kept Djola company, reading in the night and arguing as the sun rose.

"You use too much tree oil in your lamps," Pezarrat complained.

"You keep track of all my debts," Djola replied. "I pay you in enemy blood and gold for a bit of light in the night. Why pretend to be angry? Are you teasing me?"

Pezarrat laughed. "You've become so affable and amusing. Orca claims a good spirit reasons with you in your dreams, and Vandana says only *Basawili.*" Pezarrat licked his teeth. "I don't believe in good spirits or *Anawanama* jumba jabba."

A chill wind tickled Djola's neck—Samina, saving Pezarrat's life. *"Basawili* means we survive to change—"

"The gods of the crossroads are tricksters!"

"Vandana makes sure Orca and I always have good to do."

Djola never set foot in the Arkhysian Empire or any of Azizi's protectorates. His chair at Council remained empty. According to Grain, Masters groused, yet Azizi refused to name a new Master of Poisons while Djola lived. A good sign. Kyrie still provided Azizi with mountain herbs and secret counsel while smuggling reports from Grain to Djola. Most of the news was bad: poison desert encroached; grain stores dwindled; rebels raided and citizens rioted. Kyrie's Mountain Gates held as did her hope. Nobody had seen the bodies of Djola's children.

Djola practiced patience. Whenever he drank a mild seed and silk potion and flew to Smokeland, Samina spoke of days to come.

She swore greedy fools had yet to conquer the future. She loved the world and held to hope like sister Kyrie. Samina never let Djola apologize for past arrogance or terrible decisions, never let him talk of revenge or speak of the children. She'd made peace with their actions and insisted all was not lost.

One smoke walk in the middle of Djola's seventh year in exile, Samina put icy fingers on his lips. "You know the cause of the poison and a cure." Djola gaped at her. "You wrote a scroll of spells long ago." She used the voice not to be argued with. "You still whisper that spell in dreams."

"I can't remember my dreams."

"Do what you need to do, then come to me, at Mount Eidhou."

"If I knew what to do, I'd already be free."

"To be free, you live for change, not revenge. Conjure the future *as if it were past*."

He gasped. "To dance *Xhalan Xhala* for Pezarrat I should see the gold dust or turquoise his plunder brings?"

"That's one future." She put icy fingers on his heart. "You say we do this to ourselves. There are other futures. See these as well. And offer void-smoke to crossroads gods."

Smokeland was what might be, what could be, yet never very far from what was happening right now. *Xhalan Xhala* brought Smokeland to the everyday and the void too, the lost possibilities. Before they could speak more, Djola was rushing across the light bridge, swirling through a comet's icy tail, his mind reeling, his heart quaking. He came back to himself shivering and sweating on his bunk.

The sick bay was empty. Vandana and Orca had left his breath body unprotected. Somebody could have killed him or worse, poisoned him and made him a spirit slave. Djola jerked up. Vandana and Orca were spies, but loyal to him, always on the lookout for assassins. Something was wrong.

His Aido bag, kora harp, and mountain of books had disappeared. Vandana's bag sat next to him in the sunlight from a porthole. The blades Orca had confiscated from Djola circled the bag, tips pointed outward. A scroll and Djola's latest maps for Jena City and Bog-Town lay on top of the bag. A message was scrawled in *Lahesh* on the scroll.

> *If the way is open, run.*
> *I should have left sooner, but didn't want to abandon you and Orca.*
> *Now you go to home and I have good to do elsewhere. That is living.*
> *I am too sentimental to face farewell.*
> *I hold your Kora harp and Aido bag. This* Lahesh *bag, your bag*
> *now. A library.*
> *Keep it safe. Add to it. Pass it on.*
> *Remember, these are good people on the wrong ship.*
> Dochsi, *you do love the world.*

Dochsi—the *Lahesh* no to negativity. His heart pounded; blood sang in his ears. Aside from *Weeds and Wild Things,* Orca and Vandana were the only ones *living* who touched him inside the fortress he'd made of heart and mind. Djola hid the knives in boots, sleeves, and belt, then snatched up bag, scroll, and map. He tore through the ship, searching for his friends.

Pirates, captives, and the cook claimed ignorance, but they lied. Djola burst into Pezarrat's cabin. The walls glowed in the light of many lamps. Ten swords and two bows were aimed at Djola, and still the guards stank of fear. Maps and velvet throws were strewn about the chamber. Two naked women shivered on the bed. A hot pot under a messy table warmed Pezarrat's feet. Djola dropped the Jena City map on the table next to a knife-catapult from the floating cities. Pezarrat, wrapped in a dead black bear, looked up from his fish eggs and oysters, his face a mask of cool. A lie.

"They told me nothing of use," Pezarrat declared. "Well, Orca said you'd lost your wits trying to master *Xhalan Xhala,* but the spell of spells would not yield to you. Vandana said you'd finally found what you were looking for, right when *Mama Zamba* hosted spring." An eyelid and a nostril twitched. "Somebody had to be lying."

Djola shook his head. Vandana and Orca spoke truth.

"Either way, one betrayed you and one betrayed me, so both deserved death." Pezarrat scratched beads of hair on a sun-bronzed scalp—what he did when fearful. "I sold that *Mama Zamba* healer bitch. A snake in my house, like you. She was worth a new ship. Orca said I would choke on my treasure and die." He swallowed an oyster. "What captain allows that from a useless fat whore? I cut his uppity head off." He laughed.

The women on Pezarrat's bed clutched each other's bruised arms. The guards trembled. Pezarrat was lying, testing, joking, and telling awful truths. Distractions.

Despite waves of revulsion and rage, Djola kept his face blank.

"Feeding Orca shark stew and floating-city scrolls"—Pezarrat smirked—"your fault he's dead, you arrogant son of savages."

"Why should I care what you do to your spies?" Djola danced his mind still. With each spin and stomp, Samina's chill filled him. As the temperature dropped, the women scrambled to cover themselves with velvet. The guards lowered swords and bows, entranced. Pezarrat fingered his knife-catapult. Djola squinted his right eye at the Jena City map and touched the corner with his bare left hand. *"Xhalan Xhala."*

At the crossroads of crossroads, he imagined Pezarrat's future rising from the flames. There were many futures; Pezarrat's was easy to render. White flames flared then a gold nugget materialized. Everyone gasped. Djola's breath was cold mist. He pushed the nugget toward Pezarrat. A cloud of void-smoke, of possibilities lost, gusted out the window.

"I'll raid Jena City and pay off the last of what I owe you." Djola smiled.

"You'll join a raid?" Pezarrat fingered the gold. "What of your mission for Azizi?"

"What remains in the Arkhysian Empire for me?" The truth was the best illusion. Pezarrat clutched the gold. Greed warred with reason on his face and greed won. Djola would feel no remorse when Pezarrat died. "If it's a trick, you can set your guards on me." The guards trembled. Djola leaned close to Pezarrat. "Or we can get rich enough to retire to the floating cities. I've mapped Jena City's wealth."

"You speak truth." Pezarrat prided himself on reading men's hearts. "Our last raid."

2

Trickster

Dawn. The sea was gray glass. Thick fog tasted sour in Djola's mouth as he and Pezarrat's guards headed out in six large supply canoes. Muscular rogues with pirate pants cinched at the ankles, they all looked like Pezarrat: tight knots of hair, beady dark eyes, a greedy sneer on full lips. Men like this dragged Samina to a transgressor hut and abandoned his children to the desert without blinking. Men like this could sell Vandana and chop Orca's head with a chuckle and a fart. They deserved a poison-desert death.

The canoe slid onto a golden beach as fog burned off. Djola and the pirates strode along a boardwalk into Jena City. Nobody patrolled the sea entrance to the city, not even a dog—lazy arrogance. A cluster of mud-brick buildings was surrounded by warrior-statues carved from black lava rock. Flying beasts died on the warrior's blades; naked women were curled at their feet. Deserted merchant stalls swayed in the sea breeze. A stone well inlaid with crystals dominated the market square.

"Water is life—the greatest treasure." Djola touched cool wetness to his forehead.

Captives huddled in their own filth by the well. They waited for

a dousing and sale. Women, men, and young ones were locked together, but not guarded. They observed Djola with dull eyes. Thief-
lords did swift trade in human flesh. They deserved a poison death
too. Railing at the crossroads gods for their indifference, Djola
touched the captives' chains.

In the midst of murky tomorrows, he glimpsed a free future:
*people stepping off a waterwheel boat in the floating cities, enchanted by
garden barges and sky windows.* Locks burst open in a flare of light.
Crystals in the stone well swallowed void-dust. Djola barely had
time to register this. The captives shrieked. Djola used a *Lahesh*
blade to slice through shackles. "Run!" He pointed at the beach.
"Today we're free."

They gaped at his oozing eye and smoking hand. Nobody
moved. Djola couldn't reach the locks on their spirits. Shrugging,
he danced *Xhalan Xhala* around the market square and called
to the future of the thief-lord city. Whatever merchant house or
abode he spied with his right eye and touched with his left hand
burst into white-hot flames. After a blast of heat, cool treasure
glittered: a humble bakery became ten gold nuggets; a merchant's
palace turned into a bloody garnet; a spirit house dissolved into
yards of cloud-silk. Reckoning fire swallowed one building after
another. Samina's chill kept him frosty. The spell of spells had finally yielded to him.

"Run!" Djola shouted again at captives who trailed after him.
They squealed at flames roaring through Jena City's towers and
humble abodes. Djola shouted in *Anawanama* then *Zamanzi*. This
time many captives headed for the water. Pezarrat's crew wanted
to dash away too. "To me," he commanded. The pirates fell in behind him.

Terrified barbarians abandoned their homes and market shops.
White-hot flames seared those who were too fascinated, too slow,
or too dazed to escape. Half-naked folks, lugging children or an

armload of possessions, stampeded out of Jena City into the sweet desert. The city watch ran ahead of everyone, drunk, but swift.

Pezarrat's men gathered the precious metals, noble crystals, and numinous cloth that appeared when the flames winked out. "Throw a bit of fire, and thief-lords puke and piss themselves."

"Don't waste time laughing at cowards," Djola said. Void-swirls appeared from shimmer. "When this noxious air disperses, only toxic ground will remain." A small price to pay. Or that's what he told himself.

The pirates hurried back to the beach, weighed down with Jena City booty. Djola trotted behind them. His right eye ached; his head throbbed. His mind was a jumble, but Samina's chill eased pain. The sun was setting, the day over so quickly. Dancing *Xhalan Xhala*, Djola felt blistered inside. Relieving himself, his piss burned.

The pirates launched the canoes and paddled through choppy waves, glaring at him. Blood dribbled from his right eye as he glared back. Nearing the fleet, the guards fingered weapons. Djola sang a lament, and geysers of seawater erupted around them. Behemoth eyes glowed below the surface. Two giants breached, grinning and flapping fins. The pirates stared at shell-encrusted maws and froze.

"Hold your weapons. My friends jump at the flash of iron," Djola said. "Pezarrat wanted to assure the arrival of his booty, so, you have orders not to skewer me before I set foot on deck." Four behemoths circled the boats. "My large friends would be sad if you spilled my blood, so I'll stay in this canoe." A cloud broke apart and ice fell from the sky, stabbing everyone but Djola. One pirate bled from his eyes. The others cursed Djola for the storm. "Take the booty. Tell Pezarrat, I keep my word. Our last raid. I'll find my own way in the storm."

The pirates shook slush from their hair and scuttled up the ladder onto the flagship. Djola felt blank. *Xhalan Xhala* had hollowed him out. He bobbed in the water, free yet dazed, like the captives in the square. He'd found what he sought, but perhaps lost everyone he loved.

The behemoths ferried him up a river of ice to Bog-Town's docks. Nobody pursued him. Instead, pirates celebrated victory with music, wine, and the bodies of slaves. If Orca was dead, at least he wouldn't have to endure the victory party.

In the night, a high tide of hot seawater melted the ice in the Bog River. Djola paddled back to open sea. Seeing his canoe, captives jumped from the flagship and swam to shore. Nobody knew what had happened to Vandana and Orca. The women from Pezarrat's cabin insisted, "If he cut off Orca's head, he'd put it on display. If Vandana wanted to go to home, who could stop her?"

Djola wanted to imagine escape or a quick death for his friends. Not knowing was worse than seeing a body. Haints and restless spirits wandered the fortress he had made of his mind and heart.

Samina said: *End torture in the huts, on the sea, in the woods and fields.*

"Captain, I come to pay my debt," Djola shouted in *Anawanama.*

Pezarrat opened a porthole. "What jumba jabba are you talking? Have you come to kill me?" He was sober. Good. "Trickster, I don't know why I didn't kill you long ago."

"Greed," Djola said. The years on the pirate ship were vivid in his memory:

Buildings and ships dissolved into sludge.
Young boys drowned in their own blood.
Battered captives and pirates begged for a miracle in this life or
*   mercy in the next.*
On barren shores, old women pulled out hair and wailed over the
*   bones of the future.*

"You raid the future for trinkets." Following a rogue impulse, Djola touched the flagship and danced *Xhalan Xhala*. Reckoning fire engulfed the hull before Pezarrat could scratch the beads of hair on his sun-bronzed head. When the fire subsided, colorful baubles floated on dark water. Djola felt no joy, thrill, or even relief at Pezarrat's demise, still blank and jumbled. He paddled from one ship to the next and turned the fleet into pearls and glass beads. Those who jumped into the sea and left treasure behind survived. They avoided his canoe. In the morning, beads and pearls washed up on Jena City's beach. Survivors left these trinkets in the sand.

Djola wasted no time celebrating a hollow victory. He thanked the behemoths, turned his back to the sea, and, not quite right in his mind, paddled upriver to inland strongholds. Cutting a swath of reckoning fire through thief-lord realms, he handed out the poison-death the barbarians deserved, till he reached the border-lands and protectorates of the Arkhysian Empire.

On his march north, Djola called on Samina's chill but shunned Smokeland journeys to see her. Samina would think he sought re-venge and try to argue him out of his plan—an awful plan, yet he had no choice or that's the lie he chanted. Word of his deadly conjure reached Arkhys City. A letter from Grain was full of his exploits—exaggerated by griots, but true enough.

Xhalan Xhala showed the disaster barbarians and good citizens made of their world, and finally, the People listened—to the con-jurer who turned Pezarrat's fleet into trinkets and thief-lord cities into sky-stones. They cheered the master who promised a new world was coming. Yet, every day silvery haints cursed at him from moun-tain mist, sounding like Tessa or Quint. They asked who Djola had become.

"A clown," he told them. "Tricking people to their right minds."

Grain reported that enemies on Council babbled lies to Azizi. With no more pirate booty to fill Empire coffers, Azizi finally gave in to corrupt masters. He gathered mercenaries to protect grain and oil stores. He barred non-citizens from entering Arkhys City except on festival days and called for Hezram's Dream Gates around the capital. Illusion solution. So, Djola planned a carnival of destruction at the temple hall of the mountain gods during the Sun Festival.

What better place for reckoning fire than inside Holy City's Dream Gates?

3

Sentinels

A wa was barely awake, sleepwalking through the morning, a sunny day in Holy City, but on the forest floor, chill and murky as twilight. A splash of sunlight caught ferns and moss by surprise. Cathedral tree leaves rustled, pleading for mercy. Awa closed her heart to leaf-song. With hammer and blade, she chopped thick roots that anchored soil to Ice Mountain's rocky shanks. Interlocking roots ran from the edge of snowfields down to the Amethyst River. Ice Mountain was a family tree, twenty thousand years old according to Iyalawo Tembe.

Tembe wandered through the grove as too many transgressors climbed three-hundred-foot trunks to harvest seedpods or hack boughs. Freckle-skinned, yellow-haired Meera climbed higher than anyone and lopped off new red leaves for high priest Hezram's dream conjure. Meera was tough. Nobody caught her off guard and pinched her seedpod sack. She'd have kicked them out of the tree. Besides warhorses and bees, Meera was Awa's only friend in Holy City. Who could count trickster crows?

Iyalawo Tembe urged Meera on. Tattoos on Tembe's dark face lit up. She had northlander and floating-city ancestors, yet turned against her mountain, her people, herself. She urged everyone to climb higher for Hezram. Middle-aged trees fell over and rotted, a catastrophe for the soil, crows, and bees. Muddy mountain streams ravished fields in the valley. The Amethyst River complained, groaning day and night. Tembe ignored the wailing river and trees. She loved Hezram more than her mountain. Love was strange.

Cathedral tree oil for most of the Empire and beyond came from Holy City. The spirit debt for chopping and draining healthy trees to death was high, so this work was forced on transgressors who faced torture to the edge of death if they refused. Shrieks echoing inside mountain cells kept transgressors awake at night and hard at work killing trees in the day. Awa, with only one strong arm and a crooked leg, siphoned oily resin from the roots. After breathing tree-oil fumes for hours, she passed out. Meera hauled her to the temple for bleeding, and the afternoon shift took over root work.

After being bled twice in three days, Awa was no good for an evening shift siphoning oil. Hezram sent her to the fruit groves beyond the Green Gates to tend warhorses. These temperamental beasts were two hands taller than ordinary horses, strong as elephants, and fast as cheetahs. They stomped everybody—priests, acolytes, transgressors, but never Awa. The ancient Master of Horses was grateful for help the warhorses tolerated. Awa buried her face in Fannie's red mane—a shock of color against shiny black. Fannie nickered, happy to see her.

Cleaning hooves and brushing out burrs was the delight of any day. Fannie and the others enjoyed Awa's calm strokes, Green Elder songs, and occasional gush of sentiment. Nobody else dared to hug Fannie. Why not gush? The Sun Festival was coming. On this feast day, fickle ice gods might smile on anyone, even transgressors. Awa could hold on that long.

As the sun set, she whispered her hopes to Fannie, then limped unnoticed through twilight gloom to the mango grove for lookout duty. Her horses would wander back to the corrals on their own. Fannie would nose the latch shut. Awa scrambled into a squat tree, barging through waxy leaves and pendulous green fruit. One arm was useless for climbing, the other worn out, and she almost fell. Flailing, she squished a banana rotting in the crotch of the tree. Pulp spurted into her nose and eyes. With no time for an antidote, she was flying toward Smokeland for the first time since barbarians brought her to Holy City forever ago.

The border-void was endless, longer and denser than she remembered. Even holding to fear was hard. Finally, the cathedral tree forests of her first trip appeared. Smoke-walkers, with dull hair and empty eyes, stumbled about, bashing into each other. Their breath smelled of rotten eggs; their hearts were feeble embers, barely beating. They left a trail of rot and ruin in their wake. Awa almost choked. Her home region was crawling with spirit slaves in the thrall of a witchdoctor or priest.

Cathedral trees yanked up roots and raced away from creeping rot. Awa followed them, sliding into another region, then another and another. Devastation greeted her. Ashes clogged every wind, and the seas were putrid swamps, choked with rubble. Worst of all, spirit slaves overran the six regions of her heartbeat. Awa returned to her home territory and huddled behind a giant elder tree that sheltered a beehive the size of an elephant. Her first Smokeland hive, it buzzed with life. Tiny bee hearts made a cloud of sparks around Awa's face. The banana smell of alarm almost suffocated her.

"What can I do but run back to the everyday," Awa told the bees. "No escape there."

Spirit slaves grabbed any sentinel who flew too close and sucked down the tiny spark. Void-smoke drifted from vacant eyes as the fiends fed feverishly. Awa swallowed a shriek. This was how the border-void increased! Yari never told her that. She called the bees close. Spirit slaves shuffled toward her, nightmarishly slow, yet tracking the bees somehow. She tried to squash panic. Too much fear or fascination and she'd lose the speed of thought. Bal was not there to save her, but—

A conjure woman with purple dawn eyes and sandy skin tinged green, marched through Awa like a cold shiver, a strange sensation even for Smokeland. The woman's silver hair was streaked with red mica. Intricate tattoos snaked around her eyes. She smelled of buttery raintree blossoms. Her heartbeat was silver lightning bolts. Awa trusted that over embers. "Greetings . . ." Awa's tongue knotted up on words she'd rehearsed for Mother.

"Your breath body lies in Holy City. Dangerous." The woman spoke Empire vernacular with the musical accent of the floating cities. Her breath had the tang of a lightning storm. Cold radiating from her skin cut into Awa. "We should leave this region." She scanned the surroundings. Spirit slaves lumbered toward them. "Now."

"They'll devour the hive!" Awa balled her fists. "I won't abandon the bees without a fight."

"You'd die for bees?"

"Green Elders say, *I am the bees and the trees, I am the wind and the songs, the rocks and the dew, I am me and also you*," Awa replied. "Many bees have died for me."

"You're bold," the conjure woman said, "but no need to die." A spirit slave lunged from stink bushes, granite teeth bared. The woman jabbed something through transparent skin into an ember heart. Indigo sparks filled the fiend's body. Color returned to a kind face; the heart beat lightning bolts and brown eyes filled with tears. The fiend hugged a heaving chest, perhaps a fiend no more.

A *veson* nodded at the conjure woman and disappeared. "Free the heart, free the spirit." She lifted the giant hive and set it in a circle of cloth on her head as if it were a water pot. Sentinels swooped close, ready to sting her and perish. "Calm your friends." Awa danced with the light of a setting sun and urged bees into the hive. The conjure woman smiled. "Travel with me?"

Dazzled by her craft and beauty, Awa would have done anything she asked. "Yes, but spirit slaves roam the six regions." A few lumbered their direction.

The woman pressed Awa to a cold breast with her free hand. They rose up through green aurora to a cascade of stars and raced along a light bridge to a seventh region with a complex, blurry rhythm. Light reflecting off snowfields and frosted trees made Awa squint. The woman set the hive down on heather-covered cliffs by a crystal waterfall. "You and your bees are safe, for now."

Awa's exhalations turned to icy fog. She'd never been all the way to winter, never climbed Ice Mountain to its glaciers. She marveled at columns of ice growing in the stream that rushed over a cliff. Rainbow spirits played in curtains of mist. Cold burned her skin. She shivered. "Is it too chilly for bees?"

"They can rest, sleep, until warmth comes again." The woman wrapped Awa in a cloud-silk cloak. "Winter won't last forever."

Awa strained to catch the rhythm of this seventh region. The pattern escaped her. "Must be a difficult place to find."

"Impossible, almost." The woman circled the hive. "Have you seen the Master of *Weeds and Wild Things*? Djola he is called." She reached her hand deep inside the layers of honeycomb. "Djola is lost, but not his name, not his true spirit."

Awa shook her head. "I don't know him."

"You love the world." The woman dropped to her knees, cradling a sluggish bee the size of a hummingbird with three hot stingers on its butt. "We must find Djola before it's too late." She stabbed Awa's chest with a stinger the size of a dagger. Awa yelped at venom jolting her heart almost to a standstill. The woman kissed Awa's burning ears and whispered, "Do you promise to bring him to me?"

Water doused Awa as she said yes.

4

Lovers' Lookout

Through a blur of golden frizzy hair, rough hands slapped Awa's face. She was back in the everyday. "Wake up," Meera said, worry on her freckled face. Good friends were a rare treasure in the huts. "You're burning up."

It was night. The moon grinned at Awa. She had fallen from the tree with unripe mangos. Her head was on fire, returning to the everyday too fast. Horse-keeper Rokiat, a handsome acolyte who lusted after Meera, ignored sparks in Awa's hair and shook her so hard her thoughts banged into one another. "Wake up!"

"No real escape that way." Meera dumped a second bucket over Awa's head. Steam carried away the burnt smell. "Don't you leave me here alone."

"I wouldn't think of it." Awa lied. She'd thought of killing herself this afternoon, if only for a second.

"Well just don't." Meera hugged her.

"I said I won't."

They were outside the citadel's Dream Gates. Lying in warhorse meadows brought no punishment. Few realized this. Hezram conjured Illusion Gates in people's minds. Awa had mapped the limits of his power.

"Some lookout." Rokiat shook her again. "What were you doing?"

He was the banana culprit. He often brought fruit, nut bread, and coconut wine, then kissed Meera's lips and squeezed her breasts. Meera enjoyed the wine, and pretended to pine after Rokiat's silky black hair, almond eyes, and hungry lips on her pink nipples. Meera gave Awa half the feast to stand lookout. Since acolytes were forbidden to touch transgressors, they snatched new detainees behind dung heaps or shoved their victims into a crack in a wall where priests could ignore them. Few were so bold as to dump a dead girl in the temple or to pile on a transgressor with Hezram standing there.

Rokiat brought food or conjure books as payment and a blanket for the grass. Meera said this—and Rokiat's shining eyes—meant love. Awa was happy to eat feast food and read forbidden scrolls, but she didn't trust love. Rokiat thought he was a hero because he wasn't a fiend shoving Meera in dung and leaving her bloody. A true hero would burst from Ice Mountain on a winged beast and set Meera, Awa, and all transgressors free.

"What if I get caught because of you?" Rokiat scowled at Awa.

"I told you, never a banana," she shouted.

"Farts and fleas! Quiet." Rokiat peered through unripe mangos. "The rocks have ears. The grass tells tales."

"Who wastes night eyes on this grove before harvest time?" Meera said. "Fleas and farts?" She laughed at his colorful language.

Filled with awe, Rokiat tugged Awa's singed hair. "Did you fly off to Smokeland?"

"Green Elder drivel," Awa said. "Too many nights doing lookout. I fell asleep."

Rokiat frowned. He wouldn't tell anybody her secret. He'd do anything for Meera or his horses, and Awa was friend to both. "What's that?" He pointed to a Smokeland honeycomb and two dagger-sized stingers clenched in Awa's fingers.

"Oh. Look. See?" She displayed a fresh gouge on her leg to distract him.

"Whayoa!" Rokiat closed his eyes. Priests bleeding transgressors made him sick to his stomach. He cleared warhorse dung from the sundial courtyard, buried dead acolytes who had no family and weren't worth proper funerals, or oversaw any disgusting transgressor-duty instead. Other acolytes were glad to trade with him. Awa hid the bee-daggers in Bal's Aido bag hanging at her waist.

"That leg wound festers." Meera frowned at an old wound that wouldn't heal.

"Honey helps." Awa smeared a thin layer on her leg and the burnt arm that had oozed pus for two years. Smokeland honey dulled pain and prevented fever.

"Bees don't sting you?" Rokiat glared at the honeycomb.

"This cloud-silk cloak is beautiful." Meera stroked it. "Where'd you get it?"

"I don't know really." Awa folded the cloak again and again, until it was no bigger than a thin honey cake.

"Don't let anybody find that." Rokiat blinked as it disappeared into Bal's Aido bag.

"I won't." Awa drizzled more honey on her leg. Nobody, not even Hezram, had ever noticed Bal's shadow-warrior bag, which still held the golden wheel and marble eye from Smokeland. Great treasures.

"Come." Meera gripped Awa's squishy arm without gagging. Meera was as wide and strong as Awa used to be. Meera dug nails into tender flesh. Awa grimaced. Every step hurt, even on spongy grass. "We have almost a league to go." A league should take a person an hour to walk—Awa needed two. "Next week is the Sun Festival to the gods of Ice Mountain. The day of short shadows." Meera ran through mango trees toward Ice Mountain's rocky flanks, tugging Awa along.

"Preparations begin tomorrow." Rokiat ran beside them. "You'll work for me, burying the dead. A sickness takes many acolytes. Every day in the temple somebody pierces himself instead of a transgressor and then creeps off to die in our cottages."

"They lose their wits." Meera shuddered. "It's scary."

"Hezram doesn't want their bodies to fester." Rokiat ran ahead. He could do a league in half an hour. "I'll protect you from sickness and rogues."

"What could you do against Jod and his set?" Meera let go of Awa and danced around him, showing off the cocoon and carapace anklets Awa made for her. She shook the rattles at his crotch and tickled him with her toes.

"They're all thugs, still . . ." Other acolytes would have tormented Rokiat for his soft ways, but he rarely left the meadows, and everybody feared his warhorse friends. "I'm not afraid of Jod or the rest."

"Jod and his crew have no pity, no heart," Awa said. "You should be afraid."

"I'm not." Playing a brave man and risking all for Meera thrilled Rokiat. Lovesick fool. He could end up cut and bled too. Who would tend his precious horses then? Oblivious, Rokiat sang an epic in a dead language about a *veson* shadow warrior who defied emperors, had many, many lovers, and became one of the first Green Elders, roaming free, talking to the ancestors, and recovering lost wisdom. Someone like Yari!

Rokiat could make anyone's heart ache when he sang. He even charmed high priest Hezram. Next week after the festival, Hezram would put the old Master of Horses out to pasture and give Rokiat keys to *every* meadow lock. All the priests and cooks trusted good-natured Rokiat. He was the perfect lover if Awa and Meera were ever to escape. Awa tried to like him. She sang tree harmony to his song.

"Here we are." Meera ran for a tunnel hidden in prickly bushes. It led to the transgressor huts. Awa limped behind her.

Rokiat smiled at Awa. "You sing like whispering leaves." He turned to Meera. "You taste like sunshine." He unlocked the tunnel gate then kissed Meera's navel.

Meera pulled away. "We have to go."

Rokiat groaned, wanting to lick Meera all over. He watched her with a greedy eye, then came to his senses and locked the passageway behind them.

"I started off pretending with Rokiat . . ." Meera shivered with lust as they picked their way through the dark.

"Do you love him?" Awa was jealous, even though she didn't want Meera the way Rokiat did. A swarm of demon-flies flashed green and blue, lighting the way.

"Torch-bugs mean we deserve good luck." Meera smiled, in a grand mood.

"Everyone deserves luck." Awa sighed. "We call them demon-flies."

Meera squeezed Awa. "Something is about to change. I feel it."

The days before the festival, high priest Hezram freed transgressors at the ice god's whim; acolytes also bled some transgressors to death to fortify Dream Gates for the next season. Acolytes joked that Hezram might spare Meera. She was ugly—brassy yellow hair and freckled skin, but perfect body—big belly, breasts, and thighs. Or Hezram might spare Awa because she was beautiful—sable skin and midnight eyes, but broken—a burnt arm and crippled leg. Sacrifices should be one thing or the other, not a mish mash. Too much hope made Awa stomach-sick. Not knowing was torture.

"We don't want anybody to know about our tunnel adventures," Meera said, her feet flying over rocky ground.

"No." Awa gritted her teeth and kept up.

"Jod says, Iyalawo Kyrie is against bleeding transgressors to death. He worries she'll ride into Holy City on feast day with a troupe of spark demons to burn priests and acolytes and rescue transgressors. I told him not to worry. Kyrie won't do this."

"Why talk to Jod?"

Meera sighed and took Awa's good arm. "Kyrie only cares about *her* mountain and *her* trees, and *her* haint people. Ice Mountain is Iyalawo Tembe's concern."

Awa leaned into Meera. "Iyalawos marry their mountains."

"That wrecks the heart for everyday men." Meera shuddered. "Floating-city Babalawos plotted to poison Kyrie, but she made her one true love drink the lethal brew instead, and he died."

"I heard a different story." Awa couldn't remember the details.

"Kyrie is black lava and bitter ice," Meera insisted. "She eats her enemies' hearts and makes demon gates from stolen phalluses. Tembe is not that bad."

"Really?"

"Tembe loves Hezram. Kyrie loves no one. She calls up earthquakes and bad weather. A monster." Meera quivered, happy to have someone to rage against as they slipped from the cave into the back of their hut—a dead end for anyone without the key Rokiat let Meera steal. "We don't need monster Kyrie rescuing us." Meera kissed Awa's cheek. "We'll save ourselves."

Awa grunted at this fantasy, then touched Meera's smile and relented. "Yes, we will."

Sometimes illusions were torture. But not always.

5

Gifts from the Crows

The Crows watch as people throw good food in a deep hole and cover it with dirt. They screech and caw at stupid waste. They drop feces on faces and heads. An archer sends an arrow their way and only nicks one wing. The Crows take to the trees, blending into shadows to avoid his bad aim. They hope for carelessness, for bits of flesh left lying.

The sun is almost gone and people are tired from filling holes all day. They sweat and curse and gripe and finally drift back inside the gates. The Crows count. Three remain: Rokiat, Meera, and Awa. Rokiat and Meera roll in the grass, caressing and sucking one another. They are no danger. Awa uncovers the last dead bodies. She strips off yellow robes and caws, not the nonsense most humans do. Awa knows how to speak of *good food* or *danger* or *all is safe*. Awa sits in grass, chattering as Crows swoop down, watching as they pick and peck at a feast.

A wild dog pokes his head in her crotch and sprawls in her lap. Awa rubs his big gray head and keeps him occupied as Crows fill empty bellies. She knows their hungry days in endless desert that once was many, many forests. Too many forests to count, gone.

Awa knows sweet water and poison berries that humans can't eat, but Crows love. In these dry times, Crows face great dangers feeding anywhere. A hawk or night owl has better aim than Holy City archers, so Crows come whenever Awa caws. She never forgets them, never leads them astray.

A Crow with several white wing feathers does not feed with the others. This Crow flies close to Awa. She sits up, quiet and still, and the Crow hops toward her, despite the wild dog. He snores, lulled to dreams by Awa's fingers.

"I'm not dead meat yet." Awa says what many humans say to a curious bird.

This Crow aches from barbs caught in the chest and face. Eating is hard and pain is constant. Awa has hands that have plucked berries from bushes and honeycombs from a hive. The Crow has also seen these hands pull barbs from the wild dog and warhorses and from Meera and Rokiat. The Crow hops on a boulder, close enough for Awa to reach the barbs and pluck them out. Awa holds her breath. The Crow caws, speaking of pain, asking for help, hoping Awa is not stupid like most other humans.

The wild dog stirs and the Crow almost flies away, but Awa leans in, squinting at the barbs and shaking her head. A bee buzzes in a puff of hair. The Crow caws and caws. Awa reaches her hand out. The Crow pecks her fingers to make sure she will be gentle. Awa jerks away from the beak. The Crow caws again. Quick as an arrow, Awa pulls a barb from the Crow's white feathered breast. The Crow pecks her thumb.

"Zst!" Awa hisses.

The Crow pecks Awa after each barb, but she even tugs out one buried in the Crow's face. Relief.

"Farts and fleas!" Awa shakes bloody fingers. "Thanks to you too."

The wild dog jerks awake. His big head tilts to the side and his tail slaps the dirt. He dips down on his elbows and sticks his hind parts in the air. An invitation. The Crow spreads iridescent wings (which hold only a memory of pain) and struts toward the dog who lunges. The Crow flies just out of reach of powerful jaws and lands on the dog's back. Awa laughs as the Crow walks toward the tail. The dog twists around, catching a few wing feathers in his mouth. He tugs gently then releases. The Crow soars high and swoops down to tug the dog's tail before flying off to join the feast. Some succulent flesh remains. Awa holds her sides, laughing. Meera and Rokiat are laughing too. The dog licks Awa's fingers and trots into mist rising from the Amethyst River.

Rokiat and Meera take out a picnic of fruit bread and coconut wine. They enjoy a good meal in moonlight with the Crows. They leave many crumbs. There are warm updrafts and sparkly threads and stones from the yellow robes to play with.

Awa shoves the bones into a hole and covers them with rocks. "Green Elders bury the dead on high biers or in a rocky stream bed. This is where they buried Neth. Why take forever to become dirt?" She sings to the wind.

Meera and Rokiat listen before another roll in the grass. Awa has no human to roll with, not even the dog. She caws a lonely song. Crows answer and toss shiny stones at her. She catches one and smiles.

The Crows have seen what Awa did for the piebald one. They tell everyone her story. More Crows will follow her. She is famous, a friend to Crows, horses, wild dogs, and bees. As the moon rises, Awa sings human songs and hobbles away with Meera and Rokiat in a shower of glittery gifts.

6

Blood Conjure

Laughing with crows and the wild dog lifted Awa's spirits. She was out of breath keeping up with Rokiat and Meera, but the ground was soft and the moon smiled. The temple-mountain's ice-blue peaks looked serene, hopeful. Iyalawo Tembe had left Awa and Meera a pot of scraps and a sack of stale bread and bruised fruit instead of feeding it to the pigs. Perhaps Tembe was better than Kyrie. Awa and Meera might live through the week and dance at the Sun Festival. Rokiat was a fool for love and after the festival he'd have any key they needed.

Fannie was fearless. The warhorse would carry Awa far, beyond Hezram's reach. Good citizens shunned runaway transgressors or dragged them back to the huts. If Awa and Meera rode warhorses, folks would think twice before giving chase. Griots claimed warhorses could outrun death. Awa would head for the Bog River Gorge or the sweet desert and look for Bal and Yari. If she had survived, surely they had too. She felt stupid giving up hope when escape was so near.

Rokiat led them from the burial grounds past the warhorse corral to the temple. No need to sneak through a tunnel—they were a work detail. He stopped at a side gate and whispered to the guard, a drunken fellow who laughed too loud at whatever Rokiat said. Stringy hair covered his face and fluttered as he made rude noises with his lips.

"Burial detail is better than blood watch," Rokiat insisted.

"I'll bet." The guard leered at Awa and Meera. He reached for Meera's breasts.

Awa smashed him with Tembe's pot. "Not tonight," she yelled, as surprised as he was. "Not tonight."

"These two are mine," Rokiat said. Awa punched the guard hard, for emphasis.

"Fine." The guard swallowed wine. "I like watch. Nobody bothers me." Inside Green Gates, he was safe from marauding barbarians, and acolytes avoided the warhorse meadows. He could drink himself senseless. "I never do blood work."

They marched on. At the temple door, Rokiat kissed Meera one last time and fumbled with his keys. An acolyte barged out the door and down the steps. He vomited on sacred crystals in the square. Rokiat gagged at the man's misery or perhaps at the stench wafting from the temple. Rokiat was used to meadow air. Awa and Meera steadied him and they wound through the Temple's back corridors.

Preparations for the Sun Festival were in full swing. Dim chambers were filled with the breath bodies of Hezram's spirit slaves. They lay on straw mats and were chained to the walls, eyes open and unblinking. They smacked slack lips, struggling for air, and tore at rags covering their bony figures. Skin and muscle dissolved into dust. Soon there would be nothing for a smoke-walker to return to. Void clouds hovered above the wasted bodies.

Rokiat covered his mouth. Awa and Meera held their breath as they passed chambers with gurgling cauldrons where acolytes poured Hezram's tree oil and blood concoction into the mouths of new spirit slaves chained to stone benches. Awa looked away from limp bodies. Why carry their last pains with her? Better to remember people when they were alive. A careless acolyte got his finger chomped to the bone. He howled.

"We'll be burying him next week." Rokiat shuddered. "How many tonight? Ten? Breathing void fumes, acolytes rot inside—blood's not even fit for Hezram's conjure."

Awa grunted. Acolytes deserved sickness and death.

Jod stuffed a rag in the wounded man's mouth and dragged him out. Hungry spirit slaves strained against chains to drink the trail of blood. They were deadly in Smokeland *and* the everyday. Awa stumbled to a halt at the last chamber before the Temple Hall and the front door. She leaned against a scraggly cathedral tree, fascinated, disgusted. Rokiat and Meera tugged her in vain. Hezram was claiming a new spirit slave. Awa had never seen this.

A smoke-walker's breath body jerked and thrashed. Hezram drizzled poison in *vie*'s mouth and whispered a spell, until jerks became twitches, until eyes emptied out and breath was a puff of void-smoke. Jod poured blood and oil down the spirit slave's throat. Hezram moved on. He drizzled poison and whispered chants, renewing his hold on spirit slaves whose bodies had withered only a little. Jod fed each one, careful to keep his fingers clear of gnashing teeth.

A flash of indigo light filled the chamber. Hezram startled and scowled. Jod and other acolytes feeding spirit slaves halted as their charges became more agitated. "Someone got free," Rokiat whispered. "In Smokeland."

Awa was thrilled to hear this.

Jod loomed over Meera. "What are you gaping at?" He pulled her close. He sniffed her neck and licked her chest. "After blood conjure, a man needs something soft and sweet." He buried his face in frizzy golden hair and grinned at Rokiat. "Some burial detail."

Rokiat clenched a hand behind his back and held his breath.

"Look, another one." Awa pointed to an indigo explosion. When Jod turned and cursed, she snatched Meera away, and jumped in his face.

He turned back and looked right through her as he always had. "Fatazz! Who is doing this conjure in Smokeland?"

Awa shrugged—the conjure woman in the seventh region or someone else who knew a cure. "What's Hezram going to do? That's the question." She forced a smile.

"Yes." Jod raced to a dead smoke-walker—heart still, indigo light leaking from her eyes. Death was a doorway.

"Kyrie's work. Or someone like her." Hezram patted Jod. "Don't worry. Kyrie can't get to spirit slaves holding my Dream Gates. I'd eat her alive first."

Rokiat, Meera, and Awa raced through the glowing Nightmare Gates that trapped Hezram's spirit slaves. Lost souls got caught in the filigree of crossroads Vévés, but not forever—a third indigo explosion and someone was free. Hezram cursed.

"What happens to Dream Gates when Hezram runs out of smoke-walkers?" Meera asked as they slipped out the front door.

"Hezram says smoke-walkers hide among us. He looks for a spell to expose them." Rokiat winked at Awa. "Tembe says, no such spell. Anyone could smoke-walk. We just have to learn how. I believe her. Tembe is Hezram's keeper of spells." Rokiat unlocked their transgressor hut—a hovel built into the mountain behind the temple. Straw and rags were strewn on filthy ground. Dung burned in a fire pit. Folks huddled around dying flames. Rokiat dropped his voice—spies were everywhere: "Tembe's conjure book is what Hezram uses for everything."

"Why?" Awa asked. "Why help a monster?"

"Love," Meera whispered. "It makes women weak and men strong." Yet Meera let herself love Rokiat. "The people love Hezram too. He feeds on their love."

Rokiat squeezed Meera's hand. "Love is also a good thing." He locked them in.

The hut smelled like a festering wound. Awa shivered in the damp. Meera hugged her, radiating heat. Other transgressors eyed them. Awa passed out the scraps of goat and yam she'd gotten from Tembe. People snatched bread and gristle from her hands, muttering at how little she had. A big man barged through the crowd, grabbed the pot, and disappeared into shadows, before everyone got a taste.

Awa had considered hiding the food, not sharing, to spite the greedy ones, but she feared what they might do to her or Meera if they came back empty-handed. She also feared feeling so cruel. Every day new cruel thoughts. That's why she'd tucked mango in her Aido bag for the newest arrivals—*Zamanzi* twins, a boy and a girl, acrobats from a carnival troupe. She wanted to hate them, but they reminded her of Bal, muscular and fierce, balancing on one arm, dancing on high branches. What lies had folks told on them to land them here?

"Do you juggle fire? Shapeshift? Tease peaceful haints?" Awa offered the fruit.

They stared at her, surprised by *Zamanzi* words in her mouth. "We're warrior-clowns and we see what you do for us," the boy said. He was sharp angles.

"We remember this," the girl added. She was intense and earnest. Wearing Aido cloth robes, they almost faded from view, but weren't quite shadow warriors yet. They grabbed the last of the mango, nodded thanks, and swallowed quickly. Who had time to taste sweetness?

Meera pulled Awa down in the drafty corner near the door.

"You sleep first. I'll keep watch," Awa said.

"They fear you." Meera nodded at transgressors scuttling away from them.

"Me? You're the fierce one."

"You speak with crows and horses and the river. They don't know what other tongues you have, and Tembe trusts you."

"Tembe thinks we can be redeemed from the huts, like some of her drummers. Then we'd be loyal to her, even after death." Awa sneered. "That's not trust."

"You scare them. That means we can both sleep."

Awa groaned. "Someone could jump us in the night and—"

"All right. I'll keep watch. You're exhausted. Put your head in my lap."

Awa curled up against Meera. "If we die before the festival—"

"We're almost there." Meera stroked Awa. "Think of smoke-walkers escaping, indigo fire on their last breath."

Awa held up her Aido bag. "If I don't make it. Keep this. A shadow warrior gave it to me."

Meera put a hand to Awa's lips. "You get worried at night, but I say Hezram will choose someone else to sacrifice, not us. Someone worthy of the gods."

"He doesn't do it for the gods."

"I'll sing Rokiat's song. You'll dream of green hills and sea creatures dancing and you and me riding to Arkhys City." She sang softly in Awa's ear. Not the best singer, yet Awa drifted off and dreamed of Holy City exploding. She and Meera rode warhorses through indigo sparkles.

To have found such a good friend was impossible luck. Begrudgingly, Awa thanked the crossroads gods.

7

Yari

The Wild Dog whimpers. Yari shoos him away. The Dog woofs and stands his ground. He must warn Yari. They tussle outside a clay cottage built over a stream of water from Ice Mountain's glacier. Hezram's cottage. It reeks of the witchdoctor, of blood and oil, void-smoke, and the power piss of a big predator.

The Dog jumps up and licks Yari's face. *Vie* turns from his reassuring tongue and sets paws on the dirt. *Vie* smells of cinnamon, jasmine, and desert rose. Nut bread crumbles in a pocket and goat skin on *vie*'s talking drum tenses in the chill. Dry cocoons on swollen ankles smell of bugs long gone.

Yari should leave. The Dog sniffs fresh blood conjure on the wind. Hezram approaches, from a nearby waterfall. The temple stink clings to him despite a shower. It is still dim. The sun hides behind the mountain, lighting the sky, and not the bushes. They could run away. Hezram would not catch them. The Dog is strong. He jumps against Yari's chest, knocking *vie* to the ground. He grips a sleeve and tugs *vie* toward an escape route.

"Stop," Yari says. *Vie* glares at the pathway from the temple.

The Dog sits and sniffs. Yari is a jumble of feelings: anger, fear, frustration, and other scents the Dog can't quite read.

"You're a loyal friend." Yari scratches the Dog's head. The Dog puts a paw on *vie*'s shoulder. "I must persuade Hezram, trick him to his right mind."

The Dog tilts his head, whining. Yari should prepare for a hunt, a fight to the death.

"If I can't talk sense into this witchdoctor, go find our friends and get them far away from here. Survive!" Yari hugs the Dog's neck, tears rolling down *vie*'s cheeks. The Dog whines too. "You don't understand me, do you?"

The Dog wags his tail and growls. Hezram is close. The Dog turns his head into the scent. Too close. The Dog wants to rip Hezram's throat out.

"He's coming." Yari grabs a handful of the Dog's neck fur and drags him to the bushes. "Stay here, out of sight, even if something bad happens." Yari shakes *vie*'s finger at the Dog's nose. "Hezram would put a bolt in your heart."

The Dog crouches in shadows, ready to pounce if Yari needs him. He knows this hunt, one out in the open, one downwind from the prey. Hezram is startled by Yari and halts at the edge of the clearing, uncertainty on his breath. Yari marches toward him.

Hezram has a hand on a knife. "Is this an ambush?"

"No." Yari steps close. "You trusted me once. Trust me again."

"I was young and you seduced me out of my right mind. I'm a grown man now." Hezram pats Yari's cheek. "I hear you made fools of *Zamanzi* war chiefs and escaped."

Yari pulls Hezram's hand away. "Your spies are wrong. *Zamanzi* are rebels now. Warrior-clown allies."

"Forgiven?" Hezram wags his head. "How do you do that?" His voice is hollow.

"You talk your way into people's minds too." Yari's face twists. A smile fails.

"*Zamanzi* raided your enclave and murdered Isra. Why not kill the bastards?"

"I forgive them for myself." Yari tries to relax. The Dog tenses. "*Lahesh* diplomacy."

"The *Lahesh* have been wiped out." Hezram wants to bite someone.

Yari should bite him first. "You aren't the only master of illusion."

"I know why you've come." Hezram claws his hair. "You're against my gates."

"You invite the void to the everyday."

"Not just me." Hezram backs away from Yari. "Everybody is doing that."

"I can't reach everybody. I start with you, then the pirate master."

"Your wayward Sprites." Hezram laughs, but he smells sad. "I thought you gave up on the Empire and ran away, beyond the maps to make bridges to the future."

"The rebels are finally getting organized. I join them."

"Of course you'd join the clowns!"

They sniff each other, panting to stay cool. Hezram kisses Yari, but it is a lie. There is only fear in Hezram's sweat and bloodlust on his breath. A hunter hugging a deadly prey . . . Yari's breath is sour, a tangle of emotion. *Vie* clutches Hezram. "Let me show you what you've done, what you're doing."

"All right." Hezram leads Yari into the cabin and shuts the door. A bolt slides. The Dog runs close, whines, and paces. He hears murmurs and catches a jumble of scents coming from under the door—joy, fear, lust. They argue and laugh and curse. Silence. The scents fade. The Dog jumps against the door and scratches. He digs in the dirt till his paws bleed. He can't get in. Tunnels under the cabin take mountain water to the Amethyst River and also lead to the temple. The Dog has wandered there trailing Awa and caught Hezram's scent. If he goes to the temple he might find Yari and Hezram, before Hezram sucks Yari's blood and eats *vie's* heart.

The Dog races off as fast as he can run. He hates the temple: thrashing breath bodies, caldrons of oil and blood, clouds of void-smoke. He slips through an open door, looking like a gust of soot. Dazed acolytes almost trip over him, but he stays away from clumsy feet. They breathe too much void-smoke. It's killing them. Awa and Meera were here yesterday with Rokiat. The Dog will find them later.

Wandering without a pack in the temple is dangerous. Heavy doors slam shut at night. Some tunnels lead to nowhere. Priests hunt dogs and pierce them with swords or throw fire. Spirit slaves tear dogs to pieces. The Dog smells this, but can't turn back. He has Yari's scent and Hezram's, from moments ago. He runs, knocking down an acolyte who doesn't get up. Others trip over the boy and also don't get up. The commotion is camouflage. Nobody sees the Dog stick a nose in Hezram's chamber.

Too late. Hezram hugs Yari's thrashing breath body. He drizzles poison in Yari's mouth and chants in *vie's* ear. The Dog lunges for Hezram's throat. A pack of breath bodies reeking of Hezram leap up and block the Dog. No chains hold them to stone benches. Hezram barks and Yari joins the attack. A mass of fists and teeth try to bite the Dog's neck. They rip mouthfuls of fur from his back. Spirit slaves are awkward and confused in the everyday.

The Dog knocks Yari down and other spirit slaves fall on *vie*. Before they regroup, the Dog dashes out the door. Spirit slaves are too inept to trail him. They chase their tails and barge into one another, blocking Hezram. The Dog runs along the Dream Gates to the outside. Dazed acolytes don't notice him slipping out the citadel. He picks up Awa's trail and runs and runs until he sees her. She is beyond the warhorse meadows with Rokiat and Meera. They bury bodies—dead men who reek of temple conjure and void-smoke. The Dog charges into Awa and almost knocks her down.

Awa pets him. "What's the matter?"

The Dog pants and snorts, howls and whimpers. Yari is lost and it's his fault. He tries to crawl into Awa's lap.

"What happened to you?" She laughs, and the Dog nuzzles her, whining. "You're usually cheering me up." She lets him sit on her.

"We need a break anyhow." Meera strokes his back. He whimpers when she touches bare skin. "Did something try to eat you?"

Meera and Rokiat sit close. They talk softly and stroke the Dog's head as Awa puts bee spit on his wounds. Nobody licks him though.

"It's all right." Awa kisses his nose. "You got away to us."

The Dog licks her and falls asleep. In his dreams, he chases Yari and Hezram through Smokeland.

8

Holy City

Obsessed, relentless, and not quite right in his mind, Djola marched into Holy City. He hadn't been in his right mind since Zizi exiled him. No seed and silk potion dulled his senses and although Samina's chill cooled his temper, rage fueled his resolve. He pushed that thought away. It was noonday when Ice Mountain's highest peak cast the shortest shadow. Only Mount Eidhou near Arkhys City had a peak so high with ghost-blue glaciers frozen year round.

Barbarians, northern tribes, and citizens would gather this evening to receive blessings from fickle mountain gods. At the festival's end they'd pay tribute to high priest Hezram and his lapsed Elders and Babalawos, his witchdoctors. This was money snatched from the emperor's coffers, from roads and bridges, armies and waterworks. Water was fluid treasure, the Empire's greatest currency. Holy City squandered water, blood, and the wind too.

Hezram and his gang of liars deserved what was to come.

During noonday heat, people in Holy City withdrew to cool cellars for siesta, love play, or meditation. Only women's societies toiled to prepare feasts and dances while transgressors did penance labor—what no righteous person would soil their spirits with. Transgressors swept streets in Holy City clean of dung and set out flowers that seduced a riot of rare songbirds.

Djola donned a silver-mesh blindfold and headed for the festival plaza in front of the temple built into Ice Mountain. He tapped counterpoint to the hummingbirds with a blind-man staff. Cheerful cooks offered him fragrant honey cakes. Warrior-acolytes guarding the citadel's Dream Gates laughed at an unarmed, disabled supplicant. They assumed he'd arrived early to be nearest the water altars.

"Hope to catch a wayward miracle, do you?" one sneered and let him pass.

Sweating and muttering in character, Djola picked his way around clay cottages perched atop underground streams. Holy men stayed cool even with hundreds of lamps burning. Transgressors provided a steady supply of tree oil, wild goat, and ice from the mountain. Northlanders brought books, maps, and tapestry from across the world. Barbarian thief-lords offered children to bed. The holy men had no complaints.

Blindfolded, Djola was not distracted by luxury or other power-spells. Passing through the frosty metalwork of Hezram's Dream Gates, his skin prickled at cold conjure. He zigzagged over the stone altar square to the sundial courtyard. Lines of crystals marked the sun's transit across the sky. Whether Djola could see them or not, rainbow spirits from the crystals danced across his white robes. They were tricksters, playful one moment, deadly another. Djola's heart thundered in his ears as he praised the crossroads gods and strode over sharp facets poking his boots.

Nestled below jagged cliffs just beyond Rainbow Square was the only temple to the supreme god and his gang of minions outside of Arkhys City. This spirit house guarded the mouth of the

Amethyst River. Water for all green lands in this region flowed a thousand leagues from Ice Mountain to the Salty Sea—a perfect site for reckoning fire.

The stench of boiling blood and oil hung in the air. How did anybody get used to that? Tapping a crossover rhythm on the bottom step to the temple, a call to death and new life, he proclaimed, "I will bring your spirit hall down. Come to the sundial courtyard and witness defeat." He loosed a stiff wind to carry his words and awaken Hezram, once a carnival witchdoctor of dreams, now risen to high priest of Ice Mountain and, according to Grain's last letter, a candidate for Azizi's Council. Hezram had risen as far as Djola had fallen. Everyone in the city awakened to Djola's words echoing in the streets. Nobody believed their ears. Only a man wishing death would wield a weapon or weapon-spell inside the citadel's Dream Gates. Unafraid, folks abandoned cool cellars to go witness the miracle of god striking down foolishness.

Djola waited patiently for his audience who no doubt saw themselves as good citizens of the Empire. Few men were evil in their own minds, but Djola saw Holy City dwellers as bloodsucking demons destroying green lands. He savored their last breaths. The terror he was about to unleash would force everyone in the Empire and beyond to heed his words and change.

As feet stampeded through the Dream Gates, Djola called up an image of the spirit house in his mind's eye. Cathedral tree columns rose five hundred feet, anchoring glass walls and forming archways to the glory of the supreme god. The skulls of martyred saints leered at him from massive porticos. The flags of rich merchants and thief-lords fluttered on iron spires. Water rumbled through culverts and dams to the Amethyst River. The teeth of supposed traitors rattled in glass jars. Djola's teeth could have been there. Tree oil and transgressor blood bubbled and coagulated in iron pots—food for power-spells and dream conjure.

Djola's audience reached the stone altar square with a roar.

"Every midsummer, savages and fools come to curse the festival."

"This clown is too crazy to wait for evening cool."

"He'll be cold as a ghost soon."

Djola sucked up their enthusiasm for his imminent demise, removed a silver-mesh glove, and touched the bottom step to the temple with his bare left hand. He took a breath. Blindfolded, he relied on his mind's eye to dance *Xhalan Xhala* and show them their future. The mob halted fifty yards from him and hushed. Even men were wary of treading on crystals in the sundial courtyard. Only priests and warhorses were so bold.

A geyser of flame as wide as the spirit house spurted beyond blue sky to the stars. A chaste fire, it did not spread to nearby trees, but whirled tight against the temple walls. With each twist and turn, it consumed a wooden portico, glass facade, or stone tower. The mob groaned.

"So much fire. Does the fool burn?"

"I don't think so."

Djola pulled off his blindfold. Coppery skin burnished on pirate ships was salt streaked and taut with contempt. Full lips ran red with blood. His left hand throbbed. His right eye oozed burning pus. He must look like an angry demon. Confusion and disbelief spread through the mob. The temple was now a mound of sky rocks nestled in yards of cloud-silk—toxic baubles, like in Jena City. Brutal deities were trapped in the spidery orange veins of the turquoise. Four afternoon worshippers, three miners, and two acolytes tending transgressor blood in a front chamber were vapor. Only those deep in the mountain on the other side of Hezram's Dream Gates survived. Djola let out a breath of cold mist. He refused the hapless

278   **ANDREA HAIRSTON**

dead a heartbeat of regret. He hoarded regret for the deaths of his family.

"The temple didn't burn, did it?"

Ashes fell on their heads, but the good citizens resisted the evidence of their senses.

9

Witchdoctor

High priest Hezram, frantic, blue robe tangled, head and feet bare, raced across the sundial courtyard toward the whirling poison master. Hezram swallowed pride and fell to the ground by the mound of turquoise. Dragging silky brown hair and beard in the dirt, he kissed dung-coated boots and begged for mercy.

Witchdoctors, lesser priests, and groggy acolytes surged past the water altars onto the sundial. Sumptuous yellow robes cushioned clumsy falls as they dropped down behind their leader. Citizens, northern chiefs, and barbarians seethed behind the holy men. Warriors left armor and weapons outside the Dream Gates. They looked naked and foolish. A few howled. Behind the men, women dancers and cooks in festival robes hugged each other at the edge of the plaza. The women were careful not to desecrate the stone altar square with female flesh lest they call down more catastrophe.

"Festival conjure," Iyalawo Tembe declared. A wise woman with floating-city ancestors, she was the only woman who'd dare speak in the priestly citadel. "Nothing else burns. Impossible, a mirage, a carnival-spell." A robust figure, Tembe's skin was darker than Djola's, her hair a dusky cloud with streaks of gold.

She had green-flecked black eyes, like Djola. A fortress of knowledge pledged to Hezram, Tembe scowled at Djola and calmed the crowd. Those who still wanted to run from catastrophe were jammed in too tight to move.

"Don't worry." She spoke with a musical lilt. "The supreme god won't turn a blind eye and abandon the faithful."

The holy men knew better. The gods—if they existed at all—cared only for power. "Mercy! Mercy!" Hezram and his inner circle chanted, a few in barbarian languages.

"Mercy?" Djola had ancestors from north and south. Mercy rescued none of them. "What good is mercy or fickle gods or corrupt priests and lapsed Babalawos living on people's fear?"

Several books wrapped in *Lahesh* metal-mesh tumbled down crumbling steps. They landed by Djola's feet and raised a cloud of sand that stung his shins. The holy men choked on their chants as he thrust scrolls and books into the small bag slung across his shoulder. Vandana's bag, his bag now.

"Mercy is salvation in every religion. Why steal ancient books no one can read?" Hezram gripped Djola's thigh. "We welcome all gods in Holy City. Join us. Surely, Emperor Azizi would—"

"You're a pampered, backwater protectorate, sacrificing children." Djola shook Hezram off and dropped turquoise sky rocks into his bag—proof for Council. "Thief-lords pay tribute but tell you lies."

A musician beat her talking drum to say: "Lying in the citadel means certain death."

"You're a stranger, from the floating cities perhaps?" Hezram glanced at the dwindling mound of turquoise and a bag no bigger than a calabash. His mustache wilted and his smile cracked. "Inside the Dream Gates, it's suicide to lie. Weapons kill the men who wield them."

"Yes." Djola blinked aching eyes. Without a blindfold, he too was vulnerable to void-spells. "Barbarians and northern chiefs don't lie inside the citadel. They say nothing. They even avoid stabbing each other on the streets of Holy City. Beyond the city, anything goes." He dabbed his oozing eye with cloud-silk that fluttered back into the small bag of its own accord—Orca's spell. "Who believes in mercy? Tell me you don't worship catastrophe and power."

"What is this conjure?" Hezram gestured at Ice Mountain. Cathedral trees shuddered down burl-mottled trunks to leagues of roots. Branches flailed in the wind.

"These steps"—Djola pointed—"they go to the peak?"

Hezram nodded. "Climbing is prayer. The mountain is the supreme god's temple."

"Literally." A hairline crack zigzagged around Djola's heart fortress. Had he gone too far? No change without risk. The mountain quaked in the aftershock of his spell. The steps were shivering, crumbling. The devastation he called up ran deep.

"I don't understand what you've done." Hezram was curious despite rage.

"I only amplify what you do. *Xhalan Xhala.* What everyone does . . ."

"Impossible. *Xhalan Xhala* is a *Lahesh* tall tale." Hezram burnt his hand on encroaching sand. "Who are you?" Few witchdoctors or masters wielded more power than Hezram and they sat on the Emperor's Council in Arkhys City.

"You've been blissfully ignorant in Holy City." Djola barged past Hezram and addressed the crowd. "Floating cities and archipelagos refuse passage to Empire caravans and trading ships unless we hand over half the cargo at each port. Pirates steal what remains and sell our own goods back to us for profit and sport." There had been no sport in it for him. "Spies slip into our villages, poison wells, and pollute young minds, inciting rebellion for love of this god or that delusion." He tapped his blind-man staff against a clay urn. "War rages on every border. Tribes fight each other over goats and cheese, over stolen women and wounded pride. Over water and air . . . Poison desert encroaches on green lands, starving us all."

"Poison desert?" Hezram pulled blue robes tight against his muscular physique. "Why punish Holy City for other people's crimes?"

"You bleed even children for your power," Djola shouted. "Children!"

Tembe's drummers drowned him out. She danced and spoke. "Hezram conjures with transgressors. Their spirit debt is so high, dying in the huts is a blessing. We're not to blame for their crimes."

"We're all to blame."

Djola should never have offered Council his map to tomorrow without iron proof. His family paid for this arrogance. Tessa, Bal, and Quint were bone and ash, scattered in the desert where he could not mourn them. Samina walked only in Smokeland. Their suffering was Djola's fault, yet Samina helped him solve the poison desert mystery and asked him to *end torture in the huts, on the sea, in the woods and fields.*

"I live for change, not revenge." Djola smashed an urn in Rainbow Square. Water cascaded down the altar to the ice gods. "You celebrate lies rather than seek truth."

"What truth?" Hezram shouted.

Djola shoved him onto the crystal sun lines. "Your Amethyst River floods even high farmland during first planting and dries up before first harvest. The mountain god is angry. All will be desert soon. Yet for cool afternoons, scented thighs, and goat cheese, you chop down the mountain and doom your people." He'd said as much to Council, but now he had undeniable proof—a mound of poisoned turquoise. *Xhalan Xhala!* They'd have to listen to him.

"Don't lose faith." Tembe closed green-flecked black eyes and chanted. "This cannot be real. A demon conjure show." Good citizens closed their eyes and whispered with her. In a few moments the whole mob refused to look.

Hezram stood up. "We fight with nobody and pay Empire taxes. We are free lands." He leaned close. "For the secret of the Dream Gates, Emperor Azizi has offered—"

"All the People and the *Weeds and Wild Things* are free?" Djola said. "No. You lie inside your Dream Gates."

The Vévés rendered in *Lahesh* metal-mesh on the gates sparked and shuddered. Hezram clutched a necklace of poison snake heads. His spirit body got sucked to the borders of Smokeland. Djola watched him tumble through jellyfish spitting toxic barbs and fiends sucking heart spirit. Hezram jabbed viper fangs into his own breast. In a spurt of fire, his spirit body escaped the borderlands, but his heart stopped in the everyday. Wheezing one last breath, Hezram passed out at Djola's feet.

"What have you done, fiend?" Tembe hovered at the edge of the plaza, not willing to desecrate the stone altar square with female flesh even for love.

"Mercy!" Priests and acolytes pleaded with the mountain god to grant their leader sense again. The god was crumbling. No time for mortal woes.

10

Transgressor Carnival

Djola hovered over Hezram's glassy eyes and motionless chest. Many would die this day. Why save a scoundrel? Samina would never forgive Djola if he let Hezram die for revenge. She'd be furious about Tembe's mountain crumbling, no matter that Tembe was deluded, a curse to the mountain she served. No matter that bringing down the mountain was an accident.

Djola thrust a cloth soaked in aromatic salts in Hezram's mouth and pounded his chest until his heart found a steady beat in the everyday. The witchdoctor coughed, spit out the sharp medicine, and stood up. The lie had singed his beard and left a cataract in one eye. Hezram blinked and gestured at Djola's healing cloth. Even witchdoctors were obliged to pay spirit debts, but no man wanted to be beholden to his enemy. Reluctant gratitude twisted on Hezram's burnt lips and got mired in a curse.

"I'm already cursed." Djola tramped across what had been a temple to the sooty flanks of the mountain. Using a diamond-tipped blade from his boot, he sliced chains and kicked in the doors of hovels that had been concealed behind temple walls. Transgressors cowered in the dark, some ancient and white-haired, others not yet full-grown. All were bloodless and feral. Djola bashed doors until his muscles trembled and blood soaked the inside of his boots.

"Stop!" Hezram chased behind him, careful to dodge sparking dust demons from Djola's bring-down-the-temple spell.

"How much transgressor blood do you drink?" Djola pressed his staff against Hezram's racing heart.

The witchdoctor sputtered and froze.

Djola smashed in more doors. Samina had died in a hut like this. She'd pulled Djola into her final living journey to Smokeland and urged him to end transgressor torture. *Do this for me,* she said as they walked a starway over poison desert to mountain forests where evergreen woods and snowfields claimed her spirit body. These cold memories shielded him during *Xhalan Xhala,* yet tormented him afterward. He knocked the last door open. "How much blood and tree oil?" He hissed in Hezram's face.

"Those people do penance—" Every hovel door stood wide. Hezram shook his head. "For grave offenses—"

"Singing tree songs? Talking to mountains and dirt? Hush. I might have to break your neck if you talk on. That isn't part of our plan. Samina told me . . ." Djola spoke his wife's name out loud for the first time in two years. His tongue ached. "Samina said change, not revenge, is salvation."

"Samina? I do know you." Hezram scrutinized Djola from tattooed skull to booted ankle. "Emperor Azizi banished you. The Master of Poisons?"

"I am changed." Following another rogue impulse, Djola barged past Hezram. Prostrate priests rolled aside as he strode to the Green Gates. Tall as cathedral trees and wide as the courtyard, the ancient entryway was covered in rust and moss. With both hands bare, Djola pressed against the copper and iron lacework. The massive structure shivered and shrieked.

Nobody had entered the Green Gates from the courtyard in over a decade. Wild green lands were ruthlessly guarded treasure. Priests used secret underground passages to tend livestock or harvest groves. Witchdoctors opened the south gates to the Empire Road from the inside with keys, drummed incantations, and an army of warrior-acolytes.

Hezram chanted a witchdoctor spell calling the Green Gates to full power. Poachers who broke through metal lacework or scaled corral fences first lost control of their bowels, then their hearts beat out of rhythm as jumbled minds wandered. Raving and shitting blood, would-be thieves died of heart failure. Their spirit bodies increased the gates' power. As Hezram sang the last line of his spell, keening echoed in the courtyard. Djola shrugged at haints drifting through him—his heart and mind were a fortress. Still, challenging the gate-spell, the hairline crack around his heart twanged. He could live with that and a few farts. The gates swung open, tearing apart a snarl of vines and bushes. Rodents scurried from ruined nests, yammering with the good citizens whose eyes popped wide open.

A cathedral-wood corral enclosed a maze of meadows and groves. Fruit trees with heavy crowns nodded in bright sun. Wild flowers scented the breeze. A string of weaver ants bent leaves for a nest. Plump birds from the south splashed in a pond. A fat creature with a pink snout rooted in mud, squealing at worms. The hidden bounty silenced the mob and angered Djola.

"Even Azizi doesn't feast on ducks and pigs," he fumed. Would the world ever change? He answered this bleak question by touching his left hand to each side of the wooden corral, and without considering consequences, sent reckoning fire in a circle. He whistled to warhorses scattered about the fields. The fierce beasts gobbled one last bunch of fruit and clump of clover before trotting toward his Green Elder melody. He grabbed the halter of a hefty black mare with a startling red mane and tail. Tall and imposing, when she halted, so did the herd.

"Listen," he shouted at transgressors still hovering in dank doorways. "Now is your chance for escape. Leave Holy City as fast as a horse can run."

"No," Hezram shouted. "These horses belong to Emperor Azizi, for his farms and armies. They're long-lived and tireless, priceless. I can't allow you to steal them." He raised a hand as if to cast a weapon-spell.

"I'm no lapsed Babalawo to be felled by common conjure. Within your Dream Gates any weapon-spell you chant will target you first. I don't wish your death, but I won't save you again."

"A true Babalawo, a wise man, claiming the power of ancestors?" Hezram glared at Djola. He couldn't figure a way around his own conjure. "You planned this well."

"Actually," Djola said, grinning, "kicking in doors was an impulse."

"Transgressors are well-marked." Hezram smiled too. "They'll be slaughtered on sight or they'll starve. Sane people won't shelter them."

"I'm not sane." Djola heaved a large chunk of turquoise at Hezram's feet. "Payment for their freedom."

Nobody in the hovels moved even as Ice Mountain crumbled behind them. Djola heaved the last five rocks at Hezram. What else to do? Prisoners and slaves did not always welcome liberation. Samina set fire to her hut rather than leave it. Her ashes scattered—no memorial place to grieve her. Regret was where Djola buried his family. Cliff faces trembled and the supreme god wept icy tears. Cathedral tree roots wouldn't hold the temple mountain much longer. The Green Gates and corrals crumbled inexorably into toxic sand. Holy City was doomed.

"Time favors no one," Djola said. He must get to Azizi.

Two young transgressors, a boy and girl, *Zamanzi* twins from the north, scrambled from a hovel into the courtyard. Djola recognized new detainees from their nut-brown color, thick locks, and sweet sweat scent. They leapt from altar to altar.

"That's the idea," he cheered.

As the twin acrobats jumped onto a red gelding, a skeletal figure stumbled out a hut. Pasty skin hung from wasting muscles. Blood-crusted rags reeked. Wiry hair was patchy on a burnt scalp.

"Samina?" He reached for a ghost haunting him in bright sunlight. A man, not dead Samina, gripped Djola's hands, muttering gratitude. Attending to his next breath, Djola gathered his wits and pulled away. "Go on, man, escape."

Lesser priests and acolytes bolted up and chanted curses. The skeleton hesitated. Billowing robes blocked his path to the horses. Other transgressors grumbled and stepped farther back into the hovels.

"They're wiser than you," Tembe shouted. "They refuse to abandon the supreme god's judgment and desecrate our horseflesh."

Djola wanted to curse them all, but refrained from wasting heart spirit. Leading the black mare, he stomped through witchdoctors and priests to the hovels. Other horses followed. "Death comes one way or another. This way is freedom too," he shouted. A few brave souls ventured from every door. "Escape! Claim your lives!"

"What life would that be?" A transgressor yelled from the shadows, a girl. "We saw what you did." Unusual to hear an adolescent woman speak where grown men had lost their voices. "You might be worse than what we already suffer. Why follow your orders?" She asked a good question.

"There are better gods than these mountain fiends," he replied. "Somewhere there is free air to breathe. Time runs out for Holy City."

A horse stepped among the transgressors, unafraid. A storm of a woman, sporting a mop of golden hair and freckled skin, threw her arms around its neck and wept. The horse nuzzled her heaving sides. Priests and dancers howled outrage, but transgressors poured from the hovels. They hobbled around the sundial courtyard and gripped amiable steeds. Stumbling over priests, they pulled each other onto even frisky beasts. Bushy tails whacked bald heads; dung splattered naked feet. Horses dumped a few transgressors onto sharp crystals then nibbled shoulders, but trampled any priest who came near—like pratfalls from a carnival act. Tembe seethed at desecration as the golden-haired woman hauled herself onto her horse's back and trotted off.

"Wait." A young witchdoctor tried to calm a skittish yearling and got dragged toward the trees. A handsome fellow with long black hair and almond eyes, he threw himself onto the horse and charged after the golden-haired woman. "Wait for me."

"Ride fast, ride far, across the river." Djola spooked the horses into a gallop.

Racing across the meadows, they jumped disintegrating corral walls and charged onto the Empire Road. Ragtag escapees clung to their steeds as if it were a matter of life and death. They hadn't lost all spirit. When thundering hooves were a distant echo, the few remaining transgressors retreated into their hovels. The festival crowd hooted.

"Did that Kyrie witch send a demon to free transgressors?" someone yelled.

"Kyrie would never do something like this to Ice Mountain," Tembe yelled back.

Barbarians reached for absent weapons and clutched air.

Northern chiefs made signs to ward off evil. Priests and acolytes tore at their beards and wailed. Tembe and the cooks ululated. Drummers accompanied their distress. Finally believing their eyes, the good Empire citizens stomped over each other to escape the doomed plaza.

11

Garden Sprite

Djola allowed himself several belly laughs. Mirth banished ghosts and cleared his head, but the hairline crack around his heart widened. He exhaled slowly and pulled a travel cloak from Vandana's small bag. He'd done what he could, more than he thought possible.

"The trees weep," the feisty young transgressor said. She held a withered arm close to her body and dragged a wounded leg. An Aido bag hung at her waist, barely visible. Crystals cut her bare feet. Wiry black hair was filled with straw and clumps of mud or worse filth. Red rivulets streaked a once-green shift. Priests had bled her recently. The black mare lifted her head and neighed. The girl staggered toward her.

"What are you?" Djola squinted at dangling seed earrings and an anklet fashioned from catalpa pods, beetle carapaces, and dead bees. "A Garden Sprite?"

"They don't see"—the girl's wide nostrils flared—"but I know what you did."

The last of Djola's audience grumbled useless death threats at her for desecrating the sundial courtyard. Hezram hushed them with a sweep of his arms. An acolyte stuck out a foot to trip her. She stomped him and, from the crunch and yelp, broke bones in his leg. Djola grinned at this emaciated young survivor. She hobbled to the mare's nose, getting a tongue across her cheek and a nip on her ear.

"Everyone should run." The girl's voice cracked. "The mountain falls to its knees and poisons the Amethyst River. The air turns bitter." She clung to the mare's luxurious red mane, wheezing. Her body was weaker than her spirit. "You make a wasteland. Across the meadow, trees moan. The dirt dies and honeybees are wailing."

High priest Hezram took a sharp breath, and Djola nodded. This was proof Council could not deny. This Sprite saw what others could not. "Was your transgression flying with bees?" Or smoke-walking like Samina? No. The girl would be dead or somebody's spirit slave. Maybe her crime was withered limbs and a sharp tongue.

Hezram lurched into the green-land meadow. He hugged muddy blue robes to heaving ribs and spoke priestly nonsense. His prayer couldn't stop disaster that he and good citizens had begun years before this festival of reckoning. Hezram scurried from encroaching sand onto still green grass. His ankles were red and blistered. "What have you done?" Fruit trees crumbled.

"Don't blame me," Djola replied. "Not a curse or weapon-conjure, but what you've been doing for years, what everybody does across the Empire and beyond, only faster."

Hezram gazed down at dying grass. "What do we do like this?"

"You know better than I do."

"Escape!" Tembe led drummers along the edge of the stone altar square and through Green Gate rubble. Barbarians, priests, and cook women stumbled behind her toward the Empire Road. "Our world comes to an end."

"The wise woman speaks truth," Djola said. "The end of days. Change or die."

Djola tucked two yards of blind man staff into Vandana's bag and leapt onto the black mare. He gently pressed his legs into her sides. The horse took a reluctant step then rested her head on the young transgressor's shoulder. Djola pressed the mare again. She didn't budge. The girl clutched the thick red mane. They were old friends.

"I guess you're meant to come with us. I ride to Arkhys City to the emperor." Djola extended his right hand. The girl glared at silver-mesh and stepped back. "The glove is protection. Besides, my left hand calls reckoning fire."

"And your right eye sees it." She grimaced. "I watched you."

"You have nothing to fear from me."

"I would ride with death."

"Would you rather stand with death?"

The courtyard quaked. Cliffs collapsed into the Amethyst River's underground channels. Green leaves turned to golden ash in a whirlwind. The girl changed her mind and gripped Djola's wrist. He hauled her up behind him and sang a Green Elder melody. The mare gnashed her teeth and rose up on powerful hind legs, a warhorse ready to chase death. They rammed past Hezram who fell on his face as the mare charged down the Empire Road.

The girl never understood why the Master of Poisons decided to take on a transgressor at the start of his triumphal return to Arkhys City and the emperor's court of power. All he would tell her was:

"I'm the end of a story. You are a prelude to change."

12

Escape

The outskirts of Holy City rushed by in a blur. Awa was sick with dread. She couldn't see, couldn't think. She wanted to leap off Fannie and run. A sliced-up leg wouldn't carry her far, and the warhorse scrambled through rocky terrain too fast. A fall would break Awa's neck. And could she abandon Fannie? Trapped behind a monster, Awa balled her strong fist and moaned. That was better than silence. She and Meera had dreamed a different escape. They'd stashed coin, clothes, and food in the meadows and planned to steal Fannie and Bibi.

Meera had people to run to across the Amethyst River, far away north near Arkhys City. Rokiat was one ceremony from Master of Horses and witchdoctor of the Green Gates. He could have unlocked another future for them tomorrow. Awa understood Rokiat abandoning her, but Meera rode Bibi down the Empire Road without a glance in Awa's direction. They'd shared food, dreams, and secrets, even despair. In fact, Awa was more a hero than Rokiat. She'd risked herself several times to save Meera's life. Awa swallowed a scream.

Actually, she was mad at Meera for not being Bal. "Zst!"

"Do you curse a hero?" the poison master shouted into the wind.

He was a tall man, muscular, fierce, confident in his power and used to respect. Blue and green tattoos on his smooth bald head shimmered with silver. He had made his mind a fortress. Silver tattoos must cover his heart. Awa shuddered. She rode with a handsome fiend who felt nobody else's pain or joy.

"Too often, the heroes or gods we bow down to become the monsters that stomp our bones and drink our blood." He translated a line from *The Green Elder Songs for Living and Dying* into Empire vernacular. Awa was unimpressed. Everyone made fun of Green Elder wisdom. She had done so herself as a young Sprite. But *The Songs* were no longer blather she mouthed to satisfy Yari, Isra, and other Elders. Too much had come clear to her for easy laughter.

"Our hearts betray us," the poison master said. "Do you understand?"

Awa shook her head. Her heart ached from Meera abandoning her and even more from older wounds. She couldn't blame Father, Mother, or her brothers for all her misery. Awa was the fool who had abandoned Bal and Yari.

"You spoke freely before, child. Why be silent now?" the poison master said. "Fatazz! I bet you're older than you look with a good story to tell."

"I'm soon twenty." Awa clutched Bal's Aido bag. "Life in a Green Elder enclave was a good story, but that time is gone, a griot tale for children."

The poison master startled Awa with Green Elder song-conjure:

Gray is the day—bleak is the way—cracked is my heart, yet—
Every breath a wonder, every moment thunder
Miracles crashing the night
Offering a blaze of light

He did harmonies, polyrhythms, and overtones.

Where do we start—lost is my art—cracked is my heart, yet—
Every beat a wonder, before we're torn asunder
Miracles crashing the night
Offering a blaze of light
Dance and sing while the wind blows
Where our ashes land, who knows?
Leap and soar while the rain falls
We must be ready when the spirit calls

Winded, Fannie slowed down, despite conjure music. Even a warhorse couldn't run forever. They trotted along the tree-lined banks of the Amethyst River. The surrounding green lands were not as lush as Hezram's preserve, yet the smell of goat manure, mangoes, and corn soothed Awa.

Farm laborers, who had no time for festivals, dotted the fields, threshing a second harvest. They halted as talking drums warned outlying villages and farms of disaster charging their way. Awa looked back at Holy City. Dream Gate towers and blue treasury cupolas were still in sight. Fear and death rode the wind and stung her eyes. As she blinked, blue cupolas blurred into red-tinged sand.

"Good citizens guzzled transgressor blood; it explodes through their skin," the poison master said without looking.

Awa marveled. "The gates hold fast."

"Of course. Silver lacework is cold conjure and impervious to fire and dust storms."

"And when no acolytes feed spirit slaves blood and oil?" Awa bit her lip.

"They become void-smoke. I could teach this spell to one such as you in an hour."

"Why teach me?" Awa asked.

"You see what hides in plain sight."

Awa squinted back at the city. "Why teach anybody a nightmare spell?"

The poison master bristled. "Ignorance won't save us."

"Neither will arrogance." Fannie flicked her tail, as if she agreed.

Cottages and bridges collapsed on dancers, priests, apprentices, and laborers. White flames scorched the sky, claiming crows, hawks, and rare songbirds who'd come for the festival. Sand fell instead of afternoon rain, searing the dead and dying. Trees couldn't get up and run in the everyday. Seeds flung into the wind burned. Few people or animals would escape. The devastation was too quick-moving. Awa's brothers might be poison dust if they hadn't already moved on to Arkhys City, Meera and Rokiat too, if their horses weren't fast and sure. The trees wailed mourning. Awa croaked a harmony to the burning branches and crackling leaves.

"Do you curse a hero?" The poison master asked again, low in his chest. A threat?

"What hero?" Awa said. Was he truly deluded? "You?" She bit her tongue too late. Living in a transgressor hut, she usually sassed in her mind, keeping her spirit alive without risking her neck. Tree song made her reckless.

"Heroes are fools," he said. "I curse them too."

Farm laborers ran around Fannie, heading toward disaster, toward families trapped in a city turning to poison desert. The poison master warned them to turn back, but they continued going in the wrong direction. The poison master finished his song:

Lost is my art—cracked is my heart, yet—
Who knows what tree grows
I say, who knows what tree grows
In all our lost art
In the crack in my heart

The piebald crow soared and dipped in time with his melody, warning the flock. Awa wanted to urge crows to peck the poison master's eyes or call bees to sting him.

"Green Elders say folks who curse others waste passion," he said. "Worse, they curse themselves. Squandering heart spirit on ill will supposedly hastens death."

"In Holy City, I never saw curses turn back on anybody, even *inside* Hezram's Gates—except a weapon-spell." Still, she'd refrained from cursing priests, *Zamanzi*, barbarians, Father, Mother, or brother Kenu. Conjure was a long game. Power for spells was borrowed from the same well that nourished heart spirit. Blessings *might* fill the well; curses drained the heart for sure. "Reckoning fire awaits conjurers who abuse borrowed power."

"Maybe," he growled. "How did you survive the huts without curses?"

Awa unsettled stomachs or called bees to sting bald heads, outside the Nightmare Gates. She put the vilest characters out of commission for days, provided a respite for everyone, and never killed a soul. Wielding a polyrhythm of curse *and* blessing, she let people poison themselves. Even stomping Jod in Rainbow Square had been self-defense, not revenge. Hopefully she hadn't wrecked her heart spirit slaughtering so many cathedral trees.

"I poured libation to crossroads gods." Awa lied with truth, a Holy City habit.

"Curses lurk inside you," the poison master said, "for fathers and witchdoctors."

"I curse nobody," Awa said. The poison master was probably beyond her modest skill, like Hezram. "A little torment. Trickster crows are happy to oblige."

"Good girl." He nodded as they left grain fields behind and rode into a scrub brush wasteland. Cathedral trees hugged the riverbanks. "When I was a captive on a pirate ship, I cursed too many folks—ruined my heart."

Awa considered him with new interest. Such a powerful medicine man had been a captive? Despite the fortress-spell, he rubbed his chest as if his heart ached for the evil he'd done. Rumbles under the roadbed interrupted her inspection. "Do you hear?" she said, a challenge as much as a question.

The poison master tensed. "The roots warn us, warn everyone."

Trees swayed as if in the grip of a tempest. The Amethyst River twisted around a bend and swelled over its banks. Torrents of mud-brown water inundated its placid blue-green currents. Swarms of insects rushed ahead of feasting bats.

"Zst!" Awa said.

"What? Do the roots say more?"

Awa shook her head. "My friends Meera and Rokiat raced off on warhorses. I don't know which direction they took." She was furious with them, yet still hoped they'd made it across the city bridge. "Meera and I would have ridden off *together*, tomorrow."

"What about the other transgressors tomorrow?" His anger was a smack.

How was Awa responsible for them? "We planned an escape, not a rebellion."

"Apocalypse on our heels. We must all hurry." Singing conjure music, he urged Fannie to a fast trot.

"Even she won't last at this pace," Awa said. "Flesh and blood have limits." Escape with one rider would be faster.

This must have also occurred to the poison master. "I can't

abandon you, child. The mare loves you. A broken heart won't take me far."

Fannie slowed to a pace she could maintain without breaking her heart.

13

Glory and Love

A few hours of freedom and Awa's head throbbed and her butt ached. The poison master reminded her of compelling fiends in the border-void who could unravel the best minds. Yet the headache was her own fault. She could never help thinking a knotted thing apart. This was her genius and also torment. Most Sprites played first thought against second and third thoughts and, no matter the clash and confusion, held the polyrhythm for truth. Awa never stopped at a clash of three or five or seven or . . . How else to survive Smokeland or a transgressor hut? She hadn't forgotten herself after all.

Fannie hesitated, wary of sludge surging across the Empire Road. The poison master caressed her neck and ears and melded his body to hers as she scrambled into brush away from deluge. Monster and all, he was a true horseman. Awa pressed her face into his icy cape and clung to his waist, praying he wouldn't get thrown.

"Just water," he murmured, coaxing Fannie back to the road. "Water will save us. Water is life." He whispered about the wonders of wetness and the miracle of muscle and bone. Was he a lapsed Elder like the traitors who helped *Zamanzi* raid her enclave? Or a

Babalawo, a father of mysteries from the floating cities gone witch-doctor rogue? "You know water," he said, calming even the screeching crows. "You are water."

"We're all water," Awa mumbled, "still—" Too much water ripped and roared toward the narrows and the only bridge outside Holy City for leagues and leagues, a triple-arch stone structure on disputed land that nobody tended to. "We could be trapped in this valley between a flood and a deadly sandstorm."

"I know." The poison master didn't seem like a suicide. This flood must be more destruction coming faster than he had expected.

Awa couldn't really fathom what he had expected.

"Rogue impulses." He talked to her thoughts. Hopefully he wouldn't make that a habit.

Fannie stumbled on through refuse battering the road. Rather than worry about drowning, Awa lost herself in the polyrhythm of blood beats. The horse's heart was a bass djembe drum, half the pace of the man's. The crows' treble hearts went too fast for counting. Awa's heart played among these beats. Sprite discipline rescued her again. Still alive, why fear death and spoil your moments? They managed to reach the narrows before an exhausted mount dumped them in brush or the flood swept the road away. Awa smelled Holy City deluge gaining on them, a burnt blood and raw sewage odor. Cathedral trees bellowed as the ground quaked and tore up their roots. Across the river, the distant foothills of the Eidhou mountain range beckoned.

The Narrows Bridge was a worse wreck than Awa recalled. Abutments, piers, and arches were missing stones. Railings dangled over the side and got buffeted by debris rushing down the river. Muddy refuse skittered across the roadway. One more flood would wash this bridge away. That could happen this afternoon. Crows chattered worry and hope. Fannie took one step onto the bridge and balked.

"So much water. And the bridge wobbles like a loose tooth," Awa said. "Too risky for her."

The poison master glared at a whirlwind of ash and sand coming their way. "More risk if we don't cross." He jumped down and urged the mare a step at a time to the middle of the roadway. Slow going.

Uprooted baby cathedral trees, crashing and banging like giants at play, careened around a sharp bend in the river five hundred feet from the bridge. Rubble from cottages, libraries, and granaries had gotten caught in a rush of roots and branches. The tangled mass surged forward and smashed the center piers. Books went flying and glass shattered. Branches exploded into splinters. Grain fell like rain. The bridge shuddered as if it meant to come apart. Fannie kicked the poison master's leg. He stumbled to the edge. Gripping Fannie with her thighs, Awa leaned over and yanked the strap of his bag with her strong hand before he tumbled into the water. Horse, man, and young woman slid through mud along a gap in the railing.

"Whayoa!" The poison master spread his cape wide, catching a rush of wind and slowing them down. He hurried them away from the railing over soggy scrolls and choking fish. Shrieks made him halt and turn. "Zst!" He tugged Fannie's halter, but she wouldn't budge.

A ten-story tower bashed into cathedral trees wedged in the river bend. Bright faces peered from barred windows. Rich, blood-sucking southerners were weeping and wailing at the mountain gods. Feeding on tree oil and transgressor blood, they'd expected protection from catastrophe and a long, long life. They clawed at bars meant to keep danger out. Awa hated their rosy, well-fed cheeks. A boy of thirteen or fourteen bled from his eyes. Awa gritted her teeth against a thrill of pleasure. In a moment, tree trunks would snap and the tower would smash the bridge. They were all doomed. Her last thoughts should not be spite or fear.

When *Zamanzi* raided the crossover ceremony, Awa should have chosen warrior, like Bal, no matter the risk. Soldiers ignored the mysteries and trained to survive destruction and death. They experienced glory and love. But no matter her bad choice, Awa had puzzled impossible questions, collected life and death stories as a griot might, and smoke-walked to a seventh region of snow and ice. Drunk on Rokiat's coconut wine, she and Meera had sworn never to leave the other alone. Even if Awa had faltered recently, she'd meant every word. That was glory and love, no matter what Meera did in return.

"You there! Help us!" Southerners shouted in the staccato tongue of barbarians. "Please, have mercy."

Nothing to do even if Awa wanted to. Fannie was paralyzed. Heartbeats raced out of time. Tree trunks with thirty-foot diameters snapped like twigs. A servant jumped from an open balcony and got smashed by debris.

"Run!" The poison master smacked the mare's haunches. "Run or die!"

Fannie leapt forward. Awa clung to her mane. Her heart quickened to an impossible pulse as fear flooded her despite Sprite discipline. Solid ground and stout tree trunks shimmered like a mirage. The opposite shore was too far, even at a gallop. The tower rushed for the bridge. They would need wings to escape the collision alive.

"No! Please! *No!*" Awa screamed with the blood-sucking southerners. "Mercy!"

The tower rammed the bridge.

14

The Amethyst River Speaks

Mercy? You have stood on my banks, oblivious. Who are any of you to ask for mercy?

I am your sweat and spit, and tears of joy, but you do not know water.

For a thousand thousand years and more, winding through rocks, slipping downhill to the Salty Sea, I cut gorges and pounded out waterfalls. I hewed these green lands from barren rock and brought mountain riches to meagre soil. This valley was my garden grove. I nourished roots, called up clouds.

The wind whispered its secrets to me. The sky rode my back, blue, green, and white froth. Falling stars cooled in my mud. The moon tugged me toward its cold bosom. I hosted rainbow spirits, brought the dead back to life, again and again.

What do you know of mercy? Do you mourn waterfalls or gorges become barren cliffs? I have drowned hopes and swallowed despair. For a thousand thousand eons, I ferried life more leagues than you can count. You say, we are all water; water is life. Empty talk.

I am three thousand leagues all at once, ocean too, reaching the floating cities and beyond. I am glaciers and steam and clouds and blood. You are fools, come and gone in a blink, stuck in one small splat of time, running *in circles, ruining wherever you touch down. Your poison in my water has killed many with no return from death.*

A hairy mammalian weed, why should I offer mercy to you?

You let loose a fury in my stream, breaking the pattern of my patterns, drying up my dreams. Who will hold me? What will guide me? Water is life, but what do you care that I am river no more, but a deluge, and afterward dry dead land making a lethal storm of the wind?

Mercy? Hosting this last rainbow, I—

15

Monsters

Darkness swirled behind Awa's closed lids. The pattern of her be-ing was faint. She might have slipped into the death lands, except irritating river talk made her heart pound, made her gasp in breath.

"Mercy is a miracle," Awa croaked at the Amethyst River. "To give or receive . . ."

And who believes in miracles? The River replied.

"I should be dead, I was dead, but . . ." Awa's temples throbbed with the beat of hooves on solid ground. "I'm alive again."

Yari claimed that every moment was a gift, a miracle, yet de-spite dazzling experiences in Smokeland, Awa never understood miracles until now. Coming back from the dead, she found joy in needles of rain cutting her skin and in panic sweat drying under her arms. Bird shrieks from up, down, and sideways were a sere-nade. Crow slurry sailed past her nose and jolted her eyes open. The poison master sat behind her now, holding her up, and she was thrilled to be cradled by a monster.

"A wonder . . ."

The sky spun more than darkness had. She blinked a gray hori-zon into its rightful place. Night was coming. The sun was pink haze behind a high canopy of trees. Dry fields had given way to the foot-hills of the Eidhou mountain range. Cathedral trees covered every ridge. They'd traveled far. Awa must have been dead to the world for a long time.

"I wasn't sure you'd come back to yourself," the poison master murmured, relieved.

He pulled things from her hair and tossed them to the wind before she saw what filth it was. He thought himself kind. Were all monsters deluded? He touched her withered arm with a soothing balm. She flinched all the same. Gravelly-throated crows swooped up from the valley and chattered about survivors trotting toward them.

"We're only a few leagues ahead of good citizens who might want to stone us," he said. "The carrion-eaters celebrate every-body's heartbeats." He had a smile on his tongue. "Hearty folks from Holy City ride warhorses also."

Perhaps Meera and Rokiat had ridden impossibly far too. Awa smiled. "Miracles."

"Yes. We're on high ground," he said. "Safe."

Awa frowned. "No matter what miracle you did on the bridge, we're not safe. Did you hear the Amethyst River? Your death-spell hounds us still."

"Not *my* death-spell. The People die from their own poison." Rage burned through his icy cloak and stung her. "Reckoning fire does not consume a good heart."

Fannie snorted as the incline got steeper. Her hot breath fogged in cold drizzle.

"But—" Awa's tongue was heavy. "So many die who were not to blame."

"A person always has a choice."

"Living in a transgressor hut, we—"

"Can you swear you did nothing to cause poison desert?"

"No, I, I . . ." She chopped roots and tried to forget herself for two years.

"Did you resist? Any of you in the huts?"

Awa shrugged. "We just survived."

"I thought as much," he muttered. "Throughout the Empire, people are *just surviving* and so water, air, and earth become poison."

"What do you know?"

"Denial is worse than poison sand."

Awa shuddered. "Everyone has spirit debt . . ." She never imagined resisting, only escape—an impossible dream each night that sometimes included Holy City crumbling into poison sand. Prayers danced to the crossroads gods were always for sweet revenge that wouldn't trouble her heart spirit with more debt. The poison master's bring-down-the-mountain spell had answered these prayers.

"What happened on the bridge?" She changed the subject. "Tell me."

"You saved me," he said. "Thank you."

"I didn't mean to."

He chuckled. "Rogue impulse."

"How did we escape the tower collision? How could we—" She almost threw up. He patted her shoulder. She tried not to cringe at the silver-mesh glove.

"Look to that ridge." He pointed. "Our destination will keep your stomach down until we can take a proper rest."

The horizon was a steady seam of gray. A grove of young cathedral trees rose above a rocky outcrop. Bushy new growth was burnished bronze. Awa's dizziness faded. Acres of trees at the base of the hills had been felled. The scarred landscape was infested with toxic brush and strangle vines. Soldier beetles thrived, eating exposed heartwood.

"Thief-lords." The poison master spit out hatred.

"Crows feast on fat soldier beetles. They're happy."

"Too many beetles decimate everything. Barbarians steal today and tomorrow too."

Cathedral trees supposedly belonged to the emperor. Precious oil, wood, seedpods, leaves, and roots were his living treasury. Sickly trees were chopped with an imperial license. Hezram held the license for Holy City and environs. He guarded his groves with warrior acolytes and Dream Gate conjure. The lands beyond the Narrows Bridge were disputed, so no licenses had been issued. Empire patrols were too scattered to keep thief-lords from raiding groves and hacking down trees.

"Barbarians will return with elephant brigades and fire bows to claim this young grove," Awa said. "I hate them also."

"Forgive my anger. It is old and unwise, leaking through a crack. My wife warned me . . ." The poison master shook his head. "Southern thief-lords are no better or worse than anyone. We must forgive—"

"I don't forgive them." Awa clutched her burnt arm. "I can't."

"Do you forgive yourself?"

"Do you?" Awa shouted. "Is reckoning fire and poison sand forgiveness?"

The poison master stiffened.

Awa leaned on Fannie's neck, away from his anguish. "Your forgiveness is hollow."

"At the crossroads we can always change direction."

Awa's stomach howled at Green Elder jumba jabba.

"Every choice you make could be wrong," he continued. *"Forgiveness replenishes your heart spirit."* He reminded her of Yari, playing conflicting truths against each other.

"I'm too faint to think." Her belly was touching her backbone. There were no scraps from Tembe's cook pots until the end of a festival day. Perhaps she could scrounge something to eat in the grove above.

No one owns the trees

The poison master sang Yari's favorite song as the mare high-stepped through strangle vines creeping across the Empire Road.

They belong to themselves
Or maybe to the bees
No one owns the dew
Another's heartbeat
The rays of a setting sun
Drifting through the leaves

"People belong to themselves too." Awa shivered in the cold drizzle. "Does that stop thief-lords from selling anyone? Nonsense we sing for stupid children."

"My children are dust, scattered on the wind." He drew Awa into his warmth and pulled his cloak around her shoulders too. "So I sing for my haint children, growing old in the shadows."

No one owns our hearts
We can give love away
Or share it in our arts
No one owns my soul
Your tears of joy
The rays of a rising sun
As the new day starts
No one owns the trees
We belong to ourselves
Or maybe to the bees

Another miracle. Awa felt sorry for a monster, for treading on his wounds. She ached with the pain of ghost children loved and lost. "You must tell me how you called a miracle to save us," she said. "And how we have traveled so far. It's a thirty-day ride from Holy City to the foothills of the Eidhou mountain range, even on a warhorse."

"Forty-day ride, and if I *must* tell you," he said, "I'll tell, when you're stronger."

Awa sat up on her own. "I'm strong enough for any story."

"You need much heart spirit for the Iyalawo language of miracles."

Awa felt dizzy again, remembering the opposite shore shimmering like a mirage. The poison master must have folded the distance from the Narrows Bridge to the Foothills Bridge. "You conjured a wise-woman passageway." Awa had never believed the tales of conjure women folding space and bending time and light to hide their comings and goings. But there was no other explanation. "I would love to see such a wonder. Why would Tembe share Iyalawo secrets with *you*?"

"Not Tembe. Another."

"Who?"

Someone battered at the seals around his heart. Awa felt this and flinched. He exhaled a cold breath and mumbled in a dead language as Fannie trotted uphill past tree stumps and rotting roots.

16

Taking Measure

The oily expiration of young cathedral trees filled Djola's mouth. The grove must be around the next bend, beyond a rocky outcropping. New red leaves fluttered in the wind, catching the last of the sun. Trunks and ferns undulated in the shadows, a trickster's dance. Gray forms with granite teeth, smoky hair, and spark hearts floated between the trees. Haints.

Djola's breath grew shallow; his eyes burned with unspent tears. Samina was the chill at his neck, the cold in his bones. *Kill nobody in my name.* Using Samina's spell to open a wise-woman corridor had been foolhardy, and then singing from *The Songs for Living and Dying* . . . Bold haints broke from the forest of shades and taunted him for reckless conjure, whispering with the leaves.

"How else could we escape the deluge?" He yelled in *Anawanama*, what his mother's people used, before the Empire and after, to talk to the stars and trees, to ancestors and spirits. "I couldn't choose death on the Narrows Bridge. Not time yet."

"Why shout in words nobody remembers?" the transgressor girl asked in Empire vernacular—once a minor trading language and these days filling everyone's mouth.

"I remember," he replied in Empire talk, glad to focus on her. "We're not all dead to this world." The transgressor girl twisted around to face him. Haints ventured closer. He almost made out a round familiar face. The crack in his heart throbbed. "So much I cannot say or see unless I speak *Anawanama*."

"Ancestor tongues conjure other worlds." The girl followed his gaze. "What?"

His eldest daughter, Tessa, wavered in front of him, a shaft of evening mist with blue-violet eyes like Samina. Tessa was wide-hipped and forthright like her mother and arrogant like Djola. She chastised him for leaving the way open to scoundrels and fools. Quint, a smoldering ball of ash, echoed his sister.

"No time to close the wise-woman passageway," Djola told the haints in *Anawanama*. Opening corridors was easy, no danger of getting caught in a collapsing fold; closing one could take a month. "The enemy snapped at our heels." Tessa and Quint hissed at his excuses. Djola had never seen his dead children so clearly. As he marched from the coast to Holy City, they'd come as blurs, torment, as wishful thinking. He'd dispelled them easily. In the shadows of Mount Eidhou, on ground they'd walked and near rivers they'd tasted in life, his children claimed the power of ancestors to challenge him. Where was Bal? They should all be together, unless Bal was ashamed of her father, unless Bal refused to haunt a monster. "I'm not a common murderer raining down terror on the Arkhysian Empire." Speaking this lie in *Anawanama* burned his mouth. What was he then? "Tell your sister."

Tessa's and Quint's hissing replies got snatched by the wind. Djola only heard *last breath*. Cathedral saplings wove these words into their red-leaf song. The transgressor girl added a soothing harmony. She patted his thigh and startled him.

"Not yet the hour for my last breath," he said. *"Basawili."* One word in *Anawanama* yet so much to do. "In Arkhys City, I must lay disaster at Azizi's feet and force Council to give up the Dream

Gate illusion, before it's too late to save anything. Years they've wasted." Haints whistled from behind rocks and bushes. "Stop! I promised your mother. She still loves the world. I do what she asks." Time enough for his death after that. "Where is your sister, where is Bal? She must honor her father."

His haint-children went silent and dissolved into cold shadows, leaving a reproach rustling through the leaves. The warhorse pricked up her ears and swiveled them.

The transgressor girl narrowed her eyes. "What?"

"Azizi banished me. Masters killed my half-brother, and . . ." Djola licked dry lips. "Since my wife and children were . . . Since they died, I'm not always in my right mind."

"I knew a Sprite named Bal." Love and longing colored these words. The transgressor girl leaned back against him. She smelled of horse dung, cinnamony tree oil, and rot. He should tend her wounds when they made camp.

"Where my people are from," he said evenly, "Bal is the name for a second child, born under a mango moon, a gift of fire and wind."

"Bal went off to soldier, when lapsed Elders and northlanders raided our enclave."

"Northern tribes raided Green Elders?"

"To kill *vesons* or convert them, and Bal was fearless, resisting—"

"No glory or love for soldiers these days, only destruction and death."

"How do you know?" The girl let anger flare. "Bal is a shadow warrior, determined to survive. She loves life. No matter her fate, that is glorious."

"I suppose."

"What happened to your Bal?" the girl demanded.

"I don't wish to speak of her." Hope was a pointless distraction. He squinted down the road. Abandoned cathedral stumps rotted in the gravel. The lush young grove was farther up than he thought.

The girl stroked the horse. "How many more leagues?"

The road looked endless. "This steep incline and whispering shades saved those trees above from elephant brigades."

"Just say you don't know." Her boldness was strange comfort. "Sorry . . ."

"Keep speaking your mind. It's refreshing, like cathedral tree song."

The warhorse sidestepped pink fungus glowing in twilight and got tangled in strangle vines creeping around rocks. The barbs were sharp enough to tear up her legs. The warhorse halted, snorting steam. Sweat foamed on twitching flanks. She was too hot even in icy drizzle.

Djola stroked silky ears. "Standing still on the road, I feel like a target too, but nobody ambushes us now. Just ornery weeds seizing an opportunity." He drew the thin blade with a diamond tip from his boot and hacked at thorny stalks and creepers. "We need to reach the highest ground no matter how far. The other horses followed our scent through the wise-woman corridor. They track us still."

"Kurakao!" The transgressor girl perked up.

"You give praises for an ambush?"

"Reunion. My friends galloped off on Fannie's friends. Those horses would follow her into fire—"

"Fannie?" A cloud burst overhead and fist-sized hail battered them. Freed from barbed vines, the warhorse charged up the almost vertical road as if she hadn't already carried them too many leagues. "Good girl," he said as the road wound through a thicket of bushes and boulders and levelled off. "The weather is wrong in the valley, but here—"

Supple young trees swayed in the storm. Seedpods waved a welcome. The warhorse slowed to a walk under whispering branches. An umbrella canopy of elephant leaves, nut vines, and weaver-ant nests kept the rain and hail out. The air was oily and warm. The warhorse snorted relief but wouldn't go much farther. Crows circled above them and cackled joy. He cackled back.

"Your friends?" the girl asked as the crows disappeared behind leaves. "Not my favorite birds."

He chuckled, his chin grazing her head. "They always know something we don't."

"Crows make me think of death."

"We all live by death," he sang, *"yet we hold hope for the lives to come."*

"You're not making fun, are you? Of *The Songs,* I mean."

"What you say you become." Without thinking, he stroked her head.

"You sound like a Green Elder."

"I was never much more than a Garden Sprite like you." He scanned for a campsite.

"Do you *believe* we all cast a spell with our words?" She was earnest, like Tessa.

"I did once. I believed all *The Songs,* all the old ways." He closed his eyes. "Today forgotten Elder words return to me." He shivered at visions of his youth with Yari then opened his eyes. "Conjure is a long game. Maybe if I chant the verses, I'll believe again."

"What twisted you into a monster?" The girl bit her bottom lip.

"Sometimes monster is the only choice," he whispered.

She whispered also. "Many times in the huts, I came to a life-and-death crossroads and chose monster too."

"I don't believe that," he said. "Take better measure of yourself."

She spluttered. "Yari speaks through you."

"The famed griot? No. Yari speaks no more." Grain reported this in his last letter. Djola got this news just after he started for Holy City. Grief laid him up for days. *"Vie* is lost to us."

"Dead?" The girl squirmed. "Are you sure? Did you see a body?"

"Iyalawo Kyrie saw Yari surrounded by a mountain of spirit-slaves in Smokeland. She couldn't reach *vie*. A priest holds *vie* captive in Smokeland. Dead would be better."

Tears burst from Awa's eyes.

"Ah. You knew sweet Yari, fierce Yari." Djola was flooded with old passion and grief. "I wish it weren't true."

The girl crumpled, her anguish hot on his chest. Djola hugged her close, marveling that a new someone had slipped through the fortress around his heart. A miracle.

17
Names

The road ended at a cliff face. The warhorse halted by a giant elder tree. Muscles trembling, sides heaving, she stepped inside the trunk-tower. The girl blubbered grief into her mane. High up, bees buzzed around a hive sculpted between several knots. Circular tiers of bright yellow honeycombs reminded him of festival flatbread. Several bees flew close. One landed in the girl's tears. It climbed from cheek to forehead, settling in wiry hair. Another bee poked a wiggly birthmark. The girl swallowed sobs.

"Better? Good. Yari lives on in our hearts."

"Survive," she muttered with a *Lahesh* accent.

"We'll have to go around the cliff." He scanned the dusky environs, weary. "I don't know if we've come far enough to camp. The other riders are close."

"We have the high ground." The girl cleared her throat. "A forest of shades and a wall of brambles protects us. They won't let our enemies through."

"You felt the spirits, saw them too?" Kyrie had extended her Mountain Gates this far. "Still, we should not underestimate our pursuers."

The girl clenched her jaw. "Fannie needs food and rest."

The warhorse lifted her head.

"You really named this warrior mare Fannie?"

Fannie pawed the ground, neighing.

"Let us rest. The tree cave is a boon." The girl looked around. "I've seen it before."

"In Smokeland?"

"Crow-distance is sky measure. By road, the riders could still be far. Don't worry."

He snorted. "Will you protect us with visions?"

"Meera and Rokiat will rest also. They won't ride their horses to death."

"Hezram and his priests would."

"Hezram and his horde are no match for the conjure on your hands or in your bag. Your heart is a fortress. They are pampered fools who should fear you."

He studied her, shaking his head. "You have a sharp mind."

"But a sharp tongue is a fool's tool."

"You're no fool. You can read, conjure, and speak with rivers, crows, and trees. Perhaps even these bees. Do they fly with you to Smokeland?"

The girl froze.

"Don't worry. I mean you no harm." He patted her shoulder, delighted—someone worthy of ancestor spells and conjure from the floating cities. "A miracle that our paths crossed. I'm the end of a story. You are a prelude to change." He untangled a piece of who knows what knotted in her hair. Silver-mesh gloves made him clumsy.

"Thank you," she muttered.

"You've saved my life." He carried song cloth from the ancestors, a library from the floating cities, and conjure scrolls from around the Golden Gulf. This girl-woman who knew the language of bees, rivers, horses, and dirt might actually be able to bear the weight. He squeezed her shoulder. "What do they call you?"

"Awa. And what shall I call you besides the Master of Poisons?"

"My name is lost. I'm only what I do. You're bold, naming soldier horses Fannie." He chuckled. "Call me whatever you like."

Awa sputtered at him.

"Crow distance?" He nodded. "And shade sentinels. Sound reasoning. We'll rest here before heading on to Arkhys City." He swung a leg over Awa's head and dismounted.

Startled, Awa slid from the wet horse onto slippery ground. Her battered leg crumpled. She clutched Fannie's bushy red tail and leaned against sturdy haunches. "You're strong and brave." She stroked the exhausted horse.

"So are you." He pulled bandages and healing herbs from his bag. "May I?"

Awa stared at him wide-eyed. "I'm filthy."

He pointed at water gushing from a hole in the trunk-tower.

Awa took off bracelets and a snake-head necklace. She undid her belt and Aido bag, wincing as her tunic got tangled. "I can't manage the rest. My bad arm is caught."

He pulled his diamond-tipped blade and sliced the shoulders of the filthy green shift. It landed in a heap at her feet. Skin hung from her bones; her breasts were as flat as a child's. She thrust the Aido bag at him and closed her eyes, shuddering, yet trusting him. Unlike good citizens, Green Elders saw no shame in naked bodies. In Holy City, acolytes and priests abused transgressors regularly. What torment had she survived? Avoiding rage, he removed the mesh glove from his right hand and drew her under the warm, fragrant water. The bees flew back to the hive, and Awa sighed as filth and crusted blood washed away. He stuck his head in the spicy wetness too.

"You crack my heart." His voice was rough. "I . . . I feel you."

"High praise," she replied. "I feel you too."

"For hunger cramps." He made her drink an herb potion then drizzled a healing salve onto her festering arm and leg. She flinched but tolerated cloud-silk and silver-mesh bandages. He pulled a black robe and pants from his bag, smooth outside, furry inside, what Vandana wore for mountain travel. "A *Mama Zamba* cloak." He cut a foot from the hem using the thin blade.

"A Green Elder knife." She struggled into the pants. "This can slice rock."

"The *Lahesh* first crafted such knives." He slipped the robe over her head; it caressed her ankles—a perfect length. "Better?" he asked.

"Hmm." She hugged the robe close with her good arm as he cinched the waist with her belt and Aido bag.

"Shadow-warrior's cloth." He touched the bag. "A gift from your Bal?"

Awa nodded. She wiped a squall of tears with the bandaged arm and gazed at him defiantly. He put the viper's necklace back around her neck. A recent kill, the venom sacs were full. She could have poisoned him and ridden off on Fannie.

"That arm will heal, but the bones in your leg have grown crooked—potions and mesh won't fix that." He handed her a pair of Vandana's boots. "Stuff in rags if they're too big." He turned to the horse with a brush from his bag. Using firm, gentle strokes, he cleaned away the journey's dirt and debris. "Did they break your leg in the huts?"

She slipped the boots on. "No, before the huts, a wedding gift from northlanders."

"Which people?"

She furrowed her brow. "*Zamanzi.*"

"Mmendi and Thalit's desert clan, freedom fighters, harrying the Empire."

"*Zamanzi* stole me from a Green Elder enclave, not an Empire village."

He combed Fannie's mane. "*Zamanzi* wouldn't have sold you to Hezram. They despise Hezram more than they hate *vesons*."

"Open-minded thief-lords raided the *Zamanzi* and sold me to Hezram."

"Of course." The crack in his heart throbbed. He shook grain and sweetgrass from his bag. Fannie buried her nose in the food. Awa eyed the rough oats and straw, spit drooling from her lips. "I'm surprised the boots fit. Vandana is . . . or *was* a tall woman." He held out nut bread and hunks of mango for her.

She grabbed the food. "Everyone in my family has big feet, tall or short."

"Tell me how you managed not to lose yourself in the huts."

"You need much heart spirit to hear such a story." She swallowed great chunks, barely chewing. "You're not eating?"

"Food dulls my senses. I'll eat again when we're out of danger."

"You should eat before then. I'm sure you're well stocked."

Laughing, he threw off cape, pants, and a sweaty tunic of leather and copper-mesh. He even removed the glove from his left hand and stood naked in the water pouring into the tree cave.

A polyrhythm of emotions played on Awa's face. She pointed at the wheel of flames tattooed over his heart. "*Vie* who sees every direction." Interlocking stars formed the wheel's center and glowed in the dimness.

"And *vie* who does not burn out, who shines ever bright." He gingerly touched the signs. "Vévés to call down the gods of the crossroads."

"We should all fear you." Unafraid, Awa crammed a last hunk of mango into her mouth. She nodded at the leather-and-copper-mesh tunic. "I thought conjure armor from the *Anawanama* had been outlawed and their spell-scrolls burned."

"I'm an outlaw who traveled to the floating cities where Iyalawos and Babalawos aren't witches and witchdoctors, where many are *vesons*, and no one burns wisdom. Yet." He gave her more nut bread and donned pants and smock of Aido spider-weave cloth.

Awa paused chewing to exclaim, "I know that pattern. Stars and eyes. It means something wonderful."

"All patterns hold meaning. To see new patterns, you need new eyes."

Awa smiled. "One of Bal's favorite weaves."

"Your Bal is a wise warrior."

Spider-weave cloth, every color strong, was dress well-suited to renegades and free spirits. Easy to fade into shadows or dazzle in sunlight. His achy skin was grateful for a light touch. He put silver-mesh gloves back on. No need to risk rogue impulses or accidents. The *Anawanama* travel cape was a breeze on his shoulders and impervious to weather and weapons. When climbing boots had been cinched, he shook out a few figs for Fannie then slung Vandana's bag across his chest. It felt heavier.

Outside the trunk, crows fussed and fumed. The thicket of brambles and haints slithered across the road—Kyrie's Mountain Gates were closing tight—against what threat? The crows screeched. Sighing, he pulled two large rat corpses from the tree roots and shoved them outside for the crows. Azizi would have left the rats to rot in peace and feed the roots—

"But I am the Master of *Weeds and Wild Things*."

"Djola?" Awa almost choked.

"How do you know my name?"

"Watch over us, Fannie." Bees flew down from the hive toward their heads. "Guard our breath bodies." Fannie shook her mane at Awa and gobbled the last fig.

"How do you know what you shouldn't know?" Djola said as Awa strode toward him, a crown of bees in her hair. "Answer me." Djola backed out of the tree cave.

Awa and Fannie followed. "Master of *Weeds and Wild Things*." Awa gripped his arm. Her heartbeat rang in his ears. The rhythm made him swoon. "You've been lost, but not your name or true spirit."

BOOK IV

1

Debts

Before Djola could protest or resist, before he realized what was happening, Awa lifted his spirit body up. He marveled at her craft and audacity as they flew above rocky cliffs, higher and higher. *Lahesh* crystals filled with trickster spirits were scattered in Kyrie's thicket of leaves, vines, boulders, and haints. Her Mountain Gates were a weave of Smokeland and the everyday without a wisp of void-smoke thanks to the crystals.

"I promised," Awa said. Her heart was even stronger than he thought.

A sliver of moon lurked beyond the mist, a crooked smile in the dark. Djola longed to wipe the awful grin from the sky. Samina had always loved the scar moon, especially when it dangled low over the Salty Sea. *A wound in the night, it tugs my spirit* she would say and paddle Djola into waves higher than their house. This was reckless conjure on a flimsy raft, and he'd loved her for taking his breath away . . .

"Promised who?" Djola demanded.

Green aurora smudged the dark. Awa sped toward these

shimmering undulations. "I don't know her name. The conjure woman who lives beyond the light bridge."

Djola quivered. For two years, whenever Samina's favorite lights wavered in the sky he'd refused to look. He'd brew an almost lethal sleeping potion, don a blindfold, and hide in a hole. Tonight he was transfixed. The moon was red on its outer edge and more blade than wound, a weapon hacking at Djola's heart. The aurora pulsed, and his left hand throbbed against the mesh glove; his right eye oozed pus. Spirit debt for *Xhalan Xhala*.

"Your thoughts are heavy." Awa drizzled honey into his mouth. Haloed by the aurora, she looked like a demon of old. "I have you. And Fannie guards our breath bodies. Don't worry." The sweet taste and her graceful wind dance soothed him. A thousand thousand bees, gossamer wings roaring, hot stingers sparking, surrounded them. Faceted eyes reflected green iridescence and red moonlight. "She calls us."

"Who? Tell me," Djola pleaded.

"I think you know who." Awa had carried them through luminous clouds to—

"Smokeland." Djola had avoided crossing the border-void since he turned Pezarrat's fleet to pearls. Samina might see his actions as revenge. He had never dared to smoke-walk without drinking a seed and silk potion. "Stop!" A gelatinous creature exploded, showering them with muck. He pawed slime from his face. "My spirit debt, Hezram will—" The void seeped through his skin, engulfing betrayal, anguish, regret, cloaking even hidden caches of joy. "Hezram, he will find . . . He . . ."

"What?" Awa said.

Djola forgot that he had anything to say.

"We can't linger." She pulled them into a whirlwind of smoke and poison dust.

Djola resisted, bashing her with silver-mesh fists and booted feet. Void-smoke made it hard to breathe, hard to fight or think. As he got tangled in himself, only one thing remained clear: he should never leave the border realm.

"Hold to your feelings." Awa gripped him to the bone. Her good arm was muscled and strong, too strong for his dull resistance. "We make the void and we can unmake it." Bee hearts glittered around her face as they escaped the whirlwind. "See?"

They drifted over land shrouded in shadows. Anguish returned, a mountain, a deluge. "Sugar on dung." Djola felt flimsy, yet as heavy as a broken promise. "We're carrying too much weight for Smokeland." A tendril of border-void chased after them. "Cowards couldn't bear a return to the everyday—too many possibilities frightened them. Trying to eliminate harsh futures, they conjured the border-void and got trapped in their own spells."

"The void is lost possibilities?"

"Or stolen ones."

Awa soared on toward a distant blue horizon, Djola trailing behind her like a banner. "Yari never said people conjured the void."

"The griot of griots always tried to see past the gloom," Djola grunted, "and what good was that? Scoundrels poisoned Yari while *vie* roamed Smokeland."

Awa trembled. "If there is no hope, only fools willingly return to torment or death."

"Exactly. Who told you that?"

"I figured it out for myself." She scanned the skies, steering clear of void tendrils.

"So, living in the huts has granted you great wisdom—"

"Living anywhere. We could all be lost souls. We must never give up looking for each other."

Djola scoffed. "Should I write that down for the Elder book? *Every day a new page.*"

"I'd be honored if you included me in any book or song." Awa jammed a honeycomb in his mouth. "Clear your thoughts. The void lingers in you."

Djola chewed reluctantly. The honey was full of swamp blossom and fireweed that dulled torment. Smoke cleared from his mind. "Smart girl, friend of bees and horses . . ."

"Don't sneer. That slows our progress. And there's nowhere to land." They flew over fields of rotting strangle vines and cathedral tree carcasses, not the steamy swamplands or tall grass prairies he recalled. Despite their breakneck speed, blue sky was no closer. Awa groaned. "Reaching the winter region is a trick."

Something hissed in the wind.

Djola jerked every direction. Beyond the rotting fields was poison sand. No trees or grass, no wild dogs, warhorses, or smokewalkers in sight. "Zst! What region is this?"

"Poison desert of the mind."

The honeycomb fell from his mouth. He cursed. "The void encroaches on *every* region with the blessings of witchdoctors and high priests."

"Every region except the seventh." Awa chomped her lip. "An impossible rhythm to find in my heart."

"I know the way. Through the aurora to the starway, a light bridge."

"Do you see one here?"

He looked up. Tendrils of smoke chased after them from every direction and covered the sky. On the ground, scurrying through tree ruins and poison sand, emaciated spirit slaves jabbered. Dark holes gaped where eyes and mouths should have been. Beneath translucent skin, collapsed lungs shivered and heart embers had almost gone dark. A few fiends sprang high, tangling worker bees in sticky hair. Sentinels came to their rescue, poking hefty stingers into bony chests. The fiends, and sentinels too, dissolved into a pool of indigo. Djola was transfixed by bee sacrifice.

Awa shook him. "Don't think down. Think up. We must fly higher."

"Who are those people?" Djola muttered.

"Spirit slaves."

"I know that, but I've never seen so many . . ."

"Smokeland is no longer just a waste of space." A deep voice jabbed Djola's ears.

"Do you hear that?" Djola scanned a ravaged valley. A dead river cut a black ribbon through gray rubble. The last trickle of water boiled away. "Where's it coming from?"

"Nowhere. Don't listen." Awa gritted her teeth. "You'll be too heavy to fly."

Below them, the upturned faces of over a hundred spirit slaves wore the same smirk: Hezram. Worker bees flew into vacant eye sockets and exploded. The fiend's ember hearts flickered brighter. Djola snorted wing filaments and bitter venom as he and Awa plummeted down through smoke toward the dead riverbed.

"Master of Poisons"—Hezram's horde spoke with one melodious voice—"why carry so many heavy ghosts?"

Displaying great Smokeland skill, Awa slowed their descent. The blast of light from her heart made Djola squint. "We all carry ghosts," she proclaimed, "and still fly."

Hezram's horde shouted over her. "Djola, you think you're better than I am, better than us all, yet you'd sacrifice anybody or anything for your cause."

"I'm not like you," Djola insisted. He gagged on a mouthful of void-smoke. "You would destroy our world."

Denial is worse than poison sand. More worker bees exploded in dark fiend mouths. "Your words. Look in your bag of death."

"Don't." Awa pulled him close as they stalled in midair. "It's a trick."

"Your only shield is a swarm of bees." The horde snickered.

"Lugging a library of lost languages and a dead mountain, you're too heavy to fly."

"Ice Mountain too?" Djola squinted in Vandana's bag. The turquoise rocks turned into crumbling cliffs jammed between dry waterfalls and silent songbirds. Citizens' bones rattled in glass jars. Icy mountain tears turned to muck.

"Witchdoctor illusions." Awa shook Djola. "Look away."

"To where?" Djola asked. "Smokeland is never very far from the everyday." Ice Mountain's ghost glaciers got heavier with each breath. Tessa and Quint were shadow and ash among burning cathedral trees. Where was Bal?

"Hezram is the rogue Babalawo who lost his way on the Empire Road, not you." Awa cinched the bag shut. "He tries to snare us in your despair."

"I do that myself." The bag banged Djola's hip, a hammer smashing his bones.

Awa slugged him too. "Tell a different story."

"You're a true child of Yari, of the griot of griots—"

"You're not?"

"Sometimes, there's only one story to tell."

"Never." Awa clicked and warbled like a cheeky crow. Her breath tasted of honey and bananas. *"I am feathers,"* she sang. *"My bones are air. I am the wind."*

Djola scowled. "Green Elder jumba jabba."

Awa tugged his murderous weight straight up. "The Empire tongue twists meaning. To northern ancestors, jumba jabba means *speaking miracles is grace, for we are what we say.*" She sucked in a deep breath. Her heart was like a volcano pumping lava. "Say who you mean to be."

Djola's tongue felt too thick for words.

In the riverbed, Hezram's fiends joined other spirit slaves building a tower with cathedral tree carcasses and slaves whose hearts were almost dark. Djola observed them, fascinated, dazed. Haphazard and clumsy, the tower collapsed twice, and the sweet-sour scent of decay and death rose in a cloud of smoke. Vandana's bag got heavier and heavier, dragging him and Awa down. He tasted blood on Awa's breath. By the fourth attempt, the fiends were careful, even cooperating with each other.

"Empty out your bag before it's too late for you both," Hezram's voices whispered.

Rising quickly, the tower was less than ten feet away. Sentinel bees exploded with a flash of indigo, but made little difference—too many spirit slaves. Djola tried to pull free of Awa.

"Stop." She held on. "We are miracles together."

Djola shook his head. "Not here." His left hand glowed inside the silver-mesh glove.

"Remove your glove," Hezram's horde said sweetly. "Touch the transgressor's cheek. You will bring her down like Ice Mountain."

Awa's face fractured in his right eye. The left eye saw only smoke. As she spoke, her words also broke apart. Meaning escaped him.

"This monster murdered innocents." Hezram's voices were as clear as glass shattering. "You're a witness, girl."

"He speaks truth. I'll exhaust you, destroy you," Djola said.

"Save yourself. Abandon the Master of Poisons and his bag of demons and haints before he abandons you. Everyone always abandons you."

Awa babbled and her grip tightened.

Panicked, Djola thrust his lethal left hand back and forth between her face and his own. "With me, no escape," he said over and over.

2

Family

Smokeland was jumbled up. Demon voices and void-smoke confused Awa, made her wonder if she should honor a wild promise to a stranger, made her doubt that she could carry Djola to the seventh region and back to the everyday. But the conjure woman saved her life, saved the bees too. *"Basawili!"* Awa put a hand to Djola's lips, silencing jibber jabber. He was heavier than Bal. Hovering with him over the dead riverbed was a challenge. Flying on seemed impossible. She couldn't find the rhythm of the seventh region in her heart, still, "I can hold you and not lose myself." She said what she wanted to believe, speaking Djola's ancestor tongue, *Anawanama*.

"Be reasonable," Djola spoke *Anawanama* also, intelligible again. "I'm begging you."

They wobbled, thrown off balance by the conjure bag dangling from his shoulder. Awa glanced at the fiend tower, so many wasted bodies and dead trees. Djola's fault, her fault also, still, "If I abandon you, I'm lost."

"I should have smelled a smoke-walker so close." Hezram's fiends jabbed Awa with Empire talk. "Friend to bees, to horses and crows too. Jod said beware."

"I need your long life not your sacrifice, Awa." Djola's *Anawa-nama* was a caress.

"You can't hide in yesterday's words," Hezram's fiends shouted. A lie. Hezram feared what he couldn't understand.

Awa shouted, "*Anawanama* is today and tomorrow too."

Djola clenched his lethal hand. "The Empire conquered the old ones. What good are their words?"

"That's void talk," Awa countered.

"I speak from the crack in my heart, not the void," Djola replied.

She squinted a hundred hundred leagues through haze and dust, looking for clear sky. "Every language changes your mind." Green Elder talk.

Hezram laughed. "I'll find you two anywhere." Priests and witchdoctors hunted smoke-walkers to use for gate- and weapon-spells. Hezram knew Djola's and Awa's blood rhythms. Tracking them in Smokeland and the everyday would be simple.

"Hezram can't chase you to the winter region, no spirit slaves to serve him there. Kyrie's Gates protect our breath bodies in the everyday." Djola talked to Awa's thoughts, one of his most irritating gifts. "So, drop me and fly on."

Awa rubbed burning eyes. "The conjure woman said bring you—"

"Save one of us."

"Does he tell you to drop him?" Hezram asked. "Listen to wise counsel."

"We save each other." Using a polyrhythm of dissonant voices, Awa sang over the single voice coming from a hundred mouths. She wasn't as skilled as Bal, yet the fiends clutched their ears and Hezram's chorus of one disintegrated into cacophony.

"Smart conjure." Djola almost smiled.

Awa touched her forehead to Djola's like a good daughter to a wise father. *"Every soul a miracle, every maggot, every rotten leaf."* Green Elder jumba jabba, saying who you mean to be.

A fierce wind twisted along the riverbed, painting the horizon black and red. Djola jerked and spit at the storm charging toward them. "Hezram is not our only threat. The Amethyst River and Holy City chase us too. No mercy." Poison sand from the storm spiraled up the fiend tower and blasted them. Djola's eyes rolled in their sockets.

"Stay with me." The crown of bees in Awa's hair grew silent. The sentinels were dead—nobody left to protect them. A wound on her belly opened, and blood oozed through cloud-silk bandages. Many old wounds split open. Her leg was on fire, as if a *Zamanzi* woman had smashed her bones again. *Survive!* What choice but to abandon Djola? Awa curled in a ball around him and pulled his cloak over them and the bees. In the darkness, Yari's favorite song dropped from her lips:

> *No one owns your heart*
> *We can give love away*
> *Stolen love tears you apart*
> *For no one owns the trees*

If Hezram conjured his way through Kyrie's thicket of haints and stormed the elder tree, Fannie would stomp their breath bodies before she let the witchdoctor near. No living death in Smokeland. Awa filled herself with warhorse ferocity:

> *No one owns the sky*
> *No one owns the question why*
> *I say, stolen love tears you apart, but—*
> *We can give love away*
> *Make a bridge of the heart*

In the storm's fury, ember hearts burned out and spirit slaves turned to poison dust. The fiend tower sank a few feet. Awa stroked Djola's feverish face and sang in his ear.

No one owns the clouds or the dew
The mountain rocks, the color blue
No one owns the leaves or the breeze
The rushing river, the frothy seas
We belong to ourselves
Or maybe to the bees

Djola roused from his stupor. "A new version?"

"Yari could never leave a song be."

The strap on Djola's conjure bag sliced his shoulder. Blood dribbled into the mouths of fiends below. Their heart embers sparked brighter. They leapt up, sucking the air for more blood. Djola shook her. "Take a good look at what chases us."

Hezram's sneer on a hundred faces chilled Awa more than empty eyes. Drunk on stolen dreams, Hezram had lost himself, lost the world. "I promised and—" Djola might be Bal's father, a master forced to slave on a pirate ship and give his daughter to an enclave to save her. Awa needed to fly Djola to the seventh region for Bal. "And . . ."

"What?" Djola asked. "Can you see beyond the void?"

Awa closed her eyes and willed them away from the fiend tower. Hezram couldn't be everywhere; that was a bluff, an illusion to steal the speed of thought from her. Awa opened her eyes to a grove of flowering trees untouched by creeping void. She dropped them into the bushy crown of a young raintree. The supple branches dipped low and flung them into a black velvet sky. Fragrant petals cleared her mind. "The conjure woman smelled of raintree blossoms . . ."

"Zst!" Djola's bag slid down his bloody left arm.

Awa grabbed the strap. "I can carry this for you." The bag weighed nothing. She slung it over her shoulder. Beyond a splash of green aurora, she spied the bridge of stars. Endless arches of light cut into the deep dark. "I see a way."

"Good." Djola twisted free and flung her toward the aurora. His cape fluttered about him, giant black wings. Without the conjure bag he glided easily.

"What are you doing?" Awa chased him.

"Hezram tracks us still. Take my bag. Escape." Djola feinted away from her. He was fast again. "Get to Emperor Azizi. Warn him against disaster before it's too late. Build no Dream Gates in Arkhys City."

"What do I care if the Arkhysian Empire crumbles away?" Awa shouted. "Warn him yourself."

The fiend tower burst beyond smoke into black sky.

"Here I am," Djola shouted, and the tower tilted toward him. "Take me if you can."

Clambering to the top, a spirit slave with a bright heart smashed others out of the way using a double-headed talking drum. Awa stared at bells and seeds on the rims and faltered. The fiend leapt at her, light as ashes and faster than thought.

"Get out of here." Djola collided with the fiend, shoving it off course. He fumbled with the mesh glove on his left hand. The fiend gripped Djola's cape, tugging him toward granite teeth. They twisted and whirled and got tangled in rippling fabric. "Fly!" Djola yelled.

But Awa hovered close, gaping at mottled goat strands connecting the drumheads and Aido cloth decorations. She knew only one person with such an instrument. The fiend caught Djola's right foot, bit through thick boot leather, and sucked greedily. Djola howled and kicked the fiend in the face to no avail. As they spun away from Awa, the drum hit her cheek and twanged a familiar tone.

What did it matter who this spirit slave had once been?

Awa snapped the viper's head from her neck. She thrust her hand through the fiend's back and stabbed the sparking heart. Pain shot up her arm and she almost fainted. Venom burst into indigo sparks that spread through chest, abdomen, legs, and arms. When sparks flared from dark eye sockets, Awa pulled the fangs out. The fiend unclamped granite jaws from Djola's shredded boot and swooned. Awa clutched an almost unconscious Djola. Her hand hovered over the Vévés sealing his heart.

"Don't abandon me," she pleaded with him.

Djola pressed her hand close. The Vévés glowed—a cool light. "I'm here." His cape fluttered as he tucked the mangled right foot against the back of his left knee.

Thrashing in indigo sparks, the fiend drifted toward the aurora. Hezram's visage faded, and color blossomed on the smooth cheeks of a *veson*, a Green Elder whose heartbeat was silver lightning bolts. Bloodshot eyes were outlined in black kohl. Thick gray hair was knotted with *Lahesh* flame-cloth, seeds, and carapaces. Red mica glittered on broad palms as *vie* played the talking drum.

Awa fought tears. "Yari!"

"The griot of griots?" Djola's voice cracked. "Kyrie said you'd been captured. I didn't want to believe her."

"Awa, my last gift, come to me again." Yari smiled. "And Djola, Master of *Weeds and Wild Things*. I'd hoped to find you both."

"Come with us." Awa flew toward Yari. "We'll meet Djola's friend and then—"

"*Abelzowadyo*." Yari floated just out of reach. "Sacred shapeshifter. Say it."

"*Abelzowadyo*," Awa repeated.

"The one who is changing into all things, but is never just one thing. Find Bal and offer this ancient *Zamanzi* word."

"*Zamanzi?*" Awa sputtered.

"For your crossover, your Elder ceremony. I wanted to tell you and Bal when we three were together again." Yari's eyes blazed. "Bal lives still. Tell—"

"Bal is alive?" Djola hugged a quaking chest. "Impossible."

"I don't want to be anybody's messenger," Awa said. "Tell Bal yourself."

"I must pay a spirit debt." Yari snatched the viper's head. "I'm dead in the everyday, but you've saved me, saved the other Elders too. Our family." Yari tapped and squeezed the drum, playing ancestor words, a *Lahesh* call to death and new life.

Djola relaxed, chest tremors subsiding. "A crossover rhythm." The beats were a tonic for him, yet the fiends shrieked.

"I went to Holy City, thinking to seduce a demon," Yari said, "and I failed. Hezram captured me with a kiss. I was arrogant. Bal didn't want me to go. Even the dog tried to stop me." Yari turned to the fiend tower, playing furiously. "We make the void and we can unmake it." *Vie* could drum a child into the world or a body into the death lands. "Sing my songs, tell my stories. *Basawili!*"

Djola grabbed Awa as Yari dropped low, just above the tower. Fiends snapped, snarled, and flailed yet could not reach *vie.* "Let me be one of your good stories. Promise me."

Awa should have said yes—but her tongue refused.

"We will," Djola spoke for them both. "I promise. *Basawili!* Not your last breath."

"Hezram will come for you, in the everyday, in dreams." Yari contemplated the tower of fiends. "They'll all come, a stampede. Take good measure of yourselves. Fly in your own rhythm and outwit them. *Xhalan Xhala*—see the future you want."

"How?" Awa said as her heart cracked.

"Abelzowadyo." Yari tossed the drum to her. She caught it as *vie* descended into the tower singing harmony with many, many selves. Tree carcasses exploded and fiends howled and hissed. Djola clutched Awa's waist so tightly she could barely breathe. The fiends mobbed Yari, clawing, biting, and sucking. Awa almost looked away, yet here was the hero she had longed for, saving her and Djola. Yari stabbed ember hearts with the viper's fangs. Color blossomed across the smooth faces of Green Elders from Awa's enclave. *Free the heart, free the spirit.*

The Elders joined Yari's song-conjure before plunging into the screaming fiends. The tower collapsed on itself. Yari let go of the spent viper's head and disappeared.

Awa clutched the talking drum and trembled. A blast of indigo sparks ripped from the ground to the stars and blew Awa and Djola far across the sky. Their ears rang with Yari's last words: *Abelzowadyo. Death is a doorway.*

3

Star Bridge

The air was clear of void-smoke. Under bright blue sky, grassy savannas stretched to ice-capped mountains. Awa and Djola flew easily toward the peaks.

"We've left the void behind." Djola shuddered. "This is the Smokeland I remember."

"How will we return to the everyday?" Bleary, her good arm throbbing, Awa glanced back the way they came. "Hezram's fiends patrol the borderlands and—"

Yari's drum thudded against her back. Awa longed to kill Hezram slowly, to slice his tongue, hammer his bones, and drive him mad. Sounds of torture kept transgressors awake all night. Awa wanted Hezram, his priests, and acolytes to know this same torture, even Tembe. What had she done except offer Awa and Meera crumbs?

Hezram, Tembe, Father—they murdered Yari.

"Grief often masquerades as bloodlust," Djola said as cold winds buffeted them. "A vengeful spirit makes navigating Smokeland dangerous."

"You would know." She pointed at his mangled foot. "How is it?"

"Fine."

"You lie."

Bloody pus left a brown streak in the green below. With gentle urging, bees crawled in the wound and spit cleansing venom where it festered. Only a hundred hundred bees still flew with them. They buzzed along fearlessly. *Survive.*

"We should rest." Awa veered toward a sweetgrass and wild-flower meadow.

"No." Djola tugged her up a warm updraft. She was heavy now. "Hezram will send a new horde to follow our blood." He charged up to the speed of thought.

"Yari and the Elders were my family. This is the second time I've lost them."

"You saved them."

"Where are they if I've saved them? And don't say in the crack in my heart."

"Look!" Djola spun her around. The scar moon hung low on the horizon. Sails on a mountain lake reflected green and red aurora rippling in the sky. Distant cook fires twinkled like stars. Drums and voices carried Yari's crossover rhythm.

Awa jolted, every sense alert. "Boat people. I haven't seen them in years. They've taken refuge underneath the star bridge."

"*Lahesh* rhythms shield them and us." Whispering thanks to the boat people, he flew them through the aurora into a black velvet sky. Beyond the moon, a crossroads lattice of stars arched into darkness. "The light bridge." He slipped his trembling arm through Awa's. Agitated bees made a crown in her hair and a boot for his wounded foot as they headed down the bridge.

"It goes on forever." Awa peered a thousand thousand leagues. The far end was invisible. How did the conjure woman travel to the winter region so quickly? "We're too slow. Even at the speed of thought." Awa shivered in thin, cold air.

"Everyone takes their own time on the bridge of stars." Djola flew them past a swirl of rainbow spirits to the bridge. "I was a fool to stay away. She'll help us get back to the everyday."

Rocks colliding near the bridge exploded. "Then what?"

"I sat at Council," he grinned ruefully, "more powerful than almost anyone, and—"

"Zst!" Awa was not eager for the saga of a monster.

Djola told his tale anyhow as they drifted through a blur of constellations and huddled close for warmth. He talked too fast, like a desperate Sprite defying the fates. Awa scoffed at his fatal errors. Of course greedy, foolish Council masters denied truth. They were no different than anybody. She rolled her eyes as masters betrayed Djola and Azizi exiled him. "It took you that long to realize we're all thief-lords bringing disaster on ourselves?" Unfazed, Djola spoke of pirate cunning and treachery, of whore-spies and warrior women from beyond the maps, of behemoths dancing on their tails in a river of ice. He said little about the deaths of his wife, Samina, and Tessa, Bal, and Quint. Awa was hungry for these details. "You don't know what happened to your children?" she asked.

"I know they are dead and I have nowhere to mourn them."

"Did anybody see the bodies?"

Djola complained that Kyrie conjured gates to save her mountain but did nothing for his family, then he spoke of conjure studies and vengeance barely held in check. "Poison desert is how Hezram powers his Dream Gates. Azizi would build such gates around Arkhys City and give Hezram a chair at Council. This illusion solution is disaster that could swallow all the children."

Awa sighed. "After this journey, I'll find my Bal. I can't do anything about the rest."

He clamped his mouth on a retort.

A blast of light from under their feet made her jump. A star exploded, too far for heat to touch them. She hugged herself, glad for the furry mountain attire from Vandana.

"Do you know Dream Gate spells?"

"I could teach one such as you in a snap."

She stared down the endless star bridge. "Will you teach me now?"

"You would learn this? A perverted spell really." He eyed her. "Why?"

"I'd learn anything you wanted to teach. *Ignorance won't save us.*"

"My words to you . . ." He pointed to a violet disk surrounded by blue and silver dust, a giant eye in the dark. "*The sky is empty, but full of wonder.*"

Her lips trembled. "Yari."

"Yes." His voice cracked. "Have you learned the order of things?"

"*Zamanzi* raided our enclave the day I was to cross over. I know more than you think." More than she would tell him. "Yari taught me ceremonies for trees, water, animal-people, and rocks. I sing to the land, to ancestors long dead and those to come. The order is a circle, encompassing all."

"Ahh, an Elder then."

"I don't know what I am."

"*Abelzowadyo,*" Djola declared.

"I'm a griot, not a shapeshifter." Awa squirmed. "Why a savage word?"

"The Empire stole our stories and turned us into *savage,* barbarian, citizen; they turned Iyalawos and Babalawos into witch women and witchdoctors."

"Why not call on *Lahesh, Sorit,* or *Anawanama* ancestors? *Zamanzi* stole me, Yari, and Bal from our lives." And Yari died by her hand. She didn't want to forgive herself or the *Zamanzi.* "They think *vesons* are men-women abominations. Why embrace tainted wisdom?"

"You are prelude to another world. *Zamanzi* understand change better than anyone. Yari recognized your true nature." A star disappeared into blackness, and Djola looked ready to weep. "I'll teach you what I know. For Yari."

Who could argue with that?

Djola talked and sang himself hoarse teaching her spells for what felt like weeks. He claimed it was only hours. Her mouth was dry, her stomach rumbled, but she wasn't sleepy. Weeks of no sleep would have dulled her thoughts. Time on the bridge isn't time in the everyday. Now and then trickster stars flashed blue and green, as if the end of the bridge was near. She bristled at illusions, yet learning Djola's wealth of conjure distracted her, even from the crack in her heart.

"We've come halfway." He put a gloved hand into a comet's tail. "Don't you remember these balls of ice? A belt of them . . ." He sucked a chunk.

"No." The bridge had been less than a blink on her first journey. "No."

"I do. Star ice in my mustache the last time." He handed her a chip.

"It's bitter." She swallowed nonetheless.

His heart was fainter than hers, his right eye wept blood, and his foot leaked rot. The bees gobbled this away, sparking brighter and exuding an intoxicating wildflower scent. "Tell me about yourself. What did you choose for your crossover ceremony?"

"I told you. Griot." Awa didn't want to talk about lapsed Elders and *Zamanzi* raiders. Instead, she spoke of her good life with Bal. She raced through Hezram and Holy City, talking mostly of Meera and Rokiat. "Acolytes were tormenting a warhorse foal with a crooked foot. Meera, red face and yellow hair like an angry sun, charged them, brandishing a rusty rake. I joined her, shrieking and throwing dung. The cowards ran. Fannie, Bibi, and a wild dog chased them out the back gate. Rokiat locked it, laughing so hard, he couldn't stand up. We danced and sang with him, feasted on duck and coconut wine, and counted stars till dawn."

Awa omitted the cowards' revenge behind the temple, which Tembe and her drummers interrupted. Instead she told more good-time tales of Meera and Rokiat—stealing coins from tribute plates, pulling Bibi's foal from a bog, sneaking Tembe's cook pots off to the huts and sharing feast scraps with everyone. "A transgressor told Tembe what we did. She had him bled to death for quick salvation. Nobody told on us again. Tembe left pots for us regularly and listened to our sorrows. Meera insisted we weren't her spies. Maybe we were, but Meera and Rokiat are clever and brave." Surely Bibi and her foal, a half-grown stallion now, had galloped fast and far, carrying her friends to safety. "If anybody escaped deluge and poison dust . . ."

"Crossroads gods are indifferent," Djola remarked.

"None of the gods care for us." Awa sighed. "If they exist at all."

"A skeptic." Djola touched her cheek. *"We bring love to the world."*

Another star exploded and Awa felt hollowed out. "We who?"

"We who want to get anywhere."

Djola probably blamed her for stalling on the light bridge. None of this was her fault. Awa bit her tongue on a lie—a Holy City survival tactic. Lies got you sucked into the void; truth did too. Best to keep your mouth shut sometimes.

4

Bee Dreams

The emptiness and chill on the light bridge are terrible. Gone are familiar magnetic ripples and steady gravity. The stars are too distant to feel the comfort of their heat or to waggle with their beams. The Bees try not to worry. No sentinels left to scent the air with banana fear. Instead, a hundred hundred Bees dance with Awa's and Djola's heart lights—a polyrhythmic pulse promising a bountiful future. The Bees are happy that Djola regurgitates power-food from his foot for them.

Even though this meal is sour sweet, like fermented nectar, it means the Bees won't die on such a long, cold journey back to the hive. They take turns swarming Djola's foot, careful not to sting tender flesh. Flapping their wings so furiously (for warmth) without such rich nutrients, they would wear out their hearts and expire. Nobody wants to die before they reach the hive. Nobody wants to waste wings or venom or bodies on darkness.

Time passes quickly. Cavorting in Awa's hair, they cover themselves in her queen-scent. Djola's queen-scent is weaker, but after fighting off fiends with him, after eating from his foot, the Bees know his smell. Djola belongs to the hive. He is as ready to die for the queen as they are. Anyone who loves Awa is a friend to Bees. Djola loves flowers and cathedral tree elders who offer their trunks as shelter. Awa has chosen wisely.

The Bees swarm together, full of power food and comforted by the queen-scent. They revel in this moment, glowing. The end of the bridge is near. Awa and Djola will find the hive soon—just a few more light beams to navigate. The Bees keel over, clutching each other's legs, asleep. They dream of pools of nectar, clouds of pollen, and evening dew heavy with flower scent. Why dream of anything else?

5

Spells

Darkness crept under Awa's skin and itched from the inside. Her bowels twisted around nothing; her bladder was empty. The back of each breath hurt. Toes, fingers, and the tip of her nose were numb. She and Djola huddled with the bees under his cape as they flew along the light bridge past a smear of faint stars. The cape's outlaw conjure shielded a bit against the deep chill. Furious wings and volcano hearts kept everybody from freezing. Spirit slaves with faint hearts would have faded away. That was strange comfort as Awa tried not to worry about Djola or weep over Yari or imagine revenge on Hezram. Sprite discipline held her together just barely.

"How many more leagues?" she asked for the tenth time.

"The bridge is a circle, a spiral. The end is a beginning."

Awa groaned. "You don't know—just say that."

"You repeat yourself too." Djola chortled like a fool at carnival. "The order of things."

"Will you teach me Hezram's Gate conjure or not?"

"Not Hezram's conjure. He perverted wisdom from the floating cities, from *Lahesh* and *Anawanama* ancestors actually." Vévés on Djola's skull glowed in the dark, an eerie light under the cape. "You need good smoke sense, which you already possess, and silver lattice craft."

"Like the bandages and your mesh gloves?"

"And blindfold. Insulation to keep rogue forces in or out." That was the first thing he'd taught her. Tricky, yet not impossible. "Snare a smoke-walker in his own despair and poison his breath body in the everyday. Channel his despair into the gate—a simple void-spell. The first captive ensnares other smoke-walkers."

"Yari tried to warn me . . ." Awa never got to tell Yari how much *vie* meant to her.

"Stolen hearts burn out quickly." Djola stroked his chest. "If fed blood and tree oil, spirit slaves linger and power the gate, channeling void-smoke into the everyday."

Awa flinched at the memory of blades cutting skin and slicing cathedral tree roots. "We call them Nightmare Gates. How do you stop such conjure?"

"Good question. Smart girl."

"I'm a woman now."

"You starve Dream Gates."

"Of course. Without blood and oil, Nightmare Gates crumble. No other way?"

"Bring the void to the gates." He balled his lethal hand. "It all adds to the poison desert."

Awa frowned. "So this is how witch-woman Kyrie crafts Mountain Gates?"

"No." He quivered. "All gates require sacrifice, but sacrifice need not be unwilling."

Awa kissed her teeth. "Who'd willingly give up life to power a gate?"

"You call power from recent ancestors, trees, bushes, vines, even rocks." He peered at her, holding something back. Something important, perhaps about the haints he recognized in Kyrie's gates. Had witch-woman Kyrie used Djola's children as sacrifice?

"So, teach me what Hezram does," she pleaded.

"We don't need more Nightmare Gates. Void-spells consume you and turn the world to poison."

"Is that what turned you into a monster?"

"Yes. *Xhalan Xhala*. Take care. Arrogance is strength and weakness."

"I'm not you." Elders always thought Sprites would make the same mistakes they had. She'd make her own mistakes. "What of spirit slaves who powered fallen gates?"

"If they haven't died in the everyday, they might come back to themselves."

Awa bit her lip. "Snake venom stops the heart here and every-where. Hard to come back from that."

"You didn't kill Yari."

"I know." A lie. She'd stabbed Yari's heart, killing on purpose. It seemed the only choice. She poked her head out of Djola's cape to blink away tears and spied a blue-and-brown marble just beyond a haze of clouds. "Is that the end?"

Djola poked his head out too. The marble vanished behind an hourglass of golden stars. "That looks like a talking drum."

"More like a *Lahesh* timepiece." Awa frowned. "We've seen these same stars twice."

Djola squinted, closing his right eye completely. "Three times."

"We're going in circles."

"The bridge is a spiral. This journey is a wonder. Someone should do a sky map."

"Not me." Awa was impatient with wonder. No matter how dazzling, nothing here would bring Yari and their enclave back.

"I'll teach you how to weave *Anawanama* conjure armor. You'll enjoy puzzling this."

He was almost right. The outlaw spells were intricate and mysterious. Singing metal-and glass stories, memorizing formulas to trap gasses, and learning the rhythm of rocks left little energy for anger (at herself or anyone). He also explained how to fashion a *Lahesh* bag like the one he carried, a gift, he said, from his *Mama Zamba* friend. "A wild woman with dagger teeth." He smiled. Awa had barely grasped the intricate weave of time and thread that offered limitless space when he started reciting life-and-death herb recipes and explaining the language of wind and stars. Endless, never repeating polyrhythms . . . Awa was dizzy. She ached for solid ground under her feet. "All my knowledge and spells are in that bag. Vandana's bag, yours now."

"Just until you heal." Awa didn't want his dead mountains and haints.

"Too heavy for you?" he teased in the middle of running for their lives. "I have talking books from Smokeland and Yari's stories."

"What good is the song without the singer?" Nobody conjured a choir of voices like Yari, except maybe Bal . . .

"True." Djola wiped a bloody tear. "Do a thing until it is yours. Pass the bag on when the right time comes." He taught her Orca's organizing spell and made her promise to read every scroll and watch for dangers from within and without, seen and unseen. She was to be bold and humble, cautious and loving, reckless and judicious. He exhorted her to be of many minds before acting. Always. Awa barely listened.

"Yes, hold the polyrhythms for truth." She sighed. "And if that doesn't work?"

He clamped his lips tightly and glowered, good humor gone.

Awa uncinched the conjure bag. "Is there anything for your eye or foot in here?"

Djola closed the bag quickly. "We dare not search on the bridge."

"Why?"

His breath turned sour, his heart flickered. "The bag is similar to the bridge, a fold of time and space. The folds might interfere with each other."

"That makes sense." She shifted the bag to her withered arm. The talking drum grumbled. "How did you bring down Ice Mountain? Explain that."

Djola dampened the tones on the drumheads. Bells and seeds rattled on defiantly, only quieting when bees woke and buzzed through them. "Did you know the *Lahesh* called Smokeland Jumbajabbaland, a place to think and make miracles?" he asked. "Back when the border-void was just a gasp of empty breath and a blink of smoke. Yari taught me that."

"Yari told me Smokeland had many names, and I should find one that suited."

"You must tell me about—"

She shook her head.

"We promised Yari to tell stories."

"You promised." The drum banged her back, but she didn't care.

The *Lahesh* claimed a master musician filled an instrument with heart spirit that any player could tap. Griot tales for children—a drum was just dead skin and wasted seeds. How Yari's drum played on when she barely touched it was a mystery.

6

Antidote

Fatazz!" Djola swallowed curses. The light bridge was a blur in one eye and red streaks of pain in the other. A traveler had to imagine a specific future, had to conjure the end to get there, like for *Xhalan Xhala*. Navigating Awa's grief (guilt?) and his mountain of regret—that's what was taking so long. *Tell a different story.*

"Do you want to know how I first met the griot of griots?" He managed a sly grin.

Awa clenched her mangled fist. "What good are stories?"

"Griots ask that question every day." Djola blew warmth onto her stiff fingers, and whispered *Anawanama.* Change the language, change the mind. "I was close to your age when I met Yari. Azizi's father had a demented rascal for Master of Arms who ordered a raid on a rebel enclave. He lusted after *vesons* and insisted we bring him captives, not sliced throats."

"You were a shadow warrior, like Bal?" Awa spoke *Anawanama* too.

"No, a bastard mercenary. I fought for gold and sky rocks."

"Elders defend their enclaves fiercely. You're lucky to be alive."

"I had my sword at Yari's neck, and that ax-wielding rogue

seduced me, with stories about talking books, iron horses, and cloud cities across a green sea where behemoths danced on water and sang, where shadow warriors first learned to weave Aido cloth. Jumbajabbaland, home of miracles. I dropped the sword. Yari dropped the ax, leaned against my chest, and sang like a demon choir. *Vie* added drum, and rhythms snuck in between my heartbeats, stole my breath. *Vie* left me dazed in the dirt, desire unquenched, clutching a rope of hair I'd cut. Not what the Master of Arms hoped for, but a treasure for me. I danced with myself, singing harmony to echoes, while Yari galloped away on *my* warhorse, a stallion who stomped anyone who came near except me." He chuckled. "Yari seduced the horse."

"The horse?" Awa chortled and sobbed and pounded her thighs, revving the bees into a roar. Djola hugged her as grief tore through them both.

"Folly. Not even our mission." He stroked her head. "We mercenaries and bastards had been sent to subdue the *Zamanzi,* my grandmother's people." He shivered.

Awa rubbed warmth into him. "You, *Zamanzi* ancestors too?"

"My father's father was a southern barbarian hoping to steal back his lands from the Empire. My *Zamanzi* grandmother captured him in the sweet desert. They joined forces and resisted Azizi's grandfather. Yari and the Elders also refused to be conquered. That thrilled me, and I had to find Jumbajabbaland. The Master of Arms let me join an enclave, to spy on green-land freaks. Yari taught this spy *The Green Elder Songs for Living and Dying.* A true *Lahesh, vie* answered any question and came to me for delicious nights. Make love to your enemy—a foolish creed sometimes, but not always." Heat burst through the crack in his heart.

"You're leaking light." Awa put her hands over his Vévés.

He held up a diamond-tipped blade. "This pierces the rhythm of rocks and metal."

"An Elder weapon. I saw you cut chains on the hovel doors."

"*Lahesh* conjure." Djola set the blade against his neck. "I woke one morning in Yari's bed. *Vie* put this knife in my hand, saying, *Slit my throat or join us.*" Djola trembled, cutting a line of blood on his throat. Awa gripped his hand. Startled, Djola continued. "That week, southern barbarians killed the Master of Arms. Warriors and mercenaries charged off to tame thief-lords, and I joined Yari's enclave. We traveled across the Empire and beyond. Sweet times."

The drum jingled. Muscular arms—haint arms—crushed Djola close and braids tickled his cheek. Djola swallowed a breath of coconut oil and desert rose. He luxuriated in the memory of Yari's embrace. Memory was the master of death. Awa took the knife.

"After my crossover ceremony, I returned to Arkhys City and used Elder wisdom to save Zizi's life, end the wars, and guide Council for twenty years. Zizi named me Master of Poisons for *knowing the antidote to everything.*" Djola scoffed. "Yari was Azizi's trusted advisor too, until we fought. Yari wanted me to run away from Council and bring my family to the enclave to teach the future. Instead I betrayed my family."

"Council betrayed them."

"I'm still the bastard mercenary, ruthless and vengeful. *Xhalan Xhala.* I called up Hezram's future. That's how I brought down Ice Mountain."

"You brought the void to the mountain?"

"Destroying Holy City was revenge, bloodlust." The Vévés on his head throbbed. "I'm the end of that story, but you—"

"*Loving an enemy is good for the heart.*" Awa read *Lahesh* words on the knife. "Isra said Yari could seduce a crocodile." She held the knife out to Djola. "*Basawili.*"

He stowed the blade in his boot. "Yari trusted you and me to defeat Hezram, and as long as we live—*Basawili*—not yet *vie*'s last breath."

"Yari was no match for Hezram." Awa squeezed the drum. "How can we defeat the Master of Illusion?"

"We escaped his tower of fiends, didn't we?"

"That wasn't victory."

"What does victory look like?"

Awa shrugged.

Djola tapped the drum. "Yari came back from living death because of your conjure. Never forget that."

"Our victory was at great cost."

"Like every victory." Djola's cape billowed open, wings fluttering in the wind.

The light bridge ended, and they plummeted through clouds faster than thought. The bees buzzed ahead. Awa squealed. "Glaciers. And beyond, evergreen woods and snowfields."

"Samina won't be far. This is her realm."

"Your dead wife, she calls you to your true name?"

"Samina chose a *Lahesh* way to end war: marry the enemy."

Awa sighed. "You've lost both enemy lovers."

"Samina cheats death. She'll help us defeat Hezram and save the Empire."

"Well, I won't *marry* Hezram. Kill him quickly perhaps."

"Mercy." Djola laughed.

As they raced toward the glint of glaciers, Awa pressed her forehead against his, a daughterly gesture. Djola hugged her close. Awa was the antidote he'd been looking for.

7

Gate Power

The aurora gave way to snowy plains and glacial peaks. Djola's useless right eye oozed bloody pus. He moaned, resisting the pain flaring from foot to knee to back. His heartbeat was dim. His last breath would be sooner than planned. Spirit debt for doing *Xhalan Xhala* as revenge. He let Awa take his weight. Dead weight. She charged on, ferocious and gentle, like the warhorse. "Fannie," he murmured.

Awa dropped down by a hot spring steaming out of heather-covered rocks. Even bleary with exhaustion, she was as graceful as . . . Samina riding a thirty-foot wave under the scar moon. A crow cawed, and Djola blinked this memory away. Awa dipped her feet in warm water and stuck her head into a cloud of steam. Her bee clan buzzed around an enormous hive. Would they be let in? Cathedral trees waved bushy crowns filled with rare songbirds. Purple vines crawled up the trunks. All else was the white, black, and gray of moonlight and dreams. On a ridge high above the trees, someone played a frozen waterfall. Icy tones made Djola shiver.

"Do you live for change, not revenge?"

The cracks in his heart quaked. No seed and silk potion dulled his sensibilities. Samina slid down elephant leaves like dew dripping into shadows. She was shade and memory, the afterglow of life. A cloak of sleet covered her breasts and frothed at hips and ankles. Her heart beat a lightning storm. Bare feet were whisper quiet on ash-colored grass. Djola wanted to run far away or swallow poison and die in her arms. Actually, he longed to rush through the gloom and gather her close. But her skin would feel like death; her breath would be a cold ache sucking warmth and spirit. Djola kept his distance. Samina was a haint, close kin to Hezram's fiends, deadly and unpredictable.

Unaware of Samina behind her, Awa shook mist from her hair and studied Djola. She pulled a gray marble eye from her Aido bag. "Try this." She dropped it in Djola's gloved hand. "Rogue impulse." She gestured at his blank eye.

"Nothing to lose." Djola pressed the marble into the socket. It dissolved with a flash of light and searing pain, a knife through his head. He winced as shadowy grays burst into colors. Samina looked as she did when alive. Her sandy skin was tinged green, her silver hair streaked red. Blue-violet eyes sparkled.

"Can you see?" Awa peered at him. "Better?"

When Djola nodded, Awa drew a metal wheel from her Aido bag and faster than thought pressed it through the crossroads Vévés on his chest. Howling, Djola yanked her hand out. "What is this?" He stared at a golden wheel spinning over the cracks in his heart. He took a deep breath. Vigor returned as the wheel burned bright.

"Jumbajabbaland gifts. Bal gave them to me." Awa grinned. "A conjurer stole Bal's memories to protect her from her parents' dangerous lives. Yari would do that for you and Samina, so perhaps my Bal is your Bal."

Djola wanted to disagree and agree.

"Choose what to believe." Awa sank down near the giant hive. Bees swarmed her.

"Yes, choose," Samina said, drifting close. Snowflake tattoos glinted.

Awa turned. "Kurakao! You're here." She tried to sit up. "I kept my promise."

"Thank you." Samina passed through her like mist through thin fabric. "Now rest." Awa fell asleep in the heather. Her bees flew into the hive, escorted by sluggish sentinels. Samina slithered close to Djola. Chilly breath prickled his skin. A whiff of raintree made him quiver. "Speak, my love," she said. "The dead are too quiet, but the living, I hear you crashing through the world." She circled him. "I worried you might never visit me again."

"I didn't want a fight." The wheel in his heart whirred. "Our last day, before I went to Council, we fought, and I don't know why—"

"You don't?" Samina scoffed. "Well, you've finally come again and aren't drugged." Her hand hovered over the Vévés on his chest. "What cracked your heart?"

Djola swallowed every word that came and shrugged.

She touched his foot, freezing pain. "This wound poisons your blood. It won't heal."

"I know." He drew a breath of her. The raintree aroma was faint, but not just imagined. On previous trips, potions and despair had blunted a desire to cup her breasts, kiss her navel, and draw his tongue along her thighs. This time the longing to be inside her and hold her inside of him made him gasp, gave him strength.

"The golden wheel is good medicine." Samina glanced at Awa. "An antidote to poison."

Djola gathered himself and declared, "I have a plan."

"You brought down Ice Mountain. The Amethyst River is a ruin." Samina bared granite teeth, as if to tear his flesh and suck spirit blood, like demon Yari. "You will soon be shadow and ash, a lament on the wind. What plan?"

"I thought I was rescuing a girl from the huts," he said, "yet Awa rescued me. She is the cure that Zizi needs."

Samina released a bee caught in Awa's bushy kinks. "What of Awa's own plans?"

"She'll come around. When grief dulls."

"Have you come around?"

He looked away from her. "Yari—"

"Dances with the ancestors."

"You felt this?" Djola scanned from the hot spring to the glaciers. "Are we alone?"

"Sister Kyrie came with news. She leaves her mountain and travels to Arkhys City. Hezram travels also, to sit at Council and whisper in Zizi's ear. He tells everyone you're to blame for poison desert."

"Only half a lie."

"You must arrive when Hezram does. Tembe makes corridors for him. High priest Ernold and the Masters of Water and Money welcome him." Samina's granite teeth glistened. "They lust after Kyrie's mountain."

"Twelve rivers are fed by Eidhou's peaks," Djola said.

"Zizi can't hold out much longer."

"What of the Master of Grain?"

Samina's breath had the tang of a lightning storm. "Zizi needs *you*. Kyrie too. Grain fears someone will discover *vie*'s secret. They all fight. Too proud to collaborate."

"Grain is a *veson*?" How had Djola missed this?

"You can weave peace between them."

Djola gripped Samina's hand. The cold didn't bite through his mesh glove. "You and I must talk first. About the transgressor hut, about our children."

"No."

He blew warmth into her fingers. "We never talk about them."

"They put me in a hut to torture you. Our children got lost in poison sand. What more to say?"

"Yari would have saved any one of them *vie* could find." Djola kissed her fingertips. His lips burned. "Bal doesn't haunt me."

"You want to be haunted?" She slipped free and floated up to the frozen waterfall.

"Yes." Djola followed her. "Did you see their bodies? Did Kyrie?"

"You want to believe Bal lives, but I can't help you with that." She seized a wooden mallet and played a familiar melody on hanging crystals and icicles. A few thudded, leaving holes in her song.

Djola found a mallet and played harmony. "I speak the world I want. Don't you?"

"I'm not who I once was," Samina said.

"Why didn't you live?"

"No matter how I look to you, I'm—"

"Why didn't you fight?"

"Council masters tricked me. Your half-brother said they had our children."

"Money and Water poisoned Nuar at Council." Djola's tongue ached.

"Nuar came to me in the huts." Samina swayed in melancholy vibrations. "He was dying. They'd poisoned him. I was not Kyrie. She knows better how to cheat death."

"So you sacrificed yourself. You're the power in her Mountain Gates? Don't lie. I felt you there as I passed through. Tessa and Quint as well. Why didn't you tell me?"

"Eidhou means—*all rivers flow from my heart.*" She played gurgling river music. "All gates require sacrifice, spirit blood."

"You abandoned me."

"You left us for Council, doing what you believed. Could I do less?"

"A clown's crusade," he muttered. "Kyrie saved her mountain, but not you, not Tessa, Quint, or Nuar."

"I gave my life willingly." She sighed a squall of sleet.

"Urzula betrayed you. She took her children to the floating cities while ours died in the desert."

"Don't hold the children against Urzula or Kyrie, and neither are we to blame."

"Whose fault then?" Djola played dissonant tones.

Samina's deep-throated moan echoed through the cave. "Come to Mount Eidhou. We'll tell a different story of Nuar and our children." Samina reached for his mallet. He held onto it. They struggled, flailing against icicles. Several giant ones fell and shattered. Splinters of ice and crystal passed through Samina and cut Djola's cheeks. He lost hold of his mallet as they leapt from the ice shower to the hot spring.

"You know why we fought." Samina pounded him with both mallets. "Why pretend you don't know?" She flung the mallets into the trees.

"I couldn't see another way." He sank down by Awa. A trickster crystal from the cave lodged in his foot wound, replacing one pain with another. He tugged it.

"Leave the crystal be." She gripped his hand "A *Lahesh* cure for blood poisoning."

Djola sighed. "Calling reckoning fire was not as I expected."

"The People burn. Everywhere." Samina stood over him. "Now what?"

"Awa carries Vandana's bag and Yari's drum." He stroked Awa's wiry hair.

"Exactly. You know what to do. You've always known." Samina crouched down. Her violet eyes dazzled him. Raisin navel and nipples poked through her cloak of sleet, a challenge. "Come to

Mount Eidhou." She'd begged him to do this when she lived and there was hope, and now she asked whenever he came to Jumba-jabbaland, yet—

"Impossible. I cannot walk away from the reckoning fires I have started."

Samina stabbed a large bee stinger in Awa's chest. The girl faded into the steam from the hot spring. "Work with Awa to put the fires out, then come." Samina passed through his flesh, a cold shiver, a heartache. "Isn't that what you want?"

"I've poisoned my heart spirit."

"Remember what you always told me?"

"I've told you many things." A hint of her raintree scent lingered on his lips. "Now my mind dissolves."

"Green Elders say, *At the crossroads, change. Then you find another story, another way.*"

"*Abelzowadyo,*" he murmured.

"Yes. The work is never done, but—" She stabbed Djola's golden heart and whispered, "*Impossible is a word for yesterday, not tomorrow.*"

8

Return

Awa's head was trying to catch fire. Hair sizzled and smoked in chilly mist. She was slumped next to Djola who had no hair to burn. A murky crystal was jammed in his foot. They leaned against the elder tree in the foothills of the Eidhou range just beyond a thicket of haints and vines. The sun hid behind fog, offering muted daylight. She pressed her hands into damp earth and tasted tree oil on the air. She blinked several times, happy to see brambles and weeds, delighted by crows strutting along the cliff face eating poison berries. Another miracle—she'd made it back to the everyday.

A cave mouth in the ledge near the top of an outcropping spit sparkling dirt. Awa marveled at this wonder—certain it had been a solid rock wall when they left for Smokeland. And how long ago was that? Time was different in Smokeland. Djola moaned, not all the way to the everyday. Awa refused to worry. *Everybody takes their own time on the light bridge.* Awa put her hand to his heart Vévés. She felt the wheel whirring underneath. A wild dog shoved a cold nose in Awa's crotch and licked her face. His bushy tail was familiar. Fannie reared, as if to pummel him.

"Whayoa, Fannie!" Awa struggled up and clutched the mare's

mane. "We're safe, for a moment I hope." Fannie nuzzled Awa's heaving sides. Standing up almost made her dizzy. The wild dog butted her again and she hugged him.

"While you wandered Smokeland, Fannie let nobody near, for weeks, only the cheeky dog for a sniff." Bal, in silver-mesh armor and Aido tunic, stepped from the cave mouth. Awa shouted and squealed at this vision on a ledge above her. Bal laughed and climbed down the steep incline, an acrobat still. At the bottom, she stood a prudent distance from warhorse hooves. A sword rode her hip; a bow was slung across her back. Braids threaded with leather were pulled into a tight knot. Behind Bal, the cave opened onto a corridor that wavered like a mirage. She struck a pose worthy of a carnival player. Green in dark eyes caught the light. Fierce chin and cheeks framed a crooked smile. Did Bal look like Djola or Samina? "Strays love the smell of Smokeland on you." Bal sounded like herself.

"It's always the same dog," Awa replied.

Tears streaming, she fell into Bal's arms, into the sweetgrass and iron scent, into the steady heartbeat of a shadow warrior. They stood tight, savoring each other. Fannie nosed a stranger, cautious. The dog licked Bal's knees and raced around them wagging his butt. "Two years," Awa said, "I feared you were a story, a lie I told."

"You always tell true stories." Bal kissed the nape of Awa's neck, setting off a cascade of sparks just under her skin. A thrill shivered through them both.

"I didn't think I'd ever see you again." Awa admitted losing hope. "I planned to look for you though."

Bal squeezed her closer. "Weeks we waited, worried that a witchdoctor or priest might snare you in Smokeland. This morning, Iyalawo Kyrie said you and the poison master would return."

"You know Kyrie?"

"We're the Iyalawo's guests in this mountain realm."

"Guests or—" Terror arced up Awa's spine. She stepped away from Bal. "Or prisoners?"

"Why would Kyrie take us prisoner?" Bal furrowed her brow.

"She's a witch woman who loves only her mountain."

"Yari wrote praise songs to Kyrie: *Iyalawo of Miracles*." Bal searched for a tune. "Remember?"

"No."

Bal sang, *"Kyrie, wise woman, a lightning bolt about to strike . . ."* Had Kyrie enchanted Bal? Djola banged his mangled foot and mumbled *Anawanama*, as if scoffing at Awa's fears. Bal drew her sword. "Does he fight fiends in the void again?"

"Again?" Awa stepped between them. "You saw us fight fiends?"

"A nightmare battle. Your skin sizzled and your eyes were fire. His foot withered to ash and smoke. You both turned ice-cold, breathing out snowflakes. Kyrie roamed Smokeland, but she's a terrible mapmaker and couldn't find you, or rouse you in the every-day, even calling on haints to spook you."

Awa gripped Bal's sword arm. "Djola takes his own time coming back."

Bal rubbed a scar along her jaw. "Spirit slaves are lethal even in the everyday." She eyed Djola. "No matter who they once were. We can't be sentimental—"

"I know." Awa pulled Bal away from Djola. "Better than you think."

"Tell me." Sword still raised, Bal narrowed her eyes at Djola and waited.

"Now?" Awa set down Djola's bag. It was heavy in the everyday. Yari's drum was heavier, but she held on to that. "Well, in Jumba-jabbaland—"

"Where?"

"Smokeland. It's overrun. Fiends rule the six regions of my heart."

"Zst! What do priests do with so many spirit slaves?"

"Power their gates and other nightmare spells. I had to stab a fiend's heart . . ." Awa sputtered. Bal would have found a way to save herself, Djola, and Yari too. "The fiend burned from the inside out and I . . ."

"You were brave." Bal scanned brands, scars, and crooked bones. Patchy hair ran riot across Awa's head. "A hero." She stroked Awa's snake birthmark.

"No." Awa cringed. "I'm—"

"Exhausted." Bal reached for the withered hand that had killed Yari.

Awa shied away. "This is—" not quite the reunion she'd imagined. "I am changed."

"Kyrie says you escaped a transgressor hut in Holy City."

"How does Kyrie know that?" Awa's blood boiled, her breath was steam. She wanted to smash or burn or destroy something. She turned away from Bal.

"Tell me later and I will tell you how Yari and I escaped the savages."

"You mean *Zamanzi*."

"Who else? No other savages raid—"

"You could be a northlander."

Bal sheathed her sword. "Yari enchanted the uhm, the *Zamanzi* with tales every night. Soon they were dancing to *vie*'s drum and turning into rebels." Bal wanted to say more, but instead pulled mangos, goat cheese, and honey cakes smeared with nut butter from an Aido bag. "You must eat. Still your favorites, I hope."

Awa snatched the feast and crammed her mouth. Eating was better than quarreling over who the real savages were or telling how she'd stabbed Yari.

Bal forced a smile. "We have many stories to share."

Awa scratched her patchy scalp. "I'd like to burn the last two years from my mind."

"That's what you think now." Bal wrapped Awa's head in sooth-ing cloud-silk and kissed her wiggly birthmark, the way Meera kissed Rokiat when she just felt grateful he was alive and standing close. Awa felt Bal's lips everywhere—down her face, belly, all the way to the tips of her toes, an ache, a delight. What conjure was this?

"Thank you." Awa gulped down cheese and a hunk of mango. The mango taste was sweeter than ever. "But we can't change the past."

"*Dochsi.*" Bal used a *Lahesh* word for arguing against negativity and handed her a gourd of frothy fruit wine. "The future changes the past."

"Don't sing Elder songs to me."

Bal swallowed a retort.

Awa emptied the gourd in two gulps. "Not today. Sing at me tomorrow." Bal touched the Aido bag on Awa's belt, almost empty now. For two impossible years, Awa had managed to keep Bal's treasures safe but then gave them away to Djola.

"You used to love my songs," Bal murmured, "anytime."

Stung, Awa leaned into Fannie. The mare nipped Bal's shoul-der.

Bal offered her figs and a sack of sweetgrass. "I've found my-self." She struck a carnival pose again. "I'm a *veson* and a Green Elder shadow warrior."

Joy waylaid Awa. The dancer's grace, sleek muscles, ranging choir of voices—Bal was just more of what *vie* had always been. "I thought you'd choose shadow warrior."

"And you a griot, like Yari, conjuring this world and the next." Bal brushed crumbs from Awa's nose. "You knew my story before I did."

"My story too. We're one spirit in two bodies." A lie. Awa cringed. Outside of Hezram's Nightmare Gates lies were easy.

Bal's and Awa's bodies had changed and so had their spirits. Who would they be to one another?

The talking drum grumbled, bells and seeds rattling.

Bal tapped the goatskin. "Since when do you carry such an elegant talking drum?"

"Since . . ." Awa choked on her words.

She'd never held a story she didn't know how to tell.

9

Reprieve

Crows screeched and hollered. They swooped from every tree, a storm cloud of iridescent feathers. Several pecked Djola's bald head. The crystal jammed in his foot spewed rainbow spirits and scattered the birds. Agitated cathedral trees flung seeds and spiderwebs into the wind. Fannie pawed the ground, ready to charge. Awa's skin crawled; her mouth tasted foul. The wild dog nipped the back of her knees.

"What's going on?" Awa said, happy for the distraction.

"I don't know." Bal scanned from roots and brush to the treetops.

Awa spit out the foul taste. "Not just rain in the air." The black-and-white crow circled her, squealing an alarm. She followed it to a thicket now blocking the road. "Crows always know something we don't." She fingered boulders, brambles, and a tangle of woody vines. Unruly shadows made a tight weave up into cathedral tree crowns. Weaver ants spit venom. Haints whispered ancestor words too softly for her to understand. "Djola and I came in this way. What happened to the opening?"

"The Mountain Gates close to protect us. What do the trees sing about?"

"Danger. Coming our way."

Bal nodded, unperturbed. "Good citizens lay siege to Kyrie's gates. For two weeks, I've patrolled around the mountain. Nobody has gotten through except a few days ago, *Zamanzi* twins on a red warhorse, escaping transgressor huts in Holy City. Warrior clowns."

"I know them. A boy and a girl. We shared a hut." Awa was glad they escaped even if they were *Zamanzi*. "Anyone else?"

An explosion shook the ground. Horses yelped, horns blasted, and a horde screeched and cursed. The smell of boiled blood and tree oil made Awa gag. Mango and nut butter churned in her stomach, threatening to surge back up. She bent over and sucked deep breaths. The wild dog licked her face.

Bal crept into the bushes, fearless. Fannie trotted close behind *vie,* fearless also. "Who knocks at the gates today?" Bal hissed.

"Hezram." Awa felt him. He probably felt her as well. "Witchdoctor of Illusions."

"What does he want?" Bal halted at the burl-mottled trunktower of an elder tree.

"Djola's conjure bag." Awa crawled to it. The wild dog flanked her. "I carry it."

"That's a good story, I'm sure." Bal took off the bow and sword. "Did the poison master really stuff a library from the floating cities in that?"

"Vandana did. He added song cloth from all the ancestors." Awa heaved the bag across her shoulder. Yari's songs to Kyrie would be in there, and Dream Gate conjure, maybe even a spell to find Meera and Rokiat if they were alive. Awa let Yari's drum slide to the ground. She couldn't manage both. Bal would carry the drum easily. "Yari said Hezram would hunt me and Djola, in the everyday, in dreams."

"You talked with Yari?" Bal circled the tree. "Impossible. How? When?"

Another explosion knocked Bal over before Awa had to answer these questions. Axes rang against stone-hard trunks. Oily smoke seeped through the brambles. Bal scrambled up the trunk-tower. *Vie* leapt from lumpy burls onto flimsy branches and disappeared behind elephant leaves. Awa crept to Bal's tree. The mist turned to a downpour that penetrated the canopy. In a breath she was drenched.

"I see warrior priests, drummers, cooks, and cages full of prisoners. Jod, from our enclave. Fatazz!" Bal screeched over the twang of bows. "Fire arrows! Take cover!"

Too many bolts whooshed through branches and vines. Fannie dragged Djola behind a boulder. Awa hugged the wild dog and flattened herself against the trunk-tower. Djola was right. Hezram would spread disaster across the Empire and beyond. Awa regretted not stabbing him with a viper's fang in the temple when she had the chance. She'd been a coward, saving her own life and dooming others, dooming Yari . . . Wet soot smacked her cheeks and interrupted self-pity. Blobs of ash plopped on Djola's bald head, knees, and everywhere.

"Kyrie's Mountain Gate conjure turns fire arrows to sludge." Bal cheered.

Shrieks and wails poured from the other side, but nothing more fell from the sky, except cold rain. Fannie whinnied relief. The dog wiggled free and shook off a cloud of gray. Awa patted his scruffy head. "Shall I call you Soot?" Soot wagged his bushy tail.

"Fire arrows bounce back or turn to ash in a blink. Cathedral trees refuse to burn and axes fly off the handle. Amber pitch oozes from tree trunks, paralyzing anyone who climbs." Bal cheered. "A blue-robed conjurer stumbles around in circles. One eye is covered by a blue patch."

"Hezram." Awa's heart raced. "If you see him, he might see you. Come down."

"Don't worry. They see only shadows."

Awa slowed her heartbeat. Djola insisted that nobody in the Empire, not even he, could breach Kyrie's gates. Maybe they were safe. "Worry is a bad habit."

"Since when?"

Awa sneered at Bal's ridiculous question. "I wish I could see what they're doing."

A stiff wind blew aside vines and brambles to reveal a chaos of smoking drums and burning bodies on the mountain road. Awa froze. Nobody from the other side looked her way—too busy surviving Kyrie's conjure. Warrior acolytes had been pierced by their own fiery bolts. Many lay dead because of Hezram's arrogance. Others howled and limped as rain turned to hail and battered them. Cooks smothered flames with heavy cloths. Drummers gathered their fallen weapons. Hezram had recaptured many transgressors and the warhorses they rode. Jod, in a bandage and splint, hobbled about smacking prisoner cages. He stumbled to the ground, clutched his leg, and groaned. Awa felt no pity. Jod wanted to be Hezram.

She squinted at a captive rattling the locks and chains that bound her to a cage. The woman's clothes were shreds, her golden hair singed, her face blotchy with bruises. She wore an anklet made from moth cocoons and beetle carapaces. Awa swallowed a shriek. Meera, still alive! A warhorse was tied to Meera's cage— Bibi! She stomped and snorted, chasing off a burning acolyte.

Rokiat circled the wagon-cages, riding Bibi's yearling. He winced at hail pounding his blood-crusted face. Bibi had followed Fannie here and the other horses followed Bibi. Awa whistled an alert to the herd. Bibi, and Meera too, jerked up at the piercing melody. Rokiat snapped his head around as horses whinnied and reared against restraints. Did they see Awa? Fannie dashed past her through the narrow opening to the other side.

"Fannie! Stop!" Vines and roots snagged Awa's leg and held tight. "Come back."

"An Iyalawo with gold tattoos joins Hezram's dance," Bal shouted.

"Zst! Tembe." Awa clawed at vines holding her prisoner. "The wise woman of Ice Mountain. She worships Hezram."

"Then Tembe isn't a wise woman, but a fool."

Awa whistled a come-home call to Fannie who kicked at ropes and stakes hobbling the horses. "Tembe has roots beyond the Empire in the floating cities."

"So?" Bal said. "Fools blow themselves up there too."

"Tembe might know conjure to break through Kyrie's gates."

Bal had no cheeky reply for that.

10

A Good Story

A deep voice echoed around the cliffs. "My gates will hold against Tembe."

Awa stared through a gap in those gates to Fannie and Bibi, head-to-head, conferring and gnashing teeth by Meera's cage. Bibi reared up, straining against hobbles. She shoved Fannie and nipped her flanks. Meera rattled the cage as Rokiat raced toward them.

"Do not worry." A figure in a flame-cloth robe and pirate pants cinched at the ankles jumped down from the cave of mirages and blocked Awa's view. *"Basawili."* The voice was a round, fierce woman, with silver tattoos, silver hair streaked red, and blue-violet eyes like Samina. Calm as dirt and clear as a drumbeat, she chanted *Lahesh, Anawanama, Zamanzi*, and languages Awa didn't yet know. Trees echoed the woman's songs and haints danced to her rhythms.

"Iyalawo Kyrie." Terrified, Awa wriggled free of brambles. She spread her arms wide, and bowed. Kyrie acknowledged the greeting, flicked sparks from her fingertips, and headed for Djola, who still lay slumped against the boulder. Fannie galloped through the narrowing gap just before vines, branches, and roots closed tight again. The sun broke apart clouds, and the rain subsided. Had Kyrie conjured the storm?

"Warhorses try to break free, kicking and biting. Acolytes run shrieking down the road." Bal swung down on a purple vine, singing harmony with *vie*self:

> *Warrior, warrior, why do you lament?*
> *Are the arrows in your bow all spent?*
> *My song got lost late last night*
> *Running from a quaking tongue*
> *My burnt lips refused to fight*
> *My rebel heart was undone*
> *Stiff fingers stroked deadly air*
> *Tomorrow's songs dying there*

As Bal gathered sword and bow, Fannie nosed *vie*, approving of Green Elder music. Bal scratched velvet ears and sang on.

> *Warrior, warrior, sweet enemy mine*
> *Why do we squander so much sunshine?*
> *Our songs won't run far away*
> *Just into another day*
> *Warrior, warrior, have you forgotten?*
> *Greed makes even sweet apples rotten*
> *With no stout hearts to keep time*
> *Or breath and bones for good reason and deep rhyme*
> *Doesn't really matter, your breath lost or mine*
> *No songs will save this fine day*
> *I say, warrior, warrior sweet enemy mine*
> *With no stout hearts to keep time*
> *No songs will save this fine day*

Green Elder music energized Awa. Meera, Rokiat, Bibi, and the herd were alive. Awa would free them from Hezram with Fannie and Bal's help. Somehow. Awa hugged the warrior and the horse in bright sunshine.

"Don't rejoice yet." Kyrie prodded Djola. "Hezram will head to Arkhys City. He brings Azizi warhorses, an army of acolytes, and transgressors to bleed."

"I saw my friends from Holy City," Awa said.

"Yes." Kyrie scowled at her. "The gates opened at your request."

"I made no request." Or maybe she did. Awa pushed confusion aside. "Meera and Rokiat escaped when I did, but Hezram must have captured them and the horses." Curses filled Awa's mouth. Perhaps Rokiat had betrayed Meera. He wasn't in a cage.

"Tell us about Hezram." Bal picked up Yari's drum, recognition dawning.

"Yours now," Awa said, too quickly.

Bal frowned and tied the drum to a sweetgrass belt. "Another good story." Bal stepped breath-close, straightened Awa's cloud-silk head wrap, and pouted like the petulant child *vie* used to be. "We'll help your friends."

"You will?" Awa was dazzled by Bal's ferocity.

"Of course, I would do anything for you." Bal stroked Awa's snake birthmark. "But you're a stingy griot. You owe me several stories."

"Hezram is danger," Awa said quickly. "In Jumbajabbaland he was as powerful as . . . as . . . as Yari."

"*Basawili.*" Kyrie pounded Djola's chest and shouted in *Anawanama*. "Good citizens believe poison desert won't breach Hezram's Dream Gates and they're happy to bleed other people's children. Council and Azizi too. Fools."

Djola opened his eyes, one black, one red, and scanned from

the shimmering cave to piles of ash. He jiggled the crystal in his foot. It flared. "Kyrie, Kyrie. Only bad news. It has been many terrible years. Where's the greeting?" He slurred his words and sounded drunk. Soot licked his face.

"The People eat each other. Time for salutations is past," Kyrie replied.

Awa escaped Bal and ran to Djola. "Are you all right?"

He laughed at her stupid question. Death wheezed at the back of his breath. "I presume you've introduced yourselves."

Kyrie shook her head. "No need. Everyone has heard of me, and Bal told endless tales on her beloved Awa."

Embarrassed, Awa leaned her forehead to Djola's and whispered, "I worried you might get lost in the void."

He patted her cheek with a mesh glove. "You saved me. How can I get lost now?"

Awa sputtered, so much sentiment coming at her. "We saved each other."

"Haints fortifying my gates won't linger forever," Kyrie declared. "New sacrifices must be made."

Djola grunted. "I don't have much left to sacrifice."

"I don't feel sorry for you," Kyrie snapped. "We must get you to Council. I've conjured a corridor almost to Arkhys City. Tembe will do the same for Hezram when they regroup. Can you walk?"

"Not fast, not far," Djola replied.

Kyrie hauled him to standing and pointed at the mirage cave nestled up in the cliffs. It seemed distant, a steep climb over treacherous cliffs. Djola teeter-tottered. He'd never make it on his own. Kyrie kissed her teeth and poked rocks and dense brush on the ridge. Fannie wouldn't make the climb either.

"We can't leave the warhorse behind," Awa said.

"Of course not." Bal threw Djola's blood-crusted arm around *vie*'s neck and shouldered his weight.

Djola squinted. "Who are you, disappearing in bright light?"

"A shadow warrior," Awa said. "That's my Bal."

Djola gasped. Awa also attended to her breath.

"Did Awa tell tales on me?" Bal kept him from falling over. "I'm no haint or fiend."

Djola nodded at Bal's Aido cloth tunic. *To see new patterns, you need new eyes.* He tried to open his cape. "I wear the same pattern. *Lahesh* invented this in Smokeland."

"I didn't know that," Bal said mildly, "and Yari was my teacher."

Kyrie rolled her eyes and muttered a curse about tinkerers and wim-wom.

Djola sagged. "We're all fools, acting as if what we know is all there is to know." He stroked Bal's face and looked ready to weep. He dropped his hand. "Ignorance won't save us from the Master of Illusion." More words tangled on his tongue.

Muffled screeches from Hezram's side made Awa flinch.

Kyrie gripped Djola's chin. "Here's the news: Good citizens think the gods are cruel old witchdoctors living on mountaintops. They believe I power demon gates with stolen phalluses, eat my enemies' hearts, and even call up bad weather."

Luckily Awa hadn't commented on Kyrie conjuring storms. "The *Anawanama* say: *We are the weather,*" Awa declared.

"Indeed." Kyrie spat on smoldering ashes and strode to her Mountain Gates. She stroked the vines and brambles that had opened for Fannie. Hidden under leaves and in the elbows of branches were a hundred hundred knife-like thorns. Kyrie took a breath and fell. Thorns pierced her face, neck, chest, belly, thighs, and ankles.

Awa lurched toward her. "What are you doing?"

Djola lunged at of Awa. "Let her be." That move took all his strength. He dropped down on a cathedral root arching over a boulder. Bal and Awa exchanged worried glances as he spoke through gritted teeth. "Kyrie joins the mountain."

"Whatever that means." Awa worried for Kyrie *and* Djola. Bal stood behind Djola, letting him lean into *vie's* knees.

Kyrie pulled away from the thorns. "Most people believe rivers, dirt, trees, and bees have no spirit or destiny." Blood and silvery fluid oozed from many wounds, yet her voice was strong. "Even in the floating cities, the world is a dead thing. Nothing but greed and power are sacred. That's why I left."

Djola snorted. "You conjured peace with Zizi and the Empire. Floating-city Babalawos called you traitor and sent your husband to poison you. That's why you left." This wasn't the story Awa had heard.

"Yes, my one true love betrayed me." Kyrie sounded wistful. She tramped below the mirage cave and splattered silvery blood. Vines retreated and rocks dissolved. "Don't worry, Awa, we aren't people who betray the ones we love."

"You're a mountain, Kyrie. I don't know who I am," Djola and Bal said in unison and then gaped at each other.

"Griots tell wild tales about the witch of Mount Eidhou," Awa stuttered.

"Griots are the best liars." Kyrie stomped along the cliff face, dripping blood. Bushes, roots, and rocks dissolved. She was carving out a path.

"What about commandeering Samina to power your Mountain Gates?" Djola said. "Your sister, your own blood?"

"Sisters?" Awa exclaimed.

Kyrie turned a large boulder in her way to vapor. She was zigzagging up toward the mirage cave. "I conjure only with the willing."

"Samina was *willing* to do whatever you asked." Djola hugged his rage. "Why not ask her to save herself?"

Kyrie stared into the trees. "After you were exiled, I didn't know where Samina and your children were."

Djola sank down again. "In a secret hideaway I built up the coast. Nobody but half-brother Nuar knew that. And my guard."

"Ahh." Kyrie stumbled over nothing. "Samina brought the children to Arkhys City to find you."

"Of course," he muttered.

"She didn't dare smoke-walk under the eyes of priests. When we finally met in Smokeland, she wanted to find you. Who argues with Samina when her mind is set?" Kyrie paused at a bulging ledge. "I don't force rocks, trees, and people to do my bidding or command a haint army. People tell lies on me."

Djola trembled and shook his head. The crystal in his foot flared.

Awa stepped on the path Kyrie carved. It was steep and narrow, but Fannie could manage it. "Your power is not a lie."

Bal bristled. "People fear and hate power in a woman."

Awa touched a silver fleck from Kyrie's wound. Her finger burned. She rubbed it quickly in soothing dirt. "They think Kyrie is ruthless and heartless."

"Heartless for protecting her mountain, her people?" Bal shouted. "That's the nettle weed calling the prickly pear too sharp."

Awa stood breath close to Bal. "Griots say Kyrie's people are stingy haints, hiding in a green-land mountain paradise."

"They're refugees from Empire wars," Bal replied.

"Why care about refugees or their pile of rocks? Arkhysian farmers and good citizens starve and freeze. Hezram promises a sweet yesterday instead of a bleak tomorrow. Who can resist that?"

Bal's face twisted. "You defend that dung heap after what he did to you?"

"I don't defend Hezram," Awa stammered. "You're too angry to—"

"Aren't you angry?"

"We have to see how other people see." Djola's voice cracked.

"I do," Bal shouted. "Northlanders and good citizens would make me choose woman or man, or burn me alive. *Zamanzi* burned Isra right in front of us. Remember?"

"Yes, but—" Awa wanted to forget. "We—"

"Barbarians kill elder trees for temple bonfires. Good citizens suck every root dry to light the night. They let Hezram bleed a thousand thousand transgressors to death. I could—"

"What?" Awa hissed. "I siphoned oil from roots and slaughtered many, many trees." She touched a young cathedral sapling. "You'd put an arrow through every heart that bowed to Hezram's power? You'd kill us all?"

"Come!" Kyrie hugged a boulder partially blocking the cave entrance. It rolled aside until the opening was big enough for a warhorse. Kyrie's blood path sparkled in the sun, beckoning them. "I'll help with Djola."

As Kyrie raced down to them, Bal spoke in a choir of angry voices. "Where is Kyrie's stool at Council? She uses gate conjure to protect Mount Eidhou, but has no spirit slaves, bleeds nobody but herself. And they say *she* is a monster, while Hezram with his lies, terror huts, and illusions is a hero, a savior welcomed to Council by Azizi."

The crystal in Djola's foot spit murky spears of light then turned clear. He wheezed at the pain. "Let's not fight one another."

Soot licked Bal's knees. "Truth is—hard to accept." Bal swallowed more argument.

"Truth is whatever you're willing to believe," Djola declared.

"Nothing more, nothing less." Kyrie took his hand. "My true love drank poison the floating-city Babalawos gave him for me. He snatched the cup away from me at the last moment and took his own life. Without his sacrifice, I'd have never realized the danger, never escaped the floating cities, never made peace with Azizi. He loved me more than his own life. Love is power."

"Love? Power?" Awa's mouth fell open. Wounds on Kyrie's face leaked silver. Other wounds had crusted over, Vévés to mountain and forest spirits. This Kyrie was not the Kyrie of legends. "How do we change what people are willing to believe?" Awa asked.

"We must hurry. Azizi is still willing to believe Djola." Kyrie pulled him and Bal along the path. "This way to that truth."

"Why trust Azizi, Kyrie?" Bal's voice echoed around the mountain, calm once more.

"I don't," Kyrie replied. "I trust you, Awa, and people I don't know who seek to join with the *Weeds and Wild Things,* with the rocks and rain. Even Djola."

He flinched. "Trust is our wealth."

Awa shook her head at Elder-speak.

Djola touched her cheek and said, "We are Yari's hope."

II

A Mirage

They tramped up Kyrie's blood path at Djola's pace, Bal shouldering his weight now and again. Fannie pawed vines creeping back over red dirt. Soot nipped at warhorse heels and kept her moving. Kyrie regaled them with tales of good folks slogging through the void and suffering enormous sacrifices to make a better way for all. Bal argued with Kyrie's hopeful chatter but Awa barely listened to these griot tales for children.

After returning from Jumbajabbaland, Awa had planned to give the conjure bag back to Djola then leave him to his save-the-Empire quest and go find Bal. But here was Bal on a save-the-Empire quest too or something similar with Kyrie. Bal wasn't Awa's Bal anymore, and suddenly, killing Hezram and rescuing Meera, Rokiat, and the warhorses seemed impossible, even with what she'd learned from Djola.

Awa shivered in a chill wind. The Master of *Weeds and Wild Things* had one foot in the death lands and was barely able to carry himself. No giving back the conjure bag to him, it was almost too heavy for Awa in the everyday. What then? Abandon Djola and Bal to witch-woman Kyrie? One breath, Awa was full of bravado, the next full of dread. She stumbled over nothing. "Zst!" A poor griot, Awa didn't know what story to tell on her future.

"Too many people are good *and* weak. Hezram exploits this," Bal said and hauled Djola into the cave, a tunnel actually, through the mountain.

Soot scampered behind them, drooling and wagging his tail. Happy! Awa dragged into the gloom. Her breath fogged in the tunnel's icy air and her skin prickled. Cold conjure. Translucent ground and walls looked onto darkness flecked with stars, like the light bridge. The sun shone in blue sky at both ends. Fannie gnashed her teeth and shook her mane. Warhorses hated caves and tunnels, no matter how miraculous.

"Fannie, my heart, the tunnel's shorter than it looks." Curiosity shifted Awa's mood. She had been dead to the world when Djola conjured a corridor as they escaped Holy City. "This passageway is more than a trick on the eye," she shouted to Kyrie. "You've folded space and bent time and light. Is Samina's light bridge a wise-woman corridor connecting Smokeland regions?" Kyrie mumble-grumbled. Awa took that as a yes.

"When we were Sprites"—Bal leaned into Djola, bright and cheery again—"Awa could never help thinking a knotted thing apart."

"Those days are gone." Awa's insides roiled. She was ravenous. Regular feasting made hunger hard to ignore. Would she ever feel full?

Soot nosed Awa's crotch, catching her distress. He licked her fingers.

"Can you walk faster, Awa?" Kyrie yelled over a shoulder and picked up speed.

"I'll try." Each step sent shivers of pain through Awa's bad leg. Nothing else throbbed or oozed. Djola was a good healer. She thanked Vandana for that.

Bal and Kyrie lifted him over uneven ground and carried him up an incline. They went faster than Awa, even lugging his dead weight. She stumbled back into Fannie, whose ears stood erect. The warhorse was on alert for ambush. Crows circled above, mocking clumsy people. The cheeky piebald one landed on Awa's shoulder, plucked a glittery thread from the cloud-silk head wrap, and flew on.

"Djola," Awa said, "your annoying birds keep us company no matter where we go."

"Not my crows," Djola replied. "Yours."

Awa scoffed. "Of course they're yours."

"They belong to themselves," Bal sang.

"Awa's friends then," Djola said, "following her all the way from Holy City." He sounded better, but dragged his foot and left a trail of slime.

Bal laughed at crows swooping for Soot's tail. "Who has too many friends?" This sweet nature grated. Hadn't Bal been the calm, bleak one when they were Sprites? Who was this volatile, cheery stranger? Bal turned and grinned at Awa as if she were coconut wine that *vie*'d like to guzzle right now in front of everyone. "You know I'm right. Friends are wealth too." Bal loved a memory, a good story, not who Awa was now.

"Well—" Awa froze.

She didn't trust love. Mother loved Father so much, she didn't poison him after he sold her daughter. Djola loved Azizi even after Azizi had banished him, let his wife and children die, and then devastated the Empire. Djola forgave Azizi, but not Kyrie. Did he really expect more from a woman, from an Iyalawo, like Bal said? Maybe Awa did too.

Bal shot Awa another lusty look before lifting Djola over a muddy hole. "I've got you," Bal whispered, sultry, throaty, talking to them both. Which story would Bal (and Djola) choose—lost daughter who'd become a protégé of Kyrie or shadow warrior orphan with a common name? Both might be true.

A black crow snatched the silver thread from the piebald one. They swooped around a ledge, teasing each other. Their carefree banter annoyed Awa. Why crows liked her or how Soot always found her or why Djola trusted her with his bag was a mystery. And what was Kyrie up to? Too many secrets and mysteries made Awa's head throb.

"You're so quiet back there," Bal said. Bells and seeds on Yari's drum rattled in time with their march. Bal added an occasional rhythmic flourish—an invitation to hold forth. Any griot could hear that. Awa refused.

"Hoarding all your good stories." Bal kissed her teeth with mock irritation. "Spare us boredom. Tell your tales."

A fearless shadow warrior would never understand life in the transgressor huts or love such a *weak* good person as Awa, such a broken person. Her bad leg screamed pain as her foot got caught in a crevice. She wrenched muscles to stay upright.

"I need breath for speed." Awa lied with truth, a Holy City habit she couldn't shake.

"Please. What of the musician whose spirit haunts the drum? Or the goat who lost her hide for upbeats?" Bal dared Awa to tell how she came by Yari's drum.

"Sugar on dung." Awa rubbed her face. Bal wouldn't give up until *vie* extracted the snake-venom tale. "Well—"

Fannie squealed and reared. Awa clutched her mane as she backed up. An elephant lumbered their way, wavering like a mirage. Scars crisscrossed her back and one tusk was a jagged stump. The enormous beast moved fast, ears flapping, trunk extended. For an instant Awa feared she was the vanguard of a barbarian thief-lord raid. Yet Kyrie and Bal smiled and waved. Soot wagged his tail. The elephant halted before Djola and trumpeted. She extended her trunk and gathered his scents: Jumbajabbaland, honeybees, raintree blossoms, void rot.

"Mango knows you, remembers you," Kyrie said.

Djola pressed his nose to the tip of Mango's trunk. "Why name an elephant Mango?" He grumbled, happy to see the beast.

"Why not?" Bal asked.

Mango wrapped her trunk around Djola's waist and pulled him closer, rumbling. He leaned against her broad forehead, rumbling a reply. Mango dropped to one knee.

"The Master of *Weeds and Wild Things* indeed," Awa whispered.

Djola wiped blood from his marble eye and tears from Mango's cheeks, before scrambling onto her back. Ancient Kyrie climbed up, agile and practiced. Maybe she wasn't as old as lying griots claimed. Old didn't have to mean infirm, yet Kyrie defied the stories. The elephant headed out the corridor into a mango grove. The exit was closer than Awa realized. Bal leapt up on Fannie and hauled Awa up too. They trotted into warm sunlight. Awa felt dizzy, uncertain. Her thoughts were riddled with the hidden lies she was *willing to believe*. How would she ever clear her mind?

The elephant stomped away from the grove. Fannie looked back to the cave.

"Mango knows the best way to Arkhys City." Kyrie was eager to battle Hezram's lies.

"Good. Once we're there, I've made a plan with Samina." Djola was also unafraid.

"Better than the Holy City plan, I hear. No turning a mountain to poison desert." Kyrie smirked. "That golden heart wheel holds you to life. Let's not waste it."

"Golden heart wheel?" Bal poked Awa. "From Smokeland?"

"Yes," Djola said. "*Lahesh* conjure I suspect. Griots say some *Lahesh* escaped the everyday with their spirit *and* breath bodies. They roam the inner seas, tinkering and drumming."

Awa almost burst into tears. The boat people were *Lahesh*! Yari's people, living in Smokeland and Hezram hounds them.

Bal squeezed Fannie's sides to get her moving. "Where'd you get a heart wheel?"

Awa talked over Bal. "Does Samina know conjure to stop Hezram?"

"Yes. Yari did too. *Abelzowadyo*," Djola replied, and Awa lost a few breaths.

"What's that?" Bal hugged Awa's trembling shoulders. "I'm a tough blade of sweetgrass. Don't worry about tromping me down. I can hear any story you tell."

"*Abelzowadyo* is *Zamanzi* for sacred shapeshifter. Yari told us," Awa said. "Djola will explain. He's a wise man, good at explaining." Let him tell of Yari's death and their trip to Samina's cold realm. Awa leaned onto Fannie's neck, urging the warhorse to follow the elephant. She whispered, "While they save the Empire, we can rescue Meera, Rokiat, and Bibi."

Fannie snorted, not eager for this journey either. She reared and kicked before reluctantly trotting on to save their friends.

BOOK
V

1

Hidden Faces:
What Fannie Knows

F annie, my heart, we can't go back."

The whirlwind of dust, ash, and sparks leaking from the border-void blows itself out. Afternoons have the worst leaks. Fannie looks back toward the Mountain Gates.

"Not that way." Awa gestures at the Empire Road, at tree ruins in the storm's path. "Only forward."

Every day Awa says this, for many days. She sounds like clover and sweetgrass even speaking nonsense. Still, Fannie flattens her ears, angry. The elephant drops a bushel of dung and plods down the mountain toward Arkhys City, a few days' march at elephant pace. Fannie follows even though she hates leaving her herd on the other side of a bush gate with hairy cowards from Holy City. She worries she'll never see Bibi and the others again. Bibi nipped tender flanks to chase Fannie away.

Fannie knows no way to untie knots or chew through chains and rescue the herd. And why abandon Awa or Djola to become a slave, even when they head the wrong way? After traversing the light bridge too fast (and burning her eyebrows off), Awa can barely stand. Walking a great distance is impossible. Awa carries too many heavy weights—a mountain, a river, and pieces of the sky. Djola is mortally wounded. *"Abelzowadyo!"* he rasps, but no matter the wheel at his heart and the crystal in his foot, he leaks spirit into the void.

Still, Awa and Djola are hope.

Two years ago, Fannie was war sick too, ready to abandon everyone, ready to lie down and not get up, ready to be smoke in the void. Awa sang Jumbajabbaland songs till Fannie stopped jolting at every rustle or flicker. Awa cleaned the battlefields from her hooves, brushed terror off her back, soothed her from withers to tail. Awa (and her bee and crow friends and Soot too) faced down drunk acolytes to protect Fannie, Bibi, and the herd. And before Ice Mountain came crashing down and the Amethyst River lost its banks, Djola opened rusty Green Gates and called the herd to freedom. So, despite the horrors Fannie glimpses in the gloom as they march closer to Arkhys City, she matches her gait to the elephant's—an unwieldy fearless creature—who rumbles, bellows, and flaps giant ears. Rogue warriors scurry out of their way. Predators keep their distance. Fannie is grateful for elephant conjure protecting them.

The wrong direction might be the shortest way home.

Mount Eidhou hides its snowy head in mist for most of their journey, but on the fourth day at sunset, blue ice glaciers ghost above a ring of clouds. Arkhys City is a festering splotch sprawled at the base of the foothills, spewing dark rivulets into the sea. Fannie smells the riots before she hears or sees them. The wind reeks of blood, vomit, and burnt flesh. The city attacks itself. What do Awa or Djola hope to find there?

Years ago, Fannie rode into the capital, twice, with the big herd, when she was not yet leader, when she was young, and they followed a sandy mare with a golden mane and a brave heart. The city smelled of clover, oats, and ripe fruits. Baskets lined the roads, and she ate whatever she wanted. Crowds threw flowers and cheered. The morning after Fannie's second and last visit, the sandy mare went down and never stood up. Warriors hacked her legs and thrust spears into her heart.

Several brave mares died, and then Fannie was leader, charging through blood and bones, running toward spears and bows, and the herd followed her. Death came from every shadow. So many lives ambushed and lost, who could claim victory? Fannie stumbled around all night with a dead man on her back. Finally, hairy warriors, stinking of tree oil and blood, brought the herd to Holy City. Fannie chomped fingers, broke ribs, and kicked a few heads so they'd kill her quickly or leave her alone. She never trusted Hezram's gang. Raiders and thieves, blood always on their breath, they would prey on anyone, even themselves.

If nobody shows mercy, as the Amethyst River says, who should Fannie trust?

The last splinters of sunlight leave the sky. They are almost down the final hill. Awa falls asleep against Fannie's neck, snoring into her mane, trusting her and the void-smoke direction they take. Distant screams and last breaths make Fannie's ears shiver. Soot howls. Not an everyday yapper, this dog comes from beyond the smoke, from Jumbajabbaland like Fannie, or she might have stomped him already.

The emperor's warhorses all come from beyond the smoke. The *Lahesh* admired their strong hearts, loyalty, and courage. They invited a herd to the everyday, as friends. Raiders killed the *Lahesh*, stole the horses from themselves, and made them laborers and warriors. The mares who led that first journey are long dead, and young colts born recently know only the everyday. Fannie is old enough to remember life on the other side, but she is afraid to take the herd back home. What if they get stranded in the void?

And now the border-void leaks into the everyday . . .

Last week, guarding Awa's and Djola's breath bodies at the

elder tree, Fannie heard cries for help from Jumbajabbaland. She stepped sideways, skirting smoky borderlands. Whenever she'd done this before, fruit trees and sweetgrass meadows greeted her; travelers danced in cathedral branches; water creatures sang from the sea. This trip, Fannie smelled hungry spirit slaves. She spied elder trees ripping roots and running from poison sandstorms, but saw nowhere to roam free. The void swirled around her hooves and up her legs, dulling her thoughts, drinking her will. A fiend sprang at her from rotten bushes. Reacting as in battle, Fannie sidestepped back to the everyday. She shook off the itchy smoke clinging to her mane. Any fate in the everyday was better than becoming an empty-eyed fiend or adding heart spirit to the void.

Soot scurries between Fannie's feet and growls the memories away.

"Somebody behind us?" The shadow warrior twists around and puts an arrow to the bow, yet the warrior's heart does not race when they cross a rickety bridge made of woven sweetgrass. The bridge sways under their feet. Fannie hates this. Thunder River crashes far below them in a rocky ravine. Fannie wants to turn back and go anywhere else. The shadow warrior sings and caresses her sides. Fannie sways with the elephant, sick in her stomach. Then hooves touch solid ground again. Relief. She nickers.

The elephant turns and tickles Fannie with the fingers in her trunk, a friendly gesture. The shadow warrior pulls a thread and the rope bridge unravels. It whistles in the wind and smacks against rocks before splashing into water. Fannie is glad they won't return this way. Crows holler and swoop. The hairy cowards tracking them must find another crossing. Fannie snorts relief. Darkness will end soon. Sunlight is always a balm.

Djola grumbles, twitches, and moans. Awa jerks awake and sits up.

Kyrie curses. "*Veson*-sacrifices to the mountain god."

Two bodies hang in a tree, flayed flesh, burnt faces, upwind. Fannie shies away too late to avoid them. The elephant wails, vibrating the ground under their feet. The herd halts, quiet, agitated. This is not the work of hungry predators, but warriors or angry people who leave flesh to rot. Fannie is impatient as Kyrie and Bal cut the bodies down and scatter flesh and bones in the brush. When done, Bal trembles and moans, batting Kyrie away. Awa slides down to hug and kiss Bal, and they sway with the breeze. Awa knows how to stroke terror away. She sings a Green Elder song and soothes everyone. Fannie nudges Awa, not wanting to remain. The elephant wraps her trunk around Kyrie's arm before she climbs back up. Fannie wants to gallop away from death and sadness. Even the elephant manages to go a bit faster.

They trot along walls covered in a filigree of silver-mesh as in Holy City. Artisans have crafted crossroads Vévés to call down spirits and hold them. Djola curses and Kyrie sucks her teeth. Fannie neighs, agreeing with their distress. Silver-mesh corrals stretch around the city, a promise, a threat, not yet animated by haints or spirit slaves. They reach a wall that is being rebuilt with silver-mesh. Djola and Kyrie hunch down on the elephant to pass under a dilapidated archway into the city. Empire guards, tottering in a drunken stupor, motion them down cracked marble stairs. Fannie's iron shoes skid on the slick surface. She looks back to mountain cliffs and freedom.

"Rebels should stay alert," Bal hisses at the guards.

Soon there will be sober warriors and locks on sturdy corral gates. Why turn themselves into prisoners? Somehow Fannie must get Bibi and their big herd free again before Arkhys City is as dead as Holy City, before there is no escaping poison desert. She snorts stinging granules from her nose and lifts her head. Awa strokes her neck. The Amethyst River is wrong about Awa and Djola. Fannie knows their hearts. In the face of great danger, they seek help in Arkhys City to save the herd.

The city's guard towers are dim and spooky. No tree-oil lamps light the way. Too many faces hide in dark recesses. Who can tell what ambush desperate citizens might plan? As dawn colors the sky, Mount Eidhou casts circles of red light up into the clouds, a fiery crown atop blue glaciers. Good citizens in doorways and windows glower and drool as if they want roast dog, horse, or even grilled elephant for breakfast. Hunger makes fools of us all. Soot stays close to elephant legs. Fannie would stomp any fool trying to snatch him.

Musicians raise a racket in the distance. Fannie hesitates. The elephant matches her bellows to the music and picks up speed. Djola's grumbling fades. Bal adds harmony to the music as they amble closer to the market. Onion towers on the emperor's sandstone citadel gleam with hints of dawn. Tree-oil lamps in a hundred windows wink at them. Banners catch a breeze and stir up birds roosting in high windows. They fly through dust demons, squawking. Fannie hates the sand in her nostrils.

Once lush, Arkhys City is now a desert town in the rain shadow of the mountain. Fannie lifts her ears. Thunder River clatters down from glaciers through rock culverts and separates the oasis at Rainbow Square from the emperor's citadel. Deep roots drink from the river. Pendulous white and purple blossoms sway in the breeze. Raintrees in bloom on the banks of the river are impervious to void-winds. For now. Songbirds offer finicky lovers sand beetles and chirps.

Fannie isn't lulled by this tranquility. She stays alert. At the riverbanks multiheaded giants with tree trunk legs and cloud-silk robes dance around a warhorse from Holy City. At such a distance, vision is vague. Fannie rears, ready to fight foes or show allies the measure of her fury and power. From years on the battlefields,

she knows masked carnival players are unpredictable and dangerous, but warrior-clowns also might possess conjure Awa and
Djola need.

A good masquerade could save you from death.

2

Eishne, Festival of Memories

I told you," Djola sputtered at Bal. "*Abelzowadyo* means sacred shapeshifter."

Desperate, exhausted, and not quite right in his mind, Djola bounced into Arkhys City's sprawling market on an elephant's back. The market was a city within the city. Wading through clouds of dirt and dung, gawking at stalls, animals, and people from everywhere, he felt as flimsy as a forgotten ancestor. Vendors setting up shop cheered carnival rogues making a grand entrance.

Bal stood on a high-stepping mare with ribbons in a red mane and juggled four blades. *Warhorse* or *Shadow Warrior* never crossed their minds. Awa and Soot wore identical headdresses with feathers, bells, and glittery fur. They could have been *Lahesh* tricksters of old. Kyrie sat in front of Djola, wearing patchwork robes, her silver hair concealed in purple cloth. Mountain Vévés on cheeks and brows looked like face paint. Oohing and cooing, the witch of Mount Eidhou painted a yellow snake on Mango's brow. Djola's lip curled. Rage at Kyrie was maybe unjust, but Kyrie should have persuaded Samina to live.

Crows circled overhead, squawking.

"Fleas and farts!" Sparks flew from Kyrie's fingers at mercenaries with hungry eyes. "We speak *Anawanama* and listen to the birds. They'll warn us."

Hiding in Djola's mother's tongue to pass as carnival players was Awa's idea. Djola felt ambivalent. Ancestor talk was powerful conjure, dangerous even. A player with a wheel heart, marble eye, and crystal foot might lose his wits talking *Anawanama* and never get an audience with the emperor. His old friend had banished him on pain of death. Were Djola and Zizi friends anymore?

"The library has a new wing." Kyrie had been away as long as Djola. "The city shapeshifts. *Abelzowadyo.*"

"Not just buildings—" Nothing in Arkhys City *felt* as Djola remembered it. Dark-eyed towers loomed over them, whistling a reproach on the wind. Only the emperor's citadel across the river was lit by tree-oil lamps. Without supplies from Holy City or Kyrie's mountain, Arkhys City suffered cold, dark nights. The citadel's hundred lights winked out all at once, an eerie spectacle. He wrinkled his nose. "Did it always stink?"

"Doesn't smell worse than Holy City." Awa was in a terrible mood too—who could fault her? Offal from recent riots turned brown on stone streets. Sewers reeked, overflowing before reaching Thunder River or the sea. Crows descended on a corpse shoved to the roadside. Djola looked away, not wanting to know who'd been left to rot.

"This is worse than I remember." He spat out the new taste of Arkhys City.

"We've changed too. All of us, storm weary." Kyrie pointed at storm shelters along the buildings. Every stall had flaps to pull down.

Djola shook his head. "Who knows where the wind will blow?"

Mango squeezed past bedraggled farmers, thief-lord brigades, river pirates, miners, Green Elders, and pickpockets lifting purses.

Today the *Eishne* Festival of Memories began. Two hours before the sun climbed over Mount Eidhou, the gates opened to everyone, even refugees fleeing Holy City. Djola cringed at tales of the Master of Poisons bringing down Hezram's temple.

"Today is *Eishne*," Kyrie shouted. "We're all strangers, but woven from the same threads, so one family, and we remember ourselves."

Azizi and Urzula commandeered an *Anawanama* sacred day to celebrate their wedding anniversary and twenty-eight years of Empire peace. According to Grain, Council wanted to cancel *Eishne* and keep out desperate hordes running from poison desert everywhere. Azizi insisted there was no better time to remind people who they were together than in the middle of strife and war. Merchants, librarians, and carnival players were thrilled. The Master of Money lusted after tax revenue. High priest Ernold hoped for converts to his temple or transgressors for the huts. Despite official approval, the festive atmosphere was unsettled. Crowds tearing through the gates were desperate for miracles. Djola's troupe was little more than spit on a foul wind. It was folly to return to this festering place. How could they change the weather?

"Amazing." Bal pointed at Kyrie's painting artistry. When Mango waggled her trunk, the yellow snake wiggled on her forehead. Bal nudged Awa. "Mango looks like you, a snake on her brow." Awa tried not to smile, but couldn't help herself.

Mango flapped her ears, irritated at stalls, people, and animals between her and the carnival stage in the oasis garden. Elephants preferred plenty of room to maneuver. Mango turned onto a dim alleyway that meandered through northlander neighborhoods around the market. The crowd thinned to a trickle. Good citizens rarely ventured the back way to Thunder River—too dark, too dangerous, too long.

Djola tried to relax. His troupe would arrive at the bridge to the citadel before any afternoon storm. According to Kyrie, Urzula and Lilot were rebels. When poison winds roared and spectators and guards took cover, Djola's troupe would slip across the bridge to the cook's entrance. Lilot had agreed to place markers to guide them. Kyrie knew every passageway in the citadel and Lilot's jackals and hyenas avoided her. This sounded like a fine plan last night, sitting around a fire, drunk on wine. In the light of day, Djola worried that if they got past guards and dust demons, what then? Azizi might not listen to Djola or believe the proof in Vandana's bag—Awa's bag.

"You haven't told me what cure you'll offer Azizi." Kyrie glared at Djola. "If you're afraid to tell me, how will you persuade him?"

"I offer something he won't refuse." He looked at Awa and Bal. "A future."

Kyrie shrugged. The alley twisted around a steep hill. Painted clay hovels huddled against the slope. Fanciful creatures decorated doorways and walls. Raintrees struck down in a void squall leaned toward the gutter. Djola stroked their leafless crowns. His mother claimed he'd been born in this slum, on a street like this.

"I brought Samina here one night, right after we met. Raintrees were in bloom all over the city . . ." Nobody challenged the Master of Poisons as he kissed his love under a fragrant raintree. They wore transparent robes, the delights of their bodies on full display. Witch women from the floating cities had no shame. Djola loved that.

"I can imagine." Bal tapped Yari's drum.

Soot charged ahead, sniffing crevices and jumping up on dim ledges. Fannie nudged Mango's hefty haunches. No hurrying the elephant. Bal broke off drumming to nock an arrow. Red-robed acolytes ran up a side street away from Soot's raised hackles. Ernold's followers. Kyrie held a ball of fire. Acolytes snatched hapless souls from alleyways to bleed. Bal aimed at boots crunching stone on a ledge above them. A woman—assassin?—raised her hands and ran by. Bal pouted at Djola. This made no sense. Protecting him from bad people was what Bal had always wanted to do. "What does *sacred shapeshifter* mean?" *vie* asked again.

Djola groaned. This Bal, who probably wasn't *his* Bal, was as bad as Awa, digging at him, questioning everything, never giving up.

"Abelzowadyo." Bal chewed the word and scanned the alley. "Poetry ignites our spirits." *Vie* let loose two arrows, pinning a red-robed acolyte to the doorway where he lurked. A weapon clattered from a wounded hand. The acolyte howled. Bal saluted him. "On a festival day, I take your pride and leave you your life."

Djola sighed. Alley rats would have the acolyte's life.

Awa feasted on Bal's shadow-warrior prowess, in love, but fighting passion. Bal loved otherworldly Awa with abandon, drinking up her Jumbajabbaland spirit. Sweet romance had been stolen from them.

"We must be poetry in action." Bal scowled at him. "How do we live *Abelzowadyo*?"

Djola tapped Kyrie. "You write on *Abelzowadyo* in your conjure book, don't you?"

"Ernold and Money assume my gates fall when I do." Kyrie kissed her teeth. "Spirits become the gate and work without the conjurer."

"Gate conjure is shapeshifting, *Abelzowadyo*." Awa sighed.

"Haints powering gates don't linger forever." Djola nodded at Kyrie. "You were planning to sacrifice yourself, not Samina or anybody. But Samina drank poison, found you in Smokeland, and offered to watch over Mount Eidhou." Tears filled the back of his throat. "Tessa and Quint smoke-walked to you as poison desert claimed them. My family haunted your gates with their last breaths. *Basawili*."

Kyrie blinked at him, eyes blurry. "I conjure only with the willing."

"Forgive me." Djola tried to suck down tears. "I was wrong about you."

"Everyone is." Bal poked Awa.

"*Abelzowadyo* is *Zamanzi*," Kyrie said. "Shapeshift any direction, live like a god of the crossroads."

Djola wanted to hug Kyrie, but she wasn't sentimental. "Yes, be a trickster, beholden to no one, responsible to everyone. Create a new realm for all of us."

Bal sucked *vie*'s teeth with the Empire's matter-of-fact contempt for northlander wisdom. "*Zamanzi* arrogance."

Awa rolled her eyes. "Yari talked this same arrogance to us when we were Sprites."

"*Lahesh* arrogance is different," Bal countered.

Awa snorted. "Everybody's arrogance is special."

"True. And admitting you were wrong feels wonderful." Djola shook himself and smiled at Kyrie. Soot trotted back to them, tail wagging—nothing to fear ahead.

"Playing god is good meditation." Bal stowed bow and arrow. "But the gods are just stories we tell ourselves, so the sky won't seem so big and our moments too short."

"What's wrong with that?" Awa asked. "Crossing over, I chose griot, remember?"

"Fatazz," Bal cursed. "How is temple talk a plan to defeat Hezram?"

"We must make up new gods, a new yesterday and tomorrow." Awa sneered. "We must shift the shapes of the world."

Bal sang, *"We're roots to hidden treasures and seeds for something new—"*

"Do you sneer at me or Yari?" Djola snapped at them. His thighs ached from riding the elephant. The crystal in his foot burned. He uncovered it. Dust on the wind dissolved on its facets. "So much impossible work still to do."

"Awa tells me you're a very wise man"—Bal stroked Yari's talking drum—"a great teacher who can explain what the wind means, why rocks are hard and metals melt instead of burn, why this tree sings a different song than one with similar leaves." Bal licked dry lips. "She says you are barbarian, *Anawanama*, and *Zamanzi*. Ancient enemies war in your blood, yet you know how to talk adversaries to a peace fire."

"I did once. Years ago . . ." He sighed. "Or perhaps chiefs, masters, thief-lords, and pirates sat down to peace of their own accord."

"You kept them there till you had a treaty." Bal leaned into Awa. "She loves you like a father. I'm jealous."

"Do you want her love all for yourself or do you crave a father's love?" Djola asked.

Bal blinked away a tear. "Awa says you'll tell me of Yari's death."

"Not now." He tasted the wind. The afternoon storm might come sooner than expected. "That's a story for after the masquerade."

A voice like Yari's jolted Djola. "Sing! *I am Eidhou, Eidhou!*"

Griots on fast ponies paraded past them. They were smooth-cheeked Green Elders, dark eyes outlined in black kohl and wiry hair knotted around glass beads. Red mica glittered on their palms. "We celebrate tomorrow in yesterday. Sing with us."

Eidhou! All rivers flow from my heart
All the light comes from my dark
Stillness follows my fury
Love is never my worry

Bal played a rhythm that captured everyone's heartbeat. Mango was delighted and tapped Bal's nose. Kyrie and Awa leaned into Bal's music. Djola squinted through the marble eye. He wanted to peer through Bal's skin, beyond blood and bones to first moments, to origins. Awa's Bal was a grown *veson* with scars on an angular face. Djola's Bal had been round-faced, pouting the last time he saw her. Awa's Bal could braid sweetgrass rope strong enough to hold a caravan of elephants. Djola's Bal had also been a weaver, a little dancing soldier, a singer. Djola's Bal wanted to ride to the capital and protect her father from foolish, greedy men, and now Awa's Bal did exactly that.

If his Bal was Awa's Bal, could *vie* forgive Djola, could *vie* love him?

The alley came out on the river end of Rainbow Square. A rambunctious audience cheered their entrance. Someone shouted, "The horse is almost as tall as the elephant." Any of the young people squealing at an elephant with a snake brow and a mangy hound in a trickster hat could have been Tessa, Quint, or Bal grown into themselves. Djola rode to Council, for them, for all the children.

I am Eidhou, Eidhou!
When you find yourself, come right to me
When you find yourself, you have to see
Sour fruit turns to sweet in my meadows
Truth on the run hides in my shadows
Waiting for the time to rhyme
Waiting for the time to shine
Come right to me! You have to see!
I am Eidhou!

3

Yesterday's Blood

Arkhys City's Rainbow Square was more dazzling than Djola remembered. The riverstone ground was inlaid with agate, quartz, moonstone, and crystals he could not name. Sandstone buildings around the Square shimmered in hot dry air. Mercenaries marched around money houses, granaries, and tree-oil works, on the lookout for rebels but ignoring carnival clowns. These warriors-for-hire hoped to get rich plundering petty merchants and desperate farmers. Across Thunder River, sunlight snuck through the columns, domes, and towers of Azizi's citadel. After the chaotic, earthy market, the rigid splendor of rulers needled Djola. Actually, it was being stuck in the everyday that annoyed him. His wanted to fly to Council at the speed of thought.

"Wim-wom." Awa was dazzled by the *Lahesh* waterwheel that still presided over the river entrance to Rainbow Square. Creatures made of wood, metal, leather, and glass chased each other up, down, and around the wheel. Grinning behemoths, striped horses, and tentacled blobs slid along ramps, spun on tops, and leapt from catapults. Rainbow spirits from crystals in the center of the wheel cavorted around the square to the delight of men *and* women. Nobody had persuaded Azizi to ban women or replace the *Lahesh* whimsy wheel with a better power display. Djola offered a prayer to the cross-roads gods—ancient *Anawanama* words learned from his mother. She never translated the verses, but said: *Each life fills this prayer with meaning.*

Mango halted under a lone cathedral tree. Its burl-mottled trunk rose a hundred feet before hefty branches broke the vertical line. A host of animal-people chirped, squealed, and buzzed from nests, holes, and hiding places in the tree. Among the feathery green leaves was the red bronze of new growth. Rainbow spirits had protected this elder from axmen and oil merchants. Even void dust avoided this giant. For how much longer? A spring fed deep roots and burbled into a fountain altar dedicated to the crossroads gods. Mango guzzled a trough of water then raised her trunk, curious, cautious. Kyrie waved to *Anawanama* and *Zamanzi* players at the top of the oasis garden.

Djola snorted bloody sand from his nostrils. "Can we trust them?"

"They're sworn rebels." Kyrie grunted. "We join *their* cause. Can they trust us?"

Kyrie urged Mango toward the oasis garden—a green marvel at the end of Rainbow Square. The elephant stepped out, majestic, confident, but Fannie balked, rearing as Empire guards marched by the fountain with spears, swords, and bows ready.

"The battle is over." Awa stroked velvet ears. "Yesterday's blood on their swords."

"Yesterday's blood is everywhere," Djola said.

"No worries." Bal scanned for danger. "We write tomorrow."

"Is that so?" Djola wanted to argue with the green flecks in *vie*'s eyes. Not just Djola, many northland and floating-city folks had those eyes. Bal could have been Iyalawo Tembe's child, given up to Green Elders when Tembe married Ice Mountain. "What story will you make?"

Bal shrugged. "Something better than today."

"Yes." Djola forced himself to look away from *vie*. "That's usually the plan."

"Whayoa! Come no farther!" An archer guarding a tree-oil manufactory yelled Empire vernacular at a child in a rag and raffia bird masquerade tumbling his way. Mercenaries along the stone wall behind him brandished swords and spears. The archer nocked an arrow and aimed. A crowd paused to gawk and mutter. "Move on," the archer shouted, ready to lay down his life for pots of oil. He couldn't have been more than eighteen. "The show is down at the oasis garden."

The bird child nodded a wooden beak, flapped colored raffia wings, and backed away. A few gangly adults grumbled about fat mercenaries and corrupt masters. The archer aimed at their flimsy bravado, hands trembling. Djola held his breath. A carnival could become a riot on an upbeat—too many twitchy young men with weapons, too many people with nothing to lose.

Mango sucked water from the fountain and sprayed the crowd just as it was turning into a mob. People squealed and scattered; a few giggled. A hyena girl twirled, flinging droplets at those who were still dry. Mango sprayed the archer. He gaped at her, wavering through outrage, fear, and delight. She waggled her head and trumpeted. Everyone laughed. Dripping wet, his mouth hanging open, the archer lowered his bow.

"A natural clown." Kyrie used Empire talk.

Mango snatched the archer's hat and threw it in the air, then tickled his nose. The archer stifled a chuckle. "I thought the last carnival elephants died a year ago. Only barbarians and their elephant raiders left."

"Mango is a wild girl," Kyrie said. "A memory come to life on *Eishne*."

Mango put the hat back on his head. The crowd applauded.

The archer stroked her trunk. "Elephants are good luck, aren't you?"

"Yes." Kyrie beamed at him. "Today we're hopeful and celebrate peace."

Mango strode toward the library, her ears flat, her chest rumbling. Fannie trotted behind her in a better mood too. The library's onion domes were pitted and broken. Tattered banners fluttered over milky windows. Refugees from Holy City and everywhere huddled together in the portico on ragged mats and sipped a steaming brew from clay cups. Thick metal doors stood open, defiant. Djola caught the scent of mint tea, musty parchment, ink, and wax candles.

The librarians were beekeepers who loved ancient literature and welcomed everyone. Were they foolish? Naïve? Mango trumpeted a greeting. Librarians and refugees cheered her. A man in blue-violet pirate pants with a purple librarian sash across a broad chest charged down the marble steps. He looked like Orca, a bit thinner, head and chin shaved. Djola's heart wheel stuttered. The librarian grinned and waved. He had dimpled chin and cheeks.

"That's Boto, the rebel librarian." Bal waved at him. "He stands with the People."

"You," Djola shouted and shook his head. "Alive?"

"Yes, and Vandana too," Boto replied.

"Vandana? You crack my heart." Djola pressed a hand to his chest. "Boto now?"

"Abelzowadyo," Boto yelled.

"Yes." Djola shook his head, his heart wheel racing.

"How does Boto know your plan?" Bal looked wounded.

"Abelzowadyo is not just Djola's plan." Kyrie answered for Djola.

Other librarians gripped Boto, holding him back. They whispered in his ear, and Boto waved one last time before reluctantly returning to the library.

"You two are old friends?" Awa said.

"He was Orca on the pirate ship." Djola chuckled. "I worried Pezarrat might have cut his head off to spite me."

"Orca." Awa smiled too. "He saved your life many times."

"Books and Bones lost heart," Kyrie said. "He abandoned Council and returned to his lair." She sighed. "He wanders the library and leaves Council work to Boto. Azizi will gather everyone tomorrow or the next day. Boto must prepare."

Bal arched an eyebrow. "Money thinks Boto is loyal to their cause."

"What is their cause?" Awa asked.

Bal shrugged. "Staying in power and stealing what they can."

Awa sucked her teeth at this easy response.

Djola nodded. "Orca was a good spy."

"You made a rebel of him and of Vandana too," Kyrie said.

"Vandana, the *Mama Zamba* warrior woman, a rebel? Well, she already was." Djola rubbed his brow. "How big, how organized is this rebellion?"

"It's as big as all the People together," Awa said. "Kyrie told you already, when we were coming down the mountain."

"Ah. Tell me again." Djola sat up straight. "I wasn't quite right in my mind."

"Did you think all we needed was you to save us?" Kyrie teased him with truth.

"I haven't thought that for a while. But the rebels were just a mob."

"Warrior-clowns, *Anawanama* and *Zamanzi*, organized all the factions. They know how to put on a show." Kyrie chuckled. "We'll speak more later. Anyone might know *Anawanama*." She pointed at a crowd of scowling faces from across the Empire and beyond, all the People together. *Zamanzi* and *Anawanama* hated each other in the best of times. Most good citizens had contempt for *savages*, even for *Lahesh* tinkerers. Nobody trusted pirates or barbarian thief-lords who raided and plundered their own mothers.

"Fatazz!" Djola grimaced. A People's rebellion could become turf wars on an upbeat. "No getting around yesterday's blood."

4

Juggling Fire

The crows flew to the rooftops, hooting and hollering. Danger, coming their way. Big danger. Djola threw his cloak over the *Lahesh* crystal in his foot. Kyrie held a ball of fire in each hand. Soot crouched low. He and Bal were taut as bowstrings. Festival-goers scattered, screeching like the crows: angry, awestruck, and fearful.

Awa wrinkled her nose. "There." She held her breath and pointed.

Witchdoctors, priests, and warrior acolytes in billowing yellow robes poured from another alley. They raced across Rainbow Square with caged transgressors and warhorses in tow. The clatter of chains, hooves, and wheels was deafening. Djola covered his ears. With his marble eye, he spied a blue robe and a blue eyepatch moving to the head of the swarm. Hezram. Mango grabbed Soot's tail before the mangy hound could race off. He turned, fangs bared, but did not snap at the elephant.

Tembe, in golden robe and head wrap, led a band of woman drummers and a warrior acolyte around the edge of the square. They sang Hezram's praises and took care not to desecrate crystals with female flesh. No matter Azizi's edict allowing women to tread anywhere, Tembe wouldn't be blamed for ill fortune. She stopped to admire Mango. The drummers circled the troupe. The acolyte grumbled to a halt. Djola slumped behind Kyrie. Awa pulled her hat low.

Mango tickled bells on Tembe's head wrap, and the wise woman of Ice Mountain giggled. Bal stood tall on Fannie. Kyrie threw burning torches to *vie* and they juggled three, four, then five between them. Soot crouched and leapt through the circle of flames and then Bal juggled the torches alone. Tembe's women drummed a praise song: *Who dances with fire? The foolish go up in flames, but not the brave or the wise.* The warrior acolyte feigned disinterest and herded the musicians on as festivalgoers snapped their fingers and cheered.

Tembe lingered. "You must perform for Hezram and the emperor." She spoke *Anawanama* with the musical accent of the floating cities. "I'll recommend your troupe."

Vévé scars on Kyrie's cheeks flashed silver. Tembe blinked green-flecked black eyes, a question in her mouth. It dissolved as Kyrie threw Bal a sixth torch. The tight swirl of fire was hypnotic. Tembe shook herself, saluted Bal, Soot, and Mango, and dashed off to Hezram at the bridge. When the last drummer passed through citadel gates, Bal hurled each torch at the ground, scattering their audience. *Vie* sat down on Fannie and gathered a trembling Awa close. Djola had chomped his tongue; he spit out blood.

"Ah Mango, did you hear—a show good enough for the emperor." Kyrie clowned delight, slid off the elephant, and headed for the flaming torches.

A stout young craftsman with a gaunt face and a clanging belt of tools blocked her. A zigzag scar or birthmark on his cheek twitched. "The poison master brought down Hezram's Nightmare Gates." His Empire vernacular had a Holy City twang.

"What do I care?" Kyrie walked around him and doused a torch with gold dust.

Awa stared at the young man as if she knew him. "Kenu?"

"Why is my name in your mouth?" Kenu scowled. "Who are you?" Awa shook her head. He scratched a scant beard. "Do I know you?"

"Not anymore," Awa replied, her tongue thick.

"Today is the *Eishne* Festival of Memories." Djola distracted Kenu. "Everybody's past comes to Arkhys City for the carnival show."

Bal petted Awa. "The griot of griots told a tale of the dead coming back to life, roaming festival streets to find loved ones."

"I know Yari's story." Kyrie put out another torch. "The living looked too much alike: anxious, sad, and full of regret. So the haints spooked strangers, teasing till people chortled and squealed and bubbled over with mirth. The haints never found who they searched for."

A gray-haired craftsman approached. "I knew Yari. I sold my daughter to that snake. Yari is a haint now."

"I'm no carnival haint." Kenu raised a trembling fist and staggered toward Kyrie, too much wine already. "Why do you welcome Hezram and his bloodsuckers?"

Kyrie poked his tools. "Why do you build his blood gates?"

"Leave them be, fool." The gray-haired craftsman pushed Kyrie aside and gripped Kenu. They were both gaunt-faced, yet paunchy, their brown skin mottled and beads of hair close-cropped, a father and son perhaps. "Too late to regret who you are and what we do." Drunk also, the older craftsman tried to puff out his chest but staggered and coughed. "The wine's got your tongue. You don't know what you say."

"*Dochsi!* Why do we build Hezram's gates?" Kenu struggled free and blubbered. "Why?"

The old man punched Kenu's nose and blood spurted. "The Master of Poisons will beggar us all. Hezram means tree oil and turquoise. Good for us."

"Not good for Mother," Kenu shouted.

"Who told me about her? Who sealed her fate?" the old man replied.

Kenu pulled a hammer from his belt and swung at his father's head. Awa cried out and Kenu missed.

"Festival time." The Master of Arms strode between their fists and gripped the hammer. He still had a booming voice, silver red hair and beard, and a commanding presence. He was bigger than the two men put together and all muscle. "Fight next week. The carnival show is about to start."

Guards whisked the combatants away. Awa trailed them with her eyes.

"Hezram offers gate security." Arms clapped the backs of other men raring to fight. He roared, the confident center of a whirlwind. "The Master of Poisons defeated that pirate stinker, Pezarrat. Now the Salty Sea offers safe transport to Empire ships, and soon the poison desert will leave us be. That means more tree oil for everyone and plenty to eat."

Djola shook his head. Arms calmed foul tempers, but he had to be lying or worse, he'd been fed lies he believed. He marched past Kyrie without recognizing her and never glanced at Djola.

"Today people from everywhere, even Holy City, come to celebrate with Emperor Azizi and Queen Urzula who we are together. Let us feast and sing and laugh." Arms led the crowd into the oasis garden.

"How do you know that builder?" Bal asked a watery-eyed Awa. "You told me about Kenu, I think." Had Awa mentioned a brother Kenu to Djola?

"I don't care who Kenu is." Kyrie put out the last torch and glared at Awa. "No surprise to see a familiar face during the Festival of Memories. Yari spoke truth—everyone comes. So even if the dead return to you, remember our masquerade."

Awa disciplined her shock. "We juggle fire." She pulled a placid Green Elder face.

"Arms has brought good news," Djola said. "Zizi expects us."

"Fatazz!" Bal peered at the citadel bridge. "Hezram will get to him before we do."

"Hezram will take an afternoon to settle in." Kyrie stowed the torches in a bag on her back. "Unless protocol has changed, Azizi won't see him until after the storm, when the air is clear and chill, after supper."

Djola nodded. "Zizi might put him off until tomorrow."

Temple altars in the square belched oily smoke, a flagrant offering of tree oil to indifferent mountain gods. Awa gagged. "Hezram gets ready for Nightmare Gates."

Kyrie spat. "And spreads poison desert."

Djola gritted his teeth. "I found no spell to hang fallen stars back in the night or heal a rip in the sky, no conjure to return the dead to life. But—" The sun crested over Mount Eidhou and light exploded in his marble eye, a vision. "I see . . ." a fiery dust storm consuming the world.

"What?" Bal gripped Yari's drum as it rattled.

"The dust . . ." Djola muttered. "*Xhalan Xhala* plaguing me."

Mango lifted her trunk. Elephants could sense a storm fifty leagues away.

Awa pointed. "A void whirlwind, like in Jumbajabbaland, coming this way."

Kyrie squinted at a clear horizon. "At least an hour away."

"These storms keep no time. They pop up anywhere, anytime," Djola said.

Soot shook the bells on his cap and barked at the tangle of feet blocking the entrance to the garden. "Let him through," an old woman shouted and the crowd parted for the mangy hound who wagged his tail and suffered pats on his big head. Kyrie led Mango through cheers. As Fannie trotted by, intrepid elders and awestruck youths reached up to shake Bal's hands. (Rebels?) Bold singers ululated and threw flowers and seeds. The troupe marched in like returning heroes.

Djola banished terrible visions and gazed at Awa and Bal, not a cure, but hope. "Samina said: *Impossible is a word for yesterday.* We make change without a cure."

5

Void-Spells

Cheery, familiar faces welcomed the elephant troupe to the oasis garden. Hearts pounded an eerie polyrhythm. Ancestors and haints filled the back beats. Awa sang, *the past comes to carnival, and we juggle fire,* over and over, but Elder discipline was failing. The seaweed and sea island shrimp she'd gobbled threatened to come back up.

Father and Kenu had spooked her worse than any haint or spirit slave. Kenu was hollowed out, as if by working for Hezram, he'd gotten lost in the void. All of her brothers probably worked for Hezram. At least unworthy daughter Awa had been spared that fate. She shuddered to think what happened to Mother. Father had built transgressor huts *and* Nightmare Gates in Holy City and preceded Hezram to the capital to build more here. Hezram tolerated Father's insolence and paid him a pirate's ransom, probably because he needed Father to turn gate-spells into void-spells. Maybe Hezram hadn't mastered the conjure or maybe he didn't want spirit debt.

Any conjure can be perverted. That's what Father always screamed at Mother. He put the People and all the green lands in mortal danger for a few sky rocks. Kenu could be forgiven, but having such a father filled Awa with revulsion. Mother should have poisoned Father for selling Awa, even if Awa was someone else's daughter. But Mother was a coward like Awa.

Fannie nickered delight at the terraced oasis garden and dragged Awa's awareness to the here and now. They could have been stepping into a Smokeland region from her childhood. Lush fruit trees presided over an explosion of wildflowers. Bees swarmed tiers of honeycomb in several trunk towers. Tree song calmed Awa, as Fannie pranced down a winding pathway.

"No sign of poison dust damage anywhere." Bal spoke *Anawanama* like a native and snapped *vie*'s fingers at green-land bounty. "Something protects this garden."

"Yes." Raintree blossoms brushed Awa's hot cheeks. The buttery, honey smell soothed her belly. "A grove like this saved me and Djola from Hezram." Shadow warrior-clowns bounded past them in scant attire. They winked and flirted, muscular physiques and warrior prowess fading in and out of view. Bal beamed at them, and jealousy ambushed Awa. A waste of heart spirit, but what could she do? "I won't be a weak good person," she whispered. "Do you believe me?"

Bal frowned. "Of course."

"Hezram's power is illusion." Awa clutched Bal's hand. "One lying voice from many mouths. We must chant the world we want."

"Keep reminding me." Bal sounded vulnerable.

Awa leaned back into *vie*. "I'd do anything for you." Give up her life even.

"Yari enchanted the *Zamanzi* with good stories, not lies. *Zamanzi* chose to join the rebellion and stop the poison desert. We tried to forgive each other. Yari's *Lahesh* diplomacy, that was our escape." Bal hugged Awa, breathing against her ear, stroking her shoulder, a lovesick hero from one of Yari's tales. "On missions for Kyrie, Yari and I searched for you everywhere. After almost two years, I lost hope, but Yari went to Holy City, to Hezram and the transgressor huts, looking for you."

Awa stiffened. "And Yari never came back."

"Not your fault. Yari thought *vie* could reach Hezram." Bal kissed her neck. "Yari was right. We can't give up."

Awa shivered. "Agreed."

"Did you know Kenu in Holy City? Did he build huts?" Bal pulled a strand of hair and startled a bee who flew to another tight curl and settled in.

"That bee is my sentinel guard." Awa squirmed. "Leave her be."

"You don't have to say what happened in those huts. But don't be ashamed either."

"I can tell you this. We can't just blame Hezram—" Or Father who must have been young and foolish once like Awa and Kenu, who must have turned the wrong direction and when he realized, perhaps he blamed someone else and kept on going wrong.

"Yes." Bal sighed. "We all do void-spells."

"Well, not today," Awa declared.

At the bottom of the garden was a round wooden stage flanked on each side by a three-story onion-domed tower. Cathedral-trunk doors filled the center of the back wall. Storm-cloud curtains fluttered under balconies connecting the onion towers to the wall. The emperor's citadel across Thunder River looked like part of the set. Ramps ran from the stage almost to the citadel bridge and also up through the raintree groves where an excited audience gathered. Treehouses, connected by rope bridges, swayed in the breeze above the crowd. Awa thought of Jumbajabbaland lovers and tears puddled in her eyes. As a young Sprite, she'd dreamt of being a famous griot in Arkhys City, telling Smokeland tales. She'd imagined Father squirming in the audience as Mother, Kenu, Yari, and Bal applauded. Petty dreams.

"The elephant is exhausted," Kyrie said as Mango halted behind a tower. Carrying two people on her neck must have taken a toll. Elephants had enough to do carrying themselves. "After the show we cross the bridge on foot." Awa and Bal slid off of Fannie, who was also weary. Kyrie helped Djola down. With his droopy eyes, sunken cheeks, and awkward gait, the poison master resembled a bone masquerade.

"I look worse than I am." He spoke to Awa's and Bal's grim faces. "If this doesn't work and tomorrow I should haunt you—"

"Kyrie says with a *Lahesh* heart wheel, you could outlive us." Awa put her hand to his chest. The heart wheel whirred beneath her fingers. Rainbow spirits danced around his foot, doing battle with the void. "*Lahesh* conjure protects Rainbow Square and you, but the trees protect this oasis, like Mountain Gates. They make the weather here."

"Smart girl." Djola touched his forehead to hers.

Kyrie and Bal conferred with the players, sharing gossip and news. Books and Bones had gone missing. The Masters of Money and Water called for violent raids on *vesons*, rich or poor. High priest Ernold rounded up so-called transgressors (mostly *vesons*, northlanders, and noncitizens) and awaited Hezram's command. Grain feared for *vie*'s life. Riots and infighting drove Arms to his wits' end, yet he masqueraded hope. Azizi trusted nobody and gave into corruption. In a week Hezram could be Emperor with Father's help.

Awa choked at grim prospects. "No!"

"*Dochsi*, the players won't mind if we use their costumes." Bal scowled at her. "What are you thinking?"

"Sorry." Awa wasn't in her right mind. "I talk to myself."

"About what?"

Awa was reluctant to share her fears. "Monster garb is perfect for our storm show."

6

Moon Masquerade

The cathedral-trunk doors in the backstage wall opened up. Curtains billowed. Drummers, singers, and kora players did rousing melodies in the balconies and side towers. Spark torches flashed in citadel windows across the river, like part of the show. Three masquerades on stilts, several hands taller than Mango, clomped onstage. They wore outlaw cloaks from the north, impervious to weapons and weather like Djola's.

Mango flapped her ears at snake-eyed sea monsters with iron teeth, fat bellies, and tentacles. Diamond-tipped claws on their tentacles dripped fabric blood. Fire blasted from cavernous mouths. Bal shrieked with the children. Awa groaned. While they wasted time applauding a masquerade, Hezram could ignore protocol and topple Azizi.

"Abelzowadyo." A patchwork clown with beaded braids and a silver mustache burst onto the balcony over the stage. "Greetings." His deep resonant voice was a guest in *Zamanzi*. He winked at Awa and her troupe. "Tomorrow is now and yesterday." He jumped to a tower ledge then to the ground, where he shifted to Empire vernacular. "Hold your purse. Clutch your child. The gods of carnival are

rainbow spirits. Watch your heart. Crossroads tricksters crack you apart, and everything goes upside down and inside out, right side wrong and backside front." He spun around in billowing curtains and displayed a woman's face and form. "Nobody"—her voice rang like a bell, high and clear—"is who you think she is." The audience applauded carnival conjure.

Even Awa was captivated as an iron horse with a cloud-silk mane and feather tail glided through the curtains on a cart and bumped the shapeshifter. She and Bal squealed at the horse's ruby eyes and golden heart wheel. Smoke poured from flared nostrils and enveloped the clown who jumped up on the horse backward. His silver mustache twitched in the first face again, but the womanly form persisted. "Welcome." This voice was high with deep overtones. "We shapeshifters tell an old tale from before the void, a story learned from Yari, the griot of griots, who heard it from *Anawanama* ancestors." The audience roared their delight. Nobody jeered at a man-woman masquerade, a *Lahesh* trickster. The cart revolved and the clown proclaimed, "Today and tomorrow, we discover who we are together." *Vie* disappeared beyond the curtains shouting, *"Xhalan Xhala."* Djola jerked at *Lahesh* conjure words.

Awa patted his shoulder. "Tomorrow in yesterday need not be pain."

Djola jerked again. "Yes, Samina said that too. *Xhalan Xhala* is not just bleak visions."

Talking drums hushed the crowd. Even the noisy slurping of free festival food ceased. A warhorse pranced through the stormcloud curtains as Green Elder music wafted from the trees. Two acrobats in moon masks and black cloaks dropped from a raintree branch and landed back-to-back on the red gelding. Tiny crystals on their cloaks sparkled and moon faces glowed.

Awa recognized warhorse and players. "The *Zamanzi* twins from Holy City huts."

"Rebels now," Bal said.

"Zst!" Kyrie shushed them.

Fish acrobats burst up from stage trapdoors, trailing blue-green fabric. They tumbled underfoot, like waves rising and falling. Above the audience, Green Elders materialized in a treehouse— the griots from the back alley. They spoke the *Anawanama* legend in Empire vernacular while the moon masks and stilt monsters danced the tale:

Long, long ago, greedy demons came out of the seas and swallowed up cities, green lands, animals, people, rocks, and rivers. Wherever the demons roamed was soon barren wasteland and they were forced to travel from region to region, on and on, across the Earth. One night after eating a forest mountain and drinking a sweet inland sea, the demons were hungry still. Dying birds had whispered of the last mountain cliffs that sheltered a sweet blue lake and bush trees. The demons prepared to cross the Salty Sea to gobble these final delights.

The Moon took pity on the Earth and sang to the demons of hidden delights beyond bright peaks. Dazzled, the demons flew up on silver light beams and, feasting for a month, they ate the Moon. They swallowed every silver beam. In the darkness that followed, the demons lost their way home. Pricks of starlight carried them nowhere. Crashing about in the night sky, the demons barely resisted eating each other or the Moon as it slowly grew back, making something from nothing. The demons needed all the moonlight to return to Earth where new delights awaited them. Just when the Moon was full and fat and bright, greed triumphed, and the foolish creatures devoured the light once more. Look up in the night, the demons are at it every month. The Moon is a hero saving us again and again.

Bal joined the griots, singing:

Warrior, warrior, have you forgotten?
Greed makes even sweet apples rotten
Warrior, warrior sweet enemy mine
Will this be our last time?

The moon acrobats jumped from the red horse into the stilt walkers' fiery mouths and disappeared. The audience leapt to their feet, snapping fingers and clapping. The demon masquerades took off their masks and bounded from stilts to tower ledges to the stage floor. Moon and fish acrobats revealed their faces also. *Anawanama, Zamanzi,* and *Lahesh* players lifted their arms and the audience showered them with flower petals.

Awa sat still amidst the hullabaloo, playing a polyrhythm of conflicting ideas, trying to think a knotted thing apart. The grass terrace was soft and wet under her toes and butt. The buttery raintree scent was intoxicating. Hummingbirds fussed and fought over the best blossoms. Awa tugged Djola's arm and shouted over the cheering crowd. "What if we or you conjured Mountain Gates around Arkhys City, instead of Nightmare Gates? Not a cure, but a respite, an oasis while rebels work for change?" Djola and Kyrie exchanged glances as Awa continued. "You two must know spells we could use. *Lahesh* conjure? Something from Vandana's small bag?"

Bal was thrilled. "I knew the masquerade would give us good ideas."

"Well, I didn't," Awa admitted.

"I don't trust my hand or my vision," Djola muttered.

"Good vision takes many eyes looking every direction." Bal quoted *The Green Elder Songs for Living and Dying,* and Djola cursed. He'd quoted that song to Awa.

Kyrie grinned. "You mean to steal Hezram's gates?"

"Yes." Awa would do whatever it took to counter Father's spells. Maybe he'd never had a chance to change the weather, but . . . "I won't be a weak good person."

Bal groaned. "I'm sorry I said that."

"Without trees and bush, we'll have to commandeer silver-mesh and find a willing sacrifice." Kyrie squinted at Awa's resolve. "Why not? Let's talk more later."

"*Anawanama* perform moon masquerade before a battle," Djola said. "What are the rebels up to?"

"Reminding us what we fight and perhaps die for," Bal said, enthusiastically.

The piebald crow swooped around Awa's hat and flew off. Awa turned from the stage to watch the bird soar. The sky flushed orange and the wind moaned like a dying thing. The afternoon sandstorm raced toward the market, an hour before midday. Crows screeched and bells clanged in Rainbow Square. The audience was suddenly still. Fear scented the air. Players bowed one last time before racing into the towers and slamming windows shut.

The Master of Arms and his warriors kept panic in check. The audience mumble-grumbled but, row by row, headed to *Zamanzi* storm tents at the base of cathedral trees ringing the garden. Cotton woven with *Lahesh* metal-mesh threads glinted in the sun. Poison dust could not penetrate the shelters. Arms clutched a squealing child who'd lost his family. The boy tugged his beard. Arms whispered nonsense and waved his sword at anyone about to bolt.

"So orderly and fast." Awa marveled at the crowd.

"They dance with a dust storm almost every day," Bal said.

"Our show now." Kyrie led the troupe up a ramp to the empty stage.

Awa dropped a moon mask in Vandana's bag. Kyrie grabbed two sea-monster robes and with Bal's help draped Fannie and

Mango. The *Anawanama* weave of gold thread and sweetgrass was as powerful as the silver-mesh Djola gave out to protect eyes, nose, and ears. Awa and Soot had mesh veils in their hats.

"Abelzowadyo." The shapeshifter clown smiled at her from a treehouse then pulled down a heavy drape. Stage towers and treehouses were storm shelters too. Void whirlwinds danced everywhere in the market but avoided the wall of trees that surrounded the oasis. Only a few tendrils lapped the storm shelters. The trees made the weather here—just as Awa suspected.

"Hurry," Kyrie shouted and led Mango and Fannie onto the citadel bridge.

Bal shouldered Djola's weight. Their three-legged walk was well-rehearsed. Awa stumbled behind them, Soot at her side. Crows roosting deep in cathedral branches squawked at foolish people hobbling into danger. At the end of the bridge, dust, ash, and sparks scoured any exposed skin. Kyrie signaled a halt. If guards were posted beyond the citadel gates, they were invisible in dust squalls at the entrance. Soot snapped at Awa when she tugged the mesh over his eyes. Void dust sparked in his coat. Awa hugged him inside her cloak, then dropped the veil over her face. The eerie darkness was claustrophobic. Urzula's spark torches were gust-proof and visible through mesh, yet Awa saw nothing. Something was wrong. Chief cook Lilot should have already lit the torches. Fannie dumped a mound of manure, Mango sneezed, and Soot whined. A strong hand gripped Awa's bad arm from behind. She turned and saw two bright torches.

"Lilot, Urzula," Kyrie shouted.

The queen and her cook had come out to escort them into the citadel. Awa swallowed panic. Short, squat, and fierce like Kyrie, they had metallic-colored hair and *Lahesh* flame-cloth robes that were visible in the torchlight. Mango rumbled everybody's relief into the ground.

"Welcome," Urzula said. "Our son and daughter enjoy the wisdom and isolation of the floating cities. They've begged us to join them, but—"

"*Tschupatzi!*" Lilot grunted a floating-city curse.

Urzula shushed Lilot and continued the greeting, her voice like gentle rain wearing away at rocks. "But, like you, we have yet to cry defeat on Empire soil. Come."

The troupe followed their lights toward the cook's entrance. Soot licked Awa's hands and whined. He was worried too. What if the doorway wasn't big enough for a warhorse and an elephant?

7

A Maze of Odors

The void dust storm finally blows itself out. Soot pads close to Awa. Two pirate women, smelling of lightning, herbs, and cooking pots, lead Awa's pack through a stone courtyard. They douse the lightning on their torches with bare hands. Soot feels Awa's distress when they lead Mango and Fannie into the citadel's grassy corral. Fannie can open latches. Mango can rip up posts or chains. They are not prisoners and always happy for wide open spaces and sweetgrass. Awa buries her face in Fannie's mane and clutches Mango's trunk. She smells sad. Soot licks her hands, offering comfort.

The pirate women creep into a dank hallway. Many anxious people sneak through here, some are sick, some full of love or about to give birth, some run for their lives. Rats live in the crevices and jackals hunt them, pissing on the walls, declaring themselves. Hyenas tiptoe here and there. Soot doesn't recognize anyone. Kyrie charges ahead, flying around a bend behind the pirate women. Bal almost carries Djola on *vie*'s back and trudges as slowly as Awa, who limps across cold stone. Awa has more strength than in the mountains, yet no speed. She, Bal, and Djola breathe heavily and make no other sound, as if they hunt prey or avoid a rival pack.

They fall far behind the others. Soot stays close to Awa, ready for human ambush or hyena attack.

Many hallways intersect at the bottom of a narrow stairway, and Soot halts, catching a wind stream from a distant doorway. He smells Hezram. His heart pounds, he growls and sniffs ten times for each of his heartbeats. Bal drags Djola up the first step.

Awa hesitates and asks, "Can you manage?"

Soot doesn't hear Bal's answer. Exhaling out the sides of his nose, he maps the continuous flow of scents. The citadel is a maze of odors with eddies from yesterday, last year, and who knows how long ago. Soot concentrates, poking his nose along Hezram's pungent trail. He swallows a bark. The witchdoctor's aroma is mixed with duck fat, cathedral tree oil, transgressor blood, goat milk, snake venom, poison sand, and ash. He's been on a warhorse, down by the sea, and he drank coconut wine.

Hezram walked this way a few hours ago. A tang of Yari clings to him—sugarbush and desert rose. Hezram carries scrolls and ink, like Djola, and potions to dull the mind and trick the spirit. Hezram is unwell and has many wounds that won't heal. Soot notes sour breath, feverish oily sweat, and distress flatulence. Bal, Djola, and Awa have gone several steps up the stairs. Soot can catch them easily. He takes a moment to sort through other smells. Hezram walks with the mountain woman who worries over him and also Awa's friends from Holy City—Meera and Rokiat. They smell bloody, hopeless, defeated. They are surrounded by a hostile pack. Several men, who drink blood and tree oil like Hezram, are anxious, ready for a fight.

Soot's lips curl, exposing fangs as he races up the stairs ahead of the whole pack. At the top, Hezram's scent flows around a bend. Soot barks and barks and barks. Kyrie races up behind him and grips his muzzle. Her hands taste like a lightning storm, like the torches. The pirate women make irritation noises and pat his head. They hurry left into shadows. Soot turns right to hunt Hezram.

He is a strong old wolf, obliged to follow no one. He wags his tail to disperse power odors and frighten weak enemies. Hezram is close. Soot creeps down the sunlit hall, tail high, ears flat. The trail is stronger every step. Hezram carries pieces of Yari: a cloud-silk robe, an ancient scroll, braid beads and ties. Soot pauses, confused. Yari-odors are good time memories.

Every so often Soot finds smoke-walkers whose adventures smell compelling—Awa, Yari, and a few others, Soot does not count. The good journeys blur together. Soot remembers exciting food, novel aromas, and cliffs to climb. Awa, Yari, and Soot were always rolling in sweetgrass and riding frothy ocean waves with the boat people. Best of all was soaring over cathedral trees, static wind in his fur. Now and again, Soot ventured into the everyday with Awa and Yari for weighty, smelly fun. But since bloody Hezram started stealing people and sucking elder trees dry, there is little fun in Jumbajabbaland and too much danger. Spirit slaves suck anyone and anything to ash and smoke. Soot has been trapped in the everyday too long.

Awa gripes. "I hate secret passageways."

Soot barks at her to hurry up the stairs. He catches a hint of nut bread, honey wine, and moth cocoons. Yari wore cocoons when Hezram poisoned *vie* in Jumbajabbaland. Since losing Yari, Soot doesn't risk more than a brief trip beyond the smoke. Hezram or some priest might take him prisoner or turn him to smoke. Fiends rule most regions. Soot has only found the cold, lonely realm once or twice, by accident—running for his life, taking a desperate turn.

Awa is out of breath and sweating at the top of the stairs. Still, she scratches his head, ready for anything. Eager, Soot creeps toward Hezram. Awa points the direction Kyrie and the pirate women go. Soot sticks his nose in a pile of dead bugs and barks. Awa rubs her face. Soot whines. She drags herself toward him, glancing back at Bal and Djola. They follow Kyrie also.

"What have you got your nose in?" Awa stares at the dead bugs. She wants to shriek and jump, but looks around, wary of a hostile pack stealing Soot's find. She picks the bugs up, buries her nose in them, scenting friends. "The anklet I made for Meera." Tears blur her eyes. "She didn't want to wear nasty cocoons and dead beetles, but Rokiat liked the sound when they danced or when they . . ." Awa kisses Soot's head. "Are Rokiat and Meera here?" He wags his tail. She swallows sorrow and turns. "Soot's found someone," she calls to Bal and Djola, "I'll catch up with you."

Soot barks over what Bal and Djola reply. He wags his butt, thrilled at Awa's desire to join the hunt. He races on, following Hezram's trail. Awa drags her battered leg behind him.

"If Meera and Rokiat went this way, we could be walking into danger. Hezram . . ."

Soot growls at the name. Men with bloody weapons are coming their way, from the direction Soot wants to go. He sits by an open window, licks his nose, and tastes friendly odors riding a late-afternoon breeze across the courtyard. Going through Smokeland, he can reach the place he wants to go, but the risk would be great. Awa is with him on the hunt, eager and fearless. Soot decides stepping through the border-void is better than fighting five men with blades. Awa reaches him. Soot jumps up, puts his paws on her shoulder, and licks her face. On hind legs, he is taller than Awa. She pulls her head away from his reassuring tongue, yet wraps her arms around his back and buries her face in his fur.

Soot steps sideways with Awa into Jumbajabbaland.

"Farts and fleas! Where are we going?"

No lingering, Soot sidesteps again. Awa's heart pounds against his. She is excited, unafraid. He can't help licking her face. They're on the other side of the citadel in a small dark room. The void clings to his coat, sparking and crackling. He shakes it off and barks quietly. Who wouldn't be excited?

Awa rubs Soot's head. "Like the bees. You must show me how to do that."

Rokiat stands guard outside the cell. Soot nudges Awa to a corner where people, asleep or drugged, are tied to the wall. Soot licks Meera's arm carefully, cleaning a wound. Meera groans, pushing him away. Awa's heart jumps, but she remains quiet.

"Wake up," Awa whispers, stroking Meera's face, drizzling honey and bitter roots into her mouth. "We've come for you."

"Awa?" Meera opens her eyes, frightened, unsure. "You can't be here."

"Of course I can." Awa scans the room. "Zst! Fresh blood and spirit slaves—together."

Meera grips her. "That *was* you whistling to the horses, at the Mountain Gates."

Others from Holy City (who stink more like Hezram than themselves) lie about in rank shadows, snorting and rattling their lips. Soot growls at the mound of breath bodies filled with poison, like Yari. He keeps his distance. Spirit slaves are clumsy in the everyday, but can drink a body dry. Awa unties a tangle of ropes and drags Meera to the door. Rokiat paces outside, singing. Soot would like to sing with him, even a sad song, but this is a silent hunt. Awa and Meera hug, whimpering and blubbering.

"What's going on?" Rokiat uses keys to open the door. "How did you get in there?"

Awa clamps his mouth. Rokiat nuzzles her. Soot sticks his nose out the door. Hezram is close, a few minutes, moving away. Soot wants to run him down. He growls, impatient, yet he knows they must hunt Hezram carefully. Soot must creep up on Hezram when he sleeps, or swims in the sea, or pisses on a tree at night. Soot must rip Hezram's throat and eat his heart and liver before anyone notices.

Awa lifts his paws onto Meera's shoulder. "Take us. Somewhere safe," she says.

Scents from Mango and Fannie waft through the window. They are tense, but in no danger. Soot steps sideways with Meera into Jumbajabbaland and then to the corral. Fannie and other warhorses greet Meera. Mango stands guard, ears wide. Soot goes back for Rokiat but the man wants to stay in the locked room with fiends. Soot has to drag him to the corral. Rokiat opens his mouth as if to lick someone then shakes the void off like a dog. Soot returns for Awa. She stands over a breath body who smells like her, not Hezram. Awa has stabbed the heart with a viper's head. She killed two snakes last night and didn't let Soot eat the heads. She holds a cloth of vapors under a twitching nose. The breath body becomes more solid than shadows; cheeks turn brown like blood. If Soot had Awa's eyes he'd see red. A woman has come back to herself.

"Mother?" Awa says.

"Is it you?" Mother runs a finger over a mark on Awa's forehead. "Grown up, an Elder saving me?" Mother's heart is erratic. Venom runs in her blood.

"Yes, a griot." Awa hesitates, hiding something. "Did Father—"

Soot sneezes out the smell of venom and tries to swallow a bark. His woofing makes Awa jump. Her face is wet with tears. She is so sad, all the time. Soot whines and paces. The other spirit slaves are restless. He nips Awa's hand and growls. A sluggish fiend sits up and shakes the other bodies.

"Take us both at once." Awa lifts the dying woman away from thrashing fiends. Several clamber to standing too. "Can you do that?"

Soot is weary. Still, he puts one paw on Mother's shoulders and another on Awa. They hug him. He licks their faces and steps sideways. Fiends tug at his tail too late. Pausing in Smokeland to catch a breath, Soot smells Hezram—his sweat, his voice coming from a stranger's mouth. A fiend jumps from a tree carcass. Soot wants to rip out its throat but he steps to the everyday with Awa and Mother. The bad moments dissolve in the kissing and hugging and good mood aromas at the corral. Soot wags his tail, slapping friendly legs. Everyone is happy! Mango sprays Meera with warm water, cleaning away blood and filth.

"I should be dead," Meera says.

"I wouldn't have let them . . ." Rokiat declares.

"Miracles." Mother smiles and babbles. Perhaps she will not die right away. Her heart is steadier. "To see you again. I never thought."

Awa fusses over Mother, combing snarls from wiry hair, offering her bread and a jug of broth from the pirate cook. "I'm sorry I wasn't there to—"

"No," Mother says, patting Awa. "I'm fine. To see my beautiful daughter. Miracles." She pushes Awa toward Meera and Rokiat. "I'm fine. Go. They need you."

Reluctantly, Awa turns to Meera and Rokiat. Mother spills the broth. Soot laps it up. He eats the bread as it falls from her fingers. After many trips through void-smoke with heavy everyday bodies, Soot is a tired old hound. He sets his head in Mother's lap and she pets him. Awa puts a cloud-silk robe from her Aido bag over Meera's wet skin. The robe holds the tang of the cold region, almonds, heather, and raintree blossoms.

"I thought you'd jump on Fannie and follow us." Meera shakes her head.

"I said they were ahead of us." Rokiat strokes Fannie. "Bibi always follows Fannie."

"We stopped for the coin and clothes you and I hid," Meera says. "Then Bibi ran and ran, into mirages, and we left poison dust behind. I thought we were safe. Free."

"Like now?" Rokiat looks every direction. Soot sniffs his crotch. Rokiat wants to run, not stand and fight like Awa. "Hezram caught up with us before."

"Why were you guarding the cell and not a prisoner in it?" Awa is mad at Rokiat.

"Rokiat told Hezram he rode off chasing me and Bibi." Meera clutches his hand.

Rokiat shrugs. "Hezram assumed Meera was my prisoner."

"And made you Master of Horses?" Awa doesn't trust him.

"The old master died in the poison dust from Ice Mountain," Meera whispers in Awa's ears. "Despite everything, I do love Rokiat."

Awa stays mad. "In that cell, there were so many transgressors to bleed and spirit slaves to—"

"Hezram has twenty cells in the citadel, not all full yet." Rokiat trembles. "Rebels will bleed too, for Nightmare Gates around Arkhys City." He smells hopeless. "Hezram will find us anywhere."

"I'd rather be dead then—" Meera looks at Mother and leans into Rokiat.

Mother sits in the dirt, leaning against a post. She is smiling at them. Her breath is too slow. So is her heart.

"What are we going to do?" Meera asks.

"Not just save ourselves." Awa rubs Soot's head. "Take us to Bal and Djola."

Soot is happy to hear them planning the hunt. He raises his tail and scents the air. He is a powerful old dog and wild. Hezram should smell him and cower.

8

Sacrifice

"A wa's gate-spell idea could work." Kyrie squinted at Djola, a skeptical spark on her fingertip.

They whispered in a corner of the citadel kitchen as Djola drank Lilot's frothy medicine. Five fireplaces and three *Lahesh* stoves roared. Pots of herbs boiled; ducks on spits dripped and hissed—a barbarian feast-day specialty. Lilot's helpers—former pirates and witch women in training—stood at high tables and mixed fruits and sweetmeats with spices and vinegar. Chattering and laughing, they carried trays of hot food into the citadel maze. Soot drooled and they slipped him scraps and scratched his head. Pungent medicine wraps from the cold cellar gave off a dizzying scent.

Djola leaned against a sweaty stone wall, more tired than he ever remembered being.

"You will be the willing sacrifice?" Kyrie sounded dubious.

"A true Dream Gate spell won't work otherwise," he replied.

"You're a terrible smoke-walker."

"So?" Djola glanced at Awa.

She hovered over her mother as Lilot wrapped the old woman in medicine cloth and poured a hot brew down her throat. Urzula did the same to the transgressor girl they'd rescued. Meera? Hezram's pretty horse master stood near Meera. He flinched at doors creaking and dishes clattering then moaned as if he were at the edge of death. Kitchen crew fussed over him, icing his brow, rubbing tension from his back. Meera squeezed his hand, cooing comfort. Bal paced around them, disgusted.

"It's our best chance." Djola smacked the wall. "What else against Hezram?"

Soot growled. He growled every time someone said Hezram. Kyrie shook her head, a hundred ideas racing behind her eyes. Djola felt impatient to get going. Kyrie pounded his chest and reminded him of Samina.

"Trust me." Djola gripped her fist and kissed gnarly fingers.

"What of Awa's own plans?" Kyrie asked Samina's question.

"Awa and Bal love this world, the way I used to." This wasn't an answer. He snatched the cane Urzula had given him and headed into the hallway maze. He had to get out of this stifling kitchen, away from Kyrie's obstinance.

"Thank you." Bal appeared at his side and he halted. "For rescuing my Awa."

"She saved me. Did she tell you? Probably not. She blames herself for Yari's death." Djola pulled Bal close and told how Awa refused to abandon him when he was a deadly weight. "Awa brought Yari and a sea of demons back from the void." He savored the memory. "In a burst of indigo light, Elders turned into themselves again."

Bal stroked Yari's drum, dazzled. *Vie* leaned into Djola. "You're a story Awa told me. In the enclave, when we were young. That story saved me." Bal winked at him and Awa, bowed to Kyrie, and slipped away. Djola felt a surge of pride, despite having nothing to do with Bal's training.

Kyrie shoved him down the dark corridor. "The emperor is a difficult trick."

"I can give Azizi what he wants," Djola said. "I'm not an arrogant fool anymore, and Zizi is ready to listen to me."

"Can we afford to sacrifice you? Who will Azizi listen to after you're gone?"

Djola pressed Kyrie's sparking hand to his heart. "Let's not fight."

"It will take everything to conjure Dream Gates." She patted him. "We must be heroes."

"Of course."

"Heroes don't do what they want or get what they need."

"You're relentless, woman."

Djola hobbled away from Kyrie up the dark, twisty corridor toward Council, cursing mazes, assassins, and heroes. Lilot had wrapped his mangled foot in furry bandages that snagged on jagged stone sticking out from the wall. Urzula's cane provided sparks of light and meant nobody had to carry him, yet climbing from Lilot's kitchen, he almost passed out three times. He gulped sour air and slowed down. Whatever Lilot put in her frothy brew cleared his thoughts and calmed his belly. He'd refused pain conjure. Seed and silk potions interfered with reasoning and memory, with resolve and courage too. Facing Azizi, clarity should counter rage.

He clutched the wall, surveying a crossroads of six hallways. When assassins, spies, and Azizi's scoundrel nephews got lost in this maze, Urzula's jackals supposedly ate their traitor hearts, Lilot's hyenas crunched their bones, and Azizi's rats ate what was left. Rats ate anything.

Tessa wavered in front of him, a shaft of mist from nowhere with blue-violet eyes like Samina's, a long neck and big feet like his. Quint was a smoldering ball of ash rolling around his sister. *The living are the changes the dead cannot make.* Talking out loud to haints fortified Djola. "Trust me." Haint children nodded at his resolve and dissolved. Evening air drifted through a window.

He stuck his head out. In the citadel corral below, Mango sprayed Lilot's helpers as they brought bushels of food. Djola chuckled and walked on.

Iridescent torch-bugs flashed green and blue, a light serenade. They crawled on a *Lahesh* whimsy wheel carved into the wall. Djola leaned into the rough surface, willing it to be the Council entrance and not the jolly rat carvings up ahead. After a good shove, a door opened onto the chamber. He whispered his mother's prayer to crossroads gods and walked in.

9

A Change of Heart

Council's high ceilings, sky windows, roaring fireplace, and stone-wood table weren't as formidable as Djola recalled. Moths had eaten away at robes and helmet masks stolen from barbarian or *Zamanzi* warriors. A *Lahesh* iron horse listed to the side, rusting among sacred relics from forgotten peoples.

Azizi stood at a side table of steaming food, thin and bent, bushy eyebrows and patchy beard gone white. His left hand trembled and his right eye drooped, as if he too had danced *Xhalan Xhala*. A flimsy gray robe fluttered around a wasted form and made him look like a haint. Time had served him no better than Djola. Azizi shooed rats from the cheese and said, "Are you coming in or meditating on the whimsy wheel?"

Two emperor guards, muscled and mighty, waved double-edged swords and poison daggers at Djola. These men had wrenched Djola from his Council chair, dragged him through back alleys to the harbor, and given him to Pezarrat. The warriors trembled, confusion in their eyes. Barbarian stock, they loved their emperor and believed dying for him would be a great honor, not a waste of blood. Djola should forgive them for following terrible orders. He should also forgive himself for bringing down Ice Mountain and abandoning his family. The guards grimaced at him. Djola leaned on his cane. He needed to sit down.

"Djola's the guest I've been waiting for." Azizi motioned the guards away. They backed up only a bit. "A long wait, but the Master of Poisons has finally returned." Azizi sighed. "Just in time, my friend."

"I'm the Master of *Weeds and Wild Things*," Djola replied.

"A new name signals a change of heart." Azizi tilted his head. "Masters at my table say you want to murder me." The guards sliced the air with their swords.

Djola sucked his teeth. "Why would I murder you?"

"For what I did or"—Azizi frowned—"for what I didn't do. Council can't decide. Some say you hate the Empire. You'd see us burn and celebrate our ashes on the wind."

"Money, Water, and Ernold worry about what *they've* done and not done." Djola trembled. "They burn the world, celebrate ash, and tell self-serving lies."

Azizi ambled between Djola and his jittery warriors. "Hear a lie a thousand thousand times . . . Who recognizes truth?"

"That is the challenge to all wise people."

"Are we wise?" Azizi gripped Djola's arm, taking his weight. "Did reckoning fire ruin your eye?"

"*Xhalan Xhala.* I've done too much violence."

"So I've heard." Azizi walked Djola toward the table.

"I see wonders now." Djola tapped the red orb. "The eye is a Smokeland treasure."

Azizi set Djola down in his old Council chair with *Anawanama* ancestor spells carved on the arms and back. He found a stool for Djola's mangled foot and stroked the *Lahesh* crystal poking out of Lilot's furry bandages, unafraid. He tucked Djola in scratchy blankets stolen from a desert people. Turquoise beads dangled in the fringe. "Sky rocks heal. What happened to your foot?"

"One of Hezram's fiends fed on me in Smokeland." Djola hesitated, not ready to tell Yari's story again. He removed the mesh glove from his right hand but left the lethal one covered. "*Lahesh* crystal stops me from leaking into the void."

"What's to stop me leaking away?" Azizi turned to the guards. "Leave us to each other." He whistled over their complaints. "Djola is my old, old friend. Watch out for the other masters."

The bolder guard eyed Djola. "*Inside* the Council chamber we keep you—"

"Go," Azizi shouted. "I'm safe with Djola, an Empire hero."

Mumble-grumbling, the warriors headed for the massive doors opposite the fireplace.

"I'm not a hero." Cold filled Djola's lungs and his lethal hand burned, as if he danced *Xhalan Xhala*. "Wait, I see—"

Azizi and the guards looked around. "What?"

An ambush. The void swallowed Arkhys City. Crows turned to soot; exploding behemoths spewed amber foam. An acid wind ravished cathedral trees, toppled stage towers, and the carnival oasis was sludge. Awa, Bal, Boto, Kyrie, and Vandana also, shapeshifted into bone masquerades with Hezram's face. They muttered his lies:

Who dances with fire?
The foolish go up in flames, but not the brave or the wise.
I am the new world.
You are the old. I have only to wait for your demise.

Djola refused these visions and released his spirit body. If not hope, better to see nothing and slip away to Jumbajabbaland. He flew out the sky windows easily. The border void was thin—so much smoke had leaked into the everyday—he passed through in a gasp. The light bridge was a blink. Djola raced toward Samina's cold arms and cruel breath. Bright and bold as in life, she stood on a glacier. When he could almost smell the raintree blossom, she turned her back and faded into an avalanche.

"No," Djola yelled. "I'm almost there. Wait."

10

Lies

Wait for what?" Gruff warriors said as Djola slammed back into the everyday.

Azizi shook his shoulders and whispered, "You were just shadows and breath."

"Are you listening, poison master?" The guards detailed a slow, horrible death if any harm came to their emperor. Djola scowled at empty threats. He tortured himself worse than anybody else could.

"He's too feeble to do any harm," Azizi assured them.

Reluctantly, the warriors tramped into a Council antechamber without noticing Bal in Aido camouflage skulking by stolen mudcloth drapes. *Vie* slipped into Council with swords, bow, and talking drum before the doors locked with *Lahesh* conjure.

Azizi saw Bal easily. All Yari's lovers became *vie*'s students, noting what others might not. "I know this instrument." He tapped Yari's drum. "A shadow warrior could assassinate me and disappear, yet Lilot guided you here."

"Past her hyenas and jackals." Bal grinned, arrogant, cheeky. "Shadow warriors don't kill enemies, not even animal-people if they can help it."

"Griots get carried away. I've never seen a jackal attack a person." Azizi tapped the drum again. "Who are you?"

"Yari was my teacher. I carry *vie*'s drum." Pain rippled through the chamber. "I'm Bal. Djola is family." Bal bowed.

Azizi glanced from Bal to Djola and back. "Oh?"

"Yes," Bal replied. "I've vowed to keep him safe."

"Keep us both safe then," Azizi said. Bal bowed again and faded into the shadows by the door. Azizi turned to Djola. "Is *vie* part of your cure-spell?"

Djola clamped his tongue on *there is no cure, only change.* "Bal rides with Kyrie."

"I knew you'd talk Kyrie back to Council." Azizi stood by an Iyalawo stool at the stone-wood table. The beaded monkeys holding up the seat sniggered. "Still master of the impossible."

"Actually, Kyrie brought me back."

"A wise move." Azizi pointed to roasted goat, mashed tubers, pickled seaweed, spicy nut butters, and berry bread. "Lilot cooked your favorites. Let's talk and fortify ourselves before Council comes to fart and groan and torture us."

"Council sits tonight?" Nobody had told Djola this.

"Why drag our feet?" Azizi worshipped speed. "Poison desert creeps closer every day." He piled two plates and sat next to Djola, rubbing shoulders, banging knees, as if eight terrible years weren't a chasm between them, as if they were the same brash youths who'd dreamed and schemed behind the Elders' backs years ago. "Urzula said you and Kyrie were coming today with the antidote to our troubles."

"Awa, for Council," Djola replied. "She's the conjurer who gave me a *Lahesh* eye for clear vision and a heart wheel for compassion."

"A woman is your cure?" Azizi whistled disapproval. "Rebels worry about treacherous women. They say Tembe is a worse piece of conjure than Hezram."

"I made this same mistake, blaming Kyrie for—" For what Azizi did, for what Djola himself didn't do for his family. "Awa is *Abelzowadyo*. Bal also."

"I don't know this word." Azizi bit into the goat haunch.

"*Zamanzi* for sacred shapeshifter, a conjurer of change."

"*Zamanzi* wisdom is hard to swallow." Azizi chewed quickly, like his rats. "Who has not lost someone to *Zamanzi* poison or blades?"

"Who has not lost someone to Empire blades?" Djola attended to his breath before speaking on. "Yari gave Awa this sacred word, a crossover gift."

Azizi took another bite of goat. "Yari could see a person from beginning to end—"

"Awa is a Green Elder and carries a *Lahesh* wise-woman bag. She would conjure Mountain Gates for the capital."

"Like Kyrie's?" Azizi sucked a string of black seaweed. "Impossible without trees."

"Awa writes a new spell. She would use silver-mesh."

A faint smile twisted at the corner of Azizi's greasy lips. "How?"

"Awa conjures with a willing sacrifice—no transgressor huts, no spirit slaves. A willing sacrifice can sustain us for years. Awa should tell you herself."

"You and Kyrie believe in her. Let's drink to that." Azizi filled their wine cups, then put a hand over Djola's. "Wait. Eat first and explain the spell clear-headed."

Djola picked at the food. "You already have silver-mesh along the capital walls."

"For a year, the masons worked wonders with stone and metal." Azizi swallowed his wine in one gulp. "They'll finish that last section beyond the oasis tonight."

"Awa proposes to use their handiwork the way Kyrie uses rocks and trees."

"Council has other plans." Azizi's hands trembled. "Hezram would be emperor."

Djola shoved his plate away. "Nobody should be emperor, Azizi, ruling lands they've never touched or tasted, passing judgements on people whose songs, spells, and languages they've plundered and outlawed."

Azizi choked down a hunk of stink cheese. "The People regularly give away their power to fools and monsters who lead them into the void."

Djola thrashed in his chair. Azizi clutched his arms and held him still.

"Awa should take my chair before I break it apart," Djola said.

"An emperor must be protected from himself. That's why I need you at my table."

"With Awa you'd still have the votes you need to do right."

"Ah, the new librarian. Boto? He never seems happy voting for Money's schemes. Is Boto a rebel-spy?" Azizi poked Djola. "Bargaining and plotting, like in our youth."

"No." Djola pushed him away. "In our youth, you would have never—"

"If Awa takes the poison master chair, what will you do? What will I do?"

"Kyrie says you agreed to cut down groves and bleed other people's children."

Azizi smeared nut butter on a slab of berry bread. "You're not eating anything."

"No appetite."

"My appetite returns." Azizi swallowed the bread and gulped more wine.

"How could you allow Dream Gates? Nightmare Gates, really."

Azizi hit the table and rattled dishes. "Eight years ago, you should have lied, said you had a cure."

Djola tore off Lilot's bandages and thrust his foot on the stone-wood table. The wound oozed cloudy fluid and a rotten smell. His toes had withered to stubs. The ankle was purple and swollen. Poisoned veins crept up his calf. Rainbow tricksters in the crystal sucked down void-smoke. "Lilot says foot and crystal should come off, but the crystal and heart wheel hold me to life, for a time."

"Fatazz!" Azizi pulled his robe tight.

"Yari was the spirit slave who fed on my foot," Djola wheezed, "until Awa rescued *vie* from Hezram's void-spell."

"Nobody breaks Hezram's spells," Azizi hissed.

Djola snorted. "Does Hezram spread this tale?"

"Yari tried to seduce him in Holy City and got sucked into the void, for lying."

"A true *Lahesh*, Yari got a thrill persuading enemies to be lovers, with truth, not lies." Djola sighed. "You know this."

"Nobody survives Hezram. Nobody ever comes back to themselves."

"Yari did and saved me and Awa." Djola told the tale, relishing Azizi's tremors and twitches. Yari's drum rattled from the shadows. "Let's not waste Yari's sacrifice on Nightmare Gates."

Azizi spit out an olive pit. "Hezram was sniffing around. Savages were in revolt, and you, Yari, and Kyrie had abandoned me to a Council of traitors and cowards."

"You never listened to Yari," Djola said softly. "You removed Kyrie's stool then banished me. We never abandoned you."

Azizi jumped up, combing crumbs from his beard. "I could have executed you and Kyrie. Brought in Tembe and Hezram right then. But I waited eight years!"

"Should I thank you for my pirate adventure? Or my family—"

"Too arrogant to lie. Hezram is your fault." Azizi paced around the stone-wood table. "I didn't expect you to take so long. A few months at most." He smacked stolen robes and helmet masks. Two masks fell down—*Anawanama* sacred clowns, laughing through a cloud of dust. "I'm fending off rebels, starving hordes, and witch-doctors with demon armies, and you bring me what, a witch woman to conjure Mountain Gates?"

"Woman or not, Awa is the true Master of Poisons."

"Hezram defeated Yari. Sooner or later, he'll try to kill us all." Azizi kicked a rusty iron horse. It fell over, insides spilling out. A golden wheel rolled to the fireplace. "Even Urzula fears the Master of Illusion."

"Hezram will ambush us tonight when the gates are finished," Djola said.

Azizi stood over him. "What are you going to do?"

"Me?" Djola tried to recall why he and Azizi had been friends, why he'd sacrificed everything for him and the Empire. "We had grand plans. A better future, a just one." His head ached. "My brother, my wife, warned me. We made a disaster, Zizi."

"So it's Zizi now?" He stabbed his knife into the stink cheese by Djola's foot. "That's what Yari called me, lying in my arms, a tongue in my armpit. I loved *vie*."

"I know." Djola dropped his foot to the well-worn marble floor. "Not just Yari, I've lost everything, everyone—"

"Not everyone." Azizi gulped Djola's wine and stared at Bal. "Marry your enemy. That's what Yari said. Be the father of their children, then your enemy might not slit your throat in the night." He hurled the cup in the fire. It flared. "Masters fear my witch-woman wife and her cook lover, or I'd have been a crows' feast long ago. I only masquerade as emperor."

"I don't feel sorry for you. My half-brother was murdered in front of you. And so many others." Djola gestured at the polished marble floor. "Did Nuar die there or by the fireplace?"

"Nuar trusted Ernold and Money. A fool, like Bones and

Books." Azizi poked the fire, sulking. "Nuar betrayed Samina to save himself."

Djola choked. Vision blurred in his marble eye. Every color was a bright blade slicing him. Nuar said he'd *do anything to survive.* "Brother Nuar betrayed my family?"

"He claimed Samina plotted against me." Azizi touched Djola's hand. "You weren't here, and Samina trusted Nuar. How else would they have overpowered her? Nuar rounded your children up on the road to Mount Eidhou."

"Who told you that?" Djola stood up. The pain in his foot was a jolt of clarity.

"Ernold and Money."

"You believed them? Nuar would never do this. They told lies you'd be desperate to believe."

"Nuar spooks my dreams." Azizi's hands shook. "Grain claims Ernold's acolytes captured Tessa and Quint on the way to a Green Elder enclave or *Anawanama* village. Nobody knows what happened to your middle daughter." Azizi peered at Bal. "This shadow warrior has the green from your eyes, Samina's long legs, and your daughter's name: Bal, a gift of fire and wind." Azizi gulped wine from the jug. "So, you, Kyrie, and this Awa-witch will defeat Hezram, with the aid of rebels. Then you'll conjure metal Mountain Gates? My queen and her cook lover will help too. That could work."

"Awa's plan, not mine." Djola's lip curled. "I loved my wife, my enemy. She loved me." Rage surged out the crack in his heart. Sweet relief. He leapt on Azizi and pinned him to the ground. "You blame me, Yari, Kyrie, and Nuar for what happened, for Hezram, for my family lost, but I blame you. A coward. You betrayed us all." Djola pressed a diamond-tipped blade into Azizi's throat. Yari's blade. "I plan to taste your last breath, burn your body, then scatter the ashes so there is no place to mourn you."

Azizi waved trembling hands at Bal who had dropped bow and swords and run close. "What about forgiveness?"

"Forgiveness is a lie," Djola said.

"So many, many lies." The tremors in Azizi's hands subsided. "I was the youngest son. I never expected to rule. But you saved me, Djola. Why?"

ll

Lost

Awa shuffled behind Soot as he padded up a steep, dark corridor in the citadel maze. Urzula's sparking staff offered only fitful light. Djola's conjure bag bashed her hip, weighty again. She clutched the furry *Mama Zamba* travel cloak tight against the chill. "Where are we?"

"They said go this way." Meera dragged several paces behind Awa and Soot.

She was weary and slow; even chewing soft berry bread was an effort. With food, love, and rest, Meera would regain her vitality, but Awa feared Mother had been a spirit slave too long to recover. Mother's breath tasted like rotten fruit; her eyes were half empty, her heartbeat erratic. Awa left Mother in the kitchen, Lilot's realm, a citadel inside the citadel. Kyrie, Queen Urzula, and Lilot promised to help Mother, keep her safe. Witch women could surely do more for Mother than Awa. So much void-smoke had leaked into the everyday—nobody was safe.

Meera abandoned Rokiat to the kitchen too. He was a weak good person, afraid to bring Emperor Azizi terror tales from Holy City. Yet he was handsome, sang like a shadow warrior, and Meera loved him. Awa was also a coward, and Bal loved her. Awa's stomach fluttered. Love was strange.

"I hate secret passageways," Awa muttered. "Witch women turn jackals and hyenas loose in the maze to kill trespassers and assassins."

"Would Queen Urzula or Lilot do that?" Meera swallowed a shriek. "Hezram tells lies. An illusion-spell."

"How do you know?" Awa gulped, caught again by *lies she was willing to believe.*

"My aunt fed a hyena pack bones, gristle, and guts." Meera sounded ready to cry. "The pack left our goats alone and kept other hyenas away. We had more goats than anybody, the best cheese. Jealous herders said my aunt was a *Mama Zamba* witch and I must be too, for the hyena pups in my lap. That's how we ended up in Holy City. More witch women in the huts than men from such lies." She paused for a breath. "And my aunt bled to death our first day."

Awa and Meera had never traded stories. "Thief-lords sold me to the huts." Awa's good leg was throbbing. She walked slower. "I sang with rivers and trees. I also talked to crows and bees and smoke-walked."

"I warned Rokiat—if he told on you, I'd make all the warhorses hate him. He loves the horses more than me."

"You knew." Awa shook her head.

"Of course. Your hair was on fire!"

A window looked out on a full moon rising from Thunder River just before it would vanish behind the mountains. Awa dipped her head in moonbeams and whispered gratitude for moon sacrifice. Meera stepped close. She pulled Samina's cloud-silk robe tight over today's bruises and cuts—from snub-nose Jod or others?

"I'm sorry we rode off without you," Meera whispered. "I wasn't thinking."

Awa shrugged. "Who could think?" Forgiving Meera was easy. Nothing to forgive. "I've done worse, but now we change. We don't just save ourselves." Meera nodded.

In the kitchen, after Djola and Bal disappeared, Awa told Kyrie of Father and Kenu building Nightmare Gates. Awa promised to sacrifice herself to Djola's Dream Gates for her friends, for the *Weeds and Wild Things,* and for Bal. Djola was too valuable to lose and Dream Gates needed a willing sacrifice. Kyrie looked relieved. *Our secret* was her only reply. Every minute since, Awa wanted to take this promise back. "You're strong, Meera. You'll help me keep my promise at the gates, no matter what." She couldn't ask Bal— *vie* was too lovesick to understand. "If I falter."

"Our vow." Meera's face shone in moonlight. "I'm for you and you're for me."

Awa repeated their words and hugged her. "I love the world and I love someone, the way you love Rokiat."

"Bal," Meera said, wiping tears. "And you came for me."

Soot yapped, and they hurried up to him, their cocoon anklets banging a polyrhythm. He jumped against a *Lahesh* whimsy wheel carved into the rock. With a second lunge, a door opened, and light and warmth trickled into the passageway. High ceilings disappeared in the dark. Moonlight leaked through sky windows. Soot scampered in, barking and growling, and raced out a whimsy wheel door on a far wall.

Awa and Meera tiptoed in. Emperor Azizi lay limp on the marble floor, eyes closed, breath shallow, his heart doing a bird beat. Djola held Yari's knife to his neck. Blood trickled across the diamond tip. Bal hovered a few steps from the blade. *Vie* shot Awa a desperate look.

"Forgiveness is a lie," Djola said.

"So many, many lies," Azizi replied. "I was the youngest son. I never expected to rule. But you saved me, Djola. Why?"

"Nobody can save you now." Djola shook Azizi. "Look at me as you die."

"Stop," Awa yelled. "What are you doing?"

Djola glared at her.

Awa glared back. She marched over and crouched down. "*Djola the Assassin* is a tale Hezram would tell."

Djola snarled at her. "I'm the end. You begin a new story."

"I need a better end to begin with," Awa declared.

Bal gripped Djola's knife hand. While they wrestled, Awa and Meera dragged Azizi away. They propped him in a chair at a stone-wood table. Azizi stared glassy-eyed at his rescuers then traced the blood drizzling down his robe. Meera ripped a piece of the fancy hem and tied it around the neck wound. Awa raced back to Djola.

Bal leaned *vie*'s forehead against Djola's. The blade trembled between them. "Kill the emperor, and—Hezram will seize power tonight."

Djola stammered. "I'm lost . . ."

"We could all be lost souls." Awa put cool hands on his head and heart Vévés. "We must never give up looking for each other."

Djola let the knife fall and went limp in Bal's arms. *Vie* clutched him and rocked.

Following a rogue impulse, Awa stumbled to the emperor. "Come with me?"

"Where?" Azizi shook his head, eyes blank, breath still shallow. Blood soaked through the cloth at his neck. "Outside the citadel, I'm not safe."

"You're not safe here either." Awa squeezed Meera's hand. "Watch over us."

12

Trading Stories

Before Meera could protest or Azizi could resist, before Bal or Djola realized what was happening, Awa lifted Azizi's spirit body through the sky window and headed for Jumbajabbaland. The border-void was thin, a puff or two of smoke. Azizi kicked and screeched all the same as Awa tugged him into what might be or could be, but was certainly not far from all that was happening right now in the Empire.

"You must be Awa." Azizi batted the air in front of his eyes. "Am I drunk or is this jumba jabba real?" He gawked at the swirl of landscape rushing by and the volcano hearts pumping in his and Awa's chests.

"Jumba jabba means *speaking miracles is grace, for we are what we say.*" Awa quoted *The Songs for Living and Dying.* "*So say what you mean to be and do what you say.*" She flew faster than the speed of thought, trying to find the rhythm of Samina's realm.

"Smokeland." He pointed at wisps trailing behind them. "Yari wanted to fly me across the void once, years ago, but we never made it." Azizi pulled a tight curl at her neck. A sluggish bee crawled to her ear.

"Leave her be," Awa commanded.

Startled, Azizi jerked away. "Yari said I was too heavy."

"Djola was heavier than you at first. And Yari smoke-walked with Djola."

"Or—" He pointed at her chest. Her heart was like a star exploding. "Perhaps you're a stronger smoke-walker than Yari."

Awa snorted. "Or perhaps you've changed, gotten lighter. The *Zamanzi* say each person is many more beings than they think. That makes shapeshifting easy."

"Who listens to them?" Azizi touched his throat. "My uncle or one of my father's masters paid *Zamanzi* to poison my family. I'm the only one who survived."

Awa hid her shock that the emperor wished to trade stories with her. "My good-citizen father sold me to Green Elders and sent Mother to a transgressor hut, for love of your Empire."

"For love of jewels and coin more likely."

"Well, you and I are change and hidden strength. *Abelzowadyo.*" Awa slowed down. The seventh-region rhythm eluded her. The sky was smoke gray, no green auroras to guide her. They soared over putrid trees and black riverbeds. Rubble spilled down the hills and into the sea. Behemoths flailed in sand and warhorses rotted on the hoof. A desiccated hive sat among mounds of gossamer bee wings. Awa almost lost the speed of thought. She landed on a barren cliff. On a nearby ledge, spirit slaves with Hezram's face shuffled over one another getting nowhere, too depleted to be a threat. Ember hearts burned out, and demons who had once been people crumbled into poison dust. No good story to make of this. Awa choked on void-smoke.

"Yari said it was beautiful." Azizi looked ready to throw up. "What's happened?"

"Void-spells," Awa said. "Lost futures, like Hezram's Nightmare Gates."

The mountain quaked underneath them and a storm gathered. Azizi glanced around, panicked. "What spells do you offer?"

"I offer a moment or two." Faint music made Awa smile. "Do you hear? Someone plays a shield-spell." She pulled Azizi under her *Mama Zamba* cloak and followed the music trail through the storm to the boat people. They floated on turquoise water under cloudless skies. Colorful sailboats resembled giant birds or lizards with wings. A few jackal-boats had waterwheel butts. Behemoths leapt from the waves adding their voices to the drumming and singing. "Here is Yari's Jumbajabbaland." Awa flew low over the decks. *Lahesh* performers cavorted in carnival attire. People, who might have been Empire citizens, northlanders, or barbarians, waved.

Azizi waved to them. "Who are they?"

"*Lahesh*, and I don't know. Their friends who escaped a perilous everyday?" High in the sails of a blackbird boat, lovers with spider-web hair and cloud-silk robes folded into each other and swayed in the rigging. Treehouse refugees! Awa felt a thrill and then anger. "They're hunted in Jumbajabbaland, by Hezram's fiends and other spirit slaves. Nowhere to run and live free."

"They look free."

"In hiding? Under siege?" The music swept away void tendrils clinging to Awa's cloak.

"The voices and talking drums clear the air," Azizi whispered, fascinated, amazed.

"*We are the weather.*" Awa quoted *The Songs for Living and Dying* a second time. She was turning into the boring Elder she swore she'd never be.

"*Our thoughts make the world.*" Azizi spoke the next line and seemed lighter. He tapped his chest. "I can't catch their rhythm. Do you know these songs?"

"Bal does." This filled Awa with hope. Djola's conjure bag

weighed nothing again. Riding the crossover rhythm, she rose high and aimed for a faint glow: the light bridge. Stars and cold comets rushed by, and in no time, they stood on a rock by a hot spring. Silver trees nodded a welcome. Deep snow around them sighed and shifted as someone played an ice harp in a cave overhead. Awa pressed her cheek against the giant beehive resting in warm heather. The roar of many wings comforted her.

"Whose realm is this?" Sleet blew through Azizi's flimsy robe. Breath froze in his scraggly beard. He touched a thirty-foot icicle melting into the steam from the hot spring. Or was it growing?

"A difficult region to find. Almost impossible—" Awa sputtered.

Behind Azizi, a spirit slave with Hezram's face tumbled from the star bridge to the rock ledge, carrying a bundle of rags. This fiend had trailed them to the seventh region. Azizi turned to see what terrified Awa then shoved her against the beehive. The rag bundle the fiend carried was a limp woman. She'd been in the cell when Soot rescued Meera and Mother.

Fresh blood was quick fuel, not the slow burn of tree oil and blood. The fiend jolted at ice-harp music and slitted empty eyes against bright snow. Light drained from its heart. Awa gripped the viper necklace at her neck as the fiend chomped granite teeth into the woman's shoulder and sucked greedily. Its heart burned bright again. The woman's spirit body turned to ash and void-smoke that got swallowed by crystals at the cave mouth. Awa's lungs burned, her heart ached. The fiend crouched and blinked empty eyes wide. Azizi gazed into endless darkness, transfixed.

"No." Awa shook Azizi and focused on the fiend's bright heart. "Don't lose the speed of thought. We don't have Bal to rescue us." She pulled a snake head from around her neck and, faster than thought, flew at the grinning fiend. They passed in the air. As Awa spun around, the fiend pinned Azizi to the ground by the hive and reached down to bite a trembling hand. Awa screamed. A hun-

dred hundred bees burst from the hive, swarming the fiend, stabbing fat, hot stingers everywhere. Several sentinels were the size of
hummingbirds and had three or four stingers. Flailing, the fiend
snagged a few bees and swallowed their sparks. Before more sentinels perished, Awa raced through the blur of wings and plunged
snake fangs in the fiend's heart. Indigo sparks filled its body as it
crumpled. The bees returned to the hive. Awa snorted a puff of
void-smoke and let hot tears flow.

"Look." Azizi gasped.

Hezram's smirk faded from the fiend's face. Color returned to
the cheeks of a wizened Empire citizen with a knotty white beard.
His heart beat lightning bolts.

"A haint dead to the everyday, but free," Awa said.

"Curses on you all." He scowled and flew away.

"You broke Hezram's spell!" Azizi stood up, sweating and
shaking. "That was my cousin, the Master of Books and Bones."

"The librarian?" Awa shook her head. "Yari spoke well of him."

"Not lost in his labyrinth of books." Azizi shuddered. "Who
did this to him?"

"Hezram. The librarian wore his face."

Azizi's heart blazed as bright as hers. Anger, resolve, fear?
"With the blessings of other masters at my table."

"The bees resist." Awa stroked the hive and looked up to the
cave. Why hadn't Samina helped? "Are you there?" she shouted.
"Please. I'm Djola's friend."

The ice-harp music came to an abrupt end. Samina dropped
down to the hot spring. A cloak of sleet swirled around naked
breasts, hips, and ankles. Her eyes and lips were the blue of glaciers. Her heart beat a lightning storm.

"Samina? Can it be?" Azizi stepped back. "What are you?"

"Every day, I'm more ice storm than anything." Samina shook
a snow squall from red-streaked silver hair and walked through

Awa, like a shiver of horror—an unnerving experience. "I have few visitors. Thank you for dispatching this one. A wise woman helps spirit slaves across the star bridge."

"Tembe," Awa and Azizi said in unison, then cursed.

"I knew Tembe once." Samina ground her teeth. "My music distracted the others trying to break in. Without you two as guides, they're lost, for a while at least."

"We're all under siege," Awa said. "But Djola has a plan."

Samina smiled, granite teeth covered in frost. "Djola would come and stay with me."

"He can't, not yet," Awa declared. "Azizi needs him."

"Is that so?" Samina shook sleet from her eyes. "What do you two want from me?"

Azizi stuttered jibber jabber about spirit debt and how helpless he'd been without Djola and how helpless he still was against Hezram, Ernold, Money, and the others. "Hezram grows stronger every minute." He leaned against Awa, repeating lies and denying truth, another weak good person who'd lost his way. "Djola abandoned me, but he's come back, and— Can you forgive me?"

Samina walked through him. The blood seeping from his wound froze and he clamped his lips on more excuses. Samina's heart flashed brighter. She gathered strength passing through smoke-walkers.

"Council sits tonight," Awa said. "We want to do a Dream Gate spell, to protect the city and Mount Eidhou, the bees, everyone. To give us time to make a different story."

Samina gave her a bag of *Lahesh* crystals like the one in Djola's foot. "For the gates."

"Our last chance." Azizi sighed. "Hezram would rule."

Samina's granite teeth glinted in the sunlight. "But I am the queen of misrule."

13

Council

Mount Eidhou was a purple giant roaming midnight gloom in an ice-blue cap, settling down to sleep across Thunder River. A full moon rose above Eidhou's peaks, offering itself up to greedy demons. A breeze whispered mountain gossip to oasis trees while the river gurgled mountain secrets against the shore. Djola leaned against Mango who was damp and cool from a mud bath. They stood just inside the new city wall at the silver-mesh gates to the river. Vévés on the gates were roads and spirals, shooting stars and spiderwebs, and also the full moon rising.

Tears flooded Djola's cheeks, blurred his vision. So much to celebrate! The elephant, Vandana, and Orca/Boto had survived, had become rebels. Harsh Kyrie, proud Kyrie never betrayed Djola's family. Awa and Bal called Djola to his right mind and loved him like a father. They saved Azizi. Soon Djola would greet Samina at Mount Eidhou, perhaps Tessa and Quint also. So why so many tears and a deep ache at the end of each breath?

Mango reached her trunk around Djola to examine the gates. In his marble eye, Djola spied tendrils of void-smoke trying to lap over the silver-mesh at the top of the wall—only a thin thread

made it. Kenu, Kenu's father, and other masons were securing final hinges, latches, and *Lahesh* whimsy wheels with foul-smelling
concoctions. Tedious spells, but when done right, the gates would
hold spirits and haints to resist a void-storm or poison desert encroaching. Kenu had even put silver-mesh around the iron citadel
gates.

If Hezram conjured Nightmare Gates, Kenu and the masons
would share the spirit debt. But any spell could be perverted. If
Awa conjured true Dream Gates, Kyrie would extend her gates to
Azizi's citadel, which lay across the river and outside the city wall,
but was surrounded by trees. Azizi would gain access to Eidhou's
resources, but only on Kyrie's terms. And despite his father, Kenu
would be a hero. Which story would it be? Mango rumbled, impatient. Djola stroked her trunk and said what he desired. "Awa will
make our Dream Gates soon."

Azizi strode from the oasis garden, brandishing Urzula's
spark torch. The trip to Jumbajabbaland with Awa had invigo-
rated him. *"Abelzowadyo,"* he said to Djola. *Zamanzi* in the crowd
echoed him. Azizi raised the torch high then low, and a hundred
hundred lights in the shape of raintree blossoms lit up dark citadel windows. Floating-city conjure honored wise Samina tonight,
eight years too late. When Council betrayed Nuar and Samina,
Urzula had used her powers just for Azizi and their children. Tonight, the queen would dance an *Anawanama* moon masquerade
with the rebels. Djola might forgive the queen and all the others.
He might even forgive himself.

Stick bugs rubbed their legs together and frogs bellowed. Djola
scanned the riverbanks, taking pleasure in oozing mud, river grass,
torch-bugs, and countless mysteries unfolding in the moonlight. A
hundred crows headed for their night roost in the oasis garden trees,
squabbling and screeching. Djola smiled. He'd come to the end of
his world, and everything was new again, wondrous. *Impossible is a*

word for yesterday. He had little appetite for killing but felt ready for anything else. His spirit debt had come due. Tomorrow he'd be free, a flicker in the moonlight, a shadow on the water.

Angry voices wafted through the air. To the dismay of masters plotting to assassinate the emperor, Azizi had called Council an hour earlier than planned. He moved the gathering outdoors and invited festivalgoers and performers to attend Council deliberations and the gate-conjure ritual. Arms commandeered a stage table carved by *Anawanama* craftsmen in the shape of a winged jackal. Candles burned in its mouth and at the tail; wings were tucked against a broad flat back. Lilot's helpers hung spark lanterns along the city wall and laid out a feast—fish from the river, groundnuts, seaweed, and mountain greens.

Azizi strode to the *Lahesh* waterwheel chair that Arms set at the fiery tail. He sat down with his back to the river. Faithful guards stood behind him with Arms. Kitchen helpers brought out Djola's *Anawanama* chair and Grain's sweetgrass one. Across the river at the cook's entrance, Urzula fed a hyena pack the goat feast Djola and Azizi had picked at earlier. Warriors and festivalgoers shuddered as the beasts gobbled great hunks of meat and gristle and sang their high-pitched, rollicking odes. Griots readied a new hyena tale. Djola readied himself for battle.

The Masters of Water and Money—still silver-eyed rogues—stormed across the citadel bridge. Unnerved by hyenas and witch-woman conjure, they fumed to high priest Ernold, who was gaunt, ashy brown, and irritable too. Boto shadowed them, head bowed and eyes hooded, actually an excellent spy. The hyenas disappeared into the trees or the citadel maze. Ernold tightened his butt and chomped his teeth to walk through northlanders, barbarians, and *veson*-shapeshifters to reach the Council table.

"Fatazz!" Money swallowed more curses. "Is Council a masquerade to entertain the mob?"

"We gather around an *Anawanama* jackal?" Ernold glared at the emperor.

Azizi fed a rat groundnuts. "No one has moved the stone-wood table in a hundred years."

Dressed in Aido cloth, Grain snuck in from the trees, refusing to look at anybody or perhaps *vie* just avoided Djola's eyes. Gone was the bold young rascal. Tonight, Grain was a steely survivor, tense and guarded, yet still carrying a talking drum. *Vie* grumbled to Arms who grumbled back. Flirting.

"Grain," Djola shouted and then added a name. "Adeley!"

Grain stepped under a light. Deep blue eyes were unreadable. A purple scar ran from ear to chin on otherwise smooth, blue-black skin—a good story there. "I'm glad to see you returned from pirate exile, Djola. We need heroes more than ever before."

Djola snorted, embarrassed. "Zizi, Kyrie, and Arms spread that pirate-hero lie."

"What lie? Pezarrat no longer plagues the waters. You're the hero who saved—"

"Ha." Djola shifted to *Anawanama*, certain Grain would understand. "A friend on Pezarrat's ship said—*if it's so bad, you need gods or heroes to save your world*—" Regrets and doubts shook him and perhaps Grain also. "Well, it's time to pull together."

Grain tapped the talking drum to say: "Isn't it always that bad?"

Djola had cursed Grain's cowardice just this morning. "Thank you for the letters."

Grain also spoke *Anawanama*. "Spit on the wind."

"No. Water in the desert."

Grain drummed thanks, but was drowned out by singers and djembe drummers heralding Hezram's entrance. The old carnival hack appeared in a puff of blue smoke at the jackal's head, almost blowing out the candles. Seashells scattered in Hezram's luxurious hair framed handsome features. He wore power-blue robes, a torch-bug eyepatch that sparkled iridescent blue, and a calm-in-the-face-of-any-danger demeanor. The crowd applauded. Ernold and Money fussed and fumed. Hezram shushed them, grinned at Djola, and marched around with a *Lahesh* timepiece, prodding acolytes, masons, and everyone else. "The sooner we start, the better for the city and the Empire." Hezram sat down next to the emperor in Djola's old chair.

Azizi whistled at him. "You're not yet a master at this table."

Hezram jumped up, and pointed at the bandage on Azizi's neck. "Someone try to slit your throat?"

Arms had a blade at Hezram's head before Azizi took a breath. Hezram's acolytes readied poison darts. Emperor guards drew swords. Warrior-clowns aimed bows and spears from the shadows. Few weapons were allowed in the citadel chamber, but under the stars, Arms had little control. Azizi wore an *Anawanama* outlaw cloak like Djola's, impervious to arrows, darts, and blades. Mesh dangled from Zizi's headdress, protecting the back of his neck and forehead. Assassins would need perfect aim to bring him down. So many others could suffer if—

"Are we dead before we begin?" Sparks leapt from Kyrie's fingers and fresh Vévé wounds as she paraded in, fearless. Mountain jewels graced her hair. Cloud-silk pants and tunic accentuated her round, flowing figure. Her *Anawanama* cape snapped in the wind. Drunk on snake venom, poison sap, and rock runoff, she, like Djola, was ready for anything. She carried her conjure book. Warriors bristled and glanced about, uncertain. Mango trumpeted and touched her trunk to Kyrie's nose.

An entrance to rival Hezram's.

"You!" Iyalawo Tembe covered surprise and shook a raffia fan at acolytes till they lowered dart pipes. Her gold hair and tattoos reflected torchlight. She sat a respectful distance from the Council table on an Iyalawo stool—carved giraffes adorned with cowry shells, crystal beads, and an Aido cloth cushion. Tembe was a fortress of knowledge not to be discounted. She bowed as Kyrie sauntered toward the table. Tembe's talking drummers played a praise song for a carnival clown who juggled fire.

Kyrie bowed to Tembe. "I was sorry to hear about Ice Mountain."

Tembe's lips trembled. She'd loved her mountain. "Tonight we protect Mount Eidhou from a similar fate." She glanced from Djola to Hezram and smacked her fan against acolytes who had yet to lower weapons.

Kyrie wiggled between Hezram and Arms's sword. "Let's not waste more blood." She tugged the red beard frosted silver at Arms's chin.

"Our blood is precious," Tembe said, Iyalawo of transgressor huts. Her pronouncement made Djola's foot throb, yet others took up her words and weapons disappeared. Arms lowered his sword.

Hezram grinned. "Poison master, why stand in the trees grinding your teeth? Come over here." He put on a friendly command voice. "Sit. You're injured."

Djola wanted to shove his poison foot down Hezram's throat. "I must stand." Pain and distance from Hezram and Azizi would keep him focused.

"Djola's lost his appetite." Azizi cut cold eyes at Hezram. "You look hungry. Sit at least for food." He pointed to Djola's chair and piled fish and greens on the plate. The Master of Illusion barely skipped a beat and dropped down with a carnival smile. *Anawanama* spells in the chair made him chafe. He poked the food.

"Do you worry that Lilot might poison you?" Azizi ate from Hezram's plate.

Djola munched berry bread lest someone think he was afraid to eat with Council.

Hezram chuckled and gobbled a piece of fish. "No man wants to die this night."

"Dochsi," Djola disagreed.

"It's always a good night to die for what you believe," Kyrie and Tembe said together and laughed, deep, throaty, dangerous laughs.

Hezram smirked at the women, too confident. "Are we all here?"

"We wait on the witnesses," Azizi said. "Two women who escaped your transgressor huts."

"Perhaps they are liars, cowards who don't want to face us," Ernold said.

"They're almost here." Arms nodded at Djola. Awa and Meera would soon arrive at the oasis garden.

"Take your seats. Eat while we wait," Azizi shouted. Good citizens flooded feast tables. Hezram looked pleased by the audience. Azizi watched them anxiously. Could the emperor be trusted not to go whichever way the water ran? Djola took a sharp breath. *Nobody is who you think she is.* Mango flapped her ears, cooling them both. Masters sat down on whimsy chairs borrowed from carnival players. Kyrie crouched on a torch-bug stool. Arms sat in a monster's mouth, Money and Water on the wings of a butterfly.

Boto laughed as he and Ernold plopped between the tentacles of who could say what sea creature. He winked at Djola when no one was looking then masked his face in a blink. An excellent spy—but for whom? Djola stiffened. Boto or Grain or Azizi could be a weak chink, acquiescing to Hezram's lies and illusions. Hezram might even have launched more than one traitor. Djola scanned the masters and audience, more alert. He'd been too busy mourning the end of his life to sniff out danger coming. Nothing was as it seemed.

"Stop worrying." Kyrie scolded him in *Anawanama.* Tembe and

Hezram eyed her with fear. Good. "Clowns have to play the moment. Whatever it brings."

"I was always too serious to be a good clown or maybe too arrogant." Djola slipped into the trees, into their woody whispers and sweet breath.

14

Doubts

W hen I'm a haint in Djola's Dream Gates, I shall miss you."
Awa buried her face in Fannie's mane, relishing the scent
of salt water and sweaty horse. They loped down the long boardwalk at the harbor with Bibi and Meera as boats came in on a full
moon tide. Every mooring had a ship or two bobbing in the swell.
Sails were tucked away; waterwheels had stilled; lights winked in
windows. Bal and a legion of shadow warrior-clowns rode guard.
They joined the shadows at the loading docks, hiding in empty
stalls and behind storm curtains.

The warhorses had taken Awa and Meera on a midnight run
around Arkhys City so they could feel the neighborhoods, touch
silvered gates, and listen to *Weeds and Wild Things.* The last stop
was the docks, where they'd greet travelers coming for the Festival
of Memories. Kyrie's idea, to stop Awa dreading Hezram's next
move. *We have to get him out of your head,* Kyrie declared. *Our story,
not Ernold's or Money's or Hezram's.* In Jumbajabbaland, Hezram's
spirit slave had known what Awa was thinking before she did. If it
weren't for the bees, she and Azizi would be dead.

Awa groaned. "Zst!"

"What?" Meera chewed a hunk of fish and goat cheese. "You've said Zst five times."

A large cargo boat pulled in. *Zamanzi* and *Anawanama* clans disembarked. Thrilled to be in the capital, they donned animal masks and outlaw armor. Two more ships arrived. Tomorrow, on the final day of the *Eishne* Festival of Memories, Azizi would appoint a new five-year Council. He promised bold changes. Folks from everywhere with tales to tell and hopes to share poured into the capital—refugees, adventurers, scoundrels, and rebels, all taking advantage of open gates. As they disembarked, brave eyes met Awa's gaze. She forced a smile. Inside Djola's Dream Gates, the People, green lands, and *Weeds and Wild Things* would have time to write a different story. A few moments at least. No reason to doubt this.

Bal materialized from shadows and rode close. City buildings loomed behind *vie,* gloomy in the night. Each dark window was a promise not kept, an opening into the void, a war about to be waged. Bal touched Awa's cheek. "What's the matter?"

"Everything," Awa whispered. "Nothing."

Bal opened *vie*'s mouth, then closed it tight.

"Look at that." Meera almost squealed.

Sea sparkle swarmed below the docks. Tiny creatures turned midnight water iridescent green and purple—a miracle. Farther out, dark waves reflected moonlight. Awa had placed *Lahesh* crystals along the gates, for Djola's conjure and to honor Yari. She threw one into the sea-sparkle water for Isra.

"Yari used to sing an ode about a black sea with a shiny edge." Bal hummed, searching for a tune. "Do you remember?"

Awa had learned it without meaning to and sang it now:

When our battles are won
Who will map endless bloodstains?
When our brief days are done

What little shadow remains?
When the last wave is come
Who sings the final refrains?
Silver light creasing a black sea
That is how to remember me

"*Zamanzi* thugs and *Anawanama* whores! Savage scum!" Shouting curses, a dozen acolytes in Hezram-yellow and Ernold-red ran toward a boat arriving at the farthest dock. Froth seeped from their noses and hearts beat out of rhythm.

Sand-colored travelers ambled down the gangway. Short, squat folks in pirate pants and *Lahesh* flame-cloth robes carried spark torches and small catapult weapons. Bushy hair was streaked bronze or braided in swirls. The women had stars tattooed in half circles around their eyes—pirates, not northlanders. Isolationist floating-city folks had ventured off their island for the *Eishne* Festival. Acolytes hurled rocks and cursed foreign demons come to destroy the Empire. The pirates threw sparks at the acolytes' feet. Fannie reared. Bibi snorted and kicked too. Acolytes got tripped up by the horses. "*Tschupatzi!* Queen Urzula has invited us." The pirates displayed torch weapons.

"Urzula is a witch!" The acolytes reached under their cloaks. Before they could nock an arrow or throw a knife, Bal and the warrior-clowns hurled nets and tangled them in knotted rope. The pirates cheered, sending sparks into the sky. One red-robed acolyte fell on his own blade. His shrieks were cut short as void-smoke snaked from his wound and got sucked into Awa's last crystal. The clowns dragged him and the other acolytes into the shadows.

"Religious fanatics," a pirate said. She looked like a young Urzula. "They've swallowed the void."

"I knew we were wrong to come," replied a man who could have been her brother.

"Lilot invited us, not the queen," the woman said.

Bal jumped to the ground and spoke *Lahesh,* the diplomat's tongue. "Welcome to Arkhys City." Bal could have been a north-lander, a pirate from the floating cities, or a barbarian. "Let us take you to Lilot. She and the queen lent us these sparks." *Vie* held up Urzula's torch. "I apologize for the zeal of young men who have yet to grow into their wisdom." Bal bowed as if *vie* were the Master of Arms. The warrior-clowns bowed too. Bal stepped toward the pirates. "You see clearly. Those acolytes have swallowed too much void-smoke."

"Willingly or force-fed?" The pirate woman also spoke *Lahesh,* acting like the captain.

"Will is often an illusion." Bal grinned. "I offer an honor guard to escort you to the citadel." Clowns leapt in the air, danced on their hands, and juggled fire weapons. The travelers snapped their fingers, relieved, delighted even.

"Those acolytes are a danger to themselves," the pirate woman said, "not to us."

"Of course." Bal bowed again. "This honor guard is for our most esteemed guests." *Our?* The rebels? The Empire?

Charmed, the pirate woman marched down the gangway through cheers, somersaults, and clanging weapons. Her people followed. "We appreciate your generosity." She smiled at Bal. Warrior-clowns hustled them off into the night.

Meera scowled. "This is the third ambush." Yellow cloaks had joined Bog-towners fighting Kahartans. Red cloaks had urged a citizen mob to hang *vesons.* Bal and the clowns intervened each time. "Those acolytes are . . . are . . ."

Full of the void and acting like Smokeland fiends, but who wanted to say that?

"Hezram or Council traitors mean to deplete our ranks and rattle our spirits." Bal scanned the boardwalk. "We can't linger any longer." *Vie* leapt onto the warhorse.

Meera shook Awa. "You're not eating." She stuffed nut bread in Awa's mouth. "Don't worry. Kyrie was right to send us out. You see how easily we defeat them."

Awa chewed. "Do I?"

15

Most of All

Fannie picked up speed along the new wall that led to the Thunder River Gates. Father and Kenu had fashioned silver-mesh that gave off an iridescent light, the purple-green of sea sparkle. The latticework of moonbeam and crossroads Vévés reminded Awa of Djola's tattoos. When he called up Dream Gates, this would be fortress-conjure that held her spirit and protected everyone she loved. Awa trailed her fingers over cold latticework. Shocks made her heart skip a few beats.

"It tingles." Meera brushed fingers along the chilly surface. "Like being startled in the night or turning the corner onto a surprise."

The oasis garden was the final stop before the River Gates. They slid off tired horses and walked down a winding path. The trees were brooding columns turning bitter against creatures nibbling at shoots and leaves. Across the river, spark lights in the shape of raintree blossoms lit up citadel windows—Azizi's libations to Samina, queen of misrule. Awa sang with rustling branches and let her bones catch the rhythm of a hundred hundred roots thrumming under her feet. Meera slipped into the bushes with Rokiat. Bal disappeared with the clowns for last-minute preparations.

Crows screeched at roving owls and Fannie munched sweetgrass. Awa took a brush from Djola's conjure bag and combed burrs from her mane. She stroked the warhorse from withers to tail.

"Fannie, my heart, when I'm gone, you and Bibi take the herd, and Soot too, and run away, across *Mama Zamba* to sweetgrass fields and berry bushes, and no people riding you off to war."

Fannie nickered, happy to hear this.

Djola appeared under a treehouse, leaning on Urzula's cane. Lilot had put a fresh bandage on his foot. The crystal's facets were filled with smoke. Mango clutched the hem of his cape in her trunk, flapped her ears, and cooled them both. "Council eats while they wait for you," Djola murmured.

"I must return this to you." Awa held out the conjure bag.

"It's too heavy for me." He pushed the bag gently against her chest. "You keep it."

Awa used Elder discipline to remain calm. "If something should happen to me, I don't want Hezram or one of them to get it."

"Hezram could not carry such a bag."

Insisting Djola take it would reveal her plan to be a willing sacrifice. Azizi and Council needed Djola to check Hezram. Mount Eidhou needed Kyrie to defend it against Ernold and greedy masters. Meera could take care of Mango, Rokiat, Fannie, and the horses. Bal and Soot would protect everyone. Awa, the best smoke-walker, was the right choice to power the Dream Gates. She'd have to give the bag to Kyrie or Bal. She'd never gotten to read through its countless treasures. Someone should.

"All goes as planned." Djola stroked Fannie. Awa marveled at his faith. "What? You don't believe me?"

"I don't know what to think," she whispered.

"Your plan." Djola beamed at her. He'd get over being mad at her deceit. "Council agreed to listen to transgressor witnesses. The People have gathered to hear you too." He was warmth and love, as sentimental as Yari—what Father couldn't manage and Mother had been denied. Djola reached his bare lethal hand toward her, touching a cheek. His fingers were cool and tingled like the gates. "*Xhalan Xhala*. Your tomorrow is so bright . . . I can't see it." He brushed his lips over the palm of her burnt hand while touching her forehead, a sign of respect to a great griot. "A mountain is either being worn down or rising up."

Awa sputtered at praise for an Iyalawo wise woman. Death was near and she should take care with last words. It had been easier singing with the trees and talking to Fannie. "We'll speak the change-spell together." She pressed her forehead to Djola's, like a daughter. "I feel light and full."

"Everyone is in position." Bal dropped from a branch in front of them.

Still holding Awa's hand, Djola pressed his forehead to Bal's. "Whatever happens, I leave you a legacy of love. Share my memory." Bal was thrilled at his somber words. Djola was the story *vie* had longed for. Awa hugged them both, and then Djola hobbled away.

"Djola loves the world again." Bal watched him and Mango head to Council. Djola would help Bal with grief. "But he loves you most of all."

"No, he doesn't." Awa pressed her body against Bal's, feeling taut muscles, soft skin at *vie's* neck, and sharp bones at the collar. She drew in Bal's sweaty, spicy scent and wanted to do things she'd seen Smokeland lovers do in the treehouses. Instead, she kissed *vie* wherever she could find bare skin. "It's you who loves me most of all." An old woman clown leered at them from a branch and sang a bawdy melody. Others added harmony. Bal's lips and tongue made Awa tingle, cold conjure on her hot skin. Back from the bushes, Meera giggled at their moans and squeals. Awa pulled away. "I'd love to grab Mango and the horses, escape to Kyrie's mountain, and make good stories together, but—" She held up Djola's conjure bag.

Bal threw it over her strong arm. "What are you doing tomorrow?" *Vie* stuffed Awa's unruly hair under the head wrap. "And the next day?"

"Tomorrow is a mystery," Awa replied. "So is the day after."

"I love mystery." Bal grinned, as cheeky and arrogant as Djola. Soft, wet lips traced Awa's collarbone, tickling the hollow above her breasts.

Awa lifted Bal's chin, savoring the prickles and heat. "Any more and I won't be able to do what we have to do."

Bal nipped her nose. "So, later then."

"We should go," Meera said.

"Yari talked and drummed our way out of that *Zamanzi* camp." Bal saluted Awa. "You're the griot now and I'm the drummer, making the story we want."

"Yes." Awa slipped a *Lahesh* crystal into Bal's hand.

"What is this?" *Vie* held it up to the moon.

"My last one," Awa said. "Rogue impulse."

Bal's lips trembled. "You should keep this. For the crossroads gods."

"I'll have other protection, a potion from Kyrie." Awa shifted the conjure bag's strap across her body. She'd give it to Kyrie when Kyrie gave her the poison. "I wish I hadn't been a weak good person—"

"I wish I'd never said that to you. Together—"

Awa groaned. "Don't say it."

"But we aren't weak together." Bal said it. "We make each other strong."

Awa put her lips on Bal's and let their tongues dance, stopping more Elder wisdom. Reluctantly, Bal slipped into the shadows and Awa stumbled over roots.

Meera steadied her. "We can do this." She gave Awa a spark torch.

"You're shivering." Awa offered Meera her *Mama Zamba* travel cloak and boots. Awa smiled at her friend's big feet. "You take these. I'm too hot."

They walked arm in arm past lanterns along the city wall to the Council gathering.

16

Change the Story

The Empire's power masters squirmed in whimsy chairs around a flying-jackal table. Sitting under the stars, they shivered in fog from the river and flickered in the glare of the jackal's fire eyes. Awa chuckled, despite walking into battle, into the end of her life. This outdoor Council reminded her of the boat people and adventures in Smokeland, even if some masters picked fish from their teeth and sneered. Azizi raised his hand in greeting, and all chatter died out. Azizi's heartbeat was strong and steady. He smiled. Kyrie nodded at Awa and Meera, as fierce as her mountain looming in the background.

Two masters had blank yet identical twitchy faces—Money and Water. Perhaps they waited to see which way the water would run. Arms hardly glanced at Awa and Meera. He tracked the crowd beyond the table, the folks in the trees, and a crew at the gates. Mother sat with Lilot and floating-city pirates. She looked ready to fade away. Soot's head was in her lap; his tail thumped. Behind Mother, Queen Urzula argued with the young pirate from the docks (her son?) and the pirate captain who looked like Urzula must have twenty years ago (her daughter?).

Mother perked up as Awa and Meera walked by. Soot licked Awa's hand. Other faces in the audience displayed disgust and shock at transgressors attending such an occasion. Kenu and Father slouched against sea-sparkle gates. Kenu touched the snake birthmark on his cheek and muttered. Elder discipline allowed Awa to keep walking.

"I didn't know it would be so many people," Meera whispered. "You start."

Someone muttered *transgressor whore*, and Awa wished she'd covered bare skin. Open wounds had scabbed over, yet the scars were obvious transgressor marks. No way to conceal a twisted leg or a mangled arm. She and Meera were too thin. At least Meera had ample breasts and hips, although freckles marred her face, shoulders, and bosom. And why was Kenu still muttering at her?

Awa patted the Aido headdress Bal had fashioned for her. The pattern was a hundred *different* maps of the *same* territory: *All memory is illusion. Wise people craft truth from their illusions.* Awa shook tension from her limbs. Last thoughts should not be wasted on worrying about a traitor family or how she and Meera looked to masters, high priests, and good citizens. What mattered was the gate-spell. Bal would play Yari's talking drum and sing. Awa would lose herself in the music and find a new story. *Abelzowadyo.* This was her crossover ceremony.

"You start," Meera whispered in her ears again.

Awa bowed to Azizi, then bowed in a circle to everyone. "Greetings, we are—"

"Abominations," Hezram roared. Players straddled djembe drums bigger than Awa and beat anxious strokes that drowned out her protests. Squawking crows cut through the music. Hezram blew flames in the air, scattering the crows. "Filthy scavengers." Many applauded his carnival trick. Awa's heart ached as birds on fire plummeted toward the ground, and she didn't even like crows.

"You're the horror," Meera shouted at Hezram.

"You address Council, not the witchdoctor of dreams." High priest Ernold chastised her, his red robes billowing. "Tell your tale. You waste our patience."

Awa stammered as a crow with smoking wings flopped on the ground. Kyrie pulled fire from the bird, and threw the flames over Hezram's head. Djola wrapped the chittering creature in cloud-silk and tucked it in his cloak. Awa nodded gratitude. Truth be told, she loved the crows. Bal played Yari's doubled-headed drum. Awa's feet took up the slow, steady rhythm. Hips swung this way and that to hit upbeats. She used Urzula's spark torch to accent tricky phrases.

"We thank you, Emperor Azizi, for your patience, your time." Meera spoke in a strong voice for them both. She talked over masters interrupting her again and again. Bolstered by Bal's beats and Awa's dance, Meera detailed the horrors of transgressor huts and Nightmare Gates. Azizi and many others hung on her words, even Tembe. Meera pointed at Jod and his gang near the front of the audience. She described torture, rape, and murder. The gang smirked and made threatening gestures.

"Awa stomped me." Jod lifted up a splinted leg. "Broke my leg, and that other piece of slag sliced me." He held up a bandaged arm.

"Too bad it wasn't your neck." Meera told of cells in the citadel where prisoners were tortured and bled. "Right now, for Hezram's and Ernold's spells."

"Is that so, Hezram?" Azizi said, calm water.

"They lie," Hezram replied.

"I escaped one of your cells this afternoon," Meera insisted.

"Show us these wounds," Money shouted. A chain of coins and cowries at his waist rattled. Ernold, Water, and others chimed in. They wanted the women to strip naked.

"Is this a reasonable request?" Grain asked. Pale eyes in dark skin looked spectral.

"Denial is a drug we've sucked too long." Djola's voice boomed and silence fell. "Where is Hezram's proof?"

"Holy City's prosperity is my proof," Hezram replied.

"Holy City is in ruins because of you, Hezram." Rokiat ran from the trees, his hair blowing around the wound on his cheek. Fannie, Bibi, and other warhorses charged behind him, rearing and snorting battle cries. The crowd gasped. "I'm a witness too," he shouted.

Jod gripped his sword.

"Rokiat saved me from Jod today." Meera was exaggerating. Jod attacked her and she sliced him. Acolytes pummeled each other to get to her. In the confusion, Rokiat locked her up for blood conjure. Jod had to find someone else to abuse. But when Rokiat repeated Meera's stories, everyone groaned, as if hearing the horrors for the first time.

"Horse master, you have a beautiful voice. It rings with truth." Tembe's praise was soft and sweet as ripe mango. Meera clung to Rokiat, admiring him too. "Still—"

"We must condemn Hezram, not invite him to the table." Grain stepped forward, beating a talking drum. Hezram's supporters stiffened. Arms drew his sword.

Hezram jumped up in front of Awa. "I know you."

"You know nothing," Meera snarled.

"I hear your father sold you to Green Elders and your transgressor mother to the huts."

Awa gaped from Mother to Father to Azizi. Who told?

"I know you smoke-walk and desecrate sacred ground, and, because of you, the void leaks into the everyday and poisons our lives." A wily move to blame Awa for what he did. "Every afternoon we are devastated, because of you and other transgressors." The faithful cursed Awa and other abominations. The undecided wavered—Hezram was a compelling spectacle. "Your gate-spell would leave

Arkhys City vulnerable." He circled Awa. "My spell would require blood sacrifice, yes, but it would hold back the poison desert."

Soot crept up, growling at Awa's side.

Hezram stepped back. "Call off your wolf or he loses his head."

"Not my dog," she said as Soot licked her hand. "Soot belongs to himself." Still, she clutched a handful of hair at the back of Soot's neck to prevent a lunge.

"Green Elder nonsense." Hezram hooted and the audience joined him. "Do you believe rivers and forests live and mountains too? Do they talk to you?"

Awa's heart pounded. "Not the mountains. I'm not an Iyalawo . . ." Djembe drums drowned out her thoughts. She choked on her own tongue.

"I speak truth. Listen." Hezram stole Awa's time to talk. He blamed the ills of the world on barbarians ravaging the Empire; on northlanders and Green Elders worshipping rocks; on *vesons* and transgressors desecrating sacred ground and inviting the void to the everyday. He said nothing of everyone plundering land and sea, but vowed to turn tainted transgressor-blood into miracles. Lies people wanted to believe. Clapping and finger snapping galvanized him. He waved a *Lahesh* scroll at jeers from the back of the audience. "I deserve a seat at the table."

He pledged to sweep the Empire clean and bring back rain, beauty, and power. He promised the prosperity of old and also of never before. His acolytes perverted an *Anawanama* storm dance. No lightning graced their feet; no clouds rode their breath. They were wild eyes and a frenzy of limbs. Drunk on void-smoke, their heart rhythms were too similar. Foam dribbled from noses and ears. Hezram joined the dance and stomped until his drummers and dancers collapsed. He leapt over twitching bodies to Djola. "Poison master, you destroyed Holy City, Ice Mountain, and the Amethyst River."

Accusations and threats flew as masters insisted Hezram or Djola was to blame. Queen Urzula blasted sparks over Council heads. Everyone froze. "Let the witnesses finish," she said.

"Yes," Azizi said. "I want to hear what Awa has to say."

Meera squeezed her. "I'm for you and you're for everybody."

"Even for the animal-people?" Hezram sneered.

Lilot aimed a spark torch at Hezram's head. "Not another interruption."

Bal played a harvest rhythm. Awa walked with Soot, past scowling faces. She soaked up moonlight, let mountain chill fill her, and then turned to the crowd. "I'm one of you. Every year, right outside Holy City, farmers invited the desert to encroach on their lands. I know. Grandfather and Father did this. I am you."

She stepped in front of Kenu. "People sold neighbors, their daughters, and even sons to whoever could pay, just to save their farms another day. I was sold. Mother managed to get me to an enclave, thinking I was safe, but the Green Elders roamed the fringes, running and hiding and thinking they were free, but we were not free."

She moved on to the pirates. "Nowhere to run from ourselves. No paradise island or miracle mountain. People slaughter their herds, kill the old trees, and fish the Golden Gulf dry. More and more transgressors bleed and die in the huts, but nothing gets better. I was bled and broken, like the trees."

She approached Grain. "After the bloodletting, we had more suffering, more desert. Hezram lies. You know it. You just hope to sneak by. I know. I did this too, hoping not to be the one Hezram bled to death."

Djola tapped his cane to Bal's beats. They both sang in many voices. Soot threw back his head and howled.

Awa danced to Djola. "Few of us can be heroes. I thought once of killing Hezram, but realized it would do no good. So I didn't fight at all. I hoped to live in his shadows. But he bleeds the shadows." She raced by Bal and paused at Kyrie. "I'd rather not fight. I'd rather ride up into Eidhou Mountain and make noisy love in a goat-hair tent. Why save a corrupt empire?" *Zamanzi* and *Anawanama* clowns snapped their fingers and joined her dance. "We all do void-spells." Awa sighed. "Not just Hezram or Djola or whoever you'd like to accuse instead of yourselves. We're happy to buy slaves and cheap goods from pirates, blame *vesons* for our greed, or blame barbarians and northlanders when we eat our children. We do this. We need to write a new story."

Awa pulled the moon mask from the conjure bag, put it on, and sang more than spoke. "We brought the mountain down—we farmers, pirates, Elders, miners, masters, witch women, northlanders, ice hounds, tree-oil merchants, we good citizens and transgressors hacking the roots." She gripped Meera's hand. "For now and tomorrow, I dance a moon masquerade and sacrifice the old light to make a new story."

Grain and Tembe's women played talking drums with Bal. Rebels and carnival clowns dropped on cloud-silk ropes from the trees, tumbling and juggling. Queen Urzula, Lilot, and the kitchen crew donned moon masks and danced with Awa—an *Anawanama* masquerade for the Festival of Memories.

Meera shouted, "We brought Ice Mountain down. Awa's gates would hold back the storm and give us a respite, would give us time to conjure a new path."

"No transgressor huts, no tree apocalypse. What is the Council vote?" Djola leapt onto the flying-jackal table. Bal halted the beats. Quiet fell like a curtain. Soot crouched and bared his fangs, ready for attack. Djola marched around the table, pounding the torch cane. Mango flapped her ears behind him and threw up dirt. "Awa's or Hezram's gates? Nightmares or a real chance to dream?"

Ernold, Money, and Water voted for Hezram. They looked

ready to murder Boto as he sided with Grain, Arms, Kyrie, *and* Djola.

"No need for me to break a tie." Azizi whistled at Awa.

Djola raised his cane and chanted *Abelzowadyo* on the wind. This word echoed from the river across the city to the sea. He jumped down and backed away from the table.

Kyrie gripped Awa. "Crossing over, do you choose *Abelzowadyo*?"

"Yes," Awa said.

"Then *Basawili*. This is not your last breath. We will whisper your story into tomorrow." She pressed a vial into Awa's hand.

"The same *Lahesh* poison Samina drank—cathedral seed and cloud-silk?" Awa trembled.

"Not always poison, a conjurer drug, to help you transform."

"Will I be a snow squall or an avalanche with stone teeth?"

Kyrie lifted her cape and blocked poison darts coming their way. Warrior-clowns in the trees shot arrows into the dart blowers. Rokiat thrust Meera behind him. Fannie and Bibi pawed the ground, their eyes white and wild.

"Drink it quickly and walk on." Kyrie tossed Bal her conjure book and ran to Djola.

Faster than second thoughts, Awa swallowed what tasted like mud. She flew above the oasis garden, leaving her breath body at the edge of the trees, and headed for the crossroads of crossroads.

What happened after that, she couldn't say.

17

Xhalan Xhala—Tree Tales

The Trees whisper, *Xhalan Xhala*, across their branches. *Lahesh* learned this phrase from twigs rustling an alarm. For a thousand thousand years, elder Trees have whispered *Xhalan Xhala* whenever fire swept through a forest. Leaves also rustle *Basawili*, a word the Trees gave to the *Anawanama*, whenever they threw seeds on the wind. *Basawili*, not a word from their own heartwood, a word so old that elder Trees must have learned it from beings long gone. Roots rumble *Abelzowadyo*, a story they told the *Zamanzi* who slept on hard ground. *Abelzowadyo*—what roots learned about life from rocks and dirt. The Trees are a night chorus singing *Xhalan Xhala, Basawili, Abelzowadyo*, and words in languages people once spoke but have forgotten. A reckoning fire comes, but this is not your last breath, so change, change, change.

Crows, Bees, Goats, and Behemoths tell a story of the Master of *Weeds and Wild Things*. Mango, Fannie, and Soot report the tale too. Thunder River gurgles and froths, echoing the animal-people accounts, disagreeing now and then—rivers must twist and muddy everything. The Wind carries truth in all directions. Elder Trees are patient, adding new storylines whenever they emerge. These

People will be dead soon, thirty, fifty years, fallen leaves feeding roots, and like Rivers and Wind, they are restless, impatient, and fickle. People demand a story-song to celebrate now. So here it is:

Awa says, "Death is a doorway and you guide me through to the other side."

Three arrows pierce the Master of Arms, yet he fights on, protecting Emperor Azizi whose guards lay dead in the dirt. A patchwork clown joins Arms, riding an iron horse backward and forward, shapeshifting as arrows whoosh where *vie* no longer is.

"Traitor." Jod drives a sword through Rokiat's side and into Meera. He pulls the blade out slowly as they collapse into one another. That is the last thing Awa sees before flying off to Jumbajabbaland. She misses what Fannie and Bibi do to Jod and the gang attacking Rokiat, Meera, and her. Pirates fight with acolytes who've swallowed the void and lost their senses. Clowns carry Awa's breath body up into a house in the branches. Soot steps here and there, risking spirit blood to follow Awa's Smokeland trail.

Djola hides in bushes to drink mashed seeds and spiderwebs—a dose that will stop his heart. When he leaves his breath body, Mango stands watch. She can rip a tree from its roots. Warriors avoid the elephant and fight each other while Hezram's spirit slaves chase Djola and Awa. Ernold's fiends lurk at Jumbajabbaland borders, for ambush.

Kyrie comes through the border-void first. She is mountain heavy and plummets onto a black ribbon of dirt that was once river. She sits on a sun-bleached rock and peels off robes. The silver tattoos covering her body pulse. Kyrie impaled herself on mountain thorns before coming to Council. She knows how to milk vipers and let them live and how to imbibe their poison and not kill herself, immediately. Her blood is mostly minerals, venom, and poison seeds. She is Eidhou Mountain saving itself.

Awa arrives second and tries to give Kyrie the *Lahesh* folded space, but Kyrie refuses the small bag. Djola drops from the border-void. He snatches Awa up, and they fly on, glancing back only once. Naked and vulnerable like a bug on that rock, Kyrie turns her face to the sun. Spirit slaves, chasing Awa's and Djola's fresh blood scent, careen in and slam to a halt. In the hot sun, Kyrie stinks of the cathedral tree oil she smeared on her belly. She smells more like a tasty morsel than a deadly weapon. The spirit slaves attack. Kyrie howls.

Fiends tear each other apart trying to reach her, yet after one bite, their insides explode in clouds of indigo. Mouths that were twisted into someone else's smirk relax. Vacant eyes fill with light and expression. Hezram's visage fades from a hundred faces. Most heartbeats are silver lightning bolts like Samina's, but here and there, volcano hearts tremble and pump blood. Kyrie's wounds crust over quickly, but she winces with every move. "Flee back to your breath bodies," she rasps.

Without questioning or thanking her, revived smoke-walkers rush across the border-void. Somewhere in the everyday, a person comes back to themselves. To those who have no breath bodies to return to, Kyrie says, "You could wander a while until you fade or you could inhabit Awa's Dream Gates, do a spirit watch. What say you?"

Most fly off into the distance. Awa's mother appears, heart silver lightning. She joins a group that wants to flow into the silver-mesh. "Follow Awa," Kyrie commands, and they take off. A few indigo haints remain. They snag spirit slaves still coming for Kyrie and explode with them. Finally, nobody attacks her. Indigo haints help Kyrie into her robe. She is light and flies easily after Awa and Djola.

In the everyday, Arms and Azizi escape to the oasis garden, to the masquerade towers and treehouses with Lilot, Urzula, and their children. A few masters are with them. They tend to broken, battered bodies. Red-and yellow-robed men surround the oasis, yelling and clamoring for a fight, but a rain of arrows and a blast of sparks prevents them from advancing. Silver-mesh conjure shimmers in the everyday and in Jumbajabbaland, ready to be Hezram's Nightmare or Awa's Dream. Kenu holds the Gates open to spells and haints, and peers down a cascade of stars to a crossroads. Awa's father lies dead at Kenu's feet, acolyte arrows in his chest. Bal balances on a rope bridge above Mango, singing many voices and playing *Lahesh* crossover rhythms into the opening. Boat people in Jumbajabbaland echo *vie*.

"Burn the trees," Hezram yells. "Why waste blades? Fire and smoke will do the job."

Iyalawo Tembe of Ice Mountain blocks him. "No fire." She is a chill wind surrounding him. "These trees are sacred. I know their songs."

"Get out of my way, woman." Hezram looms over her.

"Save the day and you will have a seat at the table," Tembe declares. "Burn the trees and it will be like Holy City all over again. We do not destroy the world to save it."

"I'm winning." Hezram holds a sword to her neck.

"Then why fight me?" Tembe shatters the sword with a cold touch. "Most of your men are dead or they've come back to themselves and deserted you. Perhaps you'll be emperor of nothing. Or perhaps you'll die a traitor."

Hezram scans the battleground. Many bodies nourish the dirt. "They betrayed me."

"Tell the story you want and fight again tomorrow." Tembe leans close. "Isn't that what we've always done? We can't hand the world over to transgressors."

Hezram clutches her waist. "You could find the light bridge, the crossroads. Take me there."

"No. Smokeland is a realm of possibilities but also maybe-nots. I won't risk losing you, losing everything." She pulls away from him.

"You betray me too?" Yellow and red-robed acolytes gather around Hezram.

Talking drummers surround Tembe. "Today I go where the water runs. To survive. Show me you're the man I love."

"I'll find Awa." Hezram leaves his breath body and passes through the borderland. He wanders leagues and leagues of wasteland. Snowstorms dull his senses, chill his mind. He leaves a trail for Soot to follow but the Master of Illusion finds no trace of Awa or Djola.

At the crossroads of all the regions where star bridges lead in a thousand thousand directions, Awa and Djola rest. A moon mask is plastered against Awa's sweaty cheeks. Djola's cape snaps in a fierce wind. A snowstorm approaches—Samina. She passes through Awa, then Djola. They shiver and shudder. Samina's form solidifies with the touch of spirit she has stolen from them.

"I have finally come home." Djola hugs her close and buries his face in a snow squall of hair. He and Samina cry tears that turn to sleet. They speak a flood of words too fast to catch. Djola finally turns from Samina, pulls the crystal from his foot, and plucks the wheel from his heart. He hands these treasures to Awa. "I shall keep the marble eye and watch over you."

"Of course." Awa puts the treasures in the small bag and winks at Kyrie. Djola and Awa press hands against the gates Kenu and Father have wrought. "I sense Hezram," Awa says.

"He doesn't matter," Samina replies.

"You do the dance, speak the change-spell," Kyrie says. Her heart is a lightning storm.

Samina plays an ice-harp and Djola and Awa dance *Xhalan Xhala*. "We imagine the world we want." Awa's and Djola's voices echo through the leaves. "I have crossed over. I conjure Dream

Gates. All that remains of me rides the wind, drizzles down with the dew, sparks between the tree roots. I'm the lightning strike, the snow melting, the fire crackling. I dance in the horse's nicker. I'm the avalanche rolling down *Mama Zamba,* and the earth tugging my skin tight. I am me and I am you. Do not mourn with blame or guilt. I lost the way, wandered in the void, and found a bridge. We are all lost souls. Never give up looking for one another."

Awa swoons, Kyrie and Djola hug her as she fades back to the everyday. "No, no, no," Awa cries. "I give my life, not you."

Hearing Awa's distress, Soot leaves Hezram's trail before catching up to him to meet Awa when she comes back to herself in the everyday.

"With our thoughts we make a world." Djola, Samina, and Kyrie chant as they walk a road nobody has walked before, to a new region in Jumbajabbaland. Other haints gather behind them— Mother, Tessa, Quint, and many, many others. They sing, "*Xhalan Xhala, Basawili, Abelzowadyo.* A reckoning fire comes, but this is not your last breath, so change, change, change."

18

Dream Gates

Awa returned from Smokeland to a citadel room that smelled of herbs, wet dog, and spark torches. She was buried in cushions on a bed big enough for two. Her skin tingled, her heart was heavy, and her head ached from dancing *Xhalan Xhala*.

Bal hugged her so hard she almost passed out. "You've been gone a week."

Awa rubbed her face and stared at her hands. "I shouldn't be here."

"Nonsense," Bal declared. "The gates are glorious! The new year starts well. A week without storms, Samina's crystals suck up the void."

"I was going to—"

"Sacrifice yourself without telling me." Bal's cheer cracked. "Djola left a scroll telling me what you and Kyrie didn't."

Awa's head throbbed. Djola and Kyrie must be dead to this world. How would she stand it? "Why am I alive? They tricked me."

"Did you think Kyrie and Djola would let you throw yourself away in a gate-spell?"

"Why throw themselves away?" Grief gripped Awa's stomach. "What good am I?"

Bal stomped from the sumptuous bed to a window looking out to Mount Eidhou. "How could you just leave me like that, without a word?"

"I'm sorry." Awa staggered over and hugged *vie*. "Looking at you, saying anything, I wouldn't have been able to—" Bright light spilled in the window. Awa had never expected to see the sun rise another day or hear the river gurgling secrets to the sea. She never expected to hold Bal in her arms again. Miracles.

Bal held up Kyrie's conjure book and Djola's small bag. "We keep their spirits alive."

Grief tightened its grip on Awa's stomach. "Do they haunt the gates?"

"Nobody knows. We hoped you'd tell us." Bal put a scroll in Awa's hand. "Djola left you a letter."

Awa pressed his words to her heart. "What does it say?"

"I didn't read it." Bal splashed water in her face. "Council is in an hour."

"What?" Awa fell on carpet as soft as the cushions.

"You dance *Xhalan Xhala*." Bal sank down to her. "Azizi needs you. He's given you a chair at the flying-jackal table—they meet outside now."

"But I have to get used to being alive."

"Yes. You do." Bal laughed and cried and kissed her.

Vie helped her pull on Elder tunic and pants and wrapped her hair in Aido cloth: many maps for the same territory, a map of maps. More tears flowed and they clutched each other. Bal slipped a cloud-silk robe over Awa's head then tied a sash and Aido bag around her waist. Awa put Djola's scroll in the bag with his heart wheel and *Lahesh* crystal. Something of him to look forward to.

"If this was the best plan, why not tell me instead of treat me like a Sprite?"

"They wanted you to believe in yourself." Bal stroked the snake mark on her forehead. "You were ready to die for the world you loved, why not live for it?"

Awa painted silver snowflakes under one eye and over the other. She'd get tattoos later. "For Samina." She groaned as memories flooded her. "I saw Jod put a sword through Rokiat and Meera. I would hear harsh truth now rather than later."

"Rokiat and Meera lost a lot of blood. Lilot doesn't know if they'll make it or not."

Awa wanted to hear dead or not dead, not maybe dead or maybe pulling through. "Can I see them?"

"I thought you'd ask that." Bal thrust berry bread in Awa's mouth as they marched out of the door. Awa tumbled over Soot. He jumped up, put paws on her shoulders, and drooled in her face. Bal scratched his head. "That mangy old wolf whined and paced and drove me wild all day."

"Maybe Soot loves me more than you." Awa hugged him.

"He knows the way to Meera and to Council."

Awa buried her head in Soot's fur. "You know all the secret passageways."

The sick rooms were in Lilot's realm, not far from the kitchen. The medicine smell burned Awa's eyes. Meera and Rokiat lay next to one another, wrapped in bandages by the window. A fountain gurgled outside, a soothing melody. Bal paced among the other patients. Awa resisted asking who else was wounded, who else had died. Tomorrow. Soot whined and licked Meera's hand. Awa stroked her friend's face. "We did it," she whispered in Meera's ear. "Come back to me." She let Bal pull her out of the room.

"Council meets in the courtyard." Bal hurried after Soot.

He led them through halls and corridors for half an hour. Awa was certain she'd never find her way back. Bal talked politics. So many power plays and cutthroat deals made Awa's head spin. Dream Gates hadn't put an end to intrigue. Whatever would she do on Council?

"If I'm to have a chair, why not you?" Awa poked Bal.

"Council has changed. I'm there. I can speak, but you and Kenu are heroes."

Awa frowned. "What did Kenu do?"

"Besides take credit for the Dream Gates, nothing, as far as I can tell." Bal grimaced.

"Kenu held the gates open for your music, for the haints. I remember that." Awa sighed. "He learned from Father."

"You'll have to explain later."

They came outside into a garden with several other doorways leading off into the dark. Potted plants were in bloom, showy fragrant things unfamiliar to Awa. Water sputtered from a fountain. Arms greeted them. Wrapped in bandages, he looked stiff and sore as he ushered Awa to the flying-jackal table.

"You're the last of us," he said gruffly and patted Soot's head. Soot caught a scent and growled. He raced across the courtyard and down a murky corridor. "That wild dog knows the maze better than anybody." Arms chuckled. "He saved my life twice. Ripped a man's throat who was coming for me and Azizi."

"Soot likes who he likes." Awa looked around the table.

Boto and Grain stopped their conversation and offered a welcome. Iyalawo Tembe smiled. She sat on a stool eating mango. "Tembe's drummers fought off void-addled acolytes and helped Lilot." Bal used *Ishba* hand-talk. The chair beside Tembe was empty, a blue sea monster.

Awa choked. "Hezram still has a seat. You didn't tell me."

"Would you have come?" Bal took her hand. "Tembe claimed Ernold and rogues like Jod mounted the attack."

Awa rubbed her face. "Azizi believed her?"

"He's a politician. No one saw Hezram kill anybody. Jod, Ernold, and Money are dead. Water escaped."

"I don't believe it." Awa wanted to bolt. How could they expect her to sit with Hezram?

"Welcome!" Azizi perched in the *Lahesh* waterwheel throne at the jackal's tail. He gestured at the chair beside him—an elaborate nest, with carvings of animal-people: jackals bounding over bushes, birds taking flight, fish leaping at the moon. "You are the Master of *Weeds and Wild Things*." He saluted her. On the other side of Awa's chair, a big-boned woman with skinny gray braids and dagger teeth sat on an Iyalawo monkey stool. She played a twenty-one stringed kora harp and wore an Aido bag.

"Vandana is from across *Mama Zamba* and speaks for Mount Eidhou." Bal walked Awa to her place. "Tembe wanted the monkey stool, but Azizi gave her the giraffe." Bal stepped behind Awa next to Arms.

"Djola told me about you." Awa sat between Azizi and Vandana.

"You will tell about yourself," Vandana said.

Azizi leaned into Awa. "Vandana has agreed to take Kyrie's place."

"Who can do that? Not me," Vandana said. "To Kyrie and Djola." She poured wine on the ground. "Some of my people want to destroy your warriors and steal your land. I say no. Conquered people and slaves mean rebellions, unrest."

Azizi laughed. "I hear people beyond the maps are afraid of floating-city pirates and that's why you don't attack." He piled food on Awa's plate. "Let's eat."

Awa stared at Hezram's sea monster chair and forced herself to swallow the rich food. After being hungry for so long, it was strange to have no appetite. An *Anawanama* chief praised the ancestors and the unborn. Masters introduced themselves. Lilot brought more food, then sat down next to Queen Urzula. Azizi's children were also introduced—the pirate captain and her brother. The shapeshifter clown, flanked by the *Zamanzi* twins, represented the rebels.

Kenu represented craftspeople. "I did not forget you," he said.

"I remember you too." Awa had yet to figure out what else to say to her brother. Tomorrow or the next day.

"Council has changed," Azizi said. "More women, northlanders, barbarians, and floating city folks. Everyone ready to work." He looked pleased with himself for being a grand host.

"We should find a different word, a new name for what we do." Awa blurted this before thinking.

"An ancient word perhaps or invent a new one, to set us in the right direction?" Boto nodded at Awa, enthusiastic. "I will help you find this word."

"Where is Hezram?" Tembe spoke Awa's worry out loud and looked around.

"He drank too much," Arms said. "He makes water in the trees."

"That was an hour ago." Grain glanced at the woods.

"He should be back." Tembe sent a drummer to look for him.

Soot padded in. He licked his chops and huffed at Awa, dropping his big head in her lap. "Ew. What have you been nosing through?" Awa wiped mud and offal from his snout. Red flecks clung to his whiskers. "Were you in the kitchen?" Soot sneezed and spit blue fabric in her hand. Awa stared at the bloody scrap of an eye patch, her heart pounding in her mouth.

"We can't wait any longer for Hezram," Azizi declared. Soot growled at the name.

Tembe's breath was short. "Something has happened to Hezram. I feel it."

Awa felt nothing of Hezram. He was gone. Trembling, she tossed the blue scrap into candle fire. "Thank you." She hugged Soot.

"When Hezram comes, we tell what he missed," Vandana said.

Bal drummed thanks to the crossroads gods for all who sat at the table and all who'd given their lives. Awa shivered and looked from oasis trees to the citadel Dream Gates. Djola was a chilly edge to the wind, Kyrie an echo against the rocks. Yari was the up-beats and overtones.

"Thanks to Kenu and Awa, we have a few moments before the void swallows us." Azizi looked excited. "Where do we begin?"

Everyone talked over each other—spouting good ideas and stupid ones.

"Water," Awa interjected, "and enough food for everyone. Northlanders have seeds for drought and deluge. Grass to hold a mountain and trees to call the rain. Northland wisdom is where we start. And then freedom, of course."

"What do you mean?" Boto asked.

The piebald crow and a companion flew onto a ledge above the courtyard, building an enormous nest. They had to be pregnant. Adult crows didn't bother with nests otherwise. A crown of quiescent bees flew in sideways from Jumbajabbaland and settled in Awa's hair. After Council, she'd wake them in the oasis garden to build a hive there.

"Yes. Tell us. Freedom? What are you thinking?" Azizi asked. Awa sang:

We belong to ourselves
Or maybe to the bees

GLOSSARY

These words may have meaning in other realms and cultures.
Here is what they mean in this world.

Abelzowadyo   *Zamanzi*, change, shapeshifter, many beings at once

Aido   *Lahesh* cloth, disappears in the light

Anawanama   a people from the north

Babalawo   floating-city wise man, called witchdoctors in the Empire

barbarians   what Empire citizens call southern people

bark-paper   *Anawanama* paper made from Mount Eidhou's fig trees

Basawili   *Anawanama*, not yet the last breath

crack-cruck   stopgap or slapdash procedure

djembe   large goblet drum made from hardwood, goatskin, and tuned with ropes

Dochsi   *Lahesh*, disagreeing with a negative statement

Eishne   *Anawanama*, woven from the same threads, strangers who are family

Fatazz   curse

griot   storyteller, mapmaker, historian, praise singer, negotiator

Ishba   a northern people aligned with the *Anawanama*

Iyalawo   floating-city wise woman, called witch woman in the Empire

jumba jabba   mumbo jumbo

Kahoe   a northern people aligned with the *Anawanama*

kora   a large calabash harp with twenty-one strings

Kurakao   praise to the gods

Lahesh   a people from the north

Mama Zamba   *Lahesh*, mother's backbone, mountains at Empire's edge

Smokeland   a realm of vision and spirits, of possibilities and maybe-nots,

Sorit   a northern people aligned with the *Anawanama*

Tschupatzi   a Holy City curse

veson   *Anawanama* word for being, neither male nor female

Vévé   a sacred sign that calls down the power of the gods

vie   *Anawanama* pronoun for *veson*

whayoa   whoa

wim-wom   gadget, trinket, device

Xhalan Xhala   *Lahesh*, reckoning fire

Yidohwedo   *Lahesh*, rainbow serpent who made world from dung and water

Zamanzi   a people from the north

Zst   curse, Empire vernacular

ACKNOWLEDGMENTS

I pour libation to Eshu and the deities of the crossroads, to the Water Protectors, Animal-People, and all my Green Elders.

Thanks to my Ellis High School history teachers who let me research Nigeria, China, and the Cherokee Nation. This set me on a journey at fourteen that led to this novel.

In December 2014, I had just read that football-field swaths of Mississippi Delta wetlands disappeared every hour. People were talking about climate dystopia as inevitable. I was wondering how I could possibly respond to this without drowning in despair. Carl Engle-Laird at Tor.com Publishing invited me to write a novella, a fantasy. Thanks to Carl and my editor Ruoxi Chen who believed in the epic novel I wrote instead. Thanks to Lee Harris for making it happen the way it should. Thanks also to Pan Morigan for drawing the map of my wild visions.

At Smith College, Daphne Lamothe and Kevin Quashie and everybody in Africana Studies provided me with much-needed reality checks. My writing students and students in Shamans, Shapeshifters, and the Magic IF challenged my craft, offered me hope, and kept me sharp. Smith College's fund for faculty development supported research trips and writing retreats.

All praises to the Smithsonian Institute, particularly the Museum of the American Indian and the Museum of African American History and Culture, for access to material culture and inspiration for the future. Grace Dillon and the folks in the Indigenous Nations Studies Program at Portland State University welcomed me and Pan Morigan into their hearts and showed us marvels.

Thanks to Bobby, Mary, and Theo Welland for giving me a home away from home in Seattle. Wolfgang and Beate Schmidhuber and the whole Schmidhuber clan offered me good food, good times, and the rest needed to create. Bill Oram read a hundred hundred drafts of this book or close to it and always typed his careful and generous responses. Paula Burkhard, Kiki Gounaridou, John Hellweg, Kathleen Mosely, Daniel José Older, Micala Sidore, and Susan Stinson cheered me on through difficult moments.

The Beyond 'Dusa Wild Sapelonians: Pan Morigan, Ama Patterson, Liz Roberts, and Sheree R. Thomas supported my spirit, made me laugh at myself, and kept me writing the way out of no way.

Blessings on Pan Morigan, James Emery, and my agent, Kris O'Higgins, for believing I could work miracles.

Andrea Hairston and Daniel José Older In Conversation

This is an edited transcript of an interview between Daniel José Older and Andrea Hairston on October 1, 2020, hosted online by Porter Square Books of Cambridge, Massachusetts.

We would like to thank Leila and her team at Porter Square for hosting the interview and for their assistance in obtaining the recording from which this transcript was taken.

Older: I always love talking to you. We can just talk all day and all night. Right before we went live, we were both reminiscing about our college area because I went to Hampshire and you teach at Smith, but what I didn't know and what I learned from your introduction is that there are bears in that area, is that true?

Hairston: Oh! Oh yeah. There are many bears. I bike all the time, all over the valley. I've had many, many run-ins with bears—black bears.

Older: I'm thinking about all the time I was wandering through the woods, high at night.

Hairston: Okay, let me just say, black bears are not like grizzlies or brown bears, right? Black bears, their basic biology: the best thing to do is run and get up a tree, right? That's their impulse. It's like, "I don't really need to do this. Let me just run and go up a tree."

Older: Oh, *they're* running up a tree, not me?

Hairston: Yeah, yeah. No, no, you shouldn't run.

Older: I wouldn't be able to climb a tree in the middle of the night.

Hairston: Black bears—they're amazing. They climb trees to escape conflict because that makes more sense to them. Now if you come upon one, which I often do, I pretend that I am my bike and I rattle the bike and I make a whole lot of noise and the bear is like, "I don't need to deal with all that," and there's no food, and you're a large predator too. "I'm just going to run and go up a tree." These three-hundred-pound bears are running from me. It's really funny. By the way, I'm terrified and I make a lot of noise and I don't run. No, I stand my ground and shake my bike.

Older: That's amazing.

Hairston: Yeah, they go away. I've had many bear encounters.
   They're getting used to people, so that's a bad thing. I liked it better when they weren't used to us. Now they think, "Maybe food."

Older: Right.

Hairston: They can rip the door off your car.

Older: Are you serious?

Hairston: Yeah. They can just rip it off and get your lunch.

Older: What?

Hairston: But they're afraid of *me*? I'm like, "Why are you afraid of *me*?" Many creatures, if you pound your chest and say that you're big, it's display. It's like, "I am a giant, listen to my deep voice," so I try and do a deep voice too. I do theater on them and they think, "Power."

Older: Exactly. I've been researching a lot of pirates and the Blackbeard strategy of being terrifying so you don't have to kill as many people.

Hairston: Right, exactly.

Older: It's an evolutionary thing. He would tie wicks to the end of his beard and light them so it would look like he was on fire and a devil.

Hairston: Oh! I love it.

Older: Yeah. It's theater, it's the theater of piracy. It's so cool. Anyway: your book.

Hairston: Yeah. There is no bear in *Master of Poisons*, but there are a whole bunch of other creatures because I love creatures. I study creatures and try and get inside of them and try to feel who they are.

Older: You're literally getting inside of creatures in this book because some of the chapters are actually from the point of view of . . . and I especially love the elephant one, but there's more too. We go inside of birds sometimes I think, right?

Hairston: There are crows. There's an elephant. Bees; we go inside the bees.
There's a dog, there's a horse.
The dog is the funny one.

Older: The horse is huge too.

Hairston: Yeah, the horse is big and monstrous. A monster-sized horse, almost the size of an elephant, almost as tall.

Older: Did you have a process for that particular part that was different from your regular writing process when you were really trying to channel animals?

Hairston: Well again, it's theater. One of the exercises that I do with actors when we're going to do a show, one of our early exercises is you have to be an animal. You have to literally try and be an animal. You drop into your animal. It's deep, you've got to: "Okay, how do they move? How do they think? How do they feel? What are their senses? What do they use to navigate the world?" I even make people drop into bugs, into spiders or ants or birds. You can do this for twenty minutes. The actors are doing it and then you interact with other creatures or other people. It's really good for getting you to go from yourself to something else.
We also have permission.
If I have to be a character and I'm worried that I'll get the character wrong, or I'll do something that's maybe even potentially offensive to someone who knows a whole lot about that character . . .

but no one is going to be upset if I mess up on the ant. Right? You'll take a risk.

It's that.

Then I will drop in things like: ants don't see. Most ants don't see very well. They do mostly scent, just things like that. You suddenly realize which sense to use. Ants, they can walk upside down, so they have a different relationship to gravity than we do. They can walk up a wall and walk on the ceiling, right? Me walking on the ceiling? Oh! But the ant . . . What's my relationship to gravity?

Or bees—they can perceive magnetism. What's that like? I ask them the question and they'll just try something. The actors will just go, "Oh wow. What would that mean in the world?" and then you realize that the world you're in isn't the world that everybody else is in.

It's a really good way to get actors to realize that they may not contain their characters. The Stanislavski idea is that you look inside yourself and you find your character. Other people are like, "What if you don't have everybody?"

You've got to journey from your perspective to somewhere else and then you start to realize that when you try and be an ant or a crow or a whale or a tree—because trees move, right? They move, but really slowly. They can move, but compared to animals, we would never even hardly perceive their motion—what is that like? All of those things, I think I drop into the actor.

Older: Which makes sense, because the way dogs say, "Hey, how are you doing," is by sniffing the other dog's butt.

Hairston: Right, yes. "What you've been doing," and they sniff your butt. "Where you been? Who have you been with?" They get it all, they get it all, they know. They're like, "What you been doing? Oh, you've been doing that." For them, the whole thing of smells is less valuating. They have a different set of values about

what is offensive and what is okay. They have a world in which they
have to communicate things and they use smell, so they raise their
tails, they send out smells and say, "Look, I'm bad. Don't mess
with me!" Or, "Yes, let's get down to it."

When I get into that world, then I figure out that they all have
personalities. Mammals do have personality, so not all dogs are
alike, not all elephants are alike. They have experiences that shape
who they are. What are their experiences?

Older: I love that. I always tell my students to take a theater class
if possible; we're both theater nerds so we share that. I'm constantly
referring back to my time in education as a theater nerd when I'm
writing. I feel like nothing can compare. First of all, there's the
other piece of this too, which is that as a writer, you're going to be
required to read out loud. It's mortifying for a lot of writers, which
I understand; however, we have to do it. It's part of the job. If you
sound bored by your own work, then there's a good chance that
you're going to bore other people too. You don't have to "perform"
and do a whole presentation, but you've got to give us something,
right.

Hairston: Right, you have to lift it from the page a little.

Older: Yes, exactly, just a little. But the other piece to me is what
we're talking about, which is the idea of embodying a character.
The four years I was at Hampshire, I was doing improv the whole
time. I loved it. It was so much fun. It was really one of my favorite
things to do. It taught me so much about writing because it's not
just embodying a character whose lines you've memorized. Now,
you're making decisions as that character.

Hairston: In the moment.

Older: And you have to be funny. People are watching you waiting for you to say something funny. It's terrifying, but once you have it, you're like, "Oh shit, writing is much easier."

Hairston: Right. You get over what we call the crisis of performance. You're like, "Oh, oh my god," because the audience actually gives you a lot of energy. That's what's a little hard about Zoom because there's no audience.

Older: Yes, yes.

Hairston: I'm talking to my computer here, and I keep trying to get close.

Older: We're all sitting in empty rooms having animated conversations.

Hairston: Right, right. You can ride the audience's energy and it helps you to make connections that you would not normally make. I need an audience sometimes, and that audience can be small, it doesn't have to be two thousand people.

Older: It can be one person. Did you ever see Brother Blue perform? Do you know who he is?

Hairston: Yes, yes, yes.

Older: I love that guy. He passed a couple of years ago, I think. You guys have a lot in common, now that I think about it. I had never put you in the same room in my head, but wasn't he amazing?

Hairston: Amazing.

Older: The audience loved him. Maybe you know more about him. I used to see him as a kid all the time because he was at Harvard Square frequently. He would walk there with his white glasses.

Hairston: He was just costumed amazingly. I feel like that's the other thing I do because every day I feel like I have to costume my mood and get myself prepared for who I want to be today. To me, that the words come from this body and these clothes that can help me call the muse or the spirit that I want to me, and then reflect back on who I want to be. I felt like he was like that. He was very spiritual in his relationship to words, to people, to the moment he was in and it was amazing, like a street griot poet.

Older: Yes, all those things, doing Shakespeare, doing stuff he made up, doing whatever. I was a teenager and I saw him perform at a college once, and I think it was Wellesley, it was a women's college around Boston, I can't remember which one. It was an empty room. It was a summer program that brought him to perform and no one showed up and he just started anyway. Someone walked in and he said, "Do you play piano," and the guy was like, "Yeah." He's like, "Get on the piano," and the guy started playing piano and he told his story and by the end, the room was full. It was one hundred people in this room and I watched this whole thing. It started from literally a one-person show *to* one person and then it grew to this. His energy was the same the whole time. I will never forget that because it was so clear that he was coming from no kind of ego, from no place except spirit and story. He could have done the whole event just to me and done it with the same energy.

Hairston: And you felt the value of that.

Older: Yes, I was a kid. Do you know what I mean? It was beautiful to me.

But let's talk about *Master of Poisons* because that's what we're here to talk about.

Hairston: Okay. But all of this has to do with *Master of Poisons,* because the whole of this, to me, the griot, the storyteller, that's what my book is about, the person who's trying to conjure the world they want and they will do it for one person or for a whole group and to make a community with their words, to make a world with their words and to invite everyone in. That's Awa, that's something that I really wanted to get in the book, the power and the necessity of storytelling to who we are.

Older: Yeah, and you feel that throughout because it's in both of their stories. Djola is often wrestling with narrative the whole time.

Hairston: Yeah, he is.

Older: It feels like a doomed wrestling match, but it's not. He goes through so much, but he tries too hard. There was such a love and a compassion for him. I feel like a lot of writers would have taken a story like his and used it just as a base warning or a tragedy, just to discard him or say, "Oh, here's what happens when you don't pay enough attention," or whatever, but instead, you really turned it a different way and it felt really unexpected in such a great way. I don't know how to describe it. Did you sorta know where it was going the whole time, or did you let it guide you?

Hairston: I do both. I had a feeling, because I wanted to do: "Who are we? Who are the people we are?" and then I wanted to have a sense that I can start where we're imperfect, because it's hard to be imperfect and we're all imperfect. I wanted to start with that and see if I could get a character who did things that I didn't agree with, right? I said, "No, don't do that. Stay here, don't go over there. But I love you. I don't give up on you. I refuse to give up on you. Even if I'm dead, I don't give up on you." That was what I wanted to do with him: to not give up on the imperfect person who also is me. I have compassion because I'm like, "Oh, *I* did stuff like that," or I like to think, "Oh, I would *never* do that," but really? I wanted to just be honest about who I could have been or who I love.

I didn't want to deal with the other people who were bad because all I would do is smack them. There are people who all you want to do is smack. I don't want to write about them right now. They get enough air time.

Older: Yes. I think that is so complex. There is that moment, without any spoilers, a character who's very bad, being in this complex love affair or sexual relationship with a character who is very gray, neutral, or just different. There is no clear morality, which is what's so great, because I feel like some people would be like, "Oh, nothing matters," and it's not that at all.

Hairston: Oh, no, no, no, no, no.

Older: But without being overly moralistic at all either. It just leaves us as readers having to navigate these very complex and impossible situations, which is: that's life. That's exactly what we're all dealing with right now. There are no answers.

Hairston: Right.

Older: There are no right answers. Everyone is complicit just by existing, and how do we resist? How do we forgive ourselves? How do we move forward? I love that this book asks those questions and doesn't give us the answers.

Hairston: You and I know, and it's just something to me, because for me, writing is a spiritual act, but partly, I'm trying to forgive myself and to accept myself and to challenge myself. That's part of my task, so I try and take on characters who I have to work at that with. I want to have fun too, right?

Older: Yeah, right.

Hairston: To me, who can I have fun with? Like I said, not the people that I don't want to talk about, but to me, the things that happened to Djola are really difficult. I felt that there are some moments that are absolutely like, "Oh wow, this is amazing," stuff that on the other hand, Djola can think and do and try and be. Yeah. Yari, I think, is the character you're talking about. Who is . . .

Older: . . . complicated.

Hairston: Yeah. I like characters like that, I love that character and that character makes errors and that character is brilliant. It's fun and it's tragic. I wanted to get all of that in the book.

Older: Yeah. I think that's one of the balances that is so hard to find because: how do you get to that heaviness and also make it fun somehow. The truth is: that's telling the truth. That will always be the answer. People ask that ridiculous question, "Why are your books diverse?" They always think they're really smart when they ask it, too.

Hairston: What a world, right?

Older: Did you see what the world looks like? It's so obvious. The point is, we ask that question and the answer is that we're telling the truth. That's all we're doing.

Hairston: It's what's in my heart, right? Then I want to wrestle with what's in my heart because some of it's not good stuff.

Older: Exactly.

Hairston: I don't know about you, but I don't sit down and say, "Oh, I'm going to write a diverse book." I sit down and I'm going to write what's in my heart. I'm going to write about the people I know and the people I see and the people I want to talk to. I even want to talk to and about creatures, so I'm going to put them in the book too. These are the subjects for me of our world.

Older: Totally.

Hairston: I was talking about the fires in California and how the indigenous wisdom of controlled fires was outlawed. They outlawed that. They used to have those controlled fires to prevent the stuff that's happening. Then those practices were outlawed. The same thing happened in Australia. We had this whole conversation, I think it was with a group of faculty and we were talking about how, "Well, if we want to be diverse, we have to figure out ways of honoring other ways of *knowing* than say, your PhD." I was like, "We have stolen the idea that only a certain group of people have wisdom."

Older: Yes.

Hairston: We don't need to be throwing away any wisdom.

Older: Yeah, I always think about when I was studying to be a paramedic, there are medicines that are synthesized and created out of herbs that have been used for thousands of years.

I'm like, "Do you really think it was trial and error, that people were just walking down eating every single thing? No, there is a wisdom. There is an inherent and deep-seated wisdom that is beyond science that we need to honor and that you all do honor because you profit off it, but you don't actually want to give it the respect that other people who do honor it . . ."

Hairston: Exactly. The ways of knowing the world to me, that was the other thing I wanted to get in the book. I was a physics math major before I became a theater major. A lot of people think, "Why are you doing hoodoo or voodoo or Vodun. If you like . . . I don't know, relativity, and Einstein is one of your favorite people?" It's like, "Do we have wisdom we can throw away?" Because that's one of the things in the book, because Djola is trying to find the wisdom that people have thrown away.

Older: Yes, exactly. Right. I love that because he's really on a very mythic quest that very much has the reverberations and the energy of certain questing fantasy novels that we're used to, but in a much more holistic and natural way in tune with the world instead of the sole individual white dude—

Hairston: "Who will save the day? One man . . ."

Older: Right, that same old trope that we've seen for so long that's really, first of all, false because one person will never save the world and it certainly won't be a random white man if it was.

Hairston: Right.

Older: It's never going to be just one; the one thing is a lie. It's like that question even speaks to that, the way people frame things, it's like, "Are you this or are you that? Are you science or are you nature? Are you with spirit or are you with facts?" These lies that we've dealt with, they're all constraining and binaries that really kill people, very literally. You're writing that in the book. The book is a manifesto as much as it is an epic fantasy story. I think that's one of the things that's so great about it. We're taught to believe that you have to be one or the other. You have a manifesto or an epic fantasy, otherwise it's didactic if you try and do both. It's the opposite of didactic in every single way. You can't read this book and think didactic for a single second, because it's all those things. That's what's so amazing about it.

Do you have to consciously fight off those voices because you grew up in this world that told you that?

Hairston: Yeah. I think when I was growing up, I was really good at math, one of those people who's really good at math and everybody said, "Oh yeah, you will save the race because you can go show them."

Older: Oh no.

Hairston: Often, I would take a test and I would be the number one in the city, "See, I showed the white folk! I'm a girl, I showed the boys!" Actually the weight of that, I'm in school thinking, "Oh god, I've got to show the white folks and I've got to show up for the women." That was a deep pressure. Meanwhile, my great-aunt is hoodoo. She's working it out.

I would go over to her and she's the most powerful person I know. Everybody I know is pretty powerful and she's more powerful than anybody. Everybody defers to her even though we're all twentieth-century, because this is the twentieth century. We're all progressive twentieth-century. We don't believe that stuff. No. "Why don't you go ask Estelle? What's she say?" That was the whisperer thing, "Oh well, maybe we should check in with Estelle, she'd probably know," or, "I don't cross her, that's Estelle." All of this stuff is going on.

Estelle was my favorite, sort of like a grandparent, even though she was my great-aunt. I went to stay with her and we talked and had fun. Everything she said was amazing. I still carry it with me. *Redwood and Wildfire* is dedicated to her and my grandfather, who was a Baptist minister and he walked with Jesus. I saw him walk with Jesus and I'm like, "He walks with Jesus." Whether or not *I* can, that's another thing.

There were two guys and they were fighting, they had knives and they were doing all this craziness. We were out for ice cream after having visited the sick and the shut-ins because he would go visit people and then they would get better. They always got better. I was like, "Wow, they got better. Okay." Then we go have ice cream.

I was the only grandchild who wanted to do this because everybody else thought, "This is really boring. We're going to see some stupid sick people." I would go because I wanted to see him make them feel better.

Older: Magic, yeah.

Hairston: I wanted to see the magic, right? I didn't believe. I hadn't taken Jesus as my personal savior. I didn't get baptized. He was a Baptist minister and I didn't do the dunk because I was a physicist already. I'm like, "No, no, I can't do that." He was like, "Okay."

"But I do want to go with you when you save people."

Older: Amazing.

Hairston: I saw him walk into this knife fight. He went up, they dropped the knives, he talked them down. He took the knife and said, "Where did you get this, boy? This is a stupid knife," and he threw it. He said, "It's not weighted right," or some crap like that, I don't know. I was like, "Oh my god." Then he invited them to have ice cream with us. "This is my granddaughter. We're going to have ice cream. Do you want ice cream with us? What do you like? Do you like chocolate? I like chocolate," he's going on and on. The two boys are standing there. He's just talking and I'm like, "Hi. Are we really going with them?" "Oh, yeah, yeah. I'll pay because you all don't have any money? Okay, fine."

We go and he said, "These are two of my friends." We go into the ice cream shop and he was beloved, "Oh, we'll give them a whole lot of ice cream." They were just fighting each other with knives. He took the knives, which he still had, we were in the ice cream place and now they were honored guests who got huge amounts of ice cream. He said, "Are you all going to college? She's going to study physics." That's what he said to them, "She's going to study physics. She's going to study that. What are you all going to do?" For the next three years, he would check up on them and they went to college. Since I witnessed this stuff, and he said, "I walk with Jesus," and I'm like, "Amen." I saw the magic. I saw him do it. I went to church all the time to see him, to hear him. He was a liberation theologist. He believed in civil rights. He was always getting people to go do things. He had faith. He said, "Well, if I die, I die with Jesus." I'm like, "What's this?"

That's my early experience: my great-aunt who did hoodoo and my grandfather. I thought I was going to be a physicist and somehow not deal with this part of my life, but all the stuff I had learned from them was constantly supporting me and getting me through the moments that I needed to get through. After they had passed away, I realized that you've got to rethink; particularly doing theater allowed me access to that. Who are the people who have made you who you are? What do they believe? Why do they believe it? What is hoodoo?

My grandfather, he believed that there were many paths to God, he always said that. That was one of his big things. "I don't know the only one." That was one of his major thoughts. He never said anything to me, "Well, you're not in the church though." He said, "No, no, no. You're on your path and there are many ways to God."

Older: Man, I love that.

Hairston: He died when I was sixteen or seventeen.

Older: What was his name?

Hairston: John Hairston. There are many ways to God and you are on your path. He allowed me the space to accept whatever I could from him and whatever I could from anywhere else. My great-aunt was like that too, because she's like, "I'm not afraid of anything." I was like, "You're not afraid of anything?" "No, no, I'm not afraid of anything. I'm here in the world, I'm alive, how can I be afraid of anything?" I was like, "What is she talking about?" She said, "I'm breathing, I can do something, I have power." I suddenly realized that she was saying, not that fear was bad, but that she could wrestle with fear because she was alive. Then she told all the little kids that too, "Don't be afraid."

When she was seventy-five, she started a Head Start program; at eighty-five, she got a ten-year plaque for starting this. She had done union organizing. She was doing all kinds of things like that. These people, she had the power. Everybody said, "Oh, that's Estelle." She just would walk into the middle of the same kind of stuff that my grandfather would walk into and then she would walk out and they would be union. She walked in and they weren't, she walked out, they were. It's like, "O . . . kay . . ."

They had a vision of who I could be that was totally science fictional because nobody had done the stuff I had done before. They were futurists. They were like, "Okay, we're making this path for you. You will become someone amazing." That's what they kept saying, "You have your path. Just move all these people out of the way, yes. If you don't want to be a mathematician or a physicist, that's okay too. You can do things." It was really that, that was sustenance for me as I reviewed ways of seeing the world and realized, "Okay, we've got to open it up here because why am I throwing away wisdom? I don't need to throw it away. I need to open it up and look at who I can be and make that up myself."

With theater and all the people I knew and all the stuff going on in the seventies and eighties with people rethinking things, I was primed to reevaluate. I think we were talking in an email exchange. We have an oppressive system that we internalize and at any moment, it can go *bleurgh!* right out of us.

Older: Right.

Hairston: What we have to be ready to do is to not freak out and think that we're demons. But change. Here comes the stuff, "Oh my god, look at that stuff. What can I do?" or, "How can I change?" That is the power, that's the craft that I want to enable in myself.

I was thinking about why I was doing what I was doing and why you were doing what you were doing. It was just that's what we need, to challenge ourselves so that we can change. That's what the book is about too. Djola gets challenged. The thing is, you can hold on to stupidness that you imbibe, or you can do the hard work to disentangle yourself from it. We all have it. No one escapes it. There's nobody who's all woke for everything, right? It's not possible.

Older: Awa gets challenged too, which I love. They challenge each other in a loving way.

There's that moment when they first meet and they're rightfully skeptical of each other. She's like, "Who is this dude?" They gradually come to understand that they're actually quite connected and that there are different people in their lives that are really connected and that their destinies are connected, but not in the way of destiny that I think we traditionally see it where it's like, "You are cemented into this one path and you have to follow it." More so, it's like there is very wide-open destiny of, "You can change the world."

Hairston: Right, and you can make a new path.

Older: Right, right! A brand-new path with a brand-new language, a brand-new world of magic because the old ones aren't working and the only way you can find new ones is by challenging each other and doing the hard work. I think Djola makes his path even harder than it has to be, which is also very recognizable and understandable. I've certainly been there.

You're watching it happen and you're like, "No!"

Hairston: Right.

Older: We follow Awa too in her own journey and we just really see her growth. There's so much of growth, I think. That's really one of the things that I saw much of in the book, both characters are just so fully transformed by the end, but in a way that feels very true.

Hairston: Right.

Older: You can see that person in them in the beginning, but they haven't fully manifested until the end. That's just powerful.

Hairston: Right. One of my challenges was to write myself out of these situations. That was the challenge I had to do. That's why it couldn't be a novella. It started as a novella and I was like, "No, no."

Older: It started out as a novella that I was trying to get you to write, apparently.

Hairston: Yes, yes, you, it was all your fault. I tried to write this novella.

Older: Let's look at some of the audience questions. . . .
    "I've heard you talk about this book as a jazz riff on climate change in other interviews. What do you mean by it being a riff versus a more straightforward allegory?"

Hairston: Well, allegory to me is more like a one-to-one correspondence. You have "the sloth of despair." You physicalize some particular thing and to me jazz is you take this world and you riff on it. Jazz is, I do an improvisational riff where elements of this world and elements of other possible worlds interact. And so, there's a relationship, but it's not a one-to-one correspondence. You feel connections to our world, but there's no one thing in our world which is the same thing in the world of the book. I think sometimes people want to make fantasy into allegory. Fantasy, I think, is actually something else. Allegory isn't bad.

Older: No, but it's different. I have a negative connotation with allegory in that it's like someone being like, "You know, you really should wash your hands before you go to sleep."

Hairston: Right. Well, you get fables, Aesop's fables or you have animal characters who are to represent this part of ourselves and then you get schooled on that. I'm not doing that. To me, it's more metaphorical and symbolic. Metaphors are, by nature, rich. They move out. They're analogous, but it really is how the brain works. You take some known stuff and then you work it out to the unknown and that's what I think of jazz. Jazz takes a song you know and by the time Coltrane is finished with that song, you're like, "Whoa," but it all started with "Favorite Things," I'll just pick that one. He just goes, "Ohhhhh." There's no one-to-one correspondence to anything he's doing by the end, but he started there, he went on a journey, you can follow it. That's one of the things that I actually love about jazz or about improvisation.

Older: Mm-hmm. We were talking about Yusef Lateef earlier. I took his improvisation class and they had me working at seven in the morning on a Monday to cut down on how many people would come. Man, I would gear up. I was playing guitar at the time and I would load up my amplifier in my backpack and get my guitar and walk in this dawn, crispy, early-morning light.

Hairston: Oh my god, yeah.

Older: One of the things that he really drove home for so many people including myself was just that idea: the false notion that jazz is just people getting on horns and blowing.

Hairston: Oh yeah, no, no, no, no.

Older: That's such a terrible, horrible explanation that so many critics, prominent critics still to this day will use words like primitive to describe jazz. It's so . . . first of all, racist. Second of all, it's just not true on any level at all, and the degree in which folks like Mr. Lateef who know and knew at the time the scales backwards and forwards, all the different layers.

Hairston: Oh my gosh, fluent with every aspect of every part of the music world.

Older: Yes. He also taught a class, an overview of African American music and he would just play on the piano.

Hairston: Yep, yep.

Older: I think that was at Smith. He would sit at that piano and play. Just tell stories. What an amazing guy. Oh, he was a master. What I wanted to ask off of that question was, this is your first book that's really like a whole other world fantasy.

Hairston: Yeah.

Older: It really struck me. I love all of your books for different reasons, but this one, it felt like you took off in a different direction. I almost want to say that it felt like you felt more free in certain ways, but I feel like that's not quite the right word. Obviously there are real-world things in there. That's very clear. It's very grounded for sure, and you're very clear on the rules of the world, but at the same time, I feel like "sprawling" is a bad word for it because that has almost a negative connotation, but it just feels like you took off. You were like, "You know what? Fuck it."

Hairston: Yeah, yeah. I was feeling epic. Like I said, I was trying to cram it. I was trying to cram it into that novella, and then I went, "Come on, you can't tell this story. . . . Go for it!" There's a sense in which I went for it. I did not try to tell this story as a novella. I said, "You have to do all this world-building, do it. Do it. Go for it. What does that mean? How does that magic work? What is that over there?" A friend of mine said, "When are we going to go to the floating cities," because I hadn't gotten there yet. I said, "I'm getting there, I'm going to get there," because he kept saying, "I want to see these floating cities." I said, "I do too."

Older: That kills me, because sometimes you don't get to that stuff in a story and that's okay too. Sometimes shit is on a need-to-know basis, and if a story doesn't need or get to the floating city, you might not find out about it. You wanting to know means I did my job right, not wrong.

Hairston: Right, right. Well, I *wanted* to go, I just had to get there.

Older: Yeah, and the story needs to go there, of course.

Hairston: I love doing research, so I'd just been thinking about all of these things for a long time, so I could put them all in, all those things I'd been thinking about. I was at the African American museum at the Smithsonian and that was blowing me away. Then I was at the Museum of the American Indian and that was blowing me away. All the artifacts and all this stuff, I was like, "People are deep. People are really amazing." That's what I was thinking, not so much that I took something from that. Obviously I took it in, but I was like, "We are amazing." The whole idea of just bridges and music and all this stuff that we have done forever and ever, that I wanted to just say, "Lordy, lord. I have to make this world as amazing as our world."

Older: Amen.

Hairston: That was why it's epic.

Older: It's huge in a great way.

Hairston: And climate to me, because the whole thing, I must say, between colonialism, empire, and climate, all of those things are huge. They're not small.

Older: They're interconnected in a way. They're very naturally done in the book because it's also naturally true, another one of those: "Because it's true." You can't separate an environmental struggle from an anticolonial struggle, but they try and do that all the time.

Hairston: Compartmentalize.

Older: Compartmentalize, and it's such an injustice, even to the struggle against it, itself. How are you going to fight something if you insist on pretending that it's disconnected from today?

Hairston: Right, yeah.

Older: You can go out and talk about racism in a space that's about environmentalism, but you can't separate them, right?

Hairston: Right, exactly. To me, that's what I wanted. Again, you have to make a big book to actually do justice to how those things interconnect.

Older: Yeah, you did.

Hairston: That was my goal.

Older: You did it. Other questions . . . "Who were your biggest artistic influences, whether it's visual artists, directors, actors, or authors?"

Hairston: Oh, that's a huge list. I'll just say who's on the top of my mind, acting. Alice Childress, who's a playwright, and I'm going to mention some people that people may not know, and a novelist who wrote in the fifties. When I was a young woman, I saw one of her plays on PBS called *Wine in the Wilderness* and it starred Abbey Lincoln. I was seventeen, that age. My mother and I watched it and it was one of the first things that we saw that was intersectional; it was about class, gender, and race. That wasn't happening that much in the late sixties. She was doing intersectionality before we had that word.

Also she was bringing in Africa, and she had indigenous stuff. She was just doing all this stuff that I was . . . "Oh my god." She really touched me. She did a play on Gullah on the Georgia Sea Islands. I got to know her so I read all of her work. I highly recommend Alice Childress. She did *Wedding Band* with Ruby Dee. She's one of the early people.

Then I'll leap to Michael Ende, who's a German writer. He wrote *Momo* and *The Neverending Story*, which was made into a film, *The NeverEnding Story*.

Older: Oh, yeah.

Hairston: It was a young adult book. I liked his work so much, I wrote him a letter. I'm fluent in German.

Older: Of course you are.

Hairston: I wrote him a letter in German telling him, "Oh Michael, you're great. I love your work. Wow, this is wonderful, but your plays, they're not in English. They're all in German and nobody can appreciate them. Where's the translation?" He writes back: "You can really do good German, so why don't you translate them. Are you coming to Germany? I live here in Munich and I'll meet you."

Older: Oh my god.

Hairston: I go meet Michael Ende in the eighties and I translated his plays to English.

Older: Wow, wow, wow.

Hairston: We do one at Smith. *Momo,* which I highly recommend to everyone. The gray men have come to our world and they smoke our time. They roll it up in cigars and smoke our time and as they smoke we have less and less time and the world turns gray. Momo is a little girl who has to figure out what to do about that. She has a turtle who helps her. That's all I'll tell you, but read it. It's just a beautiful, beautiful story.

Older: That's amazing.

Hairston: Yeah, right? Then Tess Onwueme and Wole Soyinka, these are two Nigerian playwrights—amazing, amazing writers. Again, I come from the theater. Then all my theater friends said, "You should read Octavia Butler."

Kim Moore hands me *Kindred* and says, "I've been looking at your plays. I think you would like this book," and I read the book overnight. I'm like, "Ah!" and then I go and read everything I can find.

Pearl Cleage, who's also a wonderful playwright, gives me *Parable of the Sower*. She had read it. She was an artist-in-residence at Smith, and I brought her up and she said, "Oh girl, I think you need to read this." I read *Parable of the Sower* and I'm like, "Oh, okay!" I had read Ursula Le Guin and a bunch of other amazing writers, but I was like, "Okay!"

I go to Clarion West and study with Octavia Butler in 1999.

Older: Oh wow.

Hairston: That circle, all three of them, I met Alice, I met Michael, and I met Octavia and I feel like they were all telling me, "You should be writing science fiction or fantasy."

Or, "Your theater is that and in theater we don't care. It's just a play."

Then I think when I was at Clarion, I started meeting all of these people. I think I met you, Daniel, because of Sheree or something. I can't quite remember.

Older: It was Sheree. I think it was when you won the Tiptree.

Hairston: Oh, okay. Right! Yeah!

Older: I was at the table with everybody. Sheree was like, "I'm going to bring this little Cuban dude in," and I just met you.

Hairston: You had that wonderful collection of short stories that Sheree had.

Older: *Salsa Nocturna*.

Hairston: Yeah, right. It was just amazing.

Older: Thank you.

Hairston: I think the other thing is the science fiction convention has brought me together with all of these amazing writers, so now the number is huge of people who I've been on this journey with like Sheree Renée Thomas.

Older: She's great.

Hairston: Yeah. Sheree was working on *Dark Matter* while we were at Clarion. I feel like I have this wonderful community of people who were all asking similar—or completely different—but we were all in the world, trying to find a way to express ourselves. I felt supported and lifted by all of those people. Then I gave you some of the older people like Alice Childress and Michael Ende and Octavia. Octavia's not that much older than me, but she was in science fiction from the seventies and I was in theater. I was doing theater. I wasn't necessarily thinking I was going to be writing science fiction novels.

Older: And here you are.

Hairston: Here I am, right, yeah, yeah.

Older: That's the perfect way to close, I think. Thank you so much, Andrea. I love your work, I love you. You're an amazing person. I'm just glad to be on this Earth with you.

Hairston: Back at you, back at you.